541-3094

924 Engine
164 Miramar
left straight to
14th Engine devector

Luck
of
the
Draw

CAROLINA

GARCIA-AGUILERA

rayo *An Imprint of* HarperCollins*Publishers*

Luck
of
the
Draw

A NOVEL

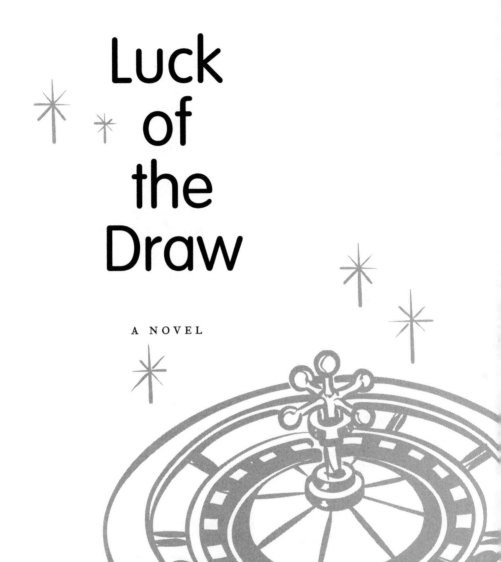

HarperCollins books may be purchased for educational, business, or sales promotional use. For information, please write: Special Markets Department, HarperCollins Publishers Inc., 10 East 53rd Street, New York, NY 10022.

FIRST EDITION

Designed by Shubhani Sarkar

Printed on acid-free paper

Library of Congress Cataloging-in-Publication Data.
Garcia-Aguilera, Carolina
    Luck of the Draw : a novel / Carolina Garcia-Aguilera.—1st ed.
        p.   cm.
    1. Cuban American families—Fiction. 2. Casinos—Fiction.
    I. Title.
PS3557.A71124 L8 2003
813'.54—dc21   2002037031

ISBN 0-06-053633-0

03 04 05 06 07 DIX/QW 10 9 8 7 6 5 4 3 2

To my Daughters, Sarah, Antonia, and Gabriella
The loves and passions of my life

And, of course, as always, to my beloved Cuba—
¡LIBERTAD!

Acknowledgments

IT IS DIFFICULT FOR ME TO believe that *Luck of the Draw* is my eighth novel. As has been the case with the previous seven books, there are certain individuals I would like to thank for making that possible. My agents at International Creative Management, Richard Abate in New York and Ron Bernstein in Los Angeles, have always been supportive of me in all my efforts. They have been my unwavering champions, and, for that alone, I will forever be in their debt. My editor at Rayo, Rene Alegria, also deserves special mention for his skills and vision. His wit and sense of humor are unique, and I treasure time spent with him. Alberto Rojas, the publicist in charge of promoting my books at HarperCollins is a true jewel, terrific at his job, and I am so grateful and appreciative of all his efforts on my behalf. Quinton Skinner, of course, in this book, as in the others, keeps my writing on track and makes sense of things I come up with that even I don't understand, and, for that, deserves my deepest thanks.

However, it is my family whom I thank from the bottom of my heart. My mother, Lourdes Aguilera de Garcia; my sister, Sara O'Connell; my brother, Carlos A. Garcia; and my nephew, Richard O'Connell, have always supported and encouraged me. Most important of all, they have consistently shown interest in the progress of the books and have praised me for my achievements.

To my daughters, Sarita, Antonia, and Gabby, what can I write here in these acknowledgments that I have not said to you in person repeatedly over the years? Thank you for sticking by me at all times, for being understanding of my foul humor when the writing is not going well, for not pointing out my shortcomings as a mother, for accepting the fact that we are not "normal" and probably will never be. (Of course, as we live on South Beach, "normal" is a rather fluid term.) Mostly, thank you for accepting me, and loving me so fiercely the way I am.

Thank you, God, for my many, many blessings. As I have done these many years, I promise I will continue to light candles to you, to thank you for all you have given me. At this rate, I will be lighting a bonfire soon.

Luck
of
the
Draw

1

I HAD JUST HUNG UP THE
phone and closed my eyes expecting to go back to sleep—always
the optimist—when it rang again. I knew this call wasn't to an-
nounce Fidel Castro's death—every Cuban exile's dream come
true—so my enthusiasm for picking up was severely limited. I debated ignoring the call and letting my voice mail get it, but I can
never let a phone ring unanswered. Instinct made me reach for the
receiver in the darkness.

I was bringing the phone to my ear when I looked over to
check out the number on the caller ID. I cursed when I saw that
it was my older sister Sapphire on the line. *Mierda!* It was barely
six-thirty in the morning, far too early to deal with a family crisis.
First my mother had called, now Sapphire. It was a bad start to
the day.

"Hey, Esmeralda, did Mama call you yet?" Sapphire launched
in without any pretense of small talk. "She called me about ten
minutes ago. I know she must have gotten to you by now."

We both knew what she was referring to. In an effort to avoid
any appearance of favoritism. Mama always telephoned her children in order of their birth. That meant she would first call Sapphire, then Ruby, then me, then our sister Diamond out in Vegas.
Our brother, Quartz, the baby, traditionally got the last call.

"What in the world is so fucking urgent that we all have to meet as soon as possible?" Sapphire asked in her shrill, staccato, migraine-inducing tone of voice. I felt a low-grade pain developing at the back of my neck.

Apparently she didn't expect me to answer, because she kept talking at breakneck speed. I groaned as I realized it was too early for her first dose of meds to have kicked in. I hated dealing with Sapphire when she was pharmaceutically free.

"I bet you a hundred dollars she's just being a drama queen," Sapphire said with delight. "There's probably no real emergency at all."

That last bit woke me up, as Sapphire knew it would. There was nothing like a friendly bet between me and my siblings. For a moment I considered taking her wager and doubling it. That's the problem with being born into a family in the gaming business— betting was in our blood. Our pool of bets on Fidel Castro's death was in the tens of thousands of dollars. As the bastard lived longer and longer, we kept rolling the bets over, extending the windows.

"I don't know what it's about," I said, making a supreme effort not to take the wager. "But it sounded important, Sapphire."

Tony, my husband, started thrashing around next to me, making sure I knew that he was irritated by all the noise coming from my side of the bed. At an earlier time I might have tried to make up with a sexual overture, culminating in a quickie before it was time to get up, but our relationship at this point was such that I didn't want to make a pass that might be rejected.

"It's too early to call Diamond," Sapphire said. "But maybe Ruby or Q will know more. I'm going to call them."

Sapphire hung up without saying good-bye. I doubted Ruby or our brother would know anything we didn't, but Sapphire didn't give me time to say so. Well, let them enjoy an early morning call from our unmedicated eldest sister. It would be interesting to see what shape they were in when Sapphire phoned. Our family doesn't do well with situations that happen in the morning—unless it is an extension of something that began the night before.

I put down the receiver and pulled the sheets all the way up to my chin. Like most people in Miami, we kept our bedroom temperature as cold as the air conditioner could go. Sometimes I awoke with chapped lips. The chill in the room was starting to make me shiver, so I gently appropriated the rest of the down comforter from Tony, careful not to disturb him further. It was too early in the day to deal with my husband just yet—that challenge would come soon enough.

I looked over at the bedside clock and saw that in two minutes the first of my three alarms was about to go off—I don't do well in the morning. Sometimes I entertained the delusion that my children might find a slot in some "exclusive" night school. It was a pretty unlikely scenario, considering the fact that they were still in elementary school.

As an interior decorator with my own company, I could set my own schedule. The only reason for me to wake up early was to roust my sons, feed them breakfast, and drop them off at school. The four of us were nearly comatose in the morning, and we barely said a word as we dressed and had breakfast. I made the boys drink double café con leches before we left the house, and still they slept in the car all the way to school. I had to yell at them to wake up and then get out and open the door myself when we finally arrived there. All three of my sons were good students, and regularly made the honor roll, but I also got notes from their teachers asking if they got enough rest. Apparently they fell asleep in class with alarming regularity. I told the teachers there was nothing wrong. It was in the genes.

The boys and I were in heaven during school vacations, because then we could sleep all day and stay up all night. My work schedule entailed my showing up at the office around noon, and I rarely scheduled an appointment earlier in the day. If the boys didn't have to be at school the next morning, it wasn't uncommon for us to have dinner at ten at night.

Tony had long since abandoned hope of regulating our schedules, and he pretty much fended for himself when the boys were on vacation. As an accountant, he had to keep regular hours, but he would have been a morning person no matter what kind of work he went into. Even on weekends, when he didn't have to go into the office, he still was up and out of bed by seven. On the rare occasions when he slept past eight—when he had the flu, for instance—he spent the rest of the day riddled with so much guilt one would think he had committed all seven of the deadly sins and shame had prevented him from arising.

When we were first married, I used to feel bad that I wasn't around to keep Tony company in the early morning hours. I soon got over it. Tony had known I was a complete night owl long before we were married, and our differences were something we used to joke about. Although he never said so, however, I knew that Tony had hoped I would mend my ways after our children were born. Unfortunately for him, that never happened. Worst of all, the boys took after me, and Tony was soon outnumbered. Every so often we tried to conform to Tony's hours, but soon we were all so miserable that Tony would beg us to resume staying up late and sleeping in.

Tony stirred next to me, his hand groping for the pilfered comforter. A few months ago, I would have assumed he was feeling for me. The way things stood now, unless he had had a really erotic dream, that possibility was a real nonstarter. If Tony had a horny dream, I probably wasn't in it.

Dawn was just breaking, and our bedroom was filling with pale light that filtered in through the white wooden window blinds. It was early May, the start of summer in most of the country and the time of year that ushered in glorious foliage and warmer weather. In Miami, it was simply the beginning of hurricane season. It was cruelly hot here most of the year, and the change of seasons was little more than an abstraction. On the few occasions when the temperature actually plunged below sixty, it was time for Floridians to break out their furs and wear them proudly. To hell with PETA—it was cold, dammit, and all those adorable furry animals had given their lives so the people of Florida wouldn't have to shiver. Never mind the fact that air conditioners were set at colder temperatures the rest of the year.

The sad truth was that, in Miami, we were aware of the climate only during hurricane season—from June to November. That was when fluorescent orange balls started showing up on weather maps, hovering off the coast of Africa and riveting our attention to the weather forecasters' pronouncements. We got so familiar with the weather people that we easily noticed when one of them wore the same tie twice in the same week, or when a female meteorologist forgot to switch earrings. We started to worry when the shadows under their eyes became more pronounced and resistant to makeup. The weather people were our security blankets in times of trouble. Everyone had their favorite, and the merits of each forecaster was a topic of hot debate.

The TV programmers knew that any mention of a hurricane in the open waters between South Florida and the Cape Verde Islands made ratings spike dramatically, and they broke into the middle of popular shows with updates on storms that might be weeks away from hitting land. They displayed lurid logos touting "Trouble in the Tropics," or some other inflammatory tag line. Even when a toddler could tell there was no way a storm was going to hit Florida, a meteorologist would somberly inform viewers that in the distant past some storm actually did make a 180-degree turn and travel ten thousand miles to lash Miami with heavy winds and rain. No one had the energy to check the history books to determine whether it was really true.

My favorite part of the programs was when the local stations switched over to on-site interviews with meteorologists at the National Hurricane Center. The reporter would desperately try to extract a prediction that a far-off storm was indeed threatening our shores. The NHC meteorologists were of course too experienced to fall into that trap. They knew nothing bumped up ratings like the threat of a hurricane, so the interviews degenerated into a cat-and-mouse game, with the local forecasters trying to pressure their NHC counterparts into predicting doom and gloom.

All of this really intensified after Hurricane Andrew's deadly visit to South Florida in 1992. After that, any mention of a big storm, no matter how far away, was enough to keep the residents of Miami glued to its TV sets. The moment a storm was given a name, South Floridians would flock to the grocery and hardware stores to stock up on supplies. Personally, it seemed to me that some of the local weather forecasters tracking storms strutted their stuff in front of the cameras in hopes of getting spotted by a scout for one of the national networks. Local TV in Miami had been the launching point for many a national news anchor. A few probably went to bed praying for big storms.

I stared up at the ceiling. I was awake, my mind was racing, and sleep was out of the question. I used my few precious moments of freedom to ponder my phone call with Mama a few minutes before. I normally tried not to use my brain before noon—I had found out the hard way that it was an unreliable organ in the morning—but I decided to make an exception. This was clearly an emergency. When Mama had called me just after six in the morning I almost had a coronary, since my mother regularly slept until after noon. She had heard my panic and assured me, in a somber and formal tone of voice, that she wasn't calling to give me bad news. The entire family in Miami was to meet as soon as possible, however, for reasons that were a mystery.

This was the first time Mama had ever made a request with such urgency. I agreed with Sapphire that my mother was a bit of a drama queen, but something in Mama's voice told me that this situation was serious. If Mama hadn't informed me or Sapphire what the meeting was about, I was willing to bet that she hadn't told my other siblings, either.

The first of my alarms went off. That's the easy one to turn off, because it was on my bedside table. The next two would require my getting out of bed: one was on the dresser across the room, and the third, and loudest, alarm was in the hall. They were set to ring within one minute of one another, giving me just enough time to shut each one off before I had to endure a symphony of bells and buzzers. I had searched long and hard for alarms with particularly piercing sounds—ones that are so irritating that they are guaranteed to get the soundest sleeper out of bed. Man, had I succeeded. No soothing FM music, waterfalls, or birds chirping for me. I needed to feel like I was in the Marines, with a drill sergeant standing over my bed screaming at me to get up. I would wake to a phone ringing or one of my children crying. Anything else had to be incredibly annoying to do the job.

Tony had come to accept my admittedly unorthodox needs for waking up in the morning, but he still hated the shrill sound of the alarms. It was a far cry from what he was used to when he was growing up. Antonio Mario Montoya was raised like a prince by his mother, whose entire world revolved around him. Until the day he left home for college, she would gently wake him with a tap on the shoulder and serve him breakfast in bed. Her behavior wasn't surprising, since she was a widow and Tony was her only child. I knew one of the regrets in his life was marrying a woman who failed to dote on him the way his mother had. I, too, was a Cuban mother, but I had long since made a vow to myself never to spoil my sons that way.

Our relationship had been pretty rocky lately, and I didn't want to exacerbate things any further, so I sprinted for the dresser and shut off the second alarm just as it began to wail. After that, I headed out to the hall and beat the third one before it went off. Then I went down the hall and pounded on each of the boys' bedroom doors. I knew I would have to beat on each one several times before they finally got up. They were definitely their mother's sons. I beamed with pride even as I was threatening them with extravagant pain if they didn't get out of bed.

Finally each one had called out to me with assurances that he was finally awake. I returned to the master bedroom and gently shook Tony.

"*Buenos días*," I whispered in his ear.

"Already?" Tony grunted. "Emmy, five more minutes. *Por favor.*"

I blinked as his words registered. His request to sleep more was totally out of character, because Tony usually bounded out of bed with an energy and optimism that were incomprehensible to me. Relations between us were worse than I had thought, or else he was having an erotic dream after all. There was hope yet, I thought, perhaps a little meanly.

It was surprising to hear Tony call me Emmy, his pet name for me. It had been weeks since he called me that. It made me start thinking again, something I normally avoided at all costs before my first cup of industrial-strength Cuban coffee. I needed my café con leche as much as an alcoholic craved his first drink, a junkie his first fix, or a nymphomaniac her first lay.

My family background what it is, it was little surprise that my body clock never adjusted to the demands of married life and motherhood. I know it's because gambling blood flows through my veins, and I'm destined to be a creature of the night. I cringe whenever one of my clients suggests a breakfast meeting—thank God, only a very few ever do that, and in Miami that demographic is few and far between. If I could, I would outlaw talking business early in the morning—if possible, with a Constitutional amendment.

Tony was warm and drowsy with sleep. His face was so relaxed that he looked like the man I had married eleven years before, the one who had made my knees shake when he walked into a room. I wondered what had happened, and why my knees were now firmly locked in place.

"I'll come back in five minutes," I told him softly. It was a small enough request, although every minute was precious during the work and school week. Our mornings were choreographed down to the nanosecond.

I went to the bathroom, took off my pink lace nightgown, and pitched it into the hamper. I peed and pulled on the clothes I had carefully laid out the night before. Even though it was only workout gear, I couldn't be trusted to dress myself in the morning. I put on black cotton drawstring pants and a gray T-shirt, then slipped into my sneakers. I made it a habit to stop by the gym most mornings after dropping the boys off at school.

I bent over the sink and, steeling myself, splashed icy cold water all over my face to drive away the fog. I brushed my teeth and looked in the mirror to see how I had fared through the night. I had just turned thirty, and the symbolic weight of the number was not lost on me. The harsh bathroom light intensified my every flaw, and I wasn't about to fool myself into thinking that the passage of time had left me unscathed.

Both my parents' families immigrated to Cuba from the north of Spain, and we shared the light coloring of the people who came from that region. Each of my parents had rosy complexions, light blue eyes, and honey-colored hair, and all their children had inherited their coloring with slight differences. What might interest a geneticist was that my eldest sister, Sapphire, had the lightest coloring, with each of the subsequent children growing progressively darker. When we were growing up, the family used to joke that our birth order could be discerned with a color meter. That was impossible now that we were adults, because we'd all fiddled around with our hair colors to the point that little was left of our original tints.

I was the third child, right in the middle, with blue eyes that changed with my mood, the weather, what I was wearing, and the light in the room. My hair, which I wore halfway down my back, had been white blond when I was a child. It had grown darker as I aged, and now I had to highlight it to maintain a light tone. For most of my life, my hair had been completely straight, but when I had children it frizzed in a sort of Raphaelite way, resulting in more than my fair share of bad hair days. Miami humidity is the eternal enemy of straight hair, but I suppose it is great for sales of defrizzing gels and hair products.

At my age, with my pale complexion, I should have had wrinkles. The reality was that I never, ever, went out in the sun, and as a result I had been spared that indignity. I was mostly satisfied with my looks from the neck up, but it was moving south that presented a problem. Though our family came from the north of Spain, my sisters and I had strictly Cuban bodies: large breasts and wide hips. No matter how much I exercised, I still felt that I sashayed when I walked. And with every pregnancy, my body had become more and more like Mother Earth. I was about average in height—five-foot-five—so every pound I gained was abundantly visible.

For as long as I could remember, I looked as though I needed to lose about fifteen pounds. Tony, being a Cuban man, liked his women with a little extra flesh. He was flatteringly unsympathetic to my plight, although my secret dream was to have a stranger ask me if I had been eating enough, and offer to take me to a restaurant immediately. All in all, though, I was pretty satisfied with the way I looked—which was no small accomplishment, in this day and age. Daily workouts were a modest price to pay.

I finished getting dressed, conscious of precious time passing, and went to gently shake Tony awake. He grumbled but shifted his weight into a semisitting position. I went downstairs to start serving breakfast to the boys.

As I approached the kitchen I heard their voices, which was somewhat unusual, since they spent many of their mornings in a silent stupor. I stifled a laugh when I heard Gabriel, my eldest, at age eleven, challenging his twin eight-year-old brothers, Alex and Carlos, to a couple of quick games of blackjack before school. It was an offer that the twins eagerly accepted.

I was so proud of them that I felt uplifted. The apples hadn't fallen too far from the tree. Their father might have been an accountant, reliable and steadfast, but gamblers' blood ran through their veins. They were mine, all mine—night owls, gamblers, jokers. Before I went into the kitchen, I lowered my head and said a quick prayer: *Gracias, Dios.*

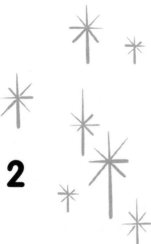

2

AFTER I DROPPED THE BOYS
off, I drove to the gym. Their school, Saint Bartholomew's, and
my gym, Sweat, were within a couple of miles of each other in
Coconut Grove. The school took students until the sixth grade, so
it was Gabriel's last year there. I really couldn't face the reality
that next year I was going to have to drive him to another
school—probably Christ the King junior high, which was ten
miles away in the other direction. I lived in a state of utter denial
about how this change was going to disrupt my morning routine.

There were moments when I let my guard down and allowed
myself to envision what things would be like next year. I would
invariably become depressed and entertain crazy thoughts. Part
of me wished that Gabriel would have to repeat sixth grade, since
that would buy me another year before having to make the daily
drive to Christ the King. Or maybe the twins could turn out to be
unprecedented geniuses, enabling them to skip three grades and
all the boys attend junior high together. Sometimes I told myself
everything would work out fine, that it wouldn't be a problem.
The latter was probably the craziest notion of all.

Getting behind the wheel in Miami wasn't for the cowardly or
weak of heart. Driving just a few blocks at certain times of day
was enough to provoke the worst sort of road rage. Not only were

our streets woefully inadequate for the volume of traffic that coursed through them, but our drivers were also the rudest and least attentive of any city's. I can still picture the morning when I followed a young woman on her way to work, speeding in her late-model BMW while she plucked her eyebrows, ate a yogurt, and carried out an animated conversation on her cell phone. I was so in awe of her audacious multitasking that I forgot to honk at her when she almost slammed into me while attempting a lane change.

Every so often I came across a motorist who actually concentrated on his or her driving, with both hands on the wheel instead of talking on a cell phone, eating, reading the newspaper, looking at the person in the passenger seat, flipping through a CD case, lighting a cigarette, playing with the dog in his or her lap, or having a game of tongue hockey with the girlfriend or boyfriend of the moment. That's how I could spot the out-of-towners.

That morning, my trip to the gym was stressful if relatively uneventful. Even though it was still early, the parking lot had filled up. I wasn't worried, though, because I knew it wouldn't be long before someone came out and vacated a spot.

Sure enough, I had waited less than a minute when a tall, hot-looking young man came out of the gym. I didn't mind driving slowly behind him as he walked to his car, because he was pure eye candy. I might not have been a morning person, but I perked up watching him walk. I started to breathe a little faster. It was reassuring to know that I could still react that way to a member of the opposite sex. I may have been a wife and mother who just broke the thirty-year barrier, but I still had eyes to see.

My guy was clearly aware that he had a nice body: he wore a tight white T-shirt, low-slung blue jeans with a rope belt, and dark work boots. He had obviously just showered because his longish, fashionably chopped black hair glistened in the morning sun. I couldn't help wondering what he smelled like. I would bet a hundred dollars he wore cologne, probably some kind of musk scent. He oozed pheromones.

I drove slowly behind him to his black Saab convertible and looked him over as he leisurely unlocked the door. I had been in a hurry to begin my workout, but since I set my eyes on macho man I suddenly had all the time in the world. I was married, but in my book that didn't preclude looking. Just thinking about the way things were going with Tony made me want to stare even longer. I needed a little joy in my life, that was for sure, and this young guy was providing me with a quick fix.

He stopped by his Saab and I turned on my blinker to indicate my claim to his parking space once he pulled out. I made myself comfortable because it looked like it was going to take a while. All indications were that the object of my attention liked putting on a show and, since I was the only other person around, his sudden stretching and flexing by his car was exclusively for my benefit. It seemed to me there was more than a little suggestion in the languid way he finally opened the car door and folded himself into the black leather seat.

I wasn't complaining. I was just trying to keep from salivating. I watched him meticulously adjust his rearview mirror, then carefully select a CD to slip into the console. He fiddled around with the dials, then arched his body to pull a cell phone from the pocket of his jeans. I was surprised anything actually fit in there, he wore his jeans so tight, but the phone was so small and slim that it hadn't created a noticeable bulge. He made a quick call, then slipped the phone into the pocket of his T-shirt. He put on his seat belt, then checked himself out in the mirror on the reverse side of the sun visor. Apparently convinced he was presentable to the world, he put the car in reverse.

He backed up, then paused before leaving. He turned, stared at me, and broke out in a wide grin. He gave me a little salute with one hand and winked, then pulled out. I was so delighted that I started to laugh. After that, I could die a happy woman.

I eased into the just-vacated slot and killed the motor. That hot guy had made me—a thirty-year-old mother of three in a Volvo station wagon—break out in an ear-to-ear smile. I had to envy his self-assuredness and sense of fun. Not to mention his body.

I walked into the gym thinking about him, wondering if he was a new member since I had never seen him before. I sure as hell would have remembered him. I contemplated the implications of seeing him regularly. My God, that would mean that I would have to seriously upgrade my appearance. I hoped not. Miami was competitive enough as far as looks were concerned. The gym was one place where I didn't have to worry about how I looked—whether my makeup was running from sweat, or whether my socks matched my sports bra. All that might have to change—I might have to start wearing perfume! I actually began to hope that the hot guy's appearance had been an aberration and that he wouldn't become a regular fixture. Not that he would even be re-motely interested in me, but hope sprang eternal as far as I was concerned.

Just before I went inside, I looked up the street to see if, by some miracle, he had forgotten something and was coming back. No such luck. Just as well, I thought. It was better to remember my last glimpse of his wave and smile. I made a mental note to program myself to dream about him that night.

I swiped my plastic membership card through the machine on the front desk, feeling as though I was back in junior high, obsess-ing about a cute guy. I thought maybe he normally worked out at night, or early in the morning before I usually came in. Maybe he had bought a one-time pass to see if he liked the gym before buy-ing a full membership. I could speculate all I wanted, but I defi-nitely wasn't curious enough to ask one of the trainers at the front desk about him. Maybe it was more fun to fantasize. I would have liked to place a bet on the reason he was there that morning, but there was no one to wager with.

Sweat was a relentlessly trendy gym in the heart of Coconut Grove, just a few miles from our house. It attracted a diverse clientele, from businesspeople cramming in a workout before their hectic days to artists and models, bodybuilders, and mothers arriving after dropping off their children at school. I belonged to the latter category. In addition, there were the men and women with no visible means of support, a demographic that described many Miamians—these were the workout fiends who never seemed to be in a hurry, who could kill an hour in the whirlpool chatting and stretching. I often felt pressed for time in the morning, but my habit of going to the gym was essential as much for my mental health as for the state of my figure. On the rare days when I missed my workout, I felt cranky and frustrated.

I took the wooden stairs up to the second floor, where I saw the reassuring sight of the cardio machines and the weight room. I waved to a few regulars without stopping to chat, instead heading straight to the treadmill. Each machine featured a small TV installed at eye level, with individual headphones. I normally watched one of the morning shows, but that day I turned off the TV. I had things to think about—what was going on with my marriage, for starters, and what was it that Mama and Papa wanted to urgently discuss. There were two places where I did my best thinking: on the treadmill in the morning, and in the bathtub at night.

It was easier to think about my parents than the state of my marriage. I replayed my early morning call with Mama while I unzipped my gym bag to organize my morning. I put my cell phone on the ledge of the treadmill, so I could easily reach it in case it rang, then I unfolded a towel and draped it over the machine's handrail.

I thought about the last time that my parents had summoned their children to make an announcement: they had become organ donors, they told us, and had made out living wills. My siblings and I had greeted the news with enthusiasm and approval, which I think secretly disappointed Mama and Papa. They probably had wanted us to cry and plead with them to be kept alive at any cost, but they should have known we wouldn't. They had brought us up with too much practicality to be sentimental about matters of life and death.

This time it probably wasn't health-related, because almost every day they issued by phone a detailed medical bulletin of their various aches and pains—real and imagined. They were a primary physician's dream, and an HMO's nightmare. Every other card they received at Christmastime was from a doctor's office. My parents' address book had extra pages added in the "D" section to accommodate all their doctors. They saw half a dozen dentists alone: a specialist for gums, one for cavities, another for veneers, one for oral surgery. They probably had more dentists than teeth, and all their other specialists put together were probably sufficient in number to field two softball teams to play against each other.

Before I stepped onto the treadmill, I did a few stretching exercises. I programmed the machine for an hour-long workout, figuring that would give me enough time to stew over my parental and marital issues. I would have to leave the gym a little earlier than usual, because I knew I was going to have to coordinate with my siblings when we were to arrive at my parents' house. None of us would want to arrive first, and alone. It would be better to show up with a united front.

I tried to reassure myself that my parents' problem couldn't be too serious. If it was, they would have wanted our youngest sister, Diamond, to fly in from Las Vegas. I wondered what Sapphire was up to. She was surely working the phones, trying to extract information from all our siblings in anticipation of our parents' revelation. Sapphire, in her unmedicated morning state, could be ruthlessly efficient.

The treadmill kicked into higher gear. Thoughts of Tony entered my mind. I checked my progress on the machine's read-out screen. I wanted to be running full-tilt when I mentally confronted my problems with my husband.

Everything in my life was always viewed in the context of my upbringing and my family. Family was, and always would be, the primary frame of reference in my life.

I remembered the cute guy in the parking lot, and how his smile made me feel. The treadmill quickened, and I breathed hard to keep up.

3

OUR FAMILY SEEMS PRETTY normal on the outside, but we've always taken pride in our non-conformist self-image. After all, how many families name their children after precious stones? It seemed perfectly reasonable to my siblings and me, but we were always explaining ourselves to our teachers and schoolmates when we were children. But, I thought as I increased the speed of the treadmill, I was getting ahead of myself. I wanted to figure out what had gone wrong with my marriage to Tony, and that meant going back to the beginning. And for Cubans, that always meant returning in our minds and hearts to Cuba itself.

The gamblers' blood that flowed through Mama's and Papa's veins influenced every decision they had made in their lives. It seemed perfectly normal for us to trust a roll of the dice to decide where we lived, attended school, went on vacation, took jobs, and whom we married. Since we were five children born within ten years of one another, we never lacked for companionship or partners to play games with. Our house was also always filled with friends—many of whom took refuge in the unorthodox environment in which we lived.

We were all good students, and although some of us found various subjects harder than others, one thing was certain: all five of us excelled at math. From the time we were toddlers, our parents had taught us how to work various number combinations in our heads—that talent, after all, was essential to being a successful gambler. We rarely needed to consult a calculator when we studied statistics, a subject we all aced. Some families had traditions of working in medicine, or law, or engineering. For us, it was games of chance.

It had started early. On Papa's side, in the 1800s his paternal great-great-grandfather won passage from the port of La Coruna, in the province of Galicia on the north coast of Spain, to Cuba by gambling at cards. Gabriel had been a penniless but ruthlessly ambitious sixteen-year-old orphan who realized he had no future in Spain; subsequently, he decided to begin a life in the New World. Since he had no money to buy his passage, he had to find some way to earn it. Gabriel considered his options and, being an honest person, ruled out getting involved in anything illegal. That would have displeased his sainted mother, who looked down on him from heaven. The only skill he possessed was a knack for playing dice, which he had learned when he accompanied his father to the *tavernas,* where the old man used to supplement his meager village blacksmith's income by gambling.

There were only a few hours left before the ship was scheduled to sail for Havana. Gabriel played dice on the dock next to the ship, throwing lucky sevens time and time again until he had won enough money to pay for the trip. The luck that had blessed him on the dock held out for the remainder of the trip, and by the time the *Santa María Santísima* reached Cuba, Gabriel had fleeced his fellow passengers out of what was, by the standards of the day, a tidy sum.

When my parents left Cuba at the end of 1958 they were able to carry very few personal mementos, but they did manage to bring out the precious pair of dice in a worn leather pouch that their ancestor had played with during that voyage. I had often held and examined them when I was a child, thinking of how different our lives might have been if those dice hadn't rolled as many sevens as they did. I also wondered what a close examination of those dice might reveal but, of course, I never gave voice to those suspicions.

Abuelito Gabriel's parents were named Melchor and Maria de Mercedes Navarro, and they surely wouldn't have given their son an archangel's name if they had known how he would make his fortune in Cuba. While he was crossing the Atlantic, he befriended three beautiful young sisters who had been sent to Havana to work as scullery maids and laundresses in the household of a wealthy Spanish nobleman. They informed Gabriel that their parents worked as house servants for the nobleman's sister in Madrid, and that they were to work as indentured servants in Cuba for five years in exchange for the money their new employer had advanced for their passage. After that term, according to the agreement, the girls would be free. Gabriel might have been only sixteen, but he doubted that the latter part of the contract would ever be honored. He knew that the girls would somehow be made beholden to the nobleman, and forced to work for him as long as they were useful.

The girls understood that their parents had entered into the agreement with their best interests at heart: they were the youngest of ten children born to penniless parents, and their future in Spain was bleak. Although they didn't openly complain, it was clear they were unhappy with being sent to a strange land, far from home, to work for a man they didn't know. Life in Spain might have been hard, but it was what they knew. They could only speculate about what awaited them in Cuba.

The girls were seasick and miserable for most of the trip, but they developed a friendship with Gabriel and came to trust him. They thought of him as a protective older brother, even though they were all roughly the same age. After a few days, the girls had opened up to Gabriel and revealed their fears about the arrangement their parents had made with the nobleman. The girls were poor, young, and uneducated, and thought they had no choice but to comply. The trip took weeks, though, and Gabriel had a lot of time to think about all their fates. Not only was he winning at dice, he realized, but also fate had placed the three charming Gonzalez sisters—Concepción, Natividad, and Milagros, aged fifteen, sixteen, and seventeen—in his path. The future was bright enough to blind him.

By the time the ship docked at Havana Harbor, Gabriel had made the sisters a proposition that had the potential to make them all wealthy. All they had to do was trust him, and work hard. As far as the Gonzalez sisters were concerned, their handsome young companion's offer was a lot more appealing than working as slaves for a nobleman. Gabriel explained that they would offer a service and help their fellow human beings find happiness in a cruel world. If they would receive financial compensation for their services, well, so much the better. The Lord said God helped those who helped themselves, Gabriel explained to the girls. And the New World was exceptionally kind to them, even if they succeeded at a profession that would have horrified their parents.

Mama's ancestors, four brothers and a sister, came from the Canary Islands, a Spanish holding off the northwest coast of Africa. They were hardy and independent, and had made their living for generations fishing the waters. After their parents died, they took stock of their situation and decided that the future held little for them at home. They were tired of the hardscrabble life their parents had carved out for them, and they decided to try their luck fishing the warm waters on the other side of the Atlantic.

Their timing wasn't good. The five Montalvo siblings landed in Cuba in 1868—just in time for the beginning of the Ten Years War for independence. It was a struggle in which Cubans fought to overthrow Spanish rule on the island, and it was at times bloody and chaotic. The brothers and sister huddled in an attic room in a boardinghouse facing the Bay of Havana. They set out to learn as much as they could about this strange, war-torn land as quickly as possible. They were strong, ambitious, and all under twenty-five, and they came to an important conclusion about their new homeland: although they were poorer and badly equipped, the Cuban fighters had the determination to eventually win independence from the mother country. Even though the war was going badly for the Cubans at that moment, the Montalvos decided to throw in their lot with the Cuban freedom fighters.

The coastal cities of the island were still controlled by Spain, so it wouldn't be possible for the Montalvo siblings to make their living fishing if they were allied with the Cubans. They were nothing if not practical, and they knew that the war couldn't go on forever. They also figured that the next government of Cuba would likely be led by the military, so it would be wise to start making connections with the troops. They looked over their options and decided that soldiers would always spend their money on amusements to forget the horrors of the battlefield. Then they began to check out the countryside for a good place to set up a business.

They ended up using all their money to buy a ramshackle farmhouse in the rebel-controlled territory of Ciego de Ávila, in the middle of the island. The brothers had grown up repairing the family's fishing boats back in Las Islas Canarias, and their facility with tools enabled them to fix up the building. Soon the Montalvos were known as restaurateurs and saloon keepers. They served rum made from the sugarcane that grew in the fields and served meat from the scrawny cattle that roamed the countryside. The brothers made the rum and tended bar, while their sister cooked and served meals. For Maria Mercedes, cooking for soldiers was no different from cooking for the men in her family; it simply meant preparing larger quantities of food. Besides, the soldiers were always more appreciative than her brothers.

The siblings just about broke even operating the bar and restaurant, but they knew they had to try something different to attract more customers. They added a room to the side of the building for games, and soon their main source of income was from gamblers. It was a fairly sophisticated operation, given the rough conditions in the countryside, with a roulette table, two blackjack tables, and a specially constructed table for throwing dice.

The war that had begun in 1868 lasted for ten years. The Spanish emerged as the victors with the Treaty of Zanjon—a document that provided for the gradual abolition of slavery on the island and some political reforms. Fighting continued after the treaty, however, and another war broke out in 1895, which terminated three years later when the Americans stepped in on the side of the Cubans. The siblings' faith in Cuban independence turned out to be well founded.

The family, growing now, was resilient and resourceful, but it was primarily their lack of aversion to paying protection money that ensured their survival. Not only did they survive; they began to survive under difficult and tumultuous times. At the turn of the century the war was over and it was safe to leave the Cuban interior. The Montalvo family moved to Havana, where they built the first Cuban-owned casino, an asset that the family owned until Fidel Castro appropriated it in 1959. By the time the brothers and sister had moved to Havana, they had all married Cubans and considered themselves thoroughly Cuban. Their past in the Canary Islands became a hazy, receding memory.

Their support of the Cubans against the Spanish paid off; they were rewarded by their many military contacts with advantages in the form of generous financial incentives. Most valuable of all to the Montalvos was the grant of a choice plot of land in the capital.

They sank all the family's money into building La Estrella, "The Star," their casino on the edge of the Malecón, the avenue that bordered the Bay of Havana. It was a prime location, in the city center, and the casino soon became a landmark. After hiding in the boondocks for so many years, the family wanted a building that stood out and claimed a place in the Cuban people's imagination. They had it painted a golden color, with flecks of precious metal that glittered in the bright tropical sun.

The building was an extravagant sight. The ceiling of the main room was designed as a planetarium, with twinkling lights that depicted constellations, stars, and planets against a midnight-blue sky. At times a shooting star would explode across the length of the room, a marvel of engineering for its time. Each adjacent room extended from the main room, making the building an architectural representation of a nine-pointed star. Each side room was named after the planet depicted on its ceiling, and each tried to outdo the one before it in opulence.

My parents had managed to bring out of Cuba some everyday pieces that had been used at La Estrella. We had glass ashtrays stamped in the middle with a color picture of the casino, boxes of matches, paper and plastic coasters, swizzle sticks, drinking glasses, playing cards, pencils, and notepads all embossed with the La Estrella logo. We also had a cut-glass ashtray with precious stones, rescued from the casino's main bar, which I used to stare at as a child until it practically hypnotized me. At the center of the cabinet, in the place of honor, was a framed photograph of Maria Mercedes Montalvo, Mama's great-great grandmother; it was a worn and faded image that endlessly captured my imagination when I was a young girl.

One of the first things Papa did after arriving in exile was to hire a carpenter to build a floor-to-ceiling cabinet. It was a massive piece of furniture, painted gold, and after it was placed prominently in the center of the living room it became home to everything he had rescued from La Estrella. No one entering the house could avoid it, and those of us who lived there were daily reminded of our family's past.

To the best of my knowledge, Papa never took those things from the cabinet once he had arranged them inside. They were preserved for eternity, or until Fidel Castro died—whichever came first. I often found Papa standing in front of the cabinet, looking at the artifacts from La Estrella with his eyes misting over. Our family had lost everything at the hands of the Castro regime—land, homes, property, furniture, jewelry, and works of art—but it was the loss of La Estrella that hurt Papa the most. It gave him an air of sadness that, hard as he tried, he could never shed completely.

Every New Year's Eve, Papa gathered his entire family in front of the cabinet, champagne in hand, and swore that he would get La Estrella back someday. Somehow. I never doubted him, especially when I was younger. But the years were passing, and Papa was growing older. I knew that, realistically, his vow had become less and less likely to be realized. It wasn't that my parents were all about doom and gloom, and always living in the past, but they always carried the loss of La Estrella with them. If we were richer, people would have called us eccentric. As it was, we were often regarded as "different."

My sisters and my brother never tired of hearing the story of how they met, fell in love, married, and lived in Cuba before the revolution. The story was so vivid and so ingrained in my mind, it was like watching a video of a favorite movie. The best part was when they described how beautiful and full of life La Estrella once was. My other favorite part was the story of how they had managed to escape the island. Compared to my mundane life with Tony, theirs seemed like an exotic adventure story.

I could close my eyes and picture it all. But I had better not, I reminded myself, unless I wanted to tumble off the treadmill. It was safer to keep my eyes open and let the video play in my head. It was escapism at its best, and I certainly needed it.

My mother and father had known each other all their lives, since their families had done business together in Havana. The family businesses were right next to each other: Papa's family owned the Cubangala, an entertainment showplace nightclub with the biggest and flashiest revue in the Caribbean, while Mama's owned La Estrella. Several times a year, the two businesses would pool their resources, close the street that separated them, and set up a huge outdoor party with music, dancing, and fireworks. The events were wildly popular and, more important, very lucrative.

Mama and Papa started checking out each other as adolescents at the street parties—first discreetly, then more openly. By the time they were in their late teens, it seemed only natural that they were considering a life together. They were married in 1950, the day after Papa graduated from the University of Havana with a business degree. Mama, three years younger and a girl, wasn't expected to pursue any kind of formal education. It didn't matter much to her, because she was so involved in the day-to-day operations of La Estrella that she was getting an education that couldn't be taught at the university.

Time passed, and Papa started spending less and less time at Cubangala, and more at La Estrella. The Montalvos relied on his knowledge and expertise to such a degree that when Enrique Montalvo, the head of the clan, retired in 1955, the family asked Papa to operate the casino. It was the first time that La Estrella wasn't run by a Montalvo. Papa modernized the business, cutting costs and increasing profits fivefold. The times in Cuba were very turbulent, with Fulgencio Batista at the head of a corrupt government and Fidel Castro in the hills of Oriente Province conducting raids into towns and cities. The situation was chaotic and lawless, with bombings, kidnappings, and state-sponsored imprisonment and torture. Papa had to pay protection money both to Batista's and Castro's men in order to run his business; as a result, it was well known that La Estrella was the safest place to gamble in Havana.

The American Mafia controlled the other casinos in Cuba, with Meyer Lansky in charge, but our family's enterprises were basically left alone. My parents never got into the details of how that was possible, but it seems likely that large sums of money were changing hands. During those years, our family was probably paying off all three competing groups in Havana: the Batista regime, the Castro rebels, and the Mob. La Estrella was making huge sums of money in order to be able to make all these payoffs and still turn a profit.

My parents knew that the situation would change if Castro came to power. He was a classic political hypocrite: on the one hand, his rhetoric denounced the casinos as corrupters of the Cuban people: on the other, he profited from their operations by extorting money not to bomb them and scare away their customers. When Castro was still limited to the hills in Oriente province, my parents could dismiss his pronouncements as hot air designed to stir up nationalistic fervor. Castro started to tell the people that the casinos were the tools of American imperialism and the Mafia, and his power started to increase. Ominously, he announced that the casinos would end when he took power.

Mama and Papa didn't like Batista or the way he governed, but they could at least operate under his rule as long as they paid—and paid—for the privilege of doing so. Castro, on the other hand, was talking about destroying the status quo. La Estrella was Cuban-owned, but my parents knew that it would probably share the fate of the American-owned casinos if Castro's revolution was successful. So, slowly, they began to make plans to salvage as much as they could of La Estrella—until things returned to normal, they thought, and the Cuban people could correct the mistake of letting Castro come to power. They turned their sights to the United States. It was impossible to move the casino north, of course, but they could take whatever they could carry.

My parents went about their daily business as normally as they could. In fact, they had begun to lead double lives. They tracked Castro's every move, reading the signs of his imminent rise to power. By the fall of 1958, they were convinced that it was a matter of weeks until rebel troops reached Havana. There would be a fight for the capital, they realized, one that Castro was going to win. The only question was when. The situation in Havana grew nearly intolerable, with kidnappings, murders, and bombings becoming everyday occurrences. Cubans walked a dangerous tightrope, because political allegiance—whether to Castro or Batista—became the source of betrayals and killings. Most people in Cuba learned to lay low and hope not to be noticed.

On New Year's Eve in 1958, when everyone was celebrating, word arrived that Castro had entered Havana. My parents realized they had to immediately implement the plans they had hatched in secret. After several months of nerve-wracking anticipation, it was almost a relief. They had been invited to celebrate that night at my tío Gabriel's house. Papa called to cancel, telling my tía Mirta that Mama had a migraine. Tía Mirta accepted this explanation without question, since the situation in Cuba was enough to give the entire population a splitting headache. It broke Mama's and Papa's hearts not to see the family one last time, but they didn't want to arouse any suspicions.

They could hear the sound of gunfire from their home in Miramar as they packed the few belongings they were taking with them. None of their children had been born yet, which they said allowed them to act so boldly. They always maintained they never would have risked any of our lives by trying to escape, which meant that if we were born earlier, we would have grown up under Castro's communist regime.

They traveled in the black van they had bought specifically for their escape, with Papa driving and Mama navigating through the dark streets of Havana. They carefully avoided the roving bands of drunken rebel soldiers yelling and firing their guns in the air, once almost crashing into a tank transporting about a dozen heavily armed young men dressed in fatigues and sporting beards to emulate their *jefe*. The scene in the city turned into a nightmare, with smoke and fire everywhere, flares from bombs going off in the distance, and staccato gunfire echoing in the night. The acrid smell of burning buildings choked them and made it hard to breathe.

Papa and Mama finally made it from their house to La Estrella. They sat quietly in the van for a moment, watching to see what was happening. There were few people around—which was surreal, given the fact that it was New Year's Eve. Their hearts pounded with fear, and their eyes burned from the smoke. Papa turned into the back driveway and guided the van into the casino basement to a loading area where deliveries were normally made. They drove inside and locked the double doors behind them, parking the van close to the two safes where the casino's revenues were stored. They turned off the motor and said a prayer in the silence of the basement. Mama held the flashlight while Papa worked the combination on the first safe; it opened, and they walked into the stale air inside.

The first safe contained pesos and dollars; the second housed gold bars and precious stones and jewelry. They opened them both, although they were primarily interested in the latter. They worked fast, loading valuables into the van. Much of the jewelry had been handed over by customers who had run up gambling debts and been forced to be creative with their payment—more than one wife, or mistress, had left La Estrella a bit lighter than she had entered. La Estrella didn't accept markers, a practice the family had established while operating the casino in Ciego de Ávila—they had been dealing with soldiers back then, who might leave a marker and then die in battle, leaving their debt unpaid. The Montalvos hadn't thrived for so long by being sentimental.

Transferring the gold bars and precious stones was difficult and time-consuming work. While my parents toiled, they could hear sounds from the casino upstairs—improbably enough, the casino was in operation, with a few brave gamblers trying their luck with a revolution going on right outside. Papa and Mama worked so single-mindedly that they didn't have time to reflect that this was perhaps the last time they would be inside their beloved La Estrella—which was probably for the best, because otherwise they would have been overcome with grief.

Once the van was loaded, Papa slammed the doors shut and closed the safes. There was no reason to make it easy for common thieves to steal the cash they were leaving behind. They hoped their employees would have the sense to open the safes and take the money for themselves.

The Archangel Gabriel must have been looking out for them, because the avenue was free of soldiers when they pulled out of the driveway. Papa had estimated the weight of the gold and jewelry, but he was still surprised by how much the van struggled under its load, and how difficult it had become to steer it. Although he had calculated every aspect of their plan, he still fretted. It was one thing to drive a van overloaded with valuables, but it was another thing entirely to cross the Florida straits in a boat that could sink under excess weight.

Dawn neared, and the streets began to quiet down. They felt as though they were in the eye of a hurricane, the air eerily calm before the winds picked up again. They knew their moment would be fleeting, and that they had to escape their homeland while they still could. They rode to the dock in silence, unable to give voice to their fears. The van groaned under its weight, and my parents were on the verge of complete exhaustion. When they finally reached the dock, they allowed themselves to exhale with relief—the boat they had bought for their escape was waiting for them.

Papa jumped onto the fifty-foot Hatteras and started the engines. Then he and Mama worked steadily, without stopping to rest, unloading the gold bars and jewelry, careful to keep the weight of the valuables evenly distributed in the craft. In about two hours, just as the sun was starting to climb in the sky on New Year's morning, they were finished.

They untied the ropes that had secured the boat to the dock. Papa put the engine in reverse and carefully backed out of the slip. Once they were clear of the dock, Papa gunned the engine and they headed north for a new life.

The only personal possessions they brought with them were the clothes on their backs and a few carefully selected mementos. Anything else would have weighed too much. However, nine months to the day from that night my sister Sapphire was born. So perhaps my parents did take something else from their homeland, although not something they planned. Conceiving a baby that night hadn't been part of my parents' careful calculations.

My siblings and I never got tired of hearing how our parents got out of Cuba, and they happily obliged when we asked them to tell us again and again. They never really explained what happened once they reached Miami, simply telling us that everything worked out. Which I guessed it had, since we never lacked for anything. We never pressed them to tell us about the early days in Miami, a subject about which they were unusually closemouthed.

I was jarred back to reality by the insistent ringing of my cell phone. I sighed, turned off the treadmill, and grabbed my towel before answering. The number on the caller ID said it was Sapphire. I hoped she had gotten around to taking her Ritalin.

"Esmeralda?" she barked out. I could tell she was still unmedicated. "OK. We're meeting at noon at their apartment."

Without another word, and without any more information, she hung up. It was about a full minute before I noticed I was standing there staring at the phone, having forgotten to restart the treadmill.

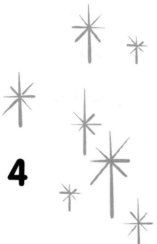

4

PRECISELY AT NOON I MET my sisters Sapphire and Ruby, along with my brother, Quartz, in the lobby of the building where my parents lived. After I left the gym that morning, I barely had enough time to race home, shower, change, and drive out to Miami Beach.

I was the last to arrive, a fact that my siblings took great pleasure in pointing out to me. We issued our standard complaints about the hellish traffic on the way over, then kissed one another and took stock of how we were all looking. There were no major surprises, which was reassuring given the general mystery of what we were all doing there.

"All right. Does anyone know anything about why we're here?" Sapphire asked. She seemed reasonably calm, and I hoped she had gotten around to taking her medicine.

I couldn't help but marvel over my sister's outfit—skin-tight royal blue pedal pushers topped by a midriff-baring cropped top in a cringe-inducing shade of blue. She wore four-inch wedge shoes of aqua-colored straw and carried a matching tote bag. Perched on her head was a fluorescent blue French beret—very Monica.

Thankfully, Sapphire had stopped getting indigo-blue highlights in her hair and allowed it to revert back to its natural blond color. It suited her much better, even if she complained that it made her look like a Republican. I knew it was just a matter of time until she gave in to temptation and started coloring it again. With everything that Sapphire had done to her hair, it was a wonder she hadn't gone bald. Sapphire was a performance artist, and she considered herself an ongoing work of art not to be constrained by societal conventions. I tried not to be judgmental about her appearance, but I secretly thought there was a point in one's life when age had to be taken into account. At thirty-five, Sapphire was starting to flirt with ridiculousness. The sad truth was that only the very young could get away with dressing like she did. Now that I had just turned thirty, I was painfully aware that I had to start thinking about myself in those same terms.

Sapphire dressed in only shades of blue. When she was twenty-one, she had visited a famous psychic who had told her that she indeed had been a Sapphire in a previous life—that is, a precious stone. I thought it was a bunch of bullshit, but if it made her feel more grounded in life, then I was all for it.

Ruby, on the other hand, was the complete opposite of our eldest sister. She was always neat and tidy, her clothes always matched, and she never had a hair out of place. She was a partner at a boutique Miami law firm and, dressed head to toe in her signature Armani, reeked of sleekness and efficiency. She was only thirty-two, but gave the impression of being much more mature than her years. Ruby was so different from the other Navarros that if she didn't look so much like the rest of us, I would have suspected there had been some kind of mix-up at the maternity ward.

Ruby had two saving graces: she loved to gamble and would bet on anything and, like the rest of us, she was a complete night owl. She was going to marry Manuel Ramirez in a few months; Manuel was a fellow attorney and Ruby's former classmate at Harvard Law School. He was a Cuban guy whom we all really liked. Ruby seemed to have it all, and her life was as well ordered and regulated as her immaculate outfits. Sometimes I tried to dislike her when she made me feel like a slob whose life was spiraling out of control, but it was no use. Underneath all her frightful efficiency, Ruby was a warm and loving woman.

I looked at Q, our baby brother, who was noticeably high. He smoked more weed than he should have but, as far as I could tell, it was a habit that was more or less under control. Ever since he turned twenty-five a couple of months ago, he seemed to have curbed his excesses a little. Sapphire, Diamond, and I had all smoked our share when we were younger, so we were reluctant to judge our baby brother. Ruby, of course, had never touched it. The rest of us had slowed down with age—at least I knew I had. Smoking grass and motherhood weren't really compatible in my book.

Quartz was dressed in basic black, very South Beach. We knew little of his personal life, and he kept all the details to himself. Still, I was reasonably certain that he was gay. He was the only boy in a family of girls, the son and heir of a Cuban family, which meant that he simply wasn't allowed to be gay. Sometimes I thought he smoked and drank because he was living a double life, having to remain closeted for our parents. Maybe it was because he had four crazy older sisters. I hoped the former was the reason, if only for my conscience.

Our brother was breathtakingly handsome, tall and thin but well built. He had hazel eyes, and blond hair that he always wore a little too long. He was one of the premiere disc jockeys in South Beach, and the clubs there competed for him. Q never went to college, instead immersing himself in music after he graduated from the Jesuit academy. During high school he had earned pocket money by hiring himself out as a disc jockey for parties, eventually doing so well that he bought his own equipment and a van in which to transport it. He had dominated the circuit of *quinceañeras,* the coming-out balls Latino families threw for their daughters when the girls turned fifteen. By the time Q turned nineteen, he had moved out of the house and into his own condo on South Beach.

Diamond, the only sibling not in attendance, was the biggest free spirit of us all. If she had been alive in the sixties, she would have been at Woodstock dancing naked in the mud and flying high on acid. She was stunningly beautiful, sporting a natural look with her nearly opalescent pale rose-colored skin. She never wore any makeup of any kind, which made her all the more striking. She was the tallest of us all, thin but with a voluptuous body, her waist-length curly blond hair streaked with natural red highlights. Diamond had extraordinary light blue eyes that sometimes bordered on gray, with silver flecks that made them look like mirrors when they caught the light just right. She favored long, flowing, diaphanous clothes that gave her a real Lady Godiva look.

Two years ago, after graduating from the University of Montana with a journalism degree, Diamond surprised everyone by announcing that she was moving to Las Vegas. We thought of Vegas as the city of plastic and artifice—which was saying a lot, coming from Miami—but ultimately we realized that her gambler's blood had drawn her out to the desert. She took a job with a community newspaper called the *Las Vegas Herald* that specialized in environmental stories.

For the first couple of months she had sent us copies of articles bearing her byline, but she had been pretty much out of touch with us for the last year. She'd come back home only twice since she moved, at Christmastime, and hadn't really volunteered anything about her life out there. She seemed happy and settled, and there had always been an air of mystery surrounding Diamond, so we knew better than to pry. When we talked about her, it was usually to express our wishes that she would come back to Miami.

I suppose I was a combination of my siblings—not as outlandish as Sapphire, as buttoned-up as Ruby, as free-spirited as Diamond, or as focused as Q. Still, I shared traits with all of them. I was the only one of us with a spouse and children, which by my family's standards made me fairly conventional and average. To my thinking, it was a façade. I was a nonconformist who lived a conformist's life. For now, it suited me just fine—although I knew my dissatisfaction with Tony meant that a change might be in my future.

For the family gathering that day, I had opted for a Banana Republic, safari kind of look. I didn't want to be overshadowed by my sisters or brother, though, and I had to admit that I might have overdone it somewhat. I looked as though I might be ready to rendezvous with Dr. Livingston in the heart of Africa, dressed completely in khaki with tan cotton pants, a camp shirt, a touch of camouflage on my scarf, and short brown canvas boots on my feet. All I needed was a canteen and binoculars, and I would have been ready for a romp around Victoria Falls.

Ruby looked at her watch. "Listen, you guys, I don't have tons of time. I have a depo at two."

I was glad that someone was going to hurry us along. "I can't stay long, either," I said. "I'm going to have to pick up the boys at school."

We walked together past Stan, the security guard sitting in his chair engrossed in doing the crossword puzzle through glasses so thick they made his face look like a puffer fish's. Stan was dressed, as usual, in his yellow uniform with gold epaulettes. He was about ninety years old, deaf, arthritic, and almost blind. It was terrifying to think about it, but Stan was actually armed, carrying a gun in a visible leather holster. I wondered how good his security firm's insurance was, because there was no way Stan could possibly stop someone from entering the building. Even I could have flicked him away like a mosquito.

I looked around the lobby while we waited for the elevator.

Mama and Papa lived in the penthouse apartment of a high-rise on Collins Avenue in Miami Beach, just a few blocks north of the Fountainbleau Hotel. They had moved there a month after Diamond left home, leaving them without a child in the house for the first time in more than two decades. We grew up in a big, traditional, two-story Spanish-style house in Coral Gables, an upscale residential neighborhood of Miami. My siblings and I had always thought our parents were happy living there because they had never given any indication otherwise. And while we weren't an Ozzie and Harriet kind of family, we blended in just fine with the rest of the neighborhood. When the other kids asked what our father did, we had been instructed to say that he "looked after the family's investments." It actually seemed pretty glamorous, what with all the doctors and lawyers running around.

Although some of our neighbors might have imagined Papa going off to an office when he got in his car and drove off, he actually spent his days and some of his nights at the racetrack. He bet on ponies and dogs, and he also frequented jai alai frontons. He took us with him whenever he could. Mama stayed at home, took care of the house, and raised us children. It didn't seem likely that Papa made enough money from betting at the track to maintain our lifestyle, but we still never wanted for anything. All five of us went to private schools and, since none of us had a jump shot, we paid full freight for college and, in Ruby's case, law school. Somehow there was always enough money for us to do what we wanted, so we never questioned the state of our family finances.

For family vacations we went to Las Vegas—and this was a long time before the town tried to attract families. Once, when I was fifteen, we went to Europe and spent a week visiting the casinos at Monte Carlo. In the fall, when our classes at school required us to write essays explaining what we did over summer vacation, our teachers received detailed reports on the assorted casinos where we had spent our time. We were the only students who came back from summer vacation without a tan. We might have been pasty-faced from too many hours spent under fluorescent light, but our math skills approached perfection.

It was an unorthodox upbringing, but all four of us girls went on to college after we graduated from high school. We all took different paths, but one thing we had in common was near-perfect math scores on our SATs. Sapphire was the first to leave home when she went to UCLA to major in theater. Ruby went north to Harvard and stayed there through law school. I went to New York to study at Barnard—I wanted to go to Columbia, but I didn't get in. I didn't know what I wanted to do in life, so I majored in English literature. Diamond wanted to live out West, so she went to the University of Montana, Missoula, and studied journalism. Quartz didn't go to college, but he was still young and made noise from time to time about applying someplace.

After Diamond followed through on her wish to move to Las Vegas, Mama and Papa immediately put the house on the market and made an offer on the Miami Beach penthouse. The house sold within hours to the first couple who saw it, and the penthouse was part of an estate sale represented by lawyers who wanted to liquidate the property as quickly as possible. Both transactions were completed within a day. The couple who bought our family house—a retired Fortune 500 CEO and his wife—liked our furniture, so my parents agreed to include it in the sale. We all knew that Mama and Papa weren't overly sentimental, but it was still a shock to see them walk away from their home of forty years without any visible pangs of regret. All they took with them were their personal possessions, their artwork, and, of course, their dogs— ever since their arrival in Miami, my parents had always owned two poodles, one white and one black. They named the dogs Día and Noche: Day and Night. By then, they were on their fifth pair.

My parents paid cash for the penthouse, sparing themselves the mortgage application process. The place was vacant, and they planned no major changes in the layout, so they moved in as soon as their new furniture was delivered. We were all stunned by how quickly this happened. Our parents had never given any indication that they were unhappy in Coral Gables, or that they planned to move as soon as the last of their children was out of the house. We weren't naïve enough to think we knew everything about their lives, but we almost felt betrayed by the extent to which they had kept us out of the loop. We didn't talk about it much, but I knew the whole episode made me wonder what else they might have hidden from us, and whether I really knew my parents.

My siblings and I spent countless hours trying to figure out why Mama and Papa moved to Miami Beach—and why they chose such a bizarre building. The only plausible explanation was that Miami Beach reminded them of Havana in the fifties. Implicit in this similarity, of course, was the influence of the Mob in both Miami Beach and Havana during that era. We knew the fifties were the golden age for our parents, and maybe they were trying to recapture lost memories. It was all pure speculation, because our parents had little to say on the subject. They said they liked Miami Beach and had always wanted to live there. With that, they considered the subject closed.

Mama and Papa didn't allow us to see their new home until they were settled in, so it was more than a month before we were invited to visit. Finally they gave us the address, and one afternoon we all met outside and stared long and hard at the building's exterior. One thing was certain—our parents had picked the strangest, flashiest place on Miami Beach in which to live. The architecture of the fifties was considered over the top, but this building was over the stratosphere. It was on Collins Avenue, the wide avenue lined with stately palm trees, right on the beach, its other side facing a canal. It stood amid dozens of other buildings, but it had no problem distinguishing itself from its neighbors.

The building was set back from the street on a small hill and was painted seafoam green with pink and turquoise accents. Set by the entrance were life-sized yellow marble statues of Roman centurions in full battle gear: tunics, sandals, helmets, and shields. They looked as though they were guarding the property and wouldn't hesitate to unsheathe their swords to protect its residents. In front of the building was a curved wall made of block glass combined with colored panels and gilt trim; the wall was ostensibly to provide privacy, but when it caught the sun it was capable of blinding passersby. A grand sweeping driveway coated with gold flecks led from the street to the building, ending in a massive portico that was truly amazing. In lieu of traditional columns, the portico featured four giant statues of Roman emperors holding up a sea green ceiling with cutouts of what were apparently amoebas. There were also palm trees painted amid the ceiling murk, leaving the impression that the artist couldn't decide between depicting an underwater scene or a beach contaminated by single-cell creatures.

The strangeness didn't end inside the front door. The cavernous lobby was a testament to its designer's love of gold. It was as though King Midas himself had had a hand in drawing up the décor. The terrazzo floor was dizzying, laid out in a geometric pattern of black and gold. The center of the room was filled by a gold fountain with rotund dolphin statues cavorting in water with jets of golden-tinted water coming from spouts that had inexplicably been set in their bellies. The dolphins looked as though they were pissing instead of blowing water out of their spouts. The perimeter of the room was occupied by nine—not one, but nine—statues of Carmen Miranda in different poses, each burnished in varying shades of gold, each carrying a plate of food on her head. I was never able to find out who had designed the place—probably because they were locked in an insane asylum as soon as their work was completed.

The building was a monument to vulgarity and gaudiness. Before they moved in there, we had thought our parents were, if not exactly refined, at least somewhat sophisticated in their tastes. All our illusions were blown away the first time we entered this house of gold. Each of us handled visiting our parents' building the best we could. Sapphire simply gaped, taking in the décor with amazement as though she couldn't believe what she was seeing. Ruby squared her shoulders and focused on her own elegant shoes. Diamond, the few times she visited, stopped at the fountain to dip her hand in the water. Quartz just shook his head and squinted, as though he was coming out of a bad acid trip and everything he saw was causing him pain. As the interior designer of the group, I tried to look around with dispassionate professional interest, checking to see if anything had changed since my last visit.

Finally the elevator chimed. The building was fifteen stories tall, but there was only one elevator. In unison, unable to bear the lobby a second longer, we all sprinted through the open door. There was little relief inside; the elevator itself was done all in gold, with sheer gauzy curtains in the back, and a mirrored ceiling. Even the buttons were coated with a gold film. All four of us averted our eyes to keep from looking at the gold cherub suspended from the ceiling above us.

Finally Sapphire couldn't stand it any longer. The elevator moved us up to the penthouse level, and she took us in with a wild stare.

"All right," she said to all of us. "Who wants to take any bets on what this is all about?"

5

their quest to recapture the fifties to the choice of the building in which they lived; their apartment also was furnished entirely in that period's style. As an interior designer, I was both awed by the authenticity and appalled. The wall-to-wall white shag carpet made me feel as though I was walking on a heavenly cloud, but I was quickly thrown down to hell by the yards of formica that covered every available surface. In addition, there wasn't a single comfortable chair on which to sit in the entire apartment. The only piece my parents salvaged from the house in Coral Gables was the floor-to-ceiling cabinet in which they displayed their precious mementos from La Estrella. It stood out even more than before in the center of the living room, because it clashed so much with the décor. Still, it was reassuring to see it there because it served as proof that my parents hadn't gone completely insane.

My parents owned the entire penthouse floor, and their living space was more than four thousand square feet. The place had one attribute that compensated for the horrible architecture and décor: a spectacular, riveting view. From their fifteenth-floor perch they could look in all directions—to the west were the mansions on Pine Tree Drive that backed onto waterways; the

Atlantic Ocean was to the east, Bal Harbour to the north, and the visual riot of South Beach to the south. The all-glass walls lent a clear and unobstructed three-hundred-sixty-degree view. I loved being there at dusk and watching the sunset, then the lights of the city coming on. The transformation was magic.

The first time I saw the place, I asked Papa how much his hurricane insurance cost; after all, the apartment was completely at the mercy of the elements. It was one of the few times in my life that Papa refused to answer a question from me. He must have had to pay a fortune because even regular insurance rates had become prohibitively high after Hurricane Andrew in 1992.

The elevator opened straight into the apartment. We walked out of the car in lockstep, but our parents were nowhere to be found. Not knowing what to expect, we simply stood there as though waiting for instructions. Then, with Sapphire taking the lead, we moved through the foyer and into the main room.

Apparently Mama and Papa wanted to be dramatic. They were waiting for us in the living room, seated on their red suede sofa with Día and Noche snoozing at their sides. They were both dressed formally, with Mama in a light pink gabardine two-piece suit—I recognized it as her favorite—and beige slingback shoes. My mouth opened in shock when I saw that she was wearing stockings; it was something she rarely did, claiming they choked her and made her feel claustrophobic. How clothing worn on one's legs could be choking was a mystery that she never successfully explained to me, but she maintained a policy of wearing stockings only on four occasions: Baptisms, First Communions, weddings, and funerals. I wondered which fit the reason for our being summoned.

Papa was decked out in a white linen crisply ironed guayabera, the formal Cuban men's dress shirt, and brown pants. I noticed he was wearing his favorite black leather loafers and—another rarity—dress socks. Papa hated socks almost as much as Mama hated stockings. My heart began to beat faster. They obviously had something important in mind.

With drawn and serious expressions, my parents offered their cheeks to receive kisses. I saw that they were holding hands—another rarity. I knew my parents loved each other deeply, but it was not in Maria Mercedes Montalvo's or Gabriel Navarro's nature to show their physical affections in front of their children. Growing up, my siblings and I wondered how on earth we were ever conceived, because the idea of my parents even touching was preposterous. The thought of their having sex was so far-fetched that we even wondered sometimes whether we had been adopted. I once theorized that my parents were the exception to the standard human rules of reproduction, and that they had somehow bumped in the hallway at home and—*presto!*—magically connected sperm and egg. I think one of the reasons I performed so miserably in high school biology was because I couldn't accept the notion that a man and a woman had to be naked together in order for reproduction to occur. Needless to say, I remained a virgin through high school.

I looked around and saw Sapphire, Ruby, and Quartz all staring at my parents' clasped hands. Somberly, we sat down on the spindly, uncomfortable chairs facing the sofa. We looked as though we were sitting in the doctor's office, waiting for the results of a particularly serious diagnostic test.

Deep breath time—I felt anxiety coursing through my body, beginning in my chest and radiating outward. I tried to reassure myself that this couldn't be a matter of life and death—if it were, Mama and Papa would have insisted that Diamond be present.

Mama didn't offer us anything to eat or drink, which was unheard of for a Cuban mother. That omission was basically as heinous as infanticide. I was about a half-step away from complete panic. All sorts of horrible thoughts raced through my mind. Were they getting divorced? Joining a cult? Becoming vegetarians? Just when I was about to burst, Papa cleared his throat. The room was so silent I could hear cool air coming into the room through the air-conditioner vents.

"You're probably wondering why your mother and I asked you here today," he said slowly. All four of us nodded, our heads bobbing up and down. Papa looked at Mama, who gave him a little nod to continue.

"You all know that I'm not very religious. But your mama is." We all nodded again. "But this case is different. This time I believe."

Papa spoke slowly, tortuously, and my brain whizzed along. Did the socks and stockings mean this was some sort of religious occasion?

Sapphire couldn't take it. She jumped out of her chair. For the first time in memory, I was glad she was such a poster child for ADD.

She let out a moan of torment and slapped herself on the forehead. "Enough!" she announced. "Papa, what in the hell are you talking about?"

Seeing that Papa wasn't doing a great job of explaining himself, Mama took charge. "Two nights ago, I had a very vivid dream," she said softly. "It was also a very important dream."

Sapphire dropped back into her chair and we four siblings sat perched. We all knew that Mama consulted psychics, astrologers, *babalawas,* and even a couple of *santeros,* but I didn't remember her seeing anyone who specialized in dreams. It was hard to imagine that she had called us there to tell us about something she saw in the night. She was far too practical for that.

"In this dream I was visited by my great-great-grandmother Maria Mercedes Montalvo." A strange, otherworldly light came into Mama's eyes that frightened me. "I saw her clearly, standing at the foot of the bed. She was so close I could hear her breathe, and I could smell the perfume she was wearing."

It took a moment for us to absorb what Mama had just said. Then, in unison, our eyes turned to the cabinet where the picture of Maria Mercedes Montalvo was displayed. Even Sapphire was speechless.

"Mama, I'm not sure what that means," Ruby said. She was using her lawyer's voice, but I could tell she was rattled.

Papa tightened his grip on Mama's hand, staring at her as she spoke. He seemed perfectly composed, which meant that hopefully he didn't think Mama had gone nuts.

Mama suddenly broke out in a familiar smile. "Don't worry. It's good news, it really is." She patted Noche, who looked up and yawned. "Because Maria Mercedes told me that we would be getting La Estrella back—and very soon."

I was ready to panic. Mama was clearly serious. She thought her long-dead namesake had come back to give her the news she and Papa had been awaiting for four decades. I decided to go along with what she was telling us, if only to learn more.

"Did Maria Mercedes explain how this is going to happen?" I asked. "I mean, the casino was taken away almost forty-five years ago and, as far as I know, Castro isn't returning any confiscated property. If anything, he's selling things off. La Estrella isn't even operating as a casino right now, as far as we know."

I hated myself for saying all that, but I had to find out whether Mama had gone completely delusional.

Mama glanced at Papa with a look that said, *I told you they'd react this way.* Then she looked at us.

"Maria Mercedes said that she would explain as soon as we are all together," she told us.

"But we *are* together," Ruby said.

"No, we're not." Mama shook her head. "Diamond isn't here."

I was ashamed of myself for not remembering Diamond. Our

youngest sister had been away for so long that I didn't often think of her.

"Surely Maria Mercedes knew that, Mama," Sapphire said. "I mean, ghosts float around all the time, so they know everything. Right?"

"So we can't find out about La Estrella until we're all in the same room?" Quartz asked, his words slow and measured because of the weed I could tell he had smoked.

We were all quiet for a moment. I knew how much my parents wanted to see their beloved La Estrella before they passed away, but I had to be skeptical of a prediction made in a dream by one of our ancestors—even if she had been one of the casino's founders.

Mama stood up. "I know you think I'm crazy and, frankly, I don't really blame you." She went to the cabinet of La Estrella mementos. "So I will prove to you that I'm not imagining things."

We all got up and followed her, arranging ourselves in a half-circle in front of the double doors.

"Look!" Mama pointed to the shelf in the middle of the cabinet.

As soon as we saw what Mama wanted us to look at, we all let out a sound of disbelief. The cut-glass ashtray containing the five stones we had been named after was in its usual place, but it was empty. My first thought was that someone had broken in and taken the stones, but I knew my parents had a powerful home alarm. Then I followed the line my mother traced with her finger, and let out another gasp of surprise. On the uppermost shelf was a detailed map of Havana with the central district enlarged. There, right on the spot that La Estrella occupied, were the five stones arranged in a neat little circle.

"See!" Mama said triumphantly. "You see—I'm not making this up. Maria Mercedes has given us a sign that we're going to get La Estrella back."

I looked over at Papa, who was sitting on the sofa petting the dogs. He nodded at me with a look of peace and contentment. It was clear that he was buying into everything Mama was saying.

My siblings and I just stood there, our mouths hanging open and our eyes glued to the stones. We had never seen the jewels anywhere but ensconced in the cut-glass bowl. As far as I knew, the cabinet door was never opened except on New Year's Eve. Papa had put the precious objects inside and closed it up until La Estrella was his again.

I was trying to get my bearings when Mama turned to face her children with a look of sudden urgency.

"Now, about Diamond," she said. "Maria Mercedes said we have to all be here together before we can learn how La Estrella is going to be returned to us. What are we going to do about Diamond?"

6

MY HEAD STARTED TO SWIM
and I reached out and put my hand on Sapphire to keep my balance. We were all now talking about what course of action we were going to take to satisfy a prophesy sent forth in my mother's dream. The precious stones moving from the glass ashtray to the map sealed the deal—never mind the fact that we had to take it on belief that Mama hadn't moved them herself, maybe while sleepwalking. The whole situation was so surreal that I might have been in a waking dream myself.

It was an awkward moment, and I could sense my siblings wrestling with the same thoughts as I. I kept staring at the five precious stones arrayed on the map of Havana. The cut-glass dish, home to the stones for decades, looked almost obscenely empty.

"Mama, we need to think about this," I offered, breaking the silence. I spoke carefully: Mama could be thin-skinned at the best of times, and I knew she would explode if she thought I wasn't taking her seriously. "I mean, this is really a shock. There are a lot of ramifications to think through."

"You think I'm making this all up, don't you?" My mother flared with indignation. "You think I was hallucinating like a crazy old lady when I saw Maria Mercedes in my dream? You think I want to go back to Cuba so badly that I'm willing to make up a ridiculous story?"

"Mama—" Ruby said.

Mama pointed at the cabinet and the ashtray. "You think I moved those stones myself?" she glared at us all. "I moved the stones, just to get you to believe me? Do you all think that I'm as ridiculous as that? A crazy old lady?"

I don't think I'd ever seen Mama so pissed off, and so quickly. She always had a temper, but she had gone from placid to enraged in about ten seconds. We were all shocked, but I had seen it coming. Anything about La Estrella was sacred to her.

"Mama, Esmeralda isn't implying we don't believe you," said Ruby, always the peacemaker. "It's just that this is all so unexpected, and we need to know more about what's happened. Please, Mama, this is all so new to us."

Mama folded her arms, her expression softening somewhat. "I am *not* making this up," she said.

"Of course you aren't." Ruby gently took my mother's arm and led her toward the sofa. "We just want to understand everything you're telling us. That's what Esmeralda meant."

Mama looked at me. "You believe me?" she asked.

"Of course," I said. "I'm sorry I made you angry. I'll listen to everything you have to say."

Mierda.

We dutifully trooped back to our seats. Papa remained quiet, petting the dogs. Now I wondered what he really thought. Part of me suspected that he was just sitting back to see how all this was going to play out. It wasn't like him to remain so aloof from something that was important to the family, although he and Mama had always presented a united front when it came to dealing with us children.

Quartz cleared his throat, obviously trying to get a grip on this strange situation. "Mama, did Maria Mercedes give you even a little hint about how the family is supposed to regain La Estrella?" he asked. He saw Mama's expression darken. "It's not that I don't believe you, of course I do. But how can Maria Mercedes expect us to take her seriously when she didn't give any concrete details about what she's predicting?"

I could have kissed my brother for finally speaking up. Mama nodded, considering his words. He had said basically the same thing as I, but in Cuban families sons have special privileges. Ours was no different. If anyone was going to reason with Mama, it was going to have to be Quartz.

"Maria Mercedes," Papa suddenly interjected. I was doubly surprised, because he had previously been so quiet and because he almost always addressed my mother as Mimi, rather than by her formal name.

"Yes, Gabriel?" Mama asked.

"I think it's time we showed the children the secret room," he said somberly. "It will help them understand everything more clearly."

Mama looked as startled as if Papa had physically struck her. "Gabriel, no. We agreed!" she snapped back with a vehemence I had never seen before.

I gasped. Our parents never, ever disagreed in front of us, and in my entire life I had never heard Mama speak so harshly to Papa. Obviously Papa had broken some kind of rule made in secret between them.

The room became sepulchrally quiet. I didn't know about my sisters and my brother, but I sure as hell wasn't leaving the apartment until I saw this "secret room"—whatever it was. I sneaked a glance at my siblings' faces and could tell they felt the same.

Our father stood. "Maria Mercedes, it's the only way they're going to believe." He reached into his pocket and pulled out a key ring, one I had never seen before. On it was a small screwdriver. "I'm going to have to show them."

We jumped up from our chairs and crowded around our father. We knew we had to press the moment because Papa was usually a pushover when it came to standing up to Mama and that he could change his mind at any moment. He was a forceful and dynamic man in all other areas of his life, but found it almost impossible to contradict his wife.

"Gabriel, if you've made up your mind, there's nothing I can do," Mama said. She stood up and, to our shock, actually kissed Papa lightly on the lips in our full view. I felt as though I was watching an X-rated movie. This was even more shocking than the ghosts, the stones moving on their own, and the secret room.

"Come on," Papa said, leading us toward the elevator at the front of the apartment. When he reached it, he stood before us and clasped his hands. "You know the story of how your mother and I left Cuba, right?"

"Of course, Papa," Sapphire said.

"And we've showed you the contents of the cabinet every New Year's Eve, and explained what our keepsakes mean to our family?"

"Every year, Papa," Ruby said.

"Now it's time for you to learn the whole story," Papa said. As soon as the words were out of his mouth, Mama joined him and, with solemn dignity, hooked her arm through his.

"Gabriel," she said, "if you're really going to tell the children the whole truth, we will tell them together."

Papa patted her arm, visibly grateful. "We told you the truth," he said to us. "But we omitted a few important facts. It was . . . it was only because we felt it was best for you."

"Gabriel, they're adults now," Mama gently scolded. "Just tell them."

Papa took a deep breath. "When you were growing up, we lived well, but not extravagantly. You never lacked for anything, did you?"

"We've always been comfortable," I told him, my voice strange and shaky in my ears.

"Your mother and I led you to believe that we lived off my winnings from gambling," he continued. "Well, I did win when I gambled. I've always done well. But that wasn't the entire source of our income."

I knew it wouldn't be long before I had to pick up the boys at school, but there was no way I was leaving. The boys could go to after-school care and I would deal with Tony later. It would be just one more thing for us to argue about, but the hell with it. Blood was pounding in my ears and I felt my skin flush. I sensed that my life was about to be redefined.

"We told you that we took some valuables out of La Estrella and loaded them onto our boat," Papa said. "But we never told you what happened after that."

"We assumed you sold them and used the cash to buy our old house," Sapphire said.

"I guess you never really explained in detail," Ruby said, obviously thinking and remembering. "But that's what I thought, too—that you sold the gold and jewels to buy the house and invested the rest."

"You were right to think that," Mama said. "We sold some of the gold bars and stones to buy the house. But not all of them."

"Not all of them?" Quartz repeated, blinking.

"Do you remember how we put the house on the market after Diamond left for Las Vegas?" Mama asked. "And how quickly we moved into this apartment?"

"*Sí, sí,*" we all said in unison.

"The reason we moved so quickly into this apartment is because we owned it all along," Papa explained. "We bought this place just after we arrived in Miami from Cuba."

I knew I looked like an idiot, but I stood there with my mouth hanging open anyway. Our parents were telling us that, in effect, they had been lying to us our entire lives.

"Mama! Papa!" Sapphire was about to lose what little composure she had been able to muster. "I don't understand!"

Mama shot a quick look at Papa that said he shouldn't have opened this can of worms. But it was too late to go back.

"When Castro was fighting in the hills against Batista, your father and I had to make a decision," Mama said. "We knew we were going to have to get out of Cuba, because Castro was going to win. That was when we decided that we had to salvage as much as we could."

"We know," Sapphire said.

"You *think* you know," Mama replied. She paused. "Look, you know we had American friends in the casino business, right?"

"You mean guys in the Mob," said Quartz. He might have been a stoner, but he was never one to sugarcoat the facts.

Papa looked annoyed. "Please don't say that. That is just a rumor. Those allegations have never been proven."

Ruby and I glanced at each other and each bit our lip. Usually Papa's denial of the Mob's existence was funny to us, but he sounded so genuinely irritated that we checked our reaction.

"Anyway, we needed help," Papa said. "So we went to an American we'd been very close friends with. He was happy to help us—for a percentage, of course."

"And what did this American 'friend' do for you?" I asked. I really had a hard time believing what I was hearing. I knew our family had to make a variety of payoffs in Havana—to the Mob, to Batista, even to Castro—but I had never heard of them dealing with the Mafia after the days at La Estrella.

"He made some important arrangements for us," Papa said. "When our boat reached Miami, there was a van waiting for us at the dock. We arrived in the morning, and we had to work quickly.

There were two men waiting to help us unload our valuables and put them in the van."

"You mean—" Quartz said.

"You had Mob guys help you unload a bunch of gold and jewels off a boat straight from Cuba?" Sapphire asked, flabbergasted. "You're lucky they didn't rob you and kill you."

Papa's eyes opened with surprise. "What makes you say that?"

"It's . . . it was the Mafia," Ruby interjected.

Papa shook his head. "You don't understand the way things worked then. With the arrangements we made, we were the safest people in Miami that morning."

"So you had a van full of valuables," I said. "What next?"

"We came here. To this building in this apartment," Mama said. "Our friend had bought it earlier in the year, and he was in the process of renovating it. Our timing couldn't have been better. We were able to have this apartment reconfigured to suit our special needs."

Special needs? Didn't they simply need a place to live? Then I remembered the secret room we were about to see. I had a lot of questions, but I decided to start with the most obvious one.

"So you brought the gold and jewels here," I said. "What happened to them?"

Mama then nodded at Papa, who stepped over to the wall to the right of the elevator. He put his hand on the bronze plate with the button that summoned the elevator and, with the screwdriver that hung from his key ring, loosened the plate from the wall. He carefully put the foot-long plate on the table next to the elevator, and carefully placed the two screws on top. And there, flush against the wall where the plate had been, was another button. This one was made of black plastic, and it was so small that it was easy to see why it had been easily concealed.

We watched Papa move the table away from the wall, then take down the big painting of a royal palm tree that had hung over the table. Then he lifted the first of the two ten-foot-tall ficus trees on either side of the table, motioning for Quartz to remove its twin. He did all this with such practiced expertise, it was obvious that he had performed this ritual on countless other occasions.

"Stand back now," Papa ordered us. Then he nodded to Mama, who pressed the plastic button. A moment later, a section of the wall the size of a regular door swung out to reveal heavy black velvet curtains. My siblings and I stood there staring at the expanse of fabric.

Mama turned to me. "Esmeralda, you asked where the gold and jewelry was." She pulled aside the velvet curtain, reached inside, and flicked on a switch. We saw a sliver of light before she pulled the curtain shut again. I caught a brief sight of a bright golden glow from within. Then our mother stepped back and gestured toward the room.

"Please," she said. "Go in and look."

That was all the invitation I needed. I pulled aside the curtain and went into the room. As soon as what I was seeing registered in my mind, I let out a gasp. What I saw probably rivaled anything in the safes of Tiffany, Cartier, or Harry Winston.

Hundreds of gold bars were stacked on cement shelves from the floor to the ceiling on three sides of the room. That was impressive enough, but it was the fourth wall that made me blink again and again to make sure I wasn't hallucinating. That wall contained five shelves, each with a glass case lined in black velvet—except for the bottom one, which was lined in white. Each case contained precious stones in a staggering assortment of sizes, ranging from the size of rocks down to little marbles. I was no expert, but I could see that sapphires were on the top shelf, moving down to rubies, emeralds, diamonds, and quartz.

I felt Sapphire nudge me aside so she and the others could come inside the cramped space. One by one, they let out their own expressions of amazement. The four of us gravitated to the wall of precious stones, each fixating our gaze on the shelf full of jewels that corresponded to our individual names. Sapphire was on her tiptoes, while poor Quartz was down on his knees.

Our mother watched from the doorway with an expression of sadness mingled with satisfaction. "And you thought your father and I gave you your names simply because we liked them," she said, sounding pleased with herself.

"This is . . . this is the treasure from La Estrella," I said, somewhat obviously.

"Not all of them." Papa said, joining Mama in the doorway. "We did sell some of them in order to meet our living expenses. But we were more successful in bringing out La Estrella's treasure than we ever revealed."

Papa stroked the gold bars on the high shelf nearest to him, much in the same manner he had stroked his dogs.

"We tried to keep as much of the gold as we could," he said. "So we sold some valuables—mostly pearls. We tried to keep nearly all of the ones we named you children after."

"Our friend helped us very much—for a cut, of course," Mama said, making sure we understood that there was honor among thieves. Mama sighed, this time with a tinge of regret. "Our friend was helpful and accommodating—we had done business before in the past, and trusted each other as much as we could. Still, we never thought this place was suitable for raising children, given its ownership, and the fact that it's in the middle of Miami Beach. We found out that Coral Gables was the place for families, so a few months before Sapphire was born, we bought a house there. And that's the home where you all grew up."

"So the reason you gambled so much, Papa, was so you could account for your income without having to declare the value of this treasure you brought from Cuba?" asked Ruby, ever the lawyer.

I thought about Tony. The accountant in him would have a heart attack. If I told him.

Papa just shrugged, as though admitting that he had done what he had to. As though feeling a need to redeem himself in our eyes, he went over to the shelf containing the rubies. "These sent you to law school," he said to my sister.

"Do you mean that literally?" Quartz asked. I could see that the shock of what he had seen was bringing him out of his fog.

"Your Mama knows her jewels," Papa said with obvious affection and respect. "When we got here with all this, we really weren't sure what it was all going to be worth. There were so many valuables in the safe the night we emptied it, but we had no idea how much. Your mother took some jewels out of their settings and took them to professionals for estimates. As far as the gold bars were concerned—well, that was easy. All we had to do was read the *Wall Street Journal* every day to keep tabs on their value."

"None of you were born yet, but I was pregnant with Sapphire," Mama said. "We set aside enough stones for seven children—four girls and three boys, we figured. All with the same value. No favorites. So when we needed money for each of you, we drew upon the stones that bore your name."

"That's why Ruby's pile is so much smaller than Quartz's or Diamond's. Your Harvard tuition really made a dent, Ruby," Papa said with a fond smile. "But I hope it will all even out in the end."

I stood there surrounded by a treasure. And then I had an epiphany. I made an admittedly dramatic gesture that encompassed all four walls.

"That's why Maria Mercedes's prophesy is real to you," I said to my parents. "This is how you know La Estrella can operate again."

My siblings looked at me. "What the hell are you talking about?" Sapphire asked.

LUCK OF THE DRAW

"Don't you get it?" I said with a laugh. "This is what they're going to use to bankroll the new La Estrella."

Mama and Papa beamed at me as though I was a student who had blurted out the answer to the day's most difficult question.

"*Sí,*" Mama said. Then she turned serious. "But remember, Maria Mercedes said none of that can happen until we're all together."

"Which means Diamond," Sapphire said.

"Diamond," Quartz whispered.

Ruby and I looked at each other and nodded. It was crazy, but we suddenly all wanted it to get crazier. And that meant finding our baby sister.

"Who has talked to her most recently?" Papa asked.

We all looked at one another. It had been awhile for all of us.

"Well," said Mama almost sadly. "Sometimes I think she's been avoiding us. But that has to stop. We have to find Diamond. The future of La Estrella depends on it."

7

TONY WAS KEEPING HIS composure—after all, we were at the dinner table, and the boys were present—but I could tell it wasn't easy. I spotted the telltale red splotch that appeared on his neck when he was fuming—and this time, it had deepened all the way to crimson. The hand he was using to hold his glass of red wine was so visibly tight that I was afraid the stem might snap. I was glad that, at least, it was our everyday crystal and not the Baccarat we'd gotten as a wedding gift. The few times Tony had looked at me during dinner, his dark brown eyes were as hard as flints. I dreaded the scene that was going to take place as soon as the boys went to bed.

The last time I had seen Tony so pissed off was when I told the boys, without consulting their father, that we could keep the mangy mutt they had found on the street. Tony's sainted mother always said that dogs were too dirty, too smelly, and that their shedding was disgusting. And, since she was never wrong, her beliefs carried a great deal of weight in our household. For my part, we had always had dogs in the house when I was a girl, and it seemed strange to live in a house without one. When a stray appeared that day, it seemed like a gift from heaven.

Buster was a puppy at the time, but it was obvious from the size of his paws that he was going to grow up to be huge. Instinctively, the boys and I knew this was our big chance to bring a dog into the family. The same afternoon we found him, we took him to the vet, had him checked out, dipped in a flea bath, and given his shots. By the time Tony got home from work that night, Buster was a done deal. Although Buster was only about four months at the time, he already weighed more than forty pounds. It didn't take him very long to add seventy more.

Buster's mother must have had a robust and lively sex life, because as far as I could tell he was part shepherd, part chow— that accounted for the black splotches on his pink tongue—and part bloodhound. All this meant that, not only did he drool, but he spread it all over as he wandered in search of different scents. The boys and I loved him to death, while Tony had barely acknowledged Buster's presence in the five years since we took him in.

Tony hadn't said anything yet, but I knew why he was fuming. Just as I had feared, I was late picking the boys up at school. To top it all off, the school had called Tony at work and told him that I was unreachable at home and at my office. From what little Tony had said to me, he claimed that he had had to leave a meeting with one of his most important clients to pick the boys up at school. The client apparently was going to endure an IRS audit the next day and, when the call came, they were reviewing his past five years' tax returns. It was just about the worst timing possible.

It wasn't that Tony was a bad man—far from it, in fact. It was just that his family background left him ill-equipped for dealing with domestic life. His mother had raised him thinking that his needs, wants, and desires always came first, and his total sense of entitlement was ingrained in him from the earliest possible age. And he was an accountant, thriving on order and predictability— two things that were hard to come by as the husband of a woman from a gambling family and the father of three young boys. Tony tried to understand me, and he knew my family was unusual when we got married, but there were limits to what I could expect of him.

Which was why I didn't just tell him the truth: that I missed picking up the boys because I was in a secret treasure-filled room at my parents' apartment, trying to fulfill the prophesy of my mother's great-great-grandmother's ghost and listening to the story of how a family friend from the Mob protected our family fortune when it was brought over from Cuba. Instead, I simply told Tony that my parents had asked Sapphire, Ruby, Quartz, and me to come discuss something about Diamond. I was vague, but specific enough to keep him from worrying that I was sneaking around with a lover.

A thought came to me: if Tony was surly now, wait until I told him about my plans.

I looked around the table at the crumpled paper that was all that remained of our dinner. I hadn't had time to make a proper meal, so I'd compensated by stopping off and picking up the boys' favorite: McDonald's Big Macs and lots of fries. I tried not to cringe as I watched them slurp down enough Coke to keep them awake for a month. Gabriel and the twins wolfed down their meals slathered with ketchup, and I avoided thinking about what all the grease was doing to their arteries. They might have been only eleven and eight years old, but I was convinced that everything in life eventually took its toll.

To feed Tony and myself, I had dropped by Pollo Tropical and brought home his favorite meal—a whole chicken with lots of side dishes. By the time I got home, my car was seemingly permanently infused with the battling aromas of American and Caribbean foods. Between the smells of garlic and grease that had seeped into my hair, I was seriously considering a Clorox shower later.

I had only had a single glass of wine, but I was so drained by the events of the day that I felt exhaustion in every inch of my body. Between my mother's predawn phone call and herding the boys to the table, my day had been nonstop. My body was screaming out for a long hot bath scented with gardenia oil, and for a glass of wine, soft music in the background, and Buster snoring softly on the bath mat next to me. It was probably a fantasy that wasn't going to come true. As much as I wanted to clear all the debris off the table, I dreaded being alone with Tony. He wasn't going to like what I was going to tell him, and I couldn't think of a way to soften the blow.

Finally I got up and started to clear away the mess. Gabriel went up to his room to do his homework, and the twins retired to the den to obsess over their computer games. I saw Tony slowly lumber off to the downstairs room that he'd converted into his home office and inner sanctum. He had claimed he needed a private place to work, but I knew the room was where he escaped from family life. I understood; after all, I liked to lock myself into the bathroom for hours. But I knew that once he was inside, I would have a hard time getting through to him. It was now or never.

I took a deep breath and followed him into the office before he closed the door.

"Hey, can I talk to you?" I put my arms around his waist and hugged him. It had been so long since we touched that he almost recoiled in surprise. I hadn't realized things had gotten that bad.

It took Tony all of one second to figure out what I was doing. He removed my arms from around his waist and looked me in the eye.

"Esmeralda, you must really feel guilty about having abandoned the boys today." His eyes narrowed, and he looked me over. "No, you're not here to apologize about that, are you? It's something else, isn't it?"

I nodded miserably. There was no point lying to him.

"I have to go to Las Vegas," I said. "To find Diamond."

Tony looked at me and shrugged. I don't know what he could have asked, but something along the lines of *Is something wrong with your sister? Do you need to talk? Is there anything I can do to help?*

"Find Diamond, huh?" he commented bitterly instead. "So go. You'll just do whatever you want, anyway."

"OK."

8

THE NIGHT SEEMED END-
less. I usually passed out the moment my head hit the pillow, but
instead I tossed and turned for hours and finally fell asleep just as
dawn was breaking. My brain couldn't stop working, analyzing,
and playing back scenes in my head as though they were recorded
on video. The scene that stood out in my memory, of course, was
the moment when I saw the secret room in my parents' apartment.
It didn't matter if my eyes were open or closed, I could still
vividly see the gold bars and precious stones stacked floor-to-
ceiling in orderly rows.

Many times during the night I looked over at Tony, who slept
peacefully next to me. I didn't really want to think about how my
upcoming trip to Las Vegas was going to affect our marriage.
Back at the apartment, when my family discussed Maria Mercedes's prediction, it was clear that Diamond was going to have to
return to Miami in order for the prophesy to come true. Part of
the reason I had missed picking up the boys at school, however,
was because my parents' story hadn't stopped there. It turned out
that bringing Diamond home might be harder than any of us
would have imagined.

The fact was, Diamond never really liked Miami. She loved
her family, of course, but that love never extended to the city of

her birth. Unlike the rest of us, she preferred the wide-open spaces and views of the mountains and the desert. It had been no great surprise to any of us when she announced she was going to college in Montana. And the fact that she was leaving home for college was no great scandal; after all, Sapphire had gone to Berkeley, Ruby had gone to Cambridge, and I had gone to New York. The difference was, the three of us older sisters never even hinted that we might be staying away permanently.

We were disappointed when Diamond went to Vegas, but we knew how much she loved the West. And she was moving to the gambling Mecca of the world, so we couldn't really say much to dissuade her. Still, while we understood wanting to live near twenty-four-hour gambling opportunities, none of us could grasp living in the landlocked desert. I thought that, in the end, we did a pretty good job of not making her feel overly guilty about leaving.

The couple of times when we went to visit Diamond, we spent most of our time at the casinos—not exactly optimal venues for getting close and personal, or finding out what was really going on with her. Since our family firmly believed that fish and house-guests started to smell after a couple of days, we always stayed at hotels. I had never actually been to her home in Vegas. She seemed happy enough with her life and with her work at the paper. Quartz had reported that she lived in a cute little town-house a couple of blocks from the Strip.

She talked about friends and, although we never met them, she never seemed lonely. I had to admit that, being Cuban, it was hard for me to comprehend how she could be happy living so far from her family. I missed her, but I also understood that she had to live the life she wanted. She seemed to have found her niche in life, and appeared to be enjoying herself. If it all was a bit mysterious at times, well, that was simply the way she wanted it.

Now, after the meeting at my parents' apartment, I was starting to worry.

Mama and Papa told us that they had called Diamond after Maria Mercedes's apparition, to tell their youngest daughter what was going on. They hadn't been able to reach her at home or on her cell phone. That didn't worry me too much—it must have been around four in the morning in Vegas when Mama called, and Diamond was notorious for turning off her phone and putting it on voice mail. She was a bit of a technophobe and could easily have been sleeping peacefully in bed with both her phones switched off.

It was the next piece of news that made me queasy. When our parents had been unable to locate Diamond, they had done what she had expressly forbidden them to do—they called her office at the *Las Vegas Herald*. Mama nearly dropped the phone when the reporter who answered told her that Diamond no longer worked at the paper. The reporter was named Oscar Maxwell, and he must have sensed Mama's desperation, because he told her as much as he knew. He said he had taken Diamond's job more than a year before and that while he didn't know Diamond personally, he had heard she was working at one of the casinos.

In the hours while they waited for us to meet at the apartment, my parents had left about a dozen messages for Diamond that she didn't return. They had even called the Las Vegas Police Department, who said that there was nothing they could do to help if there was no evidence that Diamond had been the victim of foul play. Besides, Diamond had only been "missing" for several hours. Clearly, the Vegas PD wasn't used to dealing with Cuban mothers, for whom losing track of a child for ten minutes was grounds for issuing a missing-persons report.

My parents decided that, until they heard otherwise, they considered Diamond missing. One of us was going to have to go look for her, and my parents definitely weren't up to the task. Sapphire volunteered to go, but we all knew her emotional state was too fragile. Ruby was in the middle of a trial that was going to last at least another two weeks, and Quartz, probably correctly realizing he would screw everything up, quietly demurred.

That left me as the logical person to go to Vegas to locate Diamond. I had the most common sense of all my siblings. Sapphire was the most artistic, Ruby was the smartest, and Quartz had the best business sense, but I was probably the most level-headed. In this situation, that counted for a lot. Also, I had no real business or family obligations that would keep me from going away for a couple of days. I knew my mother-in-law would be more than happy to move into the house in my absence and take care of Tony and the boys—something she and Tony loved, and which I hated. Once she was ensconced in the house, she would attack my home the way General Patton stormed the beachheads of Europe. It would take me a week to restore things for every day she spent there, and I would come back to a house full of males spoiled on homemade food and a round-the-clock cleaning service. It wasn't that I was ungrateful to Magdalena, my mother-in-law, but her very presence seemed to point out all my deficiencies as a wife and mother.

When Tony married me, he knew that I was a great girlfriend and a terrific lover. But he had no idea how I would fare in the wife-and-mother department. We were in our early twenties at the time, and lust tended to carry the day and make us both overlook what would develop into potential problems. Tony had thought my family was eccentric and amusing. He cracked up when we wagered on the weather forecast and collected money from each other the next day based on how many degrees in error the meteorologist had been. It wasn't long, though, before he stopped laughing.

I should have given more thought to the way he was brought

up. The first time I went to dinner at his house, I was flabbergasted to learn that his mother had cooked the entire meal, from the plantain soup to the coconut flan for dessert. I wouldn't have been surprised to learn that she had a coffee tree in the backyard from which she harvested beans to roast and grind by hand. My own mother hadn't exactly been in a hot race for homemaker of the year. She cooked enough to keep us from starving and, when she did, the results tasted like they had been baked in the main reactor at Chernobyl. Mostly we ate take-out, and plenty of it. It wasn't every household in Dade County that received personalized Christmas cards from the managers of Pollo Tropical, Domino's Pizza, and Tony Roma's. I grew up the product of my upbringing. I was probably the only Cuban wife and mother in Miami who did her entire weekly grocery run at the Farm Stores drive-through window.

In the early days of our marriage, I knew that Tony used to defend me to his mother; lately, though, her pointed barbs had stung more, and his protestations were less spirited. After almost a decade of marriage, I knew which battles were winnable and which weren't, so I let her comments pass. She wanted the best for her son, which to her meant a traditional wife and mother—something that, appearances to the contrary, I would never be. Besides, I needed Magdalena and, to be fair, I knew I could always depend on her if I needed help with the boys. Unless Diamond checked in with my parents in the next twenty-four hours, I had no choice but to ask for that help.

It was around dawn that I started and jerked, coming out of a fitful sleep. I squinted in the near dark and looked at the alarm clock. *Mierda.* The next few days weren't going to be easy. I just hoped I still had a marriage to come home to when it was all over.

9

I DIDN'T HAVE MUCH AT
work that needed my attention, just a few clients for whom I was
finishing up small jobs. If anything came up while I was in Vegas,
my friend and Coral Gables office partner, Dorcas Martinez,
could deal with it. I supposed that if a thirty-year-old woman
could have a best friend, for me it was Dorcas. She was two years
younger than I and, although she was also Cuban, she came from
a background totally different from mine. Still, we became friends
from the moment we met.

Dorcas had a sort of quiet beauty that became more apparent
to me the longer I knew her. She was tall and rail thin, although
she ate so much she might have been making up for all the years
she went hungry in Cuba. She had hazel eyes and thick black
lashes that never needed makeup. Her eyebrows were permanently raised, giving her a quizzical look as though she was per-
petually waiting for the answer to an unvoiced question. Her dark
brown hair was cut short and was so curly it was almost frizzy,
giving her a halo around her head. She was light-skinned and
never went out in the sun—not because she hated to get a tan, but
because she didn't want to be reminded of the three days she spent
on an open raft crossing the Florida straits.

In the four years I had known her, Dorcas had never been involved with a man. It wasn't that she was into girls, she simply considered entanglements with men to be an unnecessary distraction. She had come to this country to make something of herself, and she thought that a man might drag her down and keep her from realizing her goals. I also knew that she could never let down her guard long enough to give herself to anyone. She was a product of Castro's Cuba, where lying, cheating, and stealing were necessary for survival.

Dorcas had been one of the thousands of Cubans who fled the island in August of 1996 on boats, rafts, inner tubes, Styrofoam boxes, and anything else that could float. She shared her raft with nine other Cubans, and they were picked up at sea the day before the Americans and Castro's government signed a migratory agreement stipulating that any further refugees picked up at sea were to be sent to the Guantanamo Naval Base. Instead of suffering that purgatorial fate, Dorcas and her compatriots were picked up on their third day at sea by an American carrier cruise ship filled with tourists on its way back from the Bahamas. The passengers and crew treated her group like heroes and, by the time the ship docked at the Port of Miami, they felt as though they were rock stars.

Dorcas loved to talk about the time she had spent on that cruise ship, since it had been her first taste of American life. Her description of the first filet mignon she ever tasted was enough to make my mouth water. It would have been funny, if it hadn't reminded me that my friend had lived the first twenty-two years of her life without tasting a good piece of meat. There was no filet mignon in Cuba, except what was for the tourists and government ministers. Dorcas still loved to play the wide-eyed bumpkin marveling at the luxury of America, and after a couple of glasses of wine, she would launch into a routine worthy of Comedy Central. It was unlikely, though, that she would ever be asked to perform there. The sad fact was that few people wanted to hear about how bad conditions really were in Cuba. For Dorcas, the line between comedy and tragedy was often blurred and indistinct.

I lay in bed that morning, not wanting to get up, but with my friend's face in my thoughts. I wanted to talk about Diamond with her, because I knew she would understand my frame of mind. Whenever I had a problem that I thought was serious—my car breaking down, or my cable service getting interrupted—I put everything in perspective by reminding myself what Dorcas had been through in her life.

Dorcas had been a questioner of authority ever since she was a little girl. That was healthy for a child, and an adolescent, but it was hazardous in Cuba. She wondered aloud, for example: If Castro's Cuba was such a utopia, why had close to two million citizens braved shark-infested waters in order to escape? And why did Castro not just accept, but actively encourage, his people to take cash from the "traitor" exiles in Florida that kept his economy afloat? Most puzzling of all to Dorcas was the issue of race. Castro accused the Batista government that he toppled of being racist, but Batista himself had been biracial, and the head of the Senate had been of African ancestry. Castro claimed black Cubans were much better off under his regime, but while the population of Cuba was more than 60 percent Afro-Caribbean, there were no black men or women in top government positions. Whenever government-controlled TV in Cuba showed the men who ran the government, their faces were invariably all white.

The answer, of course, was that the government was a hypocritical dictatorship—a fact that Dorcas spoke aloud about without hesitation. Her opinions weren't much of a problem when she was a small girl, but when she refused to become a Young Pioneer and sing patriotic songs and shout political slogans, then her fate was sealed. She was denied entry to the university despite high grades, and she was therefore blocked from ever getting a job that would enable her to make a good living.

By the time Dorcas was a young woman, she was so marginalized that she survived day by day working odd jobs. She had a black-market contact who sold her hairdressing supplies, and she set up a space in her small apartment where she operated an illegal salon. This went on for a couple of years, and she was successful enough to save a few pesos before she was ratted out by a neighborhood spy. Dorcas went to her aunt for help; her mother's cousin operated a *paladar*, a restaurant catering exclusively to foreigners and operated out of a private house in Havana. Dorcas worked there as a helper for almost two years until her mother died. The aunt, no longer feeling family pressure to help Dorcas, unceremoniously fired her.

Being poor was bad enough, but what incensed Dorcas was the constant double-standard of Cuban life: anyone who had access to dollars lived on an entirely different level from those who didn't. Dorcas felt like an outcast, with no money and her record permanently smeared by the authorities. It was painful even to contemplate, but in time she came to the realization that she had to leave home. She could no longer live in a country governed by a corrupt old man, with a citizenry marking time waiting for him to die.

After Dorcas's mother died, her father quickly took up with a young girl shockingly close to Dorcas's age. She finally lost the last excuse for staying in her homeland. She was an only child, and her few relatives thought she was a troublemaker and wanted little to do with her.

In 1994 her opportunity finally came. Rumors of a mass exodus had been whispered for weeks in Havana, along with the news that the government planned to look the other way and allow the refugees to leave. Dorcas knew a young man in her apartment building who ran a thriving black-market business—she was one of his customers—and she went to him to arrange for a seat on one of the rafts that was leaving as soon as word spread that the passage was relatively safe. Dorcas told me that she paid him from the stash of money she'd been hoarding, but I suspected there was more to the exchange. I doubted that Dorcas could have survived on the few menial jobs that came her way—she had no education, no Communist Party connections, and no access to dollars. Dorcas had never said so, but I knew that in her position there was only one currency she could use for barter—her body. She wasn't a *jinetera*, one of those young Cuban girls who slept with foreigners in exchange for dollars, a meal, or as little as a bar of scented soap, but all of Cuba was for sale—and not necessarily to the highest bidder. Even boys had been known to sell their bodies, to both male and female tourists.

I also knew that Dorcas had sold herself only as a last resort—if she had done it regularly, things probably would have been a lot easier for her, at least materially. We had never discussed the topic, but I knew that she was scarred by some memories of her old life in Cuba.

Dorcas's neighbor told her to expect an unannounced knock at her door. Someone would come to tell her when and where to show up for the raft's departure. She wasn't to bring anything other than enough food and water for a few days. That was fine with her—she had nothing to bring and wanted no reminders of her old life. For two days, Dorcas sat alone in her apartment, scared to leave because she might miss the knock at the door.

On the night of the third day, the knock finally came. It was a man she had never met before, telling her to report at four in the morning at the northwestern end of the Malecón. When she arrived there, she found a group of nine men and women, with three children, all huddled together by a raft. The craft consisted of fifty-gallon steel drums welded together, tied with rope, and covered with sheets of plastic. A spindly wooden pole with bed sheets flapping in the breeze served as a mast and sail. Dorcas took one look at it and realized that she might die in the next several hours.

It seemed impossible the raft could make it out of Havana Bay, much less the ninety miles across the Florida straits. But it was her only hope, so she joined with the others as they pushed the raft out into the water. She rowed as hard as she could, deciding that it was better to die in the open waters than live another day in Cuba. She also told me she decided then that she would commit suicide if they were to be captured by the Cuban authorities.

Everyone on the raft was assigned a chore. Dorcas was a rower, and she shared an oar with a middle-aged man named Mario Fernandez. He told Dorcas he was in the funeral business; although she didn't think his line of work was an auspicious omen, Dorcas and Mario bonded with all the intensity of two people facing their own deaths. To her other side was a young woman named Adrianna, with whom Dorcas also became friendly; in Adrianna's case, though, Dorcas held back a little. Dorcas had heard talk that Adriana was involved in illegal dealings back on the island and intuited that she was someone to look out for.

The three days on the open water passed in a blur. All Dorcas could remember was waves breaking over the raft, and the children tied to the masts so they wouldn't be washed away in the heavy seas. The passengers saw the dark shapes of sharks bumping the raft; once, almost in delirium, Dorcas reached out and touched one of their fins. She and Mario clutched the oar together when the big waves came, riding the raft and trying not to fall out.

After Dorcas and her fellow rafters were rescued by the cruise ship they exchanged phone numbers and addresses—she, of course, had nothing to give, but she carefully took every name and number offered to her by her fellow refugees. In Miami, Dorcas was processed by the INS, then taken to the office of an organization that helped rafters settle into their new lives. After an interview, they took Dorcas to a motel off Biscayne Boulevard, gave her some cash, and told her they would return. They were true to their word, and returned the next day to take her to their offices near the Orange Bowl.

However nice and helpful they might have been, though, it soon became apparent to Dorcas that they had no idea what to do with her. The volunteers took her shopping and bought clothes for her—the first new things Dorcas had ever owned. After about five days of pampering, though, Dorcas decided it was time to get on with her life. Early the next morning, she got out the list of names and numbers her fellow rafters had given her—many of them were fortunate enough to have family in Miami. Her heart pounding, she called Mario the undertaker, her rowing partner from the trip across the Florida straits. She exhaled with gratitude when he sounded surprised and happy to hear from her, and even asked her to have lunch with him that very afternoon. He told her he was working at his cousin Ernesto's business and gave her the address.

Dorcas figured out which buses she needed to take and, three transfers later, arrived at the Fernandez Funeral Home. After a tearful reunion, Mario introduced Dorcas to Ernesto and the rest of the staff. Mario's family had been in the funeral business for generations, both in Cuba and now in exile. Ernesto was the patriarch of the exile wing of the family and owned and operated almost twenty funeral homes in Florida, New York, and New Jersey. The family business was doing so well that they were thinking of expanding into Texas and California.

Mario, after less than a week in America, had certainly landed on his feet. He finally got around to asking Dorcas how she was doing and—even though she had promised herself she would hold her head up—she immediately began crying. All the fear of the past weeks came out at once, and she told Mario she had no idea what to do. The motel off Biscayne Boulevard was nice, and the volunteer ladies were well intentioned, but this wasn't what she had envisioned when she risked her life on that raft.

After he gave Dorcas a couple of minutes to calm down, Mario took her in to see his cousin Ernesto. In a stroke of luck, the receptionist at the Little Havana branch of the Fernandez Funeral Home was going to be gone for a three-month maternity leave. Ernesto had figured they could manage without her, but when Mario told him about Dorcas's situation he agreed to take her on as a temporary replacement. Dorcas gratefully accepted the offer and began working that same afternoon. Soon enough the temporary job turned permanent when the receptionist gave birth to a boy, then called in to say she was quitting for good. The rumor at the funeral home was that the receptionist's mother-in-law had told her she was going to hell if she put the baby in daycare.

Dorcas absorbed every aspect of the funeral home business. She worked from early in the morning into the night, always asking questions and listening and learning. With her first paycheck she bought a series of English-language tapes and a Walkman, then proceeded to wear the tapes out by listening to them constantly. After six months of this, when her English was good enough, she signed up for business courses at Miami Dade Community College. After spending all her young life in the hopeless dead-end of Castro's Cuba, her mind and spirit began to explode with all the possibilities of life in America.

She watched the goings-on at the Fernandez Funeral Home and had an insight: while Ernesto and his staff were very efficient and professional at organizing wakes and burials, they tended to neglect the social elements of helping the bereaved say good-bye to their loved ones. Dorcas soon figured out that she had spotted a business niche. She took her time analyzing the costs and expenses of burial, and the subsequent profit margins. She put together a proposal for one of her business classes, and her professor was so delighted that he helped her come up with a marketing plan. When she was satisfied that her numbers and projections could stand up to scrutiny, Dorcas requested a meeting with Ernesto.

Ernesto figured Dorcas was going to ask for a raise and had already come up with a reasonable pay increase. What he heard instead completely blew him away. Instead of asking for more money, Dorcas wanted to offer personal services to the family and friends of the recently departed. Dorcas had seen so many shell-shocked people pass through the funeral home, individuals grieving so deeply that they were in no shape to deal with all the social details of saying good-bye to their loved ones. Dorcas drew a parallel to wedding planners—the major difference, of course, being that the funeral planner had much less lead time in which to prepare.

Once a family member contacted the Fernandez Funeral Home, Dorcas proposed, then her services would kick in. After a brief consultation with the family, Dorcas would take over. She would make sure different family members had the right clothes, she would plan the dinner before or after the wake at a restaurant or private home, and she would make sure everyone had adequate transportation. She would take care of the flower ordering for the funeral home, the church, the cemetery, and the gathering after the burial. She would see that a priest was called to comfort the mourners, pray the rosary at the funeral home, conduct the funeral Mass, bless the living, and pronounce the proper words at the burial. Her services would extend to ordering the appropriate food and drink for each occasion, and seeing to the music for each event.

Being Cuban, Dorcas would understand the trickier aspects of funerals and handle them with the utmost delicacy. For instance, if the deceased had a mistress and a lover in addition to his spouse, these women and their offspring—legitimate and illegitimate—would be discreetly dealt with. And, after everything was over, Dorcas would provide a quiet place for the reading of the will.

When the meeting was concluded, Dorcas showed Ernesto a

graphic depicting how much seed money she needed to start her business, and how much staff. Ernesto was quiet for a while, thinking. It turned out he hadn't earned the nickname "Cuban Dean of Death" by failing to take risks and letting opportunity pass by unseized. Within a week, Dorcas was set up in a back room at the funeral home—unfortunately, it was connected to the freezers where bodies were kept in anticipation of embalming, so it was freezing. After eight hours in her new office, Dorcas thought the blood in her veins was crystallizing. She soon hired three staff members, and they came to work dressed for the Miami heat then changed into outfits appropriate for Ice Station Calle Ocho.

Dorcas had told Ernesto he could cut her salary in half and that she believed in her business so deeply that in exchange she wanted equity ownership. Ernesto thought it was a great idea and was glad to see his employee grasping the essentials of capitalism. He didn't doubt for a moment that she would succeed. Her drive and ambition were almost painful to watch.

I met Dorcas after Fernandez Funeral Services had been in operation for two years. By that time, the business had grown to twenty full-time staff employees. Seeing that more office space was needed, Ernesto had at first given Dorcas an additional room in his funeral home, this time next to the crematorium. Dorcas, tired of freezing and burning when she went from one office to the next, decided it was time to move. She purchased a building right on the border of Coral Gables and Little Havana.

Dorcas asked around for a Cuban who worked in interior design and got my name after commenting how much she admired three homes whose interiors I designed. When she called me, I liked her right away. Our first lunch lasted for three hours, and what began as a professional relationship quickly turned into a personal one as well. Soon the lease on my office expired, and

Dorcas offered me a space in her building. I happily accepted. We were close enough to keep few, if any, secrets. And we spoke almost daily, even when we weren't at work.

I looked over at the bedside alarm clock. It would go off in a couple of minutes, so I reached over and turned it off. I disabled the other two on my way downstairs.

I made my way into the den and shut the door behind me. I sat on the sofa with my feet tucked under, the way I had when I was frightened as a little girl.

Diamond's home number was in my hand. I punched it in and waited. Nothing. Just her voice mail. It was four in the morning in Las Vegas.

I dialed Diamond's cell phone number. The message I heard made me shiver: *"This number is accepting no new calls."*

That meant Diamond's voice mailbox was completely full. And that she hadn't checked it in a long time.

My hand shook as I dialed Dorcas at home. She answered on the first ring, almost as though she had been expecting me to call.

"Dorcas," I whispered. "I think something terrible has happened to my baby sister, Diamond."

10

particularly vicious, so I was more than fifteen minutes late meeting Dorcas at the Versailles restaurant. When I pulled into the parking lot I saw her through the window, sitting at a table with an ever-present cigarette perched between her first two fingers. The Virgin must have been with me, because there was actually an empty spot—legal, no less, not marked handicapped—right next to the building. That had never happened before, and I decided to take it as a good omen. To seal the deal, I gunned the engine and pulled in before someone stole the space from under me.

Versailles was on Calle Ocho in the heart of Little Havana. It was always crowded and open virtually around the clock. When I turned off the engine I paused for a moment, trying to come down off my anxiety high. Dropping the boys off at school had been so time-consuming that I had been tempted to speed through several school zones. My maternal instincts had won out, though, and I had crawled along with the rest of the frustrated morning commuters cursing in a combination of Spanish and English. For me, Spanish was the language of choice when my frustration level grew and I wanted to be effective in my swearing. Spanish was so creative and flowery, capable of expressing such vivid images. It was the language of choice for insulting a fellow motorist's grandmother and her sexual preferences.

I auto-locked the car and waved at Dorcas, who glanced up from her cigarette and coffee. I sprinted inside, knowing that the sight of me hustling would be enough to make her laugh out loud. I hated to be late and, unique for a Cuban, prided myself on my punctuality. It was never easy, given travel times in Miami, and I was too proud to actually allot myself a comfortable margin getting anywhere.

When I arrived at the table I saw from the assorted paraphernalia there that Dorcas was working on her second café con leche. We kissed and I plopped down on the dark green plastic chair next to her. She looked cool, calm, and well put together. I was dressed in tattered blue jeans and a plain white cotton T-shirt, and my hair was pulled back in a ponytail. I felt disheveled, unkempt, sloppy—the very image of a stay-at-home mom who had just dispatched her carpool duties.

It was still brutally early, but Dorcas was turned out in a sky blue suit—probably an Armani, and this season's. A glance at her feet confirmed that she was wearing Manolo Blahniks. The only issue in question was what pair would she choose on any given day, since she had so many to choose from. Dorcas, the one-time refugee, was the queen of limousine pumps and any kind of fuck-me shoes.

Lately Dorcas had started to streak her hair, and in the morning sun I could discern a few discrete golden strands among her brown curls. Her nails were perfectly manicured and polished in blood red. She may have worked in the funeral business, but she certainly didn't go around looking moribund. She also didn't look like a woman who had been plucked from a raft nine years before. America had been good to Dorcas, and she showed it by dressing for success with spectacular results. For Dorcas, every Armani outfit, pair of Jimmy Choo shoes, or visit to her exclusive hairdresser was a personal act of revenge directed at Fidel Castro. Some Cuban exiles attacked the island, while Dorcas hit the stores.

"Esmeralda, calm down, honey," she admonished me. "Take a few deep breaths. I'm not going anywhere."

I hadn't realized what a panic I was in until Dorcas's words hit me. I sat back and inhaled some of the second-hand smoke from my friend's cigarette. No one in Versailles paid the slightest attention to the smoking bans in certain areas of the restaurant. Even though I worked out religiously and was in good shape, the fumes from the Marlboro a few inches from my face were keeping me from catching my breath.

Finally I calmed down enough to order breakfast from the waitress who was hovering around our table. I didn't bother to look at the menu, because it hadn't changed in decades. Every Cuban in Miami knew it by heart. I ordered café con leche—double on the espresso—scrambled eggs, heavily buttered Cuban bread, a side of bacon, and a huge glass of fresh-squeezed orange juice served so cold it would make my fillings ache. As I ordered, I had visions of the emergency room at the Miami Heart Institute—but it wasn't enough to deter me from the artery-clogging cardiac-arrest-risking meal that I wanted. Every mouthful would definitely be worth it.

It would be mere minutes until the food arrived. Versailles prided itself on fast service, which not only made the patrons happy but kept the tables turning over at a fast rate. It wasn't the kind of place where diners felt comfortable lingering after a meal. One went to Versailles to eat, and Versailles existed to make maximum profit from serving good food. It was an unspoken arrangement that suited everyone involved. Being Cuban, practicality required no explanation.

"Thanks for meeting me," I told her. The orange juice arrived, and I gulped down half the glass in a single swig. As soon as I recovered from the sweetness and icy cold, I said, "I know how much you hate to come out so early in the morning."

Dorcas puffed on her cigarette and shrugged. "No problem. Now tell me what's happening with your sister."

My food came and, in between mouthfuls, I brought Dorcas up to date. I left out the part about Maria Mercedes visiting my mother—although Dorcas had been through a lot in her life, and was hard to surprise, I didn't want her to go into information overload. Dorcas considered me to be levelheaded, with a bit of a wild streak, but if I started talking about prophesy and our family destiny she would think that I had come unhinged.

I told her what steps my family had taken to find Diamond and told her that I was going to be leaving for Las Vegas that night. Dorcas let me speak, lighting another cigarette.

"Where do you think your sister is?" she finally asked. "Why wouldn't she contact anyone in your family?"

I didn't say anything. I had no answers.

"Your parents called the Las Vegas Police, but they wouldn't help?" Dorcas asked.

I shook my head and found myself blinking back tears. Stress, worry, and exhaustion were beating down on me.

"The police said Diamond was an adult, and that there was no proof that anything had happened to her," I explained. "One of the cops said that maybe she just wanted to go away for a while. You know, get away from it all."

I finished my coffee and ordered another. I could hear my heart beating in my ears.

"Don't they understand she's Cuban?" Dorcas asked. "Cubans never need to get away from it all. They take it all with them—plus a half-dozen relatives."

We both knew what Dorcas was talking about. If Diamond had gone missing in Miami, her disappearance would have been treated very differently. Every law-enforcement officer available would have been dispatched to look for her. When a Cuban woman disappears in Dade County, it's never voluntary. She's expected to check in with her family and friends every few hours and to be reachable at all times. It's a blessing and a curse, but nothing is going to change it.

"They didn't seem to understand that," I told Dorcas. "What can I say? They don't know Cubans there. The cop basically told my mother to hang up the phone and leave him alone."

Dorcas frowned. "And no one knows anything at her job?"

"Well, Diamond quit her newspaper job about a year ago, but we didn't know about it." My words came out in a rush. It was a shameful admission to make, even to a close friend. "She didn't like us to call her at work. So we never did."

My worry about Diamond surged up in a big rush of anxiety, and before I knew what I was doing I told Dorcas about what had happened at my parents' apartment the day before—all the way to the details of the secret room. Dorcas listened with her eyes bright, lighting a new cigarette off the butt of the last. By the time I was done, the smoke hovering over our table looked like nothing less than an atomic mushroom cloud.

"So. Do you think the two things are related?" Dorcas asked me. "Your ancestor's appearance, and Diamond's disappearance?"

I didn't know. It was all too weird. Since I realized that Diamond had gone missing, I hadn't given much thought to the veracity of Mama's story. Now I knew why I had come to Dorcas. She went straight to the heart of every situation.

"I guess the thought crossed my mind," I said. I noticed that Dorcas hadn't dismissed the story of Maria Mercedes as the product of an old lady's overactive imagination. "Maybe it's too much of a coincidence, all this stuff happening at once."

Dorcas blew smoke in my direction. I loved her, but sometimes I worried that the cost of our friendship was going to be my death from second-hand smoke.

"I think it's suspicious." Dorcas reached down and started rummaging in her purse, then pulled out a PalmPilot and punched the screen with the little plastic pointer. Then she opened up a little black leather case, took out a business card, and copied down whatever information she'd looked up on her organizer.

"Here." Dorcas handed me the card. "You remember me telling you about the woman who was on the raft with me getting out of Cuba?"

"What, the one you didn't trust?"

"I thought she might have been a *jinetera*," Dorcas said.

"Did you ever find out if she was a prostitute," I asked, "or whether she was hooked up with anything fishy?"

"Her name is Adrianna Gomez," Dorcas said without answering my question. "I've stayed in touch with her. She's all right. We're sort of friends, even though we haven't spoken in a couple of years. She's living in Vegas and, from what I understand, she's well connected. She might be able to help you."

I looked at the card, staring at the name and phone number. I held it so delicately, it might have been about to burn my skin. Not only was Diamond missing, I was going to rely on a stranger to help me find her. If I was lucky. The enormousness of what I was facing hit me hard.

"*Gracias,*" I said quietly. I put the card in my wallet. "So you think she's 'well connected.' What exactly does that mean?"

Dorcas puffed on her cigarette and let out a perfect smoke ring. I had to admit, it looked pretty cool.

"Adrianna is the kind of person who gravitates to the fringes of whatever society she lives in," Dorcas said cryptically. "She's a survivor. She'll be a good contact for you in Vegas, if Diamond has gotten into some kind of trouble. I'll call her and tell her you're coming."

Dorcas started to gather her things, and I looked at my watch. I was surprised to see that we'd been sitting there for more than an hour. I had so much to do before I left, and the thought was enough to make me start to panic. I must have showed my feelings, because Dorcas reached over and patted my hand as though she was consoling a child.

"Esmeralda, I'm sorry, but I have to go," she said. She stubbed out her cigarette and started to stand. "Let's talk again before you leave, though, all right, *chica?*"

Dorcas kissed me, then left me in a cloud of Carolina Herrera perfume mixed with a thick aroma of Marlboros. Feeling dejected, I signaled for the bill. The waitress must have been waiting to clear the table, because she brought me the tab before I had the chance to lower my arm. I quickly looked at the amount, took out a twenty, and placed it over the check. The bill covered both our meals, along with a hefty tip.

As I was getting in the car to leave, I glanced back at Versailles. I was glad I met Dorcas there. It was probably going to be the last Cuban food I ate for a little while. Because, I realized all at once, I was not coming back from Las Vegas without my baby sister, Diamond—no matter how long it took.

11

MY FLIGHT FROM MIAMI TO
Las Vegas wasn't scheduled to leave until nine-thirty, but I had so
many things to accomplish before I left that by the time I arrived
at the airport, I was cutting it way too close. I entered the terminal
and, after waiting a long time to check in, hit a security line that
looked like one of the hellish queues at Disney World. I was so
frazzled, and my nerves were so shot, that I wouldn't have been
surprised if one of the security guards had pulled me aside for a
strip search before they allowed me on the airplane.

When I finally cleared security—deep breathing and concentrating on a futile search for my inner happy place—I made a mad
dash for the gate and got there just as the ticket agent was announcing last call for boarding. I shoved my ticket and driver's license under her nose and stood there, my heart pounding while
she examined them with cautious deliberation. She even looked
up, as though verifying that I matched the photo on my ID. I almost asked her whether there was a terrorist alert for thirty-year-
old Cuban mothers, but thought better of it. As things stood, she
handed back my documents and waved me on as though her best
efforts to keep me in Miami had been defeated.

I had bought the ticket earlier in the day, so I hadn't had the
luxury of reserving a window seat. But God was with me; as I

walked on and looked around, I saw that the flight was pretty empty. I found my seat in an empty row and sighed with relief that I wouldn't have to talk to anyone. It was going to be about a five-hour flight—an eternity, had I been stuck with strangers on either side. I stuffed my suitcase in the overhead compartment just as the pilot announced that we were ready to depart. I was so worried and guilty about the situation I left at home that I couldn't have said with any certainty whether I was actually glad to have caught the flight on time. I sat down, buckled my seat belt, and allowed myself to look back on my day.

To begin with, Tony had been so angry with me for leaving that he actually refused to drive me to the airport. He hadn't even bothered to be at home to say good-bye. He had never acted that way before. His message to me was starkly clear.

And, to make things even worse, my mother-in-law, Magdalena, called in the middle of the afternoon to tell me that she wouldn't be able to make it until tomorrow at the earliest. Her best friend Marta had had a heart attack and, even though she was stable, she needed someone by her side at the hospital. Magdalena had to stick by Marta's side until Marta's daughter arrived from California.

I almost had a heart attack of my own upon hearing the news. I had met Marta a couple of times, and all I could remember of her was that she was very old and seemed very frail. I hated to be so selfish, but this was not a good time for Marta's health to fail. If Marta died, Magdalena probably wouldn't be able to help me out. I had counted on Magdalena to make dinner that night, so I had nothing prepared. The boys had been pressing the number for Domino's on the speed dial as I left. I hoped Magdalena would make it by the next day. She was a miracle worker in the kitchen and could make a good meal out of Buster's dog food if she had to.

Tony could forgive many of my sins, but leaving him without a prepared dinner for two nights in a row was, by his thinking, an open declaration that I didn't love him anymore. A third time would be grounds for divorce. I think he could handle my having an affair with more equanimity than having his timely hot meals endangered.

Then, to cap it all off, the twins had announced that their science project was due tomorrow. Needless to say, this was news to me—as was the fact that they were supposed to have been working on it for the entire term and that it constituted half their grade. They dropped that bombshell on me as soon as I picked them up at school in the afternoon. I might not have been a domestic goddess, but I was pretty good at crisis management. I went into action immediately, not even wasting the time it would have taken to yell at them and threaten to ground them until they were both twenty-one. I stopped on the way home at Pearl Paint, an art-supplies store in South Miami, and bought all the materials we needed to construct a volcano that actually erupted. While we were shopping, I told the twins that Tony had a real gift for making volcanoes, a talent he had never revealed before out of modesty. The boys were smart and savvy enough to see through my surreal claim, but they nodded in agreement, knowing they were getting off easy. Tony was an accountant, and we all knew his expertise in life was largely limited to account-type activities, but the boys would have agreed to anything to save themselves from the punishment they knew they deserved.

When we got home I turned on the Weather Channel and waited for the Las Vegas forecast. I packed, then started making phone calls. I begged family, friends, and acquaintances to take my children to and from school and their various activities for the next few days. I had to make a lot of promises, but I would deal with that when I returned.

I tried to leave the house as organized as I could. Clean clothes were a high priority, so I tackled the laundry first. As I threw the clothes from the hamper into the washing machine, I looked out the laundry room window just in time to see Buster in the yard, his back rippling, suffering through an enormous attack of diarrhea. The poor dog looked so pathetic that I went outside and held his paw while he finished his business.

As I waited for Buster's suffering to subside, I wondered what would happen next to jinx my trip. First it was Magdalena and Marta, then the twins and their volcano. Now it was Buster and his disgusting gastrointestinal distress. I didn't see how it could get worse.

I felt a twinge of sympathy for Tony. He was going to be stuck with a dog he didn't like—the boys, no matter how much they loved Buster, were incapable of taking care of him. And now Buster had just finished the first of what would probably be several bouts of diarrhea. Picking up after Buster in this situation was not for the queasy. And Tony was definitely queasy. He'd probably changed fewer than a dozen diapers between all three boys.

There was only one thing to do. On my way upstairs I stopped off at the hall closet where we kept all the medicines. I took out a bottle of Kaopectate, a surefire way to stop the flood. I went outside and emptied about half the bottle into Buster's mouth. He gagged on the chalky liquid, but I fooled myself into thinking he understood that I was trying to help him. I tried not to think about the consequences of Buster's treatment—the poor dog probably wouldn't go to the bathroom for a week—but I figured leaving Tony with a constipated dog was better than the other extreme. I hoped the resulting gas wouldn't be too bad, but I knew that Buster would soon be stinking up the house. I just hoped that no one lit a match near him.

I organized and cleaned as much as I could, but Tony and the boys were going to have to do some fending for themselves. There were two big unknowns: when I was coming back from Las Vegas, and when Magdalena was going to move in. I wrote out everyone's schedule on the kitchen message board, then called for

Gabriel. I needed to speak privately to my eldest son, so I pulled him into the den and shut the door.

One look at his face was enough to break my heart. "Don't worry." I told him. "You haven't done anything wrong."

Anything that I knew of, at least.

"I'm not busted?" he said hopefully.

"No, no. Here. Take this." I took out a big roll of bills from my pocket and shoved it into his hand.

"Mom?" Gabe's brown eyes widened, and he looked at me as though I had gone completely nuts. "What are you doing?"

"Look, I have to leave for a few days to go to Las Vegas," I told him. It probably wasn't fair to spring my departure on the boys at the last minute, but I was no good at delivering bad news. "I'm going to see your tía Diamond."

"Oh, Las Vegas." Relief was palpable in Gabriel's voice. He understood Las Vegas. "But, Mom, won't *you* be needing this?"

He tried to give the bills back to me. I was so proud I could have burst. It made all the sense in the world to him that I would be doing some serious gambling in Vegas.

"Look, Gabe, I don't know just when I'll be back," I told him. "This money is for you and your brothers, in case you need to pay for anything."

I kissed him softly on the forehead, holding back tears when I smelled his little-boy scent—a bit musty, sweaty, clammy, and in need of a bath after a day of school and play.

"It's our secret," I said. "Please don't tell anyone you have this money. Put it in a safe place, and use it only if you absolutely have to."

"OK, Mom."

I kissed him again. "Don't lose it, Gabe," I warned. "It's a thousand dollars."

"A thousand dollars. OK." I saw his hand tighten around the bills. "And, Mom?" he asked.

"Yes, Gabriel?"

"Don't worry," he said in a composed voice, as though his mother gave him a thousand dollars in cash every day. "I won't gamble with it."

I knew I was relying too much on the judgment of a ten-year-old boy, but I had no real choice. Tony was a good father, but he wasn't used to being responsible for anything in the household—and that included his children. Everything would be fine when Magdalena took over, but I had no backup plan for the boys should Marta take a turn for the worse. Sometimes it felt as though my entire world relied on me and that the entire infrastructure broke down every time I had the smallest problem.

Somehow I got out of the house and into the taxi that arrived to take me to the airport. The driver wanted to chat along the way, but I cut him off by telling him that I had a migraine. It wasn't so far from the truth, but the driver took my rebuff personally and drove with such reckless anger that I was almost surprised I made it alive to the airport. It's hard to drive so badly in Miami that other drivers take notice, but my cabby succeeded, and as a result we were the targets of ongoing road rage the entire route to the airport. We didn't arrive at MIA quietly; instead, I made my entrance to the accompaniment of horns and curses all the way to the terminal.

The airplane left the ground. I looked out the window to try to pinpoint our house, but there were too many clouds. It was the first time in more than twenty-four hours that I was alone, not busy doing anything, and with my cell phone turned off. I tried to banish my anxieties when I saw the flight attendant coming down the row with the beverage cart. I ordered two wines and held out some cash. To my surprise, she waved the money away.

"The flight's so empty the pilot has told us the drinks are on him," she explained sweetly.

"How about that," I said, stunned by this good omen.

After I had finished the first miniature bottle of wine, I reached down under the seat in front of me for the oversized black leather pouch I used as a purse for traveling—it was a marvel, capable of holding enormous amounts of stuff. I took out a manila envelope, put it on my tray-table, then put the purse on the empty seat next to me.

I twisted the cap off the second bottle, poured it into the plastic cup, and sipped it more slowly than the first. I opened the envelope and shook out two photographs. The strong beam from the overhead light shone on them and made them look translucent.

The first photograph was of Maria Mercedes Montalvo, my mother's great-great-grandmother. It had been taken in a studio almost a hundred years ago. It was a copy of the original, which had been one of the few personal things my parents took out of Cuba the New Year's Eve that Castro came to power. My mother had given each of her children a copy of the photograph during one of the many New Year's Eves we spent together gathered around the cabinet full of mementos from La Estrella. Something had made me take the picture out of its frame at home and pack it in the envelope before I left for the airport. For some reason, I felt the need to have it with me.

I had looked at the picture on hundreds if not thousands of occasions. Now it was like seeing it for the first time.

Maria Mercedes must have been about seventy when the picture was taken, although she looked much younger. She wore a long-sleeved dark dress buttoned up to the neck. I could only imagine how hot she must have been, dressed that way in the heat of Cuba without the relief of air conditioning. It was hard to make out Maria Mercedes's features in the ancient photo, taken in bad lighting, but I was struck by how erectly she carried herself. Even though she was sitting down, it was obvious that she had perfect posture.

I couldn't fathom my ancestor's ghost coming back to tell Mama about our family regaining La Estrella. I had always known that Maria Mercedes was important to Mama—they shared the same name, after all—and now I wondered if my mother had carried that attachment too far. I hated to doubt my mother, but part of me did.

Maria Mercedes wasn't divulging any secrets, so I put her photograph back on the tray and, after a couple more sips of wine, picked up the picture of Diamond. I thought I might have to show my sister's photo around in Las Vegas, so I picked one that showed her face simply and clearly. The photograph had been taken by Sapphire in Missoula, when the family went there almost three years before for Diamond's graduation. I smiled as I remembered how hard it had been to make Diamond stand still long enough to have her picture taken.

Diamond was a beautiful girl—all right, woman—with her pale skin and light blond hair giving her an ethereal, almost angelic look. In the photo she was dressed in a gauzy white peasant shirt and blue jeans. She looked so young and sweet, an innocent without a care in the world. I felt my eyes begin to water when I entertained thoughts of what might have happened to her.

I looked at the photographs once more before replacing them in the envelope and then returning them to my purse. I sat back and looked out the window, letting my thoughts drift. I had some ideas about what I was going to do in Las Vegas but no definite plan. I finished off the wine and closed my eyes, trying to let the stress slip away from my neck and shoulders.

I must have relaxed a little too much because the next sound I heard was the pilot announcing our approach to Las Vegas. I blinked sleep out of my eyes and felt my heart start to race. Soon we broke through the clouds, and I saw the city spreading out below. I pressed my face so tightly to the glass that my breath clouded it. It was silly, but I hoped that maybe I would see my sister's face somewhere in those bright lights. If Las Vegas was a city of dreams, then mine was to find my baby sister and bring her home.

12

than a year since I'd last been to Las Vegas to visit Diamond; still, when I stepped out into the terminal at McCarren Airport, it felt as though I had never left. The revelation wasn't as dramatic as Proust and his Madeleines, but the sound of dozens of slot machines buzzing and ringing was enough to evoke all the trips to the city I'd taken all the way back to my childhood.

I hurried through the terminal, searching each face I saw for signs of Diamond. Of course she was nowhere to be seen, but I scanned the hundreds of faces as they raced past. I was groggy from sleeping on the airplane, but my senses came into focus amid the bustle of lights and noise.

With a shock, I suddenly realized that this was the first time I had ever traveled to Las Vegas on my own. In the past I had come there with my family, and later, after I was married, I had vacationed there with Tony. I bobbed and wove through the crowds, trying not to dwell on the circumstances that had necessitated this solo trip.

It was close to midnight, but the airport was as active and alive as the middle of the day in another place. Most of the people were gathered in the gaming areas, no doubt hoping for a little luck upon their arrival or departure from the city. Normally I would have stopped at a slot machine and dropped in a dollar—it was always my custom to check my luck within minutes of landing. Instead, I clutched my purse a little tighter under my arm and quickened my pace. I was on a mission, and hopefully there would be time to play later.

I slowed a little as I passed a middle-aged, well-dressed woman sitting on the ground. Her back was flush against the wall, her body taut, and she was openly weeping. Her tears fell and left splotches on the front of her light pink blouse. I could think of no greater display of abject misery. The city hadn't been good to her, and I couldn't even begin to imagine what had left her so totally devastated. I hurried along, muttering a quick prayer for her and for myself that I wouldn't soon end up in a similar condition.

By the time I had navigated the huge airport, I was almost dizzy from the sights and sounds that had assaulted my senses. I saw spots from the slot machine lights, the blue and red carpet, the crowds, and all the advertisements for shows and attractions. I was reminded of the state Las Vegas puts its guests in—that of being constantly overwhelmed, all the better to spend and gamble without the constraints of everyday life. When I stepped out into the night air, it was like escaping from prison. There were still people all around, but at least I was breathing fresh air for the first time in eight hours. I took out my cell phone and held my breath as I clicked it on to check for messages. Thankfully, there weren't any. There had been no emergencies at home—or if there were, Tony had dealt with them. Miami seemed so far away, like another world entirely.

I followed the signs to the taxi queue; I had decided against renting a car since I wasn't really familiar with the layout of the city. When I reached the line, though, I wondered if I had made the right decision. There were at least fifty people waiting ahead of me, although the line seemed to be moving. I snaked my way around a metal barrier and shuffled slowly behind a young couple of about twenty who were clearly on their honeymoon. I suppressed a smile when I saw that she was still wearing her wedding dress under a jean jacket and that she clutched a bouquet of baby roses in her hand. The groom, who looked barely old enough to shave, was wearing an ill-fitting tuxedo. They sported matching cowboy boots and hats. They carried no luggage, which, to me, meant that they had no interest in leaving their hotel room while in Las Vegas.

Thinking for a moment, I wondered if Tony and I had ever been so lustful and carefree. To my horror, I really couldn't remember. We must have been, at some point, but the memories wouldn't come.

I was determined not to check out the honeymooners with an eye to comparing their situation to mine a decade ago, but I couldn't help myself. The dispatcher at the front of the queue was moving things along, but there were still about twenty-five people ahead of me. The wait wouldn't have been so bad, if it wasn't for the scene that was taking place in front of me. The honeymooners apparently decided they couldn't wait to get to their hotel room to consummate their marriage, and they started going at it just a foot or so away from me. They looked so young and inexperienced, their matching gold wedding bands so new and shiny, that I was almost sure this was the first time they had been alone together. By the time we neared the front of the line, the groom had his hand under the bride's jacket and was groping her so fiercely I feared she'd become bruised. The bride was tugging at his zipper, which seemed to be stuck. I wished them well, and I hoped they got a cab before the bride got pregnant.

Finally I was at the front of the queue. I watched the honeymooners get in their cab with the realization that the driver was going to be in for quite a show—even though it would probably be nothing he hadn't seen before. The ride would be short—everything in Las Vegas was a brief ride from the airport—but I didn't think the young couple needed much time for what they had in mind.

I hopped into my own cab and told the driver to take me to the Bellagio Hotel. I knew this was going to be a hard couple of days, so I had booked myself into the most luxurious hotel on the Strip. My parents were footing the bill for the trip, and I had double-checked with them about reserving a room at the Bellagio. They were so worried about Diamond that they would have agreed to anything I asked.

I sat back to try to enjoy the short drive from the airport. I lowered my window, ignoring the driver's look of reproach as the air conditioning seeped out, and inhaled the cool, dry night air. It was a luxury—in Miami, opening a car window was foolish and reckless, if not suicidal. If the South Florida humidity and the bugs didn't prove fatal, the smash-and-grab criminals would.

We reached Las Vegas Boulevard, the main drag where nearly all the hotels were lined up in constellations of neon color. I had no trouble identifying the familiar landmarks—Caesar's Palace, the Flamingo. I flashed back to vignettes of all the time I had spent in the city. I stared out the window and realized that I was feeling like a tourist rather than the seasoned gambler I became in the company of my family.

It was shocking to realize how much I was beginning to enjoy being alone and anonymous in Las Vegas. The taxi turned off the boulevard and into the wide driveway leading up to the hotel. Along with about a hundred other spectators who were equally oblivious to the late hour, I marveled at the fountains in the artificial lake in front of the hotel. I was almost sorry when the taxi kept moving and deposited me by the front door. I glanced at my watch and saw that it was almost one in the morning. Still, people bustled in and out, and taxis and limousines were lined up all along the driveway. It all seemed chaotic at first glance, but like most things in Las Vegas, it was a clinic in service and organization.

Valets and porters worked the crowds, making sure everyone got to where they wanted to go.

I paid the driver, grabbed my bag, and headed inside to the lobby. Even though there were plenty of people around, there was no one waiting in line to check in to the hotel. I handed my American Express card to a young woman and waited for it to be approved. I let my gaze move upward in the enormous reception area, which was decorated with massive colored-glass flowers— *Fiori di Como,* a work by an artist named Dale Chihuly. I heard it had cost more than ten million dollars; to me, it was worth every penny.

The desk clerk gave me a cream-colored envelope with my room key, along with a map of the huge hotel. I looked up at the glass flowers one more time, then headed for the casino and the elevators beyond. I maneuvered through the crowds past the gaming tables, suddenly realizing how exhausted I was. I figured I shouldn't have been surprised—it was past three in the morning Miami time.

I was so tired that I didn't even stop at any of the tables to try my luck. All I wanted was a long soak in a bubble bath and then to go to bed. I wasn't even tempted to order a room-service dinner, which was a first for me.

Once I got up to my room, I started the bath and undressed. Before I got in, though, I had one thing to do. I took out the photographs of Diamond and Maria Mercedes, then placed them side by side on my nightstand. I stared at them for a while, as though looking for answers. Whatever secrets they held, they weren't sharing them with me. I was on my own.

13

BEFORE I WENT TO SLEEP, I had hung out the Do Not Disturb sign on the door. I was spent and planned to sleep in for maybe an hour or so. I had debated whether or not to call down to the front desk for a wake-up call, finally deciding not to. It was only when I finally woke up the next morning that I realized what a mistake I had made.

I opened my eyes and looked at the clock radio next to my bed. I actually let out a gasp of shock and thought that there had to be some kind of mistake. I bolted straight up and turned on the lamp on the bedside table. My curtains were shut tight, so the room had been enveloped in total darkness.

I squinted at the clock again, then reached for my watch. It took an effort to focus my eyes, but when I finally did I realized that the bedside clock was indeed correct.

It was after eleven in the morning.

I couldn't remember ever sleeping so late, not even when I was a teenager. I did the math in my head and realized that I had been unconscious for almost ten hours.

For how long had I been going through the paces in my everyday life without realizing how exhausted I was? Now that I thought about it, I never woke up on my own at home—my alarms took care of that. Tony and the boys needed me early in the morning, not to mention Buster needing love and reassurance. Then the phone would ring, or a delivery would arrive at the house. There was always something going on at home that needed my attention. Now, left on my own, I had collapsed and slept away an entire morning.

More amazing was the fact that it was almost two in the afternoon in Miami, and no one had called me. I decided to interpret this silence as good news. Still, I was disbelieving and obsessive enough to double-check the cell phone, just to be sure. I picked it up, careful not to dislodge the electrical charging cord plugged into the wall, and looked at the screen for the voice-mail logo that would tell me whether or not anyone had called. Still not quite believing the truth. I gave the phone a little tap, as though a written message was going to slip out from under the red plastic cover.

I lay back in bed and looked around the room with a critical eye. The place was a monochromatic orgy of variations on a burnt-white-cream color, along with lots of gold thrown in for contrast. The ivory patterned bedspread matched the curtains, while the creamy carpet was set off with a light caramel dotted design. The design's primary theme seemed to evoke an upscale farm in Tuscany, or maybe a lowbrow palazzo. The designer had obviously gone for a soothing effect, a stark contrast to the screaming chaos of the hotel's public spaces.

When I realized that I was still holding my watch and phone, I lightly placed both on the bedside table. I snuggled under the covers, suddenly groggy, and when I opened my eyes again it was past noon.

OK. So I was completely exhausted without realizing it. It was shocking to learn how out of touch I was with myself and my needs.

I threw back the covers and forced myself out of bed, reminding myself that I wasn't in Las Vegas to catch up on my rest. I had already wasted a morning, and I wasn't going to compound matters by letting the afternoon slip past. I opened the heavy curtains, blinking as bright desert sun flooded the room.

It took several moments for my eyes to adjust to the view. I was up on the twenty-seventh floor, and I could see far into the distance—all the way to the scrubby brown foothills and faraway peaks. I looked straight down to the jumble of highways, so complicated and intertwined that they looked like nothing more than oversized entrails. Cars sped fast in all directions, giving me an unpleasant reminder of Miami.

But when I looked up again, my eyes caught on the sight of the Sierra Nevada Mountains shimmering in the distance, their tops snowcapped. Then, as though my line of sight could encompass natural beauty for only so long, I focused on the brash Rio Hotel just a few blocks away. The massive edifice was decked out in wine blue and neon purple—not exactly an ideal color scheme, but reasonably acceptable in a place like Las Vegas. Because, after all, there was no other place like Las Vegas. I scanned over to Caesar's Palace, an architectural monstrosity that—I realized for the first time—could have inspired my parents' building in Miami Beach. The main building was incredibly massive, with huge white faces and replicated Roman columns and adornments. All around were scattered columns, statues, and an imitation Roman temple. It made me glad that Augustus and Marc Antony were spared a glimpse into the future at what they inspired. They might have reconsidered the whole thing.

I could have stood there in my nightgown all day, reveling in the mixture of awe and revulsion that Las Vegas architecture always inspired in me, but then I thought of Diamond. I quickly picked out an outfit for the day—black linen pants and a white twin set—then unpacked my suitcase and organized my things as best I could. I headed into the Tuscan-theme marble bathroom, complete with an oversized bathtub just waiting to be filled with hot water and perfumed oil. All kinds of bath products were prominently displayed on a counter next to the tub, and, recalling the luxury of the bath I had taken the night before, I could almost feel my resolve slipping away.

All right, so I was a slut for water. But there was something more to it, wasn't there? Being alone in that hotel room represented the most peace and quiet, the most time I had spent alone, in so long I couldn't remember. I hated to admit how much family life seemed to be taking out of me.

I made a date with the bathtub for later, then splashed my face with cold water and brushed my teeth. I took a quick shower, then untangled my hair and tied it back off my face. Once I had dressed and put on my makeup, I started making calls on the cell phone. I had a short list of people to contact, and I left a series of messages telling them that I was in town and would be calling back within the next couple of days.

My last call was to the concierge, to ask about the possibility of hiring a limousine for a few hours. I had asked about the procedure when I checked in the night before, but I wanted to make sure there wouldn't be any problems before I went downstairs.

"No problem," the concierge said in a deep, reassuring voice. "You can hire a car at any time by giving us ten minutes' notice."

"Let's do that," I said. "I'll call back in a few minutes."

I had considered taking taxis around the city, or renting a car and driving myself. Taxis might have been cheaper, but less efficient than hiring my own car. When I thought about it, I had realized that I couldn't deal with driving all around Las Vegas. I would end up spending half the day getting lost and the other half trying to get back to where I started.

When I was finished, I picked up the room phone and dialed my cellular, just to make sure it was still working. I couldn't believe it. No one had called me yet. I imagined they were being considerate and trying not to bother me—but then I doubted it, because consideration was never factored into decisions made by anyone in my family. I was relieved to find that my phone was indeed working. I was connected by my wireless umbilical cord; it was still there in case I needed it.

I looked around the room to make sure I hadn't forgotten anything, because I was probably going to be gone for several hours. I took the Do Not Disturb sign off my doorknob and flipped it to read PLEASE MAKE UP MY ROOM. Then I began the long trek to the bank of elevators.

My stomach rumbled with hunger, and I felt light-headed as I walked. I decided on a quick stop at the Café Bellagio, the ground-floor restaurant that was open twenty-four hours a day. I hadn't eaten since I left Miami, and I wasn't one to skip meals.

"I'm coming, Diamond," I whispered as I checked my watch. "Just hang in there a little longer."

14

I DIDN'T KNOW HOW TRULY ravenous I was until I took the first bite of the cheeseburger I ordered at the Café Bellagio. I happily scarfed the thick, juicy burger, then put a huge dollop of ketchup on the mountain of french fries I planned to attack next. I only interrupted my feeding frenzy to gulp my iced tea. It seemed as if, since landing in Las Vegas, terrifyingly pent-up needs for comfort and sustenance had taken over my body. I hadn't realized how much, and for how long, I had been denying myself.

I asked for the check and stared at my cell phone as though it was a magic totem. I would have tried to call Diamond again, but her message box was full and it would do no good. I used to turn my nose up at people who seemed to be surgically attached to their cell phones, but now I was one of them. I knew I couldn't hold out much longer without calling home, but part of me really wanted Tony and the boys to check on me first. I had to admit, however, that I didn't really miss them much yet—mostly, I was curious to find out how they were faring without me. I wanted to find out how Buster was doing, because he tended to go on a hunger strike whenever I was gone for more than a few hours. It was his dog's way of making me feel guilty for leaving him, I suspected, and I fell for his shameless manipulation every time.

When the check came, I dialed the concierge's desk and asked for a car in fifteen minutes, figuring that would give me enough time to settle the tab and make a quick stop at the ladies' room. I knew my opportunities for finding a bathroom might be few and far between the rest of the day.

I walked through the conservatory when I was finished, inhaling deeply the myriad flower scents, along with the grasses and shrubs and dewy odor of freshly watered vegetation. I remembered hearing once that every flower and plant at the Bellagio was alive—no well-crafted forgeries—and that each had been meticulously grown in greenhouses. My admiration knew no bounds. My black thumb was legendary, and many a flower and plant had fallen to cement my reputation. I stayed away from the outdoor section at Home Depot, fearing my very presence would make the potted plants die off in droves.

At the concierge's desk, I had to wait less than five minutes before a man approached with an expectant look on his face. He was tall, slightly balding, probably in his fifties, and neatly dressed in a black suit and a crisp white shirt. He stopped in front of me, his posture ramrod straight, with his eyes hidden by wraparound aviator sunglasses.

"Ms. Montoya?" he asked in a rumbling voice. I nodded, and the man extended a business card to me. "Dennis O'Shea. Your driver for today."

I read what was printed on the card: O'SHEA CAR SERVICE, LAS VEGAS. It listed a phone number. I looked up.

"Please call me Dennis," he said.

He must have noticed my shock. In Miami, I had never once had an American as a driver—either in a taxi or a car service. I certainly didn't want him to think I had any objections, so I quickly extended my hand and introduced myself. We nodded politely, if a bit warily, and stepped away from the concierge desk.

My first impression of Dennis was that he was competent and

on the ball, and I sensed already that he might make my search easier. Instinct told me that I had gotten lucky when he was assigned to me.

Dennis took off his glasses, revealing clear blue eyes and a lined face. "The concierge didn't tell me where you wish to go," he said. "So I haven't been able to prepare, or plan a route."

His flat statement let me know that he didn't like being placed in a situation that he didn't control. Now I knew I liked him.

"Well, he didn't tell you anything because I didn't give him any information," I said. "I'm not exactly here as a tourist. I'm here for a very specific reason."

I took a deep breath. OK, the search was officially beginning. I explained the situation with Diamond in stark terms, telling Dennis that my sister was missing and that my family had sent me to find her.

"I have a list of places I want to go to," I told him. "And, to a certain extent, I'll be making this up as I go along."

Dennis O'Shea listened intently, and I suddenly realized that he was guiding me through the lobby to the exit.

"The car's parked right outside," he said, his expression betraying nothing. "If it's all right with you, we'll discuss our itinerary out there."

"Fine," I said, following him out. Dennis walked me past a long line of cars parked in the driveway. He was much taller than me, and his legs were a lot longer, so I had to scurry a little to keep up. Finally he stopped in front of a Lincoln Town Car—a discreet vehicle, just as I had hoped. The last thing I needed was a pink stretch limousine with flashing lights and a Jacuzzi in the back. I looked over the car with respect for Dennis because it was so polished that it reflected the Bellagio's façade.

Dennis held the door for me while I unfolded a piece of paper and then handed it to him. After settling me in the car, he got in the driver's seat and half-turned, reading over the paper's contents.

"This is a preliminary list of places I want to go," I said to Dennis's profile. "Of course any of that could change, depending on what I find out."

Dennis nodded and, without preamble, began to explain in a calm and patient voice how all the various windows and gadgets in the car worked. I paid minimal attention, just enough not to seem rude.

"All right, we got that part out of the way," he finally said. He turned in his seat to face me more squarely. "Now. When was the last time you spoke with the police about your sister?"

"This morning," I said. "I made a follow-up call from my hotel room about an hour ago."

"Tell me exactly what has happened since you learned that your sister was missing," Dennis said.

It seemed strange to be talking this way with a limousine driver whom I had just met, but I was desperate, and Dennis had an air of authority about him. Besides, I had no one else to talk to.

"Before I left Miami, I wanted to reconfirm what my parents told me about calling the Las Vegas Police," I said. "My mother had basically said they treated Diamond's disappearance in a cavalier manner, which seemed strange to me."

"Sure would," Dennis rumbled.

"Sure enough, my mother had gotten confused and flustered when she called," I explained. "So she hadn't ever filed a formal report. She had hung up before putting the paperwork in motion."

As I spoke, I tried not to think of all the time we had lost because Mama had gotten overwhelmed on the phone.

"So I called the Las Vegas Police from my house yesterday afternoon, while I was preparing to come here," I said. "They referred me to the missing-persons department, who then connected me to the dispatch center, where the operator took down Diamond's information. I must have sounded desperate, because they transferred me to a detective who explained to me how a missing-persons case would be handled. He was pretty helpful, but I had to admit that there was no concrete reason to suggest foul play—she had never been stalked, as far as I know, and she wasn't in the habit of carrying lots of cash or wearing any expensive jewelry. The detective told me that there were no red flags in the case that would merit an immediate response. Just because we couldn't reach her didn't mean that something has happened to her."

Dennis squinted slightly, slowly analyzing the torrent of words I had just dropped on him. Finally he looked into my eyes.

"The police checked the jails, the hospitals, and the coroner's office, right?" he asked.

"Yes, at least that's what they told me when I called from my room this morning," I said. "I also have a case number that the records bureau gave me. It's right in here."

I started fishing in my organizer, but Dennis made a motion for me to relax.

"That's automatic, don't worry about that," he said. "Here's the thing. Aside from assigning a case number, there's no one set response to investigating a missing person. It depends on the case."

"I see," I replied.

Dennis was silent for almost a minute, thinking. "How long has your sister been missing, roughly?" he finally said.

"We're not really sure," I had to admit. "My parents started trying to reach her the day before yesterday. My sister was a free spirit, and she was also pretty secretive. She led her own life, if you know what I mean."

I knew how I sounded, trying to justify my lack of knowledge about Diamond's life. My feelings of guilt were betrayed by my voice.

"Well, she may or may not have a history of disappearing or

dropping out," Dennis said. "From the sound of it, you really wouldn't know one way or the other."

I looked miserably out the window. Dennis shifted, and I looked at him again. His gaze hadn't wavered.

"Well, has it occurred to you that your sister's just gone off somewhere," Dennis offered, "that she's perfectly safe but doesn't want to be found?"

"We've thought of that," I said. "But none of us—my parents, my siblings, or me—feel that's the case."

Dennis's eyes widened just a fraction.

"There are some other strange things going on," I told him. "My sister changed jobs a year ago without telling any of us. She might be private, but that's out of character."

Dennis mulled over what I had said. "Well, by now your sister's case has been formally assigned to a detective," he said. "That happens twenty-four hours after the initial report is made."

I thought for a moment about what Dennis was saying and how he was saying it.

"You seem to know an awful lot about police procedure," I said.

Dennis just grunted. I could see him debating with himself about how much of his past to divulge. I guessed I passed the test, because his features relaxed, and he said, "I used to be a homicide detective in New York. I'm retired now."

"Oh, that's terrific," I blurted out, feeling a rush of elation over my luck. As soon as the words escaped my mouth, though, I saw his jaw clench up. "Well, I mean, you can give me advice on what to do, how to proceed and all that. Right?" I asked.

Instead of replying, Dennis looked down at the paper I had given him. "I said I was retired," he growled softly, then looked at his watch. "It's already almost three. We should start at the apartment complex where your sister lives. At this time of day, it'll take forty-five minutes or so to get there."

"Fine," I said. I was so relieved to have help that I would have agreed to anything. I could see that Dennis wanted to keep out of my affairs, but I could also tell that part of him was fascinated by my story of a missing sister. *Retired,* he said. I didn't believe it.

I sat back and looked at the hotel's fountains as we pulled out. They weren't dancing yet. But they would be.

15

DIAMOND LIVED ON THE outskirts of Las Vegas in an area called Summerlin, at the foothills of the Red Rock mountain range. I tried to make conversation with Dennis during the drive out there, asking him general questions about Las Vegas, but he was gruff and monosyllabic. I didn't think he was trying to be rude; after all, he was in the service business, and it made no sense to alienate a client. I was hoping that he was thinking about what I had told him about my sister and, even though he hadn't explicitly agreed to give me advice, that he was formulating a plan for how to look for her.

I soon got tired of the semisilent treatment and just leaned back against my seat. I didn't want to irritate Dennis with a barrage of questions, because I knew how valuable he could be to me. He didn't seem the type to gladly suffer fools, and I didn't want him to decide that I was one.

Instead of talking I looked out the window and watched the scenery passing by. The more distance we put between ourselves and the Strip, the more downscale the sights became. In all the times I had visited Las Vegas, this was the first time I had left the tourist areas and headed outside the city. Even though Diamond had lived there for two years, she had come to see us at our hotel when we visited. It was almost hard for me to believe that so many people lived in the outlying areas; it was as though I had imagined that people just magically appeared at their jobs and then vanished until it was time for their next shift. There had always been an element of unreality about Vegas, and the idea of living an ordinary life there was almost unimaginable. It was like thinking of Mickey Mouse going home for a TV dinner after a long day at Disney World.

When we changed lanes for the freeway heading out to Summerlin, I spotted one of the many golf courses that surrounded the city. I remembered hearing how each of the casinos had a course reserved for their "whales"—the highest rollers who rated the most luxurious perks. My eyes lingered on the lush fairways and greens, and I dreaded to think how much water it took to maintain such perfect expanses of greenery in the middle of the desert.

The traffic was moving pretty smoothly, and it looked as though the trip wasn't going to take as long as Dennis predicted. Here, away from the big hotels of the Strip, we could have been on the outskirts of Phoenix, Albuquerque, or any major desert city. I wasn't surprised that Diamond had chosen to live away from the crowds and the bustle, because she had never really been a city girl. Still, I would have thought she would have found a place to live with more character than the flat, featureless subdivisions that rolled past my window.

What shocked me was that she was willing to live in a place so far removed from the ocean. The sea is usually a necessity for Cubans, on a par with food and air. I personally never went to the beach, and I never swam in the ocean, but it's important for me to know that it's nearby. Once, a few years before, Tony and I took the boys for a week-long vacation at a dude ranch. The place was beautiful, with vast skies and the mountains in the distance, but the hugeness of the desert had somehow made me feel claustrophobic. I was so conscious of my distance from the ocean that, by the third day, I started feeling depressed by the idyllic sights all around me. As soon as we were home again, I dropped my bags and headed for the beach. I spent about an hour just sitting there, breathing salt air with my eyes fixed on the horizon.

Diamond was the only one of my siblings who didn't share my need. Sapphire lived in California during college, and the ocean had always been nearby for her. Ruby, in Boston, had water all around, and when I was in New York I used to take the train out to Long Island to sit by the ocean. Q had always stayed in Miami and, since he lived on South Beach, the ocean was literally at his doorstep.

We had been driving for about twenty minutes when Dennis turned on his blinker and started to turn right for the Summerlin Parkway exit. Ever since I had shut up, Dennis hadn't uttered a single word to me. I was a little taken aback by his aloofness—and by the sight of his mirrored shades in the rearview mirror—but I hoped he was preoccupied with thoughts of how to help me. I certainly needed help, especially from a former homicide detective.

Although, I thought now, I shouldn't dwell too much on the word *homicide*.

My heart beat faster as we took the exit. I tried to compose myself as we drove down toward the center of the little town, but it wasn't easy. I could barely force myself to look out the window at the place where Diamond lived and all the everyday sights: the grocery store where she shopped, the gas station where she filled up her car, the health-food take-out place where she surely bought her meals. It was strange enough to see these places, and stranger still to wonder when was the last time she had visited any of them.

It was when we turned onto Town Center Drive, the avenue that led to Diamond's apartment complex, that I felt my breathing dangerously quicken. So far, the only real indication that Diamond had disappeared was the fact that she wasn't answering either of her phones or checking her messages. I could still cling to the fantasy that she might actually be at home, and simply incommunicado with her family for some reason that would make us both laugh once she shared it with me.

Get real, I told myself. She wasn't going to be at her apartment. The most I could hope for was to find something to tell me where she was. She had too many unanswered messages for her to be on some weekend nature hike in the mountains, or at some holistic spa getting away from it all. Suddenly, having agreed to search for Diamond didn't seem like such a great idea.

Dennis must have sensed my agitation, because he stopped the car before we reached the entrance to Diamond's gated community. He put the car in park and turned around to face me.

"You all right?" he asked.

I shrugged without answering. I was worried that, if I spoke, my voice might crack and I would start crying. I put my hand on the door handle, about to get out and walk the distance to the complex.

"Wait a minute. There's a security booth at the entrance. Do you have access to your sister's place?" Dennis pointed out the guardhouse next to a set of imposing black gates.

I looked out at the security guard, a middle-aged man in a brown uniform and black sunglasses. I watched him stop a car that approached the gate, a clipboard in his hand. He questioned the driver before pressing a button that lifted the gate and allowed the car inside the property. Then I saw another man, dressed in the same brown uniform. This guard was a bit older, and he sat in the shade in a golf cart parked to the far side of the gate.

The fact that Diamond's apartment complex had security was reassuring. It looked like the guards screened everyone who tried to gain access to the community. At least it was improbable that I was going to find her on the floor of her apartment, the victim of an armed home invasion. Still, the guards posed an immediate problem for me. I hadn't imagined Diamond would choose such a secure and regulated environment in which to live.

Actually, the more I looked the place over, the less likely it seemed that Diamond would ever have lived there. It was too clean and orderly, totally contrary to her granola nature. Maybe Diamond had changed since the last time I saw her, I thought. Maybe there was something about the gates and the security that she needed.

The complex was called Mountain Peaks, and it was made up of about a dozen or so three-story town houses. The buildings were relatively attractive, with stucco and wood trim, and situated on the land in a way that suggested privacy without wasting space. Each building had an outside staircase that connected the different floors. I could see the common areas of the complex, the paths and driveways. It was a pretty open plan. And anyone walking around would have been in clear sight of the other residents. The landscaping was minimal but tasteful, with grassy patches planted to surround the gravel and stone paths, and a few shrubs scattered in symmetrical patterns. I saw a few date palm trees, placed more for aesthetics than for the scant shade they offered.

Dennis was being patient, but I could tell he was waiting for me to answer. I looked up at him.

"No, I don't have access to her apartment," I admitted. "I was figuring I could contact the building manager and tell them why I needed to get inside. I figured that they'd be sure to help, once I told them that my sister was missing."

Dennis stared at me for a moment. "Well, that's as good a plan as any," he said dryly. He put the Lincoln in drive and pulled up to the line of two cars waiting in front of the guardhouse. When our turn came I lowered the window, wincing at a blast of hot air, and told the guard why we were there. The guard scratched his chin with his clipboard as I spoke. I could see the wheels in his brain turning—and they certainly seemed squeaky. I took out Diamond's picture, which he brought so close to his face that I thought he was going to taste it.

"She doesn't look familiar," the guard said.

Big surprise. He was so nearsighted, I doubt he could have selected his own mother out of a lineup. Still, I felt a pang of disappointment as I returned the photo to my purse.

The guard motioned to his colleague on the golf cart. Although this seemed like a simple request, the second guard's jaw dropped as though he had been ordered to run across the Sahara naked and barefoot. I was beginning to have serious doubts about the security detail at Mountain Peaks. I glanced up at Dennis, who sat motionless with his hands on the wheel at ten and two o'clock.

The older guard finally decided to comply with his coworker's request. Instead of walking the ten yards or so around Dennis's car, however, he started up the golf cart. It took him quite a bit of maneuvering to get around the limousine without hitting it. I looked back and saw the line of cars behind us growing longer.

I had to rehash my story with the second guard, and then watch the two men as they retreated to the open doorway of the security booth to debate what to do with me. They seemed to be having some kind of disagreement, and they started gesticulating so much that they might have been Cuban. I felt right at home, although I started to feel anxious about having my fate in the hands of these two fellows.

A couple of cars behind us started to honk. Flustered, the older guard pushed a button to raise the gate and waved us through without a word of explanation. I heard a rumble in the front seat, and it took me a moment to realize that it was the sound of Dennis chuckling.

The manager's office was in the front of the complex, and Dennis parked in one of the vacant visitor's spots and shut off the motor. He climbed out and opened my door for me.

I took a deep breath, squared my shoulders, and walked up the path to the building. I was almost to the door when I heard a voice call out.

"Good luck, Ms. Montoya," Dennis said from next to his car.

I turned and waved. I knew he was going to be on my side. I smiled for maybe the first time in days.

16

I STOPPED AT THE RECEP-tion desk outside the management office, trying not to become overwhelmed by the staggering variety of earth tones that comprised the décor.

"Can I speak to the manager?" I asked the young woman sitting in front of a computer screen.

"Maybe I can help you," she said brightly.

"Thank you, but I don't think so," I told her. "It's a very serious matter."

The receptionist took me at my word; she ushered me into a large office, asked me to have a seat, and went off to fetch the manager. In less than a minute an efficient-looking, conservatively dressed woman came in with an expectant look on her face.

"Rose Martin," she said, extending her hand for me to shake.

Rose was obviously a lot sharper than her security guards. She was about thirty, tall, with black hair tied in a sleek ponytail, and intelligent dark brown eyes. She sat behind her desk and listened as I told her about Diamond and how I needed to get into her apartment.

"You flew here from Miami?" she asked. That fact alone seemed to impress upon her the urgency of my request. She asked me to wait a moment and disappeared down the hall. A few minutes later she returned with an open folder that she read as she walked back to her desk.

"I'm afraid that I don't know your sister personally," Rose said, looking up from the folder. "Diamond signed her lease before I started working here."

"I see," I said, feeling momentarily defeated by this news.

Rose asked me a series of questions about my sister—her birth date, her middle name—and double-checked my answers against Diamond's rental application to ensure that I was telling the truth. She asked me for identification, so I took out my driver's license and handed it over. Rose called out to the receptionist and asked her to make a copy. I could see that Rose's main concern, for the moment, was the possible legal fallout from the disappearance of one of her tenants.

I asked to see Diamond's rental agreement and, to my relief, I saw that it gave permission for the manager to enter the apartment if the landlord was unable to locate the tenant. It was hard to look over the application, which my sister had filled out by hand. Every word I read in her distinctive handwriting was a reminder of how I had ended up in this rental office on the outskirts of Las Vegas.

The receptionist came back and handed me my driver's license. She then handed Rose a sheet of paper that, I could see, contained copies of the front and back of my ID. Rose gave it a cursory look before putting it in Diamond's file. She then opened up her middle desk drawer and took out a massive steel ring that contained keys in all colors, shapes, and sizes.

"Shall we go?" Rose asked, getting up from her desk.

I slung my purse over my shoulder and followed Rose out of the building. I looked over and saw that Dennis was standing next to his car, waiting. He had his dark glasses on, but I could tell that he was watching us. I touched Rose's elbow and led her over to the car.

"This is Dennis O'Shea," I said when we got to the parking area. "He's been very helpful to me since I arrived in Las Vegas."

I hadn't planned to include Dennis in my search of Diamond's apartment, but he and Rose shook hands as though nothing was out of the ordinary.

"Your sister's apartment is in the B area, past the swimming pool," Rose told me. She pointed out a three-story building that looked like all the others.

"Please come with me," I said to Dennis, who remained standing by the Lincoln as Rose started up the path. Dennis wavered for a moment, glancing in the other direction. "Please," I implored again.

The line of Dennis's mouth tightened. "All right," he said, "let's go." He started up the path with such sudden determination that I had to jog to keep up with his long strides. We joined Rose at the bottom of the landing outside Diamond's building.

"Your sister's apartment is on the second floor," she said, starting up the stairs. I watched her walk and was suddenly filled with certainty that something terrible had happened to my sister. My legs felt encased in cement, and I dreaded going inside the apartment and what I might find there.

"Let's go," Dennis barked, giving me a little shove to start me up the steps. My legs cooperated and I made it to the second floor in a daze. Rose saw the look on my face and put a hand lightly on my elbow.

"Are you sure you want to go inside?" she asked me. "If you want, I can call one of the security guards to go inside and check things out."

The idea that one of the fellows at the front gate might be the guard who Rose called was enough to snap me out of my state. "No, I'm ready," I said. "But thank you."

Rose reached out and, just to check, tried the doorknob. It was locked, so she searched through the keys on her ring until she found two that she deftly separated from the others with her index finger. She then unlocked the knob and the dead bolt. With a gentle shove, she opened the door and stood aside to let me pass.

"Diamond?" I called out, taking a step inside. "It's me, Esmeralda!"

Of course I received no answer. I didn't expect one, although it simply didn't seem right to barge in without announcing myself. I went inside, blinking, and Rose and Dennis followed a couple of steps behind.

Enough natural illumination came into the apartment from the balcony doors that I didn't need to turn on the lights to see. The first thing I saw was a wooden altar table in the foyer; on it was a large framed photo of our family in a heavy silver frame. I had the same picture, since Mama had sent us all copies a year ago. Still, I felt my eyes fill with water at the sight of it. It was comforting somehow to find evidence that we were prominent in her mind, even as she receded from contact with us.

I breathed deep and smelled something dank, like fruit left out for a long time. The place was dusty, and the air was so still that I felt each step I took disturbed a sort of solemn peace. I walked to the living room doorway and paused to have a look around.

Diamond was clearly going for a minimalist look. The living room was pretty big, but it contained almost no furniture at all. There was a single dark green canvas sofa against the wall facing the fireplace, and a low coffee table that seemed to have been forged from the trunk of a tree. I counted four dead plants scattered in front of the windows. There was a little area between the balcony and the kitchen that contained a little table with four chairs around it. The table was covered with piles of mail, a random assortment of catalogs, bills, magazines, and flyers.

I walked slowly to the middle of the room, the stillness and sense of abandonment making me feel as though I was in a dream. My first impression was that Diamond still lived much as she had in college. There were posters taped haphazardly to the walls, depicting natural landscapes of mountains and rivers. I even recognized a Yosemite vista from the bedroom of her apartment in Missoula.

I heard footsteps behind me and, rather than deal with Rose and Dennis, I went into the bedroom. The door was slightly ajar, and I gave it a little knock before I pushed it open.

The bedroom was only a little better furnished than the living room. My sister had her mattress and box spring right on the floor, the same as she had in college. She had never used a bed frame, much to Mama's consternation. The queen-size bed was neatly made, with soft yellow sheets and a flannel blanket thrown over it. In the corner, against the wall, was a big TV with a VCR and cable box on top, all perched on a stand that tilted precariously. I spotted the remote on the bedside table, next to the phone and answering machine. The red light on the machine was blinking. There was a green armchair next to the bed, so similar to the living room couch that Diamond must have bought them as a set and split them up.

I made a quick pass through the bathroom and the kitchen, making no startling discoveries. An apple and a couple of bananas were rotting in a ceramic bowl, but I couldn't tell from looking how old they were. Rose and Dennis followed. I noticed that neither of them touched anything.

"Ms. Montoya?" Dennis asked. He spoke softly, but the silence had been so thick that Rose jerked in surprise.

I was staring at some old photos—one of me—taped to the refrigerator, and I barely noticed Dennis had spoken until he repeated my name.

"I'm sorry," I said to him. "What?"

"I need to speak with you for a minute," Dennis said. Rose took the hint and walked out to the living room, leaving us alone in the kitchen.

"What do you think?" I asked him.

"I think you should ask to be left alone here for a while," Dennis told me. "So you can look through your sister's things."

"There doesn't seem to be much here," I said.

"Everything seems in order on the surface," Dennis agreed. "But unless you go through your sister's things you can't be sure. You haven't even looked through the mail, to see when she last brought it in. And you need to listen to the messages on her answering machine."

"Of course," I said, realizing all at once how much I had overlooked. "I'll ask Rose to leave us here for a while."

I found Rose looking out over the balcony. I thought for a moment how to frame my request. It was one thing for her to let me into my sister's apartment, but another thing entirely to leave me there unsupervised with a limousine driver to keep me company. She had taken everything I told her so far on faith, since I had provided no real evidence that anything had happened to Diamond. Most important, nothing we had seen in the apartment at this point suggested that my sister had come to any harm.

"Do you have a better idea where your sister might be?" Rose asked.

"Not yet," I said. "You've been a huge help to me so far, and now I have to ask you for another favor."

Rose folded her arms and looked at me intently. "OK," she said.

"I came all this way to find out what happened to my sister," I told her. "If I leave now, all I'll have learned is that she isn't in her apartment today. And that isn't enough."

Rose frowned. "And you want to stay here for a while to look for clues, right?" she asked. "You want to search the place without me around breathing down your neck."

"That's pretty much it," I said.

Rose tapped a finger against her elbow for a moment, then visibly relaxed. She seemed to have decided that I could be trusted, and I could have kissed her when she took out her business card and handed it to me.

"I'm here until seven," she told me. "Right now it's a few minutes until four. That gives you three hours. Call me if you finish early—otherwise, I'll meet you here at a few minutes before seven to lock up."

"Thank you so much," I said. I knew she was taking a risk letting us look through the apartment without anyone from Mountain Peaks supervising. I walked her to the entrance, and we shook hands before I closed the door. On the way back I paused in front of the family picture in the foyer. Then Dennis called my name, and I found him waiting in the living room.

"Put these on." Dennis handed me a pair of latex surgical gloves. I could see that he'd already put his on.

"You had these on you?" I asked.

Dennis shrugged. "I keep a box in the glove compartment in the limo," he explained. Then he gave me a little wink, almost too quick to see. "You never know when you might need them."

I put the gloves on. "I knew I was lucky to meet you," I said.

Dennis gave a dismissive nod. "All right," he said. "Let's go."

I was learning fast that that was Dennis's favorite expression.

17

"THREE HOURS SOUNDS LIKE a lot of time, but it isn't," Dennis growled. "We're going to have to move fast to do the job."

Dennis stalked through the living room, then paced a circuit of the bedroom, bathroom, and kitchen. He was practically smelling the air like a tracker following his prey. He was completely in his element. I found it fascinating to watch.

I couldn't help but wonder what the hell this man was doing working as a limousine driver. I knew that if I was ever going to find out, it would be because Dennis told me in his own sweet time. Thanks to the natural light coming in through the balcony doors, I got the full effect of Dennis's eyes—they were such a light blue, almost translucent, that they were eerie. No wonder he kept them hidden behind sunglasses much of the time.

"We'll start with the messages on the answering machine, then we'll go through the mail," he said. We went to the dining room table. "Some of this stuff you can toss—the junk mail and the flyers. But set aside any bills, especially from credit card companies. That'll tell us a lot about what your sister has been up to."

I started to do as he said, pulling a wastebasket from the corner and quickly filling it with supermarket ads and restaurant take-out menus.

"Your sister quit her job without telling your family, right?" Dennis asked, nosing through a pile of mail.

"I called the newspaper where she worked and talked to the man who replaced her," I said. "He'd heard somewhere that she was working at one of the casinos, but that's all he knew."

"Well, we'll find out where she was working if we can find a pay stub in here, or health insurance information." He put down the mail he had been looking at. "But I want to hear her answering machine messages first."

I could tell Dennis was working on his instincts and training as a police investigator. I couldn't imagine what I would have done if I had gone there alone. I doubt I would have thought to go through the mail or the phone messages. I was out of my league. I knew how to be a mother, a wife, and an interior designer—but I knew nothing about how to find my missing sister.

We walked to the bedroom and headed for the night table. Dennis and I looked awkwardly at each other; apart from the single green armchair, the only place to sit was on the bed.

"This could take a while," Dennis said. "Might as well get comfortable."

Dennis went to the dining room and returned with two chairs, which he arranged next to the bed. I thanked him and took the seat nearest to the answering machine. Dennis reached into the pocket of his suit and came out with a pad of paper and a pen.

"You ready?" Dennis asked.

I nodded, and he reached across me to press the Play button. The first thing we heard was a tinny recording announcing that the mailbox was completely full—the same annoying message that I'd endured when I called Diamond the day before.

Then the same male voice said, "You have twenty-five new messages." Dennis tapped his pen on his paper pad.

The first message was dated May 15—just four days ago—at a few minutes after ten at night. It was a man with a rough voice:

"Hey, Diamond, where the hell are you? I've been waiting a couple hours now, and you've got your cell phone turned off. Call me."

The next call was from the same gruff, disembodied voice. The man had called back an hour later, then a third time close to midnight. On the latter message he revealed his true nature: "All right, bitch, so that's the way it is. Listen good: fuck off and forget it. No woman's going to stand me up."

He called yet again, this time after three in the morning. He sounded drunk, angry, and he unleashed a tirade of profanities that had me squirming in my seat. My sister was hanging around with some bad people. Seeing that I was becoming upset, Dennis calmly pressed the Stop button.

"I can see how listening to these messages is going to upset you," he said calmly. "Ms. Montoya, I know it's not easy to learn that your sister has been leading a life where a man can talk to her—"

"First of all, please stop calling me 'Ms. Montoya,'" I interrupted. "I know you're just being polite, and I appreciate it, but I think we should stop being so formal."

Those killer blue eyes fixed on me, cold and reflective, giving me no idea what Dennis thought about what I had just said. I would have hated to be a suspect being interrogated by Detective Dennis O'Shea in New York.

"My first name is Esmeralda," I told him.

"If it makes you feel better, that's all right with me," Dennis said. "And please call me Dennis. You haven't called me by any name so far, so it shouldn't be too much of an adjustment."

"OK. Fine." I took a deep breath. Dealing with this man was like talking to my sons when they were watching TV—I knew he heard what I was saying, but I couldn't say for sure how much was sinking in. He'd visibly shifted gears, and his attention was focused somewhere deep inside.

"The man on the tape," I said. "What do you think?"

Dennis put his elbows on his knees and nodded at the machine. "Let's listen to the rest of the messages," he said.

The next message was from nine the next morning. It was from a dry-cleaner, a woman saying that if Diamond didn't pick up her clothes within the next week, then they were going to be sold or otherwise disposed of. The woman explained that the dry-cleaners could hold customers' clothes for only sixty days after they were ready and that Diamond had passed the deadline. I was so relieved to hear a normal message—and reconfirmation of Diamond's flaky side—that I actually let out a little laugh.

After that were two hang-ups. That left eighteen more to go. I knew that our family would be responsible for about a dozen of them.

The next message was from noon, the day after the threatening messages from the man. It was a young woman, from the sound of her voice. She spoke in a low, breathy way, and so quickly that her words jumbled together and made it difficult to understand what she was saying.

"Diamond, it's me, Angie," she said. "What's up? Why didn't you come to work yesterday? Mickey was so pissed! Are you sick? You really, *really,* should have called in. If he finds out I lied for you, he'll fire me. Come on, Diamond, my ass is on the line. I can't cover for you much longer. Please call in!"

Dennis pressed the Stop button. I noticed that he had big, blunt hands and that the fingernail on his index finger was as square as the face of a single dice.

"Do you know any Angie?" he asked me. "Has your sister ever mentioned anyone by that name?"

"Not that I remember," I said. "But Diamond was really secretive about her life here. I mean, I can't even tell you whether she had a boyfriend here."

"Obviously this Angie is a coworker." Dennis jotted something in his little notebook. He pressed the Play button again. "Let's see if she called back."

Angie never called back, or if she did, she found the mailbox full. The next sixteen messages were from different members of my family, all placed within a ten-hour period. I was responsible for five of these calls, and I could have cried out in frustration at the sound of my own voice. Because my family had called so many times, no one else had been able to leave any subsequent messages. Had we been more restrained, and less frenetically Cuban, Dennis and I might have been able to learn more about Diamond's disappearance.

Dennis reached over and picked up the answering machine. "I'm going to get the numbers of the people who called from the caller ID box." He laid the machine on the bed, with his pad next to it, ready to write down the numbers of the two strangers who had left messages.

I replayed the sound of the angry man's messages in my mind, especially the last one, when he had been drunk and almost slurring. Diamond had apparently failed to show up for some meeting with this guy. I was trying to imagine what they might have planned when Dennis broke the silence with a single succinct syllable.

"*Fuck!*" he shouted.

His voice was so loud that I jumped in my seat. When he looked up at me, his piercing eyes were lit like glaring bulbs.

"The fucking caller ID doesn't work," he said. "There's nothing here. Either that, or your sister never bothered to connect it."

"So we can't trace the calls," I said. "Or those two hang-ups."

"The police can do it, if it comes to that, but we can't right now." Dennis replied. He stood up, the notebook clutched in his hand, and headed for the door. "Let's work on the mail."

I followed Dennis out to the living room, where we came to the mess that I had earlier started to sort. The wastepaper basket was full, so I went into the kitchen to try to find a garbage bag. There were no plastic bags—not a surprise, since Diamond had more than once railed about the effect of plastics on the environment—but I found a couple of brown paper bags folded on the counter bearing the logo of a health-foods store.

On a whim, I opened up the refrigerator door. There was nothing inside, save for a couple of bottles of juice and a tin of Pilon coffee. I had to smile at the latter item, which told me that Diamond had maintained some of her Cuban roots even while living in the desert.

"Here," I said to Dennis, opening up one of the bags and placing it between the two chairs that remained by the dining room table. I saw that Dennis had divided the remaining mail into two neat stacks.

"Pick one," he said.

I chose the pile on the right and sat down. Dennis took the other and did likewise. We worked in silence for a while, inspecting each item carefully so that we didn't throw out anything of potential value. We finished close to the same time.

We were left with about a dozen pieces of mail, none of them personal. There was a card from the Guardian Angel Cathedral that listed its address and the Sunday Mass schedule. This surprised me, since Diamond had never been particularly religious. She had never said anything to me about becoming interested in the Church.

I found two credit card receipts. The first was dated April 30, the second May 3. There were charges for meals—$26.00 and $28.00, respectively—at a place called the Cuban Café. Diamond really did seem to be reaching back for her roots.

Still, something struck me. Diamond was a strict vegetarian, and I seriously doubted whether that had changed since the last time I saw her. And in a Cuban restaurant, finding vegetarian dishes on the menu was about as likely as finding an iceberg in Havana Bay. Sometimes, under duress, a Cuban cook would serve green peas—but only then out of a can, and as a decoration. Starches were the standard side dishes—not exactly mouthwatering offerings for vegetarians. Salad generally consisted of a few leaves of iceberg lettuce with a green tomato on top, the whole thing sprinkled with oil and vinegar. To have spent as much as she did in a Cuban place, she must not have eaten alone. That meant she had picked up the tab for someone, and more than once.

Some of the envelopes had been opened—the electric bill, home and cellular phone bills, condo fees—but none of these helped much. There were two unopened Citibank statements, for March and April, and frequent-flyer statements for American and United. Her Exxon, Visa, and Bloomingdale's bills were there as well, all unopened. Knowing Diamond, she would probably put off paying these bills until the last minute, not wanting to face the damage.

"So, should we open these?" I said, showing Dennis the sealed bills that I held in my latex-covered hand.

Dennis didn't answer right away. So far we had only separated and discarded mail. We had yet to actually open anything.

"It's tricky, Esmeralda," Dennis said. I noticed he didn't stumble over pronouncing my name, which was unusual. "Tampering with someone's mail is a federal offense. With real jail time. We want information, but we don't want to start breaking laws. That's why we can't ask the apartment complex to open up your sister's mailbox to see what's inside. We don't have the authority to do that."

Dennis took the envelopes out of my hand and looked at them

carefully. "You know what's interesting about this?" He squinted at me. "There's nothing job-related in here. I mean, she's not the tidiest housekeeper in the world. She's got flyers, receipts, and old mail all over the place. But we have no idea how she's making a living."

"I talked to a man named Oscar Maxwell at my sister's old job," I told him. "He said he thought she was working at one of the casinos, but wouldn't we find some sign of that? They're regular businesses, after all, with pay stubs, health insurance, and all the regular paperwork."

"Sure, otherwise they'd have the Nevada Gaming Commission all over them." Dennis took a deep breath and glanced out the balcony door. "Well, we know from Angie's message that your sister works someplace, and that her boss is called Mickey. That's not much to go on. Especially if she was being paid off the books."

"You mean illegally? Under the table?" I had a hard time imagining my flower-power sister involved in anything illegal.

Dennis looked at me as though I had uttered the most naïve thing he'd ever heard. "Yes, illegally," he said. He looked slowly through the mail. "Listen, there has to be more than this. You have to help. You're the only one who can shed some light on what happened to your sister. I know you said she was secretive."

I hated to use that word, but it was true. "Yes," I nodded. "Especially since she moved here."

"OK." Dennis thought for a moment. "Growing up, most kids have a secret place where they hide the stuff they don't want their parents to see. A diary, love notes from a boy at school—stuff like that—like a secret hiding place all their own."

"Right . . ." I said, uncertainly.

"But it's never all that secret," Dennis continued. "Because siblings always know where each others' hiding places are. You can fool your parents, but not your brothers and sisters."

"And I should know where Diamond keeps her secrets?" I asked Dennis, my voice rising a little.

"Exactly." Dennis looked at me with the expectant expression of a teacher facing a slow but steadfast student. I knew he was giving me invaluable help, worth much more than the hourly rate I was paying him, but that didn't preclude me feeling resentment toward him.

"If I knew something like that, wouldn't I have said so already?" I asked him.

"Think," he ordered.

I started pacing the living room. I *did* remember how Sapphire used to keep her contraband in a pencil case, which she'd stuff deep into her art portfolio. And Ruby always kept her forbidden items in her backpack, which was crammed with so much junk that no one dared look into it.

"Remember," Dennis said.

I used to keep my diary and love letters in a pair of black leather boots I had bought at a second-hand store. And Q hid his drugs in his plastic CD case.

But for the life of me, I couldn't remember where Diamond kept her stash.

Dennis got up with a frustrated sigh and went into the bedroom. I followed and arrived in time to see him lift the mattress off the bed, then run his hands in the area between the mattress and box spring. Nothing. Then he lifted the entire bed and looked under it. No luck. He went to the armchair and ran his hands along its every surface without success. He then searched the night table, going through the drawers and feeling under them. I was amazed how quickly he performed his task. When he began going through the closet, I realized that standing and watching him wasn't a particularly valuable contribution. So I walked through the house slowly, looking around, until I reached the foyer.

The big family picture stared out at me from the altar table, reminding me of my responsibility to find Diamond. It was too disconcerting to see Mama and Papa and my siblings seemingly monitoring my every move, so almost without thinking, I turned it over and lay it flat.

I moved away in the direction of the balcony and something strange happened. Looking into the afternoon light, I saw an after-image of the back of the picture frame play against the spots in my eyes as my vision adjusted. I had seen the back of the frame for maybe half a second, but now a fleeting after-image played in my visual field—and something stood out.

I turned and went back to the foyer. There it was: a little piece of white paper, maybe an eighth of an inch long, protruding from the black velvet frame backing. My heart beat a little harder when I noticed how thick the frame was and how the hinges seemed to be straining. I carefully moved the four brass hinges that held the frame backing in place.

After counting to three, I took off the backing. I don't know what I expected to find, but it sure as hell wasn't the cascade of hundred-dollar bills that fell to my feet. Then I saw the photograph of our shared ancestor, Maria Mercedes Montalvo, identical to the picture in my purse, land on top of the cash. It seemed like an ominous sign, given Mama's dream and Maria Mercedes's prophesy.

I felt a sudden chill go through my body and I shivered uncontrollably. I was in such shock that I barely noticed Dennis calling out to me from the bedroom.

"Esmeralda, come here!" Dennis shouted again. "Come look what I found."

I stood transfixed by the money and the photograph on the

floor. Dennis decided to come out and see why I wasn't responding to his summons. He found me frozen in place.

When he saw the pile of bills on the floor, he held up the results of his own search: a big bag of marijuana.

"Your sister Diamond is a fun girl," he said with a humorless chuckle. "That's for sure."

I had no answer for him.

18

AT A QUARTER TO SEVEN there was a knock at the door of Diamond's apartment. Dennis and I had finished putting everything back in place, so nothing seemed to have been disturbed. A large manila envelope was burning a hole in the zipper compartment of my bag, because it contained Diamond's marijuana, about fifty crisp hundred-dollar bills, and the picture of Maria Mercedes Montalvo. It was a good thing I carried a big purse.

Dennis and I had talked about whether we would be breaking any laws by taking this stuff. I decided that, since Diamond was my sister, she would have given me permission to hold her things for her. I thought I wasn't committing a crime, but I wasn't sure. Diamond was missing, but no evidence of foul play had been found. That meant her apartment wasn't a crime scene and that I wasn't technically guilty of taking items of evidence.

Dennis had given me a noncommittal nod in reply to my decision. We knew I was playing fast and loose with the law, but I figured I could explain myself if I had to. It would be easier for me, a civilian, but a lot harder for Dennis, a former police officer. I had him look the other way when I put the things in the envelope then my purse, so he could credibly deny any knowledge of what I had done. He neither agreed nor disagreed, simply fixing me with the stony expression that I had come to like more and more, then turning away.

We would have liked to search the place again, but we simply ran out of time. We were lucky to have the opportunity Rose granted us. We were waiting for the knock when it came, and I opened the door immediately. Rose was standing there, official, with her purse over her shoulder.

"All done?" she asked with forced cheer, obviously ready to go home for the day.

I noticed she didn't ask whether or not Dennis and I had discovered anything that explained Diamond's disappearance. She seemed to be distancing herself from the situation, which was probably the prudent thing for her to do. I wondered whether she had regretted letting me stay in the apartment, once she was back in her office.

"Yes," I said tersely. "Thank you."

I went out first, followed by Dennis. When we were all out on the landing, Rose went inside and took a quick look around, then came back out and locked the door. Before we descended to the ground floor, I looked around at the other apartments. I was hoping to spot a neighbor, someone whom I could ask about Diamond, but the place was as deserted as when we arrived. The sky was darkening when we walked around the swimming pool, none of us speaking. We then headed out to the lot where the limousine was parked. Rose escorted us the whole way, perhaps to make sure we didn't wander around on our own. We shook hands by the car.

"You'll let me know when you find your sister?" Rose asked.

"Of course," I said.

"And I'll do the same," Rose promised. "Good luck."

Rose nodded and, apparently in a hurry, bustled off. Dennis and I watched her until she turned a corner, probably headed to her car at the end of a long day.

Dennis unlocked the limo and put his hand on the backdoor handle. I cleared my throat and shook my head.

"Come on, Dennis," I said. "I think we know each other well enough by now that I shouldn't be riding in the backseat."

I went around to the front passenger seat and waited; after all, it was Dennis's vehicle, and I could tell he had a territorial sense about it. I smiled with surprise when I saw a red splotch suddenly appear on Dennis's neck, then climb up his cheeks to his forehead. It took me a few seconds to realize that the man was actually blushing.

"Well, that's up to you," he said in his gruffest voice of the day.

He came around, politely opened the door, then closed it once I got in. When he got in, he started the motor without saying anything. I turned to look at him and saw that he had at least gone from bright red to a more comfortable pink.

Just as I fastened my seat belt, I heard a muffled sound from my purse. It had been so long since my cell phone rang that I almost didn't recognize the tone. I rummaged around, and when I saw the number on the caller ID screen, it had a 702 area code—the one for Las Vegas. *Could it be Diamond?* I wondered. I pressed the Receive button as quickly as I could, before the voice mail picked up.

"Yes? Yes?" I almost shouted into the phone.

"This is Esmeralda?" asked a woman's voice that I didn't recognize.

My hands shook, and I realized how disappointed I was that my sister wasn't on the line.

"Yes, this is she. Who is this, please?"

"You don't know me, but my name is Adrianna Gomez," said the woman. "I'm Dorcas's friend. Dorcas called me and said you were in Las Vegas."

The name sounded familiar, and then I remembered: Adrianna was the woman who had fled Cuba in the same raft as my friend. I tried to recall all that Dorcas had told me about her, but I couldn't. It had been a long day, and it seemed like an eternity since I'd had anything to eat.

"Yes, of course," I said uncertainly. *"Hola*, how are you?"

Dennis pulled out of the Mountain Peaks parking lot and drove slowly; finally he maneuvered the car to the side of the road to wait until I told him where I wanted to go next.

"I'm fine," Adrianna said. "Listen, Dorcas told me about why you're here—the situation with your sister. Have you heard from her?"

"No, I haven't." I wondered how much Dorcas had told her. I knew Dorcas meant well by contacting her friend on my behalf, but I wasn't comfortable with the news of Diamond's disappearance getting around.

"I don't mean to butt into family matters," Adrianna said. "But if you're a friend of Dorcas, then I'll do anything I can to help you. You just let me know what you need."

I remembered something Dorcas had said about Adrianna. She was "well connected," whatever that meant.

"I appreciate that, but I'm not sure what anyone can do for me right now," I said. "I've just started looking."

"What have you tried?" she asked. "If you don't mind."

I paused. "Well, I've called the police, and a detective has been assigned to the case," I explained. "I have to follow up on that next."

"The detective, what's his name?" Adrianna asked.

"I don't know yet." I wondered if she was implying that she knew people in the Las Vegas Police Department. "I should know soon."

"Do you have my numbers?" Adrianna asked.

"I do," I replied. "Dorcas gave them to me."

"Call me anytime, night or day," Adrianna said warmly, with a hint of concern. "I'm serious about that. There might be something I can do to help, once you found out more about your sister. You let me know."

Without waiting for a reply, Adrianna hung up. She was all business, that was for sure. I turned around and saw Dennis watching me.

"That was a friend of a friend," I told him. "She lives here and wanted to know if she could help."

Dennis made no comment. "Where do you want to go now?" he asked.

I thought for a moment, then decided that I owed Dennis more of an explanation. I knew I could trust him.

"Back there in the apartment, I didn't tell you the significance of the photograph I found stashed with the money behind that picture frame," I said. "It's a photo of our great-great-great-grandmother, a woman named Maria Mercedes Montalvo."

Dennis stared at me, waiting for more. I didn't know how I could explain Maria Mercedes's importance to my family, so I just plunged ahead.

"I don't know why Diamond hid it there," I said. "But there must have been a reason. I want to tell you about Maria Mercedes, because I think the story might be somehow relevant to my sister's disappearance."

Dennis looked supremely puzzled. I didn't know what I was doing. I had hired the man for the afternoon and, in spite of what had happened at Mountain Peaks, our involvement would probably end when he dropped me off at the Bellagio. I simply had a feeling that if Dennis knew the deeper dimensions of what was happening, that he might continue to help me.

"Is it a long story?" Dennis asked, a little unsure.

"Yes," I said. "Long and complicated."

"Well, if it's going to take some time, we should find a better place than this car," he said.

"I couldn't agree more."

"Coffee shop or bar?" he asked.

"Bar," I replied.

The man might have been a detective in his former life, but if he didn't know which venue I would choose, then he should have brushed up on his detecting skills. No doubt about it, Dennis had as much to learn about me as I did about him.

19

tain Peaks complex, Dennis retraced the route that had taken us to Summerlin and got on the freeway heading back to Las Vegas. Soon he took an exit unfamiliar to me, then drove a mile or so until he stopped the limo in front of a small, nondescript bar. I could tell from the landmarks in the near distance that we weren't far from Las Vegas Boulevard, but the feel of the quiet street on which we were parked marked it as a place for locals. I was glad to get away from the glitz and noise of the strip, if I was truly going to attempt to tell Dennis the story behind the photo of Maria Mercedes that I had found in Diamond's apartment.

It had been just the day before that I told the story to Dorcas at Versailles, but that had been an easier matter. First of all, Dorcas was Cuban. She knew all about Cuban history, our wars of independence, and the long nightmare of Fidel Castro. I didn't have to explain to her about the players and the past. I wasn't so sure about Dennis.

We had barely spoken during the fifteen-minute ride from the suburbs back into the city. I knew what I was thinking about, but as Dennis turned off the car I began to wonder what had been going through his mind. Whatever it was, I knew this certainly couldn't have been an average day at work for him, not even in

Las Vegas. I realized how much I was coming to depend on his steady influence and hoped that the story I was going to tell him wouldn't drive him away.

I got out of the car, with Dennis holding the door open, and looked up at the pastel-painted sign above the bar's front door.

"The Clipped Chip?" I said, reading the block lettering of the sign.

Dennis sighed a little. "Want to go somewhere else?" he grunted.

"Oh, no," I said. "The Clipped Chip will do just fine."

In fact, the place fit my mood perfectly. When we walked in, the place was so pitch dark that I felt as though I had fallen into a well. The only real illumination came from signs above the bar—advertisements for liquor brands that I had never even heard of. It was one room inside, dark and seedy, with a row of near motion-less figures seemingly holding on to the bar for dear life. The place smelled like a broken dream. At a glance I couldn't even discern which of the barflies were men and which were women. Maybe they had been there so long that they weren't sure themselves.

My stomach was rumbling with hunger, but one look around told me not to expect to be able to order a meal. The clientele looked perfectly satisfied with deriving sustenance from sorry-looking peanuts and pretzels in the chipped bowls arrayed around the battered bar. Apparently the ownership hadn't dressed the place up in anticipation of a visit from the Zagats.

I blinked and blinked, but after thirty seconds still couldn't see much. That was probably a blessing. The details of the place would have had me more concerned about code violations than scanning the décor with a professional eye. Even in Miami—a city where building inspectors live in million-dollar homes and drive Mercedes convertibles—a place like this couldn't have got-ten past the most cursory inspection.

"Want to sit down?" Dennis asked. He guided me toward one of the three booths that lined the far wall. I trusted Dennis, but still I ran my hand along the seat before I sat down—the light was so dim, I was worried someone might have passed out there, and I would sit on top of a valued customer. For a fleeting moment I tried to remember when I had gotten my last tetanus shot.

Dennis watched me sit, his eyes registering my discomfort. "What would you like?" he asked, motioning at the bar. Clearly there was no table service at the Clipped Chip.

"A glass of red wine," I said. "Preferably a cabernet."

Even in the dark I could see the astonished look on Dennis's face.

"Esmeralda, they don't have wine here," he said in a hushed, patient voice. "Even if they do, you don't want to drink it. Assuming you could choke it down, the hangover would make you want to cut your own head off. Trust me on that one."

I considered my options. I rarely drank anything but wine. "OK. How about a rum and Coke?" I said, remembering my college days.

Dennis went off to get our drinks, and I settled into the booth. I felt cracked leather through the fabric of my pants and tried not to dwell on the bacterias that were surely thriving in the stuffing. I wondered how often Dennis came to this place. I didn't want to think he was a regular, but he certainly seemed to know his way around.

He returned with our drinks. "Here," he said, handing me a tall glass filled to the brim with brownish liquid and a single forlorn ice cube floating on top. He sat down and arranged his own order, which seemed to be a double scotch, neat.

"Cheers," he said, draining half of his in a single gulp.

My eyes were starting to adjust to the gloom, and I took in Dennis's incredibly blue eyes. This was the first time we had ever sat down facing each other, and I had to admit that it was more than a little disconcerting. Dennis was probably at least twenty years older than I was. I found him attractive, I had to admit, but not so much that it made me uncomfortable. I wondered what he thought of me. He had certainly put himself out for me, and I suspected that it wasn't simply because he wanted to rack up a hefty tip on top of his billable hours.

"So here we are," I said.

Dennis shot me a look that said we were beyond small talk. "Tell me about the lady in the photograph," he said.

After three rum and Cokes, for me, and four scotches, for him, Dennis knew pretty much everything about the histories of the Navarro and Montalvo families. I left out little, figuring that Dennis needed to know the whole story if I expected him to help me. He was a good listener, and he didn't interrupt me once while I was explaining. When I was completely talked out, Dennis sat for a while contemplating the contents of his glass before he looked up with those piercing eyes.

"That's quite a story," he said.

I nodded in agreement. Part of me was relieved that he hadn't gotten up and walked out halfway through.

"So what's your strategy for what to do next?" Dennis asked. I noted he was assuming I had one and was giving me more credit than I deserved.

"I guess I'm winging it," I admitted. "I mean, I'm going to go on what I found in Diamond's apartment, and what we heard on her answering machine. I've made some calls, and I'm meeting with the detective on the case tomorrow. I'm going to follow up on the guy who replaced Diamond at the newspaper, and see what he knows."

Dennis mulled over what I had said. "Seems reasonable," he muttered. "So you think your sister's disappearance is somehow tied into your ancestor's prediction."

He phrased his statement as a comment rather than a question. I had the distinct impression that I was being interviewed.

"That's what I'm going on," I said.

"Why do you think that?" he asked. The intense focus of his blue eyes gave me a feeling of warmth that wasn't at all unpleasant. For the first time in hours I thought of Tony, and wondered what he was doing at that precise moment.

"I started thinking about it in Miami," I said. "It's too much of a coincidence, the way my sister vanished at just the moment that my family needs to find her."

We had been talking for more than an hour, and I was tempted to order another drink and take my dinner in liquid form like everyone else in the place. Somehow I restrained myself.

"And now, finding Maria Mercedes's photo like that in Diamond's apartment," I said, "that nailed it for me."

"You don't really have a theory," Dennis noted. "Just a hunch."

"Call it a strong hunch," I replied. "I have to think about it."

"Be careful while you're thinking," Dennis said in a low voice. "And don't get caught with all that weed."

I instinctively reached for my purse. I had forgotten all about the fact that I was in possession of enough dope to get me thrown in jail. That would be a hard one to explain to Tony and my parents.

Dennis tossed back the last of his drink and gripped the table. "Ready?" he growled.

He caught me off guard, suggesting that we leave so abruptly. I suppose I had assumed we were going to discuss strategy, develop a plan. Anyway, that's what detectives did in bars on TV shows. Clearly, Dennis wasn't like a character on television. I wasn't even sure if he planned to keep helping me, or if we were about to part ways permanently when he dropped me off at the Bellagio.

I decided not to worry about it. I was exhausted, and the rum and Cokes had rendered me so mellow that I was close to regarding the bacteria in the stuffing of the leather seat as fuzzy little critters who would probably make great pets. The booth had suddenly become as warm and friendly as a cocoon to a moth, and I didn't really want to leave.

Dennis escorted me to the door of the Clipped Chip with a deferential manner, as though I was some kind of royalty. As far as I could tell, the four scotches he'd downed had had no effect on him. I glanced around and saw the same shady characters at the bar, frozen in the same places they'd been glued to when we came in. Maybe it was the three rum and Cokes talking, or else I was getting into a desperate emotional state over Diamond, but part of me wanted to go talk to the barflies. I was curious how much time they spent at the Clipped Chip, and whether they were friends or if they always sat in silence.

"What?" Dennis asked at the door, reading my face with a quizzical expression.

"Nothing," I said. I knew I tended to get sentimental—and amorous—when I was drinking. Neither trait was appropriate to the moment. It was time to get me back to my hotel before I screwed up somehow.

20

DENNIS HAD JUST LEFT ME at the Bellagio when my cell phone rang. I looked at the number on the screen and saw it was Sapphire.

Finally. Someone from my family had remembered me.

I pressed the button to take the call and looked down at my watch. It was almost eleven at night, Las Vegas time, which meant that it was two in the morning in Miami. I hoped Sapphire wasn't under the influence of anything stronger than her Ritalin dose.

"Esmeralda!" From the sound of my name passing my sister's lips, I knew that my hopes had been misplaced. Oh, well, I thought. After three strong drinks at a dive like the Clipped Chip, I wasn't in any position to lecture my sister about consuming mood-altering substances. The most I could hope for was that I sounded better than she did.

She repeated my name, so loudly this time that she was almost making it unnecessary to use AT&T in order to make me hear her. Anyone within ten feet of me could hear her as well.

"It's me. Sapphire!" she added, as though there was any chance of me mistaking her for someone else. I hustled over to a corner of the driveway, noticing the annoyed looks I was getting from people close to me watching the fountains. Apparently there was cell-phone etiquette, even in Las Vegas.

"What's up, Sapphire?" I found myself reflexively yelling into the receiver to match my sister's volume level. As much as I tried to avoid it, my phone conversations with Sapphire inevitably devolved into two-way shouting matches—even when we were on the best of terms.

"We decided not to call you," Sapphire explained, almost breathless. "We figured you'd be in touch as soon as you found out anything about Diamond. But I just couldn't resist."

Sapphire laughed nervously, the way she always did when she thought she was doing something that might get her in trouble.

"Don't tell anyone in the family I called, *por favor*," she added. "We all promised each other we wouldn't bother you. I mean, I know you must be busy."

"I won't tell," I promised her. "I'm just happy to hear from someone."

I moved to a place in the driveway where I could watch the dancing fountains. The fresh air was doing me good, and I felt my mood lift a little.

"So what's going on at home?" I asked. I was interested in Sapphire's answer, but part of me was also stalling for time. I knew Sapphire was calling to pump me for information about Diamond, and I had to quickly calculate how much to tell her.

"Not a thing," Sapphire said. "We're all nervous wrecks. We're just waiting to hear from you."

My family wasn't sparing in portioning out the guilt.

"There's not much to tell," I said, watching the shimmering water in the fountains. "Have you talked to Tony, by any chance?"

"Tony? No," Sapphire said suspiciously. "Haven't you?"

"No," I admitted.

"Oh, well, he's probably busy with the boys. Isn't his mother staying at your house?"

"Yes," I said. "She's helping out while I'm here."

I decided that I wasn't going to tell Sapphire about the details of what I found in Diamond's apartment at the Mountain Peaks complex. That wasn't to say that I never would spill everything, but I didn't want to get Sapphire worked up at two in the morning. That wouldn't be good for anyone.

"Listen, I went to Diamond's apartment this afternoon," I said, preempting her question.

A second of silence. "And?" Sapphire yelled in my ear.

"She wasn't there," I said. "And I didn't find anything to tell me where she's gone to."

"Nothing?" Sapphire yelled. "You didn't find out anything about where Diamond is? Listen, Esmeralda, you need to talk to people. You have to find the apartment manager and talk to him."

"It was a her, and I did," I said, a little annoyed. But then I imagined the torture my parents and my siblings must have been going through. There they were in Miami, resisting all their impulses to call me every ten minutes—and, by my family's standards, not calling all day was an extreme act of willpower. I probably should have called them, if only to say that I had no news.

I stared at the fountains as I told Sapphire about how I had spent the day—omitting information about the photograph, the money, and the weed. I told Sapphire about listening to the messages on Diamond's answering machine, leaving out the part about the man who called repeatedly, and abusively. If I told Diamond about those things, she would immediately call everyone in the family, and then they would all be awake all night talking and worrying. At least I could allow them a good night's sleep.

I told Sapphire about Dennis and how lucky I was to have his help. I also informed her of the messages on Diamond's phone from a coworker named Angie, which at least indicated that Diamond had been working someplace. I finished my account by mentioning Dorcas's friend Adrianna Gomez and how generously she had offered to help. For once, Sapphire actually listened without interrupting.

"Well, that's great about your driver being a detective," she finally said. "He's going to keep helping you, right?"

I replayed my farewell to Dennis just a few minutes before, when he said he would continue to "work with me," as he put it, and would make himself available while I was in Las Vegas. He also volunteered to try to do a little checking around on his own. I was reminded that I knew almost nothing about this man who had learned so much about me and my family. About the only personal detail I had gleaned from the day I spent with him was the fact that he didn't wear a wedding ring.

"He's picking me up in the morning to keep looking for Diamond," I told my sister. "I have an appointment with the police detective assigned to Diamond's case, and I'm going to check with the newspaper where she used to work. I don't know. There's so much to do. I guess I just have to hope I get lucky."

Sapphire sighed into the phone. "I feel so bad that you're out there dealing with all this alone," she said. "I mean, it's hard for us here in Miami, but it must be so nerve-wracking for you."

"It's going fine," I lied.

I heard Sapphire inhale deeply. "Esmeralda, where do you think Diamond is?" she said, her voice little more than a whisper. I knew the real question she was asking me. Did I think our little sister was alive?

I could have bullshitted her and told her everything was going to be fine. Instead, I said, "I just don't know. It's strange. I'm scared for her."

"We have total confidence in you," my sister said. "Remember that. Look, I don't care if anyone gets mad at me. I'll call everyone and tell them I talked to you. It'll save you the trouble of calling everyone one at a time."

"I'll let you know as soon as I find out anything," I said, my voice sounding a little hollow. "I love you."

I hung up. Suddenly I felt overwhelmed with guilt. I had started the day so late and learned so little. And all that with my family back home sitting by the phone, waiting. I hadn't even managed to talk to my sons.

I put the phone in my purse and made my way to the hotel entrance. The three rum and Cokes I'd downed on an empty stomach, combined with a day of stress and uncertainty, were making me exhausted. I needed a hot bath and room service. I looked at my watch. It was after eleven, and Dennis was picking me up at ten the next morning.

As I walked through the reception area again, I thought about the fact that Tony hadn't bothered to call all day. I knew in a flash that this was his way of punishing me for leaving him to deal with the boys and Buster.

I had to walk through the casino to get to the elevators and, for once, I wasn't even tempted to stop at one of the tables and play. I paused for a second, watching the lights and the bustle, and thought about how much fun it would be if Diamond were standing next to me.

"Hang on, little sister," I whispered. "Just hang on."

21

DENNIS WAS WAITING FOR me when I emerged from the Bellagio the next morning. Our relationship had clearly progressed past that of chauffeur and client, but Dennis was still dressed in his black suit and white shirt when I spotted him standing next to his car. He'd parked just to the right of the entrance, in the precise spot he'd used the day before.

Dennis was wearing his mirrored sunglasses, which made it impossible for me to check out his eyes. That was a disappointment on two fronts—I would have liked to see if he showed any effect from the scotches the night before, and I also wanted to see if his eyes changed color in the morning light. The latter thought came as a mild shock, but I told myself that my interest was primarily aesthetic. Not wanting to keep Dennis waiting any longer than I had to, I hurried through the small crowd waiting around the hotel entrance.

I was still trying to wake up, as I ran through what had happened since I last saw Dennis, and what I hoped to accomplish that day. I had gone straight up to my room after talking to Sapphire on the phone, and along the way I realized that I was so drained that I genuinely wondered whether or not I was going to make it. Once I was inside, I scanned the room-service menu and ordered some pasta, a salad, and a half bottle of red wine. While I waited for the food to arrive, I poured the entire contents of the bottle of bath gel that the hotel had provided into the tub. I soaked in steaming water for half an hour, getting out when I heard the knock at the door that told me my food had arrived.

I ate dinner in my nightgown, fighting sleep and watching a show on TV, which the next morning I couldn't remember. Then I put the tray outside my door, brushed my teeth, got into bed, and turned off the light. The next thing I knew the phone was ringing for my nine A.M. wake-up call. I slept so well that I wished the Bellagio allowed its guests to take their mattresses home with them after they checked out.

Fifteen minutes later, after I took a quick shower, the room-service waiter was knocking at my door with the continental breakfast I'd ordered by filling out a little card and leaving it hanging on the outside doorknob. I ate breakfast in my complimentary thick white bathrobe. If not for the reason I was in Las Vegas, I would have been enjoying so much luxury. I ate while reading the paper and watching CNN—a network I generally avoid because I think it's excessively sympathetic to Fidel Castro. Among certain ultra-rightist exile circles, that channel was known as the Castro News Network.

After a second cup of coffee, I called the Las Vegas Police to confirm my appointment with a detective that morning. The police operator gave me the station's address and told me that I would be speaking with Detective Morris at the Department of Missing Persons. I wrote everything down, trying to keep my heart from sinking.

My pulse was pounding in my ears when I made my next call, to Tony at his office. The receptionist patched me through immediately when I told her who I was.

"I'm on my way out to a meeting," Tony said by way of greeting. "I can't really talk."

No hello. No how are you. No have you found your sister.

"Has Magdalena moved in?" I asked.

"Yes. Mama's at home," Tony said in a cold voice. "We had *arroz con pollo* last night. The boys loved it."

I pictured the heaping platter overflowing with chicken and yellow rice, surrounded by *plátanos maduros*—the soft sweet plantains without which no Cuban meal is ever complete. Magdalena was a good cook.

And I wasn't. I knew what Tony was trying to say—that without me, he and the boys had finally enjoyed a home-cooked meal.

"Are you all doing all right?" I asked.

"We're doing fine," Tony said, in a way that meant he wanted me to know that my presence wasn't really missed. It was a gratuitously mean-spirited comment meant to hurt me, but I let it pass.

"The boys made it to school all right?" I asked.

"Mama got them ready early," Tony said. "There's one other thing. Your mutt has been farting so much that I'm afraid to light a match because the house might blow up. It's disgusting."

"He can't help it," I said.

"Whatever. I have to go."

"All right." I paused. "Have a good day, Tony."

"Fine. Talk to you later."

He hung up. He hadn't asked me a single question. It was comforting to know that Tony and the boys were being taken care of by Magdalena, but when I replaced the phone receiver my hand was trembling with anger. Tony knew how important my family was to me, yet he still was treating me as though I was abandoning my responsibilities at home. It wasn't as though I was on a spa with my girlfriends, or on the ski slopes, or off to the Bahamas on a booze cruise.

And calling Buster a mutt was a calculated insult. It wasn't Buster's fault that he didn't have a pedigree. And as far as his gas was concerned, I knew it was happening because of the dose of Kaopectate I gave him before I left. If I hadn't, I knew Tony would have been sopping up mounds of shit and then—because I knew Tony was perfectly capable of it—dropping Buster off at the pound.

I tried to remember if all my recent conversations with Tony were so abrupt and brusque, but I failed. It was a slow, gradual process, our not getting along, though I never thought Tony would ever speak to me without even asking how I was doing. I stared at the phone for about a minute before I snapped out of it. My only option was not to dwell on the state of my marriage. I had more immediate problems.

I got dressed in the one suit I had brought with me, a two-piece Armani skirt and top I had bought on sale at Neiman Marcus in Bal Harbour at the Last Call Sale the previous year. I finished the outfit with the one and only pair of Jimmy Choo shoes I owned. I actually took time to blow-dry my hair before going out, because I knew it would actually stay styled for a change. The Miami humidity kept my hair in a perpetual state of frizzied arousal, but the dry desert air of Las Vegas afforded me the rare opportunity to have an actual hairstyle rather than a disheveled mop.

In the mirror, I caught myself biting my lip. I was *not* going to spend the morning thinking about Tony. Diamond needed me.

It was almost ten when I made my way through the casino. The tables were filled with players, most of them looking as though they had been there since the night before. I had heard that some gamblers were so addicted that they wore Depends adult diapers—then they could piss while standing up and save a trip to the restroom. I hoped it was an urban myth but I couldn't be sure. Walking past the blackjack tables, I saw a few characters who were in such a deep gambling trance that I doubted they registered hunger or thirst, much less nature's call.

I greeted Dennis, who was standing by his car. He grumbled something, and I asked, "Sleep well?"

"Well enough," he replied. He made no effort to open the car door, which I took as an indication that he wanted to talk before we set out.

"What's up?" I said.

"No news about your sister?" he asked.

I shook my head. "I have the name of the detective who's handling Diamond's case. It's a Detective Morris. That's who I'm meeting with this morning."

"Morris, huh?" Dennis said. "Don't think I know that one."

I looked over Dennis's rugged features, which were partially obscured behind his shades. His mouth was tight and his forehead wrinkled. I suddenly realized that his look was one of deep concern for me, and I was touched.

He took a couple of steps toward the front of the car. "Front seat again?" he said, and without waiting for a reply, opened it for me. "Let's go," he growled.

Now, I figured, we were getting somewhere.

22

WE PULLED CLOSE TO THE corner of Las Vegas and Stewart Avenues, the site of the main Las Vegas Police Department station.

"Do you want to come with me?" I asked Dennis. "Maybe you could sit in on my interview with the detective."

"I don't think so," Dennis said quietly, steering us to a five-minute parking place.

I wondered again about his status as a retired homicide detective. I had thought there was a brotherhood of police officers and that, even though he had worked in New York, Dennis would want to get involved. Apparently he didn't have much use for the concept. He seemed determined to guide me along, rather than getting closely involved in the investigation. He had been a big help at Mountain Peaks, but I remembered that he had stayed in the background, especially when we weren't alone. I knew there was no point in pressing him.

"All right," I said brightly. "I'll let you know what happened when it's over."

"Fine," he said. "The main entrance is over there. I can't park here much longer, so I'll be waiting for you in the parking lot next to the building. Do you see it?"

I looked where Dennis was pointing. "I'll meet you there," I said. I paused, trying to give him an opening to change his mind and come inside with me.

Instead, he motioned at the police station. "Look, your meeting probably won't take too long," he said. "I'll probably be seeing you in a few minutes."

I got out of the car and closed the door myself, wondering why Dennis assumed my meeting with the detective would be a brief one. I almost sensed that he had disdain for what could be done through official channels.

Once inside the building, I gave my name at the reception desk. I had left the contraband from Diamond's apartment locked in my room safe at the Bellagio, but I still felt paranoid in the presence of all the police officers moving in and out of the big room. An irrational part of me feared they would sense what I had in my room, maybe take me back there and arrest me for it.

Mercifully, my wait was short. Within a minute a man came up to me and held out his hand. "Detective Mike Morris," he said. "Come with me."

He turned and started walking. This was clearly a man who was used to giving orders. I followed him, even though I had a hard time keeping up with the pace he was setting. He stopped in front of a door at the end of a long, windowless corridor and waited for me to catch up. He opened the door for me and waited for me to go in first. I thanked him and went inside.

One look around and I could tell that Detective Morris carried a huge case load; either that, or he was an incorrigible pack rat. There wasn't an inch of the room that wasn't filled. I was certain that the Department of Health had never been inside his office, because they surely would have taped it off and declared it unfit for human habitation. I had a degree of professional curiosity about how he was able to fit so much stuff into such a small space, but I sat down and told myself to focus on Diamond.

Detective Morris motioned to the one chair that wasn't covered with brown cardboard accordion files—although it was surrounded by stacks of folders and papers, piled so high that I was afraid one would tip over on me. He must have been used to the mess, because he didn't offer any comment or apology for the state of his office. I wondered whether each folder represented a different missing person. I selfishly prayed it wasn't the case—if it was, he would never find the time to look for my sister.

The detective carefully made his way to the black leather office chair behind his desk, then took out a yellow lined legal pad from a drawer. He opened a folder that was on top of a thick stack and started to scan through it. I read Diamond's name typed upside down, a sight that sent a chill through me.

When he was finished, Detective Morris picked out a pen from the assortment crammed into a coffee mug next to his lamp. He fussily arranged everything to his liking, then looked up at me. After watching the detective go through his routine, I had the depressing insight that he had been through this scene hundreds of times already.

Mike Morris was in his late fifties, thin, pale, and colorless. He had stringy silver hair plastered to his skull. His suit was an unfortunate shade of gray that didn't do much for his skin tone—if anything, it assisted him in achieving a monochromatic sheen. He seemed sharp enough, but he had a palpable air of fatigue, a weariness that I sensed he was unable to shake off. I was willing to bet that it had been years since anything shocked him.

"Ms. Montoya, I have to ask you a few questions, if that's all right with you," he said in a soft voice. I must have looked puzzled, or annoyed, because he quickly added, "I know you talked to the officer when you called, but I need to verify some of the facts. It'll be just a few questions."

"Fine," I said.

"I hope you brought a photograph of your sister," he said, almost as an afterthought.

My hands were trembling when I opened my purse and took out the manila envelope that contained the photographs of Diamond and Maria Mercedes. I selected my sister's picture and, blinking hard, examined it for a second before handing it across the desk. It felt like the last time I would ever see my sister.

I looked up and saw that Detective Morris was watching me and that he seemed to know what I was going through. I wondered how many relatives had sat in my chair, with the same questions and hopes, handing over precious photographs of their loved ones. His eyes flashed with compassion, and he gave a small sad smile.

"Don't worry," he said. "I'll make a copy and give it right back to you. I'll only keep it for a minute."

"What is it you need to know about her?" I asked. "I'll do anything I can to help you."

Detective Morris asked me some standard, routine questions about Diamond's life and last known whereabouts. I wasn't bothered by having to answer them again; I would have gone through the process a hundred times if it led to finding Diamond. The detective read from the report in front of him, only making occasional notes.

"Diamond never had a history of running away or disappearing," I told him. "She never said anything about anyone stalking her, and she didn't carry around cash or jewelry."

I figured eventually he was bound to find out that I had gone to look for Diamond at Mountain Peaks, so I told him about my visit to the complex and how Rose, the manager, had let me inside the apartment. He looked up from the file with new interest.

"How long were you in the apartment?" he asked.

"A little while," I said.

"What did you find?"

I paused. In a moment I decided not to divulge anything about the money or the grass. I didn't know what the former meant, and the latter would only get my sister, and me, in trouble.

"Not much," I said. "I looked through some mail on the table."

"Any letters, pay stubs, credit card receipts?"

Detective Morris was staring hard at me. "Nothing that told me much of anything. There didn't seem to be anything missing."

"Except your sister," the detective said.

"Right. Except for Diamond."

The bottom line was that, between the money, the grass, and the pissed-off guy on the answering machine, I was afraid that Diamond might have gotten mixed up in something illegal. I didn't want the detective to think that, because then he might start to treat her case differently.

"What about her car?" he asked.

"I don't know," I told him. "I didn't see it in the parking lot. But I'm not really sure what she's been driving."

"Not a problem," he replied. "I can run it through the computer at Motor Vehicles."

With that, Detective Morris put down his pen and let out a heavy sigh. "I have to be realistic with you, Ms. Montoya. Thirty-two million people visit Las Vegas every year. Fifty thousand of them like it here enough to relocate and take up residence."

I listened politely, but what I was hearing sounded like a pitch from the chamber of commerce. "What does that have to do with my sister?" I asked.

Detective Morris shifted in his chair, making it grate against the floor. "People here sometimes behave in a manner that's out of character." I looked into his small, beady eyes, the color of old dishwater. "Vegas does that to people. They do things that people close to them could never imagine."

It was suddenly clear to me that Detective Morris thought there was probably nothing sinister about Diamond's disappearance, that she caught some kind of Las Vegas virus that made her act strangely but wasn't dangerous or life-threatening. I got the impression he thought there was nothing to do but simply wait the situation out.

As far as I was concerned, he was full of shit. I'm sure he meant well, but my sister Diamond wasn't weak enough to succumb to some sort of wacky syndrome. For all her eccentricities, she was a solid woman who never would have put her family through all this grief.

"Please. Listen to me. I'm telling you, my sister is missing, and not of her own volition." I put my hand down on his desk with a slap. "And you have to look for her! I won't leave your office until you promise me that you're going to look for her!"

Detective Morris blinked hard and fast. I didn't think anyone had talked to him that way before. He took several deep breaths to compose himself.

"Ms. Montoya, please calm down," he said. "I never said we wouldn't conduct a full investigation into your sister's disappearance. I'm just telling you what I've seen in other cases. That's all."

"So what's your next step?" I demanded. He was backtracking, but I wasn't going to let him off the hook so easily. "What are you going to do now?"

"A notification system is set up when an individual is reported missing," he explained, still blinking. "First we check the jails, hospitals, the coroner's office—all the places a person might be located. If we find nothing there, then the search kicks off in a different direction."

"Like what?" I asked, calm enough now to focus on what he was telling me.

"First we get on the Internet and issue an alert that the person is missing," Detective Morris said. "We do this with local and out-of-town Web sites. We'll let the casinos know about your sister; we'll post her picture and vital statistics on the Web; we'll distribute flyers to cover all the angles. We'll check out her home, her job, the places she frequented. We'll conduct interviews with her friends, coworkers, neighbors. We'll coordinate with other law-enforcement agencies."

Listening to Detective Morris's laundry list of investigative tactics, I wished I could say I felt closer to finding Diamond. But I didn't. The detective was talking about going through the motions, I could just sense it, and I somehow knew that traditional methods of searching for my sister weren't going to work. Somehow Maria Mercedes was involved, but I could just imagine how Detective Morris's bland eyes would really glaze over should I mention my great-great-great-grandmother. If I mentioned Maria Mercedes, he would just assume that Diamond came from a family of hardcore nut cases. And I couldn't say that I blamed him.

He wasn't saying it, but I knew Detective Morris was counting on Diamond showing up on her own, probably embarrassed about all the trouble she had caused, with a half-assed explanation to cover up where she had really been. Until then, he would play around on the Internet and make a few phone calls.

Detective Morris closed the folder in front of him. The interview was over. Just in case I missed the hint, he stood up and extended his hand for me to shake.

"Well, Ms. Montoya, I think that's all I need for now." He patted the file. "All that's left is to make copies of your sister's picture, and then I can get to work. Please take one of my business cards. If you have any additional questions, or if you think of anything that might help my investigation, please call me right away."

I had a hard time believing the interview was over. I had come looking for answers and instead had been told that Las Vegas makes people crazy sometimes. I could have been told that over the telephone. Somehow Detective Morris's bland assurances had left me feeling more frightened than before.

"You have my number, right?" I said, almost reaching out to grab the sleeve of the detective's jacket. "You'll call me the minute you find out anything?"

"Of course," Detective Morris said, giving me what he thought was a reassuring smile. "Come on, I'll walk you out. And don't worry. Your sister is going to turn up."

On the way out, he stopped at a little room with several copy machines. He made copies of Diamond's photograph, then handed it back to me. I followed him through the building in a mental fog. When we arrived back in the lobby, we somberly shook hands again without looking each other in the eye. I walked out into the morning sunshine and headed toward the parking lot where Dennis had said he was going to be waiting for me.

All he had to do was look at me and Dennis knew I was in no mood for chitchat. He opened the front passenger door of the limo for me, then got in on the driver's side. I waited until we were on the road to give him an account of what had happened inside the police station.

"It was brief and to the point," I told him. "It was also unbelievably depressing. Say, did you know there's a virus going around Las Vegas? Apparently it infects people and makes them go nuts."

Dennis stared ahead as he drove. "And that's what happened to your sister?"

I let out a sob and felt my eyes grow hot. His eyes still on the road, Dennis reached into his pocket and handed over a perfectly pressed white linen handkerchief.

"Here," he said softly.

I took it and squinted into the sunshine. I would have given anything in the world to hear my sister's voice again.

23

MY CELL PHONE RANG JUST as I was blowing my nose with the handkerchief Dennis had given me. Sniffling, I automatically reached in my purse for the phone. My eyes were watering too much for me to be able to read the number on the screen to see who was calling.

"Hello?" I said. Even to my own ears, it was obvious from the sound of my voice that I had been crying.

"Mom!" My heart leapt with happiness when I heard the sound of my eldest son's voice. "Mom, it's me! Gabriel!"

As if I didn't know in a second. Like every mother, I knew every nuance of my children's voices. My glee ebbed a little when I realized that Gabriel didn't sound like his normal self. I started to picture all sorts of worst-case scenarios.

"Gabriel, what's wrong?" I asked. "Is everything OK?"

I switched into my mom role and automatically looked at my watch to see what time it was back home. It was just after eleven, which meant it was two o'clock Miami time. Gabriel would be in school for another hour, which meant that he was calling me on his cell phone from the bathroom before his last class of the day. No wonder his voice sounded muffled—the boy's restroom at Saint Bartholomew's wasn't the best place for a clear cell phone signal.

I sensed Dennis tensing up next to me as he listened to my side of the conversation. After leaving the police station he had turned onto Las Vegas Boulevard, and the phone had rung before we could talk about where we should go next. For now, he was driving aimlessly.

"Don't worry, everything's fine," Gabriel said. "I just wanted to talk to you. I miss you, Mom."

I visualized the way Gabriel frowned with concentration whenever he talked on the phone. His voice had sunk to a whisper. Tough guy that he was, I knew how hard it was for him to tell me he missed me.

"I miss you, too," I told him. "What's going on at home? Are you gaining tons of weight from eating your grandma's cooking?"

"Well, Dad finished my science project," Gabriel said. "He stayed up really late on it, but the volcano didn't work as well as the one you helped me make last year."

I smiled with satisfaction.

"And Sapphire's driving Dad nuts, because she keeps calling all the time to check up on us." He paused. "And don't worry, Mom. I haven't spent any of the money you gave me."

I had only been gone a couple of days, but hearing Gabriel talk made me feel as though I had been gone for three years. Then he asked me what I knew he wanted to know most.

"When are you coming home, Mom?" he asked quietly.

"I'm sorry, Gabe, but I don't know," I told him.

"OK, Mom."

"I'll come home as soon as I can, I promise," I said, heartbroken by how strong he was trying to sound for me. I wasn't going to lie to him and give him a solid date that I might have to break. "You know why I'm here, to look for your tía Diamond."

As much as I was trying to control myself, my voice was starting to break.

"Mom, are you OK?" Gabriel asked, picking up on my distress. "You sound like you're crying. Are you crying?"

"I'm fine, Gabe. It's just my allergies." I figured it was all right to tell my son a little white lie. The last thing I wanted was for him to have to worry about me. I decided to change the subject. "How's Buster? Your dad said he was farting a lot."

"Yeah, he's farting all the time." Gabriel laughed. "Grandma says the house smells like a sewer. She went to Publix and bought all this stuff to get rid of the smell. Now the house smells like flowers—really smelly, stinky, gross ones. Buster's farts are way better than that stinky flower smell, but me and the twins can't talk her out of spraying that stuff all over the place."

"How are your brothers doing?" I heard the sound of young male voices in the background, then a toilet flushing. This conversation was being carried out under less than ideal conditions.

"They're good. They really want to know when you're coming home." Without meaning to, Gabriel dug the knife in a little deeper.

"As soon as I can. I promise you guys." That was the best I could do. A moment later, I almost dropped the phone when a shrill school bell pierced my eardrum.

"Gotta go, Mom," Gabriel shouted. "Last-period bell just sounded. Gotta go. Bye."

I didn't know whether I was relieved or saddened when he quickly hung up. I didn't think I could maintain my composure much longer if he kept telling me how much he and his brothers missed me and kept asking me when I was coming home. I knew that Tony and Magdalena were taking good care of them, that wasn't the problem. What pierced my heart was that they still chose me—with my haphazard housekeeping, my disorganization, and my random meals—over their grandmother's orderly ways and delicious home-cooked food. The boys and I were cut from the same cloth: we were night owls, we loved to gamble, and we could subsist happily on take-out while wearing none-too-clean laundry. None of us really ever thrived under too much orderliness or regimentation.

"Everything OK at home?"

Dennis's voice snapped me out of my thoughts. He was still staring straight ahead and wearing his dark glasses so that I couldn't see his eyes. It wasn't that looking into his eyes ever told me much, but it was better than looking at my own reflection in his mirrored lenses.

"I guess so," I told him. "That was Gabriel, my eldest son. He just wanted to tell me he missed me, and he wants to know when I'm going to be coming home."

Dennis nodded, both hands on the wheel.

"He was calling me from school, on his cell phone." I chuckled. "He was in the boys' bathroom, so it was a little hard to hear him. There was a lot of background noise—little boys peeing and flushing, mostly."

Dennis took in what I said. "How old is he?" he asked.

"Ten."

"Your son's ten years old and has a cell phone?"

"He's had it for more than a year," I said, picking up on Dennis's incredulity. "Listen, in Miami, children having cell phones is considered a necessity for safety."

What might have been unusual in other places was commonplace in Miami. Still, it didn't seem like the best time to inform Dennis that the twins had their own cell phones as well.

I realized this was the first time I had spoken to Dennis about my children. I hadn't even told him about Tony, although I supposed he could tell I was married from the ring on my finger. I didn't know anything about his family, either, and so far it hadn't seemed particularly relevant. I noticed he didn't wear a ring, but quite a few men didn't—Tony included—so that wasn't really indicative of anything.

"So, do you want me to just keep driving around?" Dennis asked, "or do you have a specific place you want to go next?"

The way he spoke, it was clear that Dennis felt I had had enough time to compose myself after talking to Gabriel. It was time to get on with the search again. I opened my purse and took out my little notebook.

"I made a call to Oscar Maxwell, the reporter who took Diamond's job at the newspaper," I said. "I told him I'd be calling to meet him today. He didn't really sound thrilled, and he said he didn't have anything for me, but he said he'd meet me if I stopped by."

Dennis adjusted his sun visor. The sun was growing stronger, and its glare reached the eye even through shades.

"In other words, you still want to meet with Maxwell because you don't really believe him," Dennis said in a flat voice. "Otherwise, why waste the time and energy?"

"Right," I said. I was a little surprised by how well he was getting to know me and how easily he had put my vague suspicions into words.

"Do you want to call him up now?" Dennis asked.

I didn't answer right away. We were at the end of the Strip, and Dennis was going to either have to make a U-turn or we would end up in the mountains. At the next intersection, he slowed and put on his blinker. No mountains today.

"Dennis, look," I began. "I've been thinking about what we found in Diamond's apartment, and there's something that's been bothering me about it."

"Yeah, what's that?" Dennis muttered, steering us so we were going back the way we had come.

"It's . . . it's the Cuba angle." I carefully chose my words, but I knew that nothing I said could fully convey my feeling. How the hell to explain Cuba to a non-Cuban? Many had tried, but the truth was that it was almost an impossible task.

"Look, if this is going to be a serious discussion, I'm going to have to pull off," Dennis said, glancing over at me and smiling in a surprisingly intimate way. Even though he was still wearing his dark glasses, his entire expression changed; he looked softer, and a lot more appealing. I almost executed a double take at the suddenness of his smile and the attractiveness of the result. If he had coupled that smile with his amazing eyes, I think I might have passed out. That's how suddenly affected I was. From the way Dennis usually behaved, that smile was a more tender gesture than if we'd just made love.

"Then I think you should pull over," I said. I was so flustered that my words tripped on one another coming out of my mouth. I felt like a sixth-grade girl who had just been kissed for the first time. My reaction to Dennis's smile was so absurd, embarrassing, and inappropriate that I could only pray he hadn't noticed it.

At that moment, we were right in front of the Bellagio, so Dennis slowed down and parked. "This OK?" he asked me.

"Sure. Fine." What was I thinking? I obviously wasn't totally in control of myself. I gave myself a stern talking to: it was time to rein in. And now.

Unaware of all the turmoil he had caused, Dennis turned into the driveway and drove slowly up to the entrance. "You want to go inside the hotel?" he asked. "Or just talk out here in the car?"

"Outside is fine, but can we get out of the car?" I asked. The way I was feeling, it would do me good to get some fresh air and to stretch my legs. I just hoped they wouldn't be shaking once I tried to stand. I didn't even want to think about how I had been affected by Dennis's smile. I hadn't even looked at another man in the years I'd been married to Tony—all right, except for the guy at the gym earlier in the week, and maybe one or two others. I had had my share of propositions, so I knew that I was still attractive to some men. But why was I even thinking about this?

Dennis drove slowly past the hotel entrance and waved to a

couple of porters who were helping hotel guests out of their cars and taxis. He pulled over to the place reserved for limousines, the place where he had parked his car earlier. Once we had slid into a designated spot, Dennis turned off the motor.

"Whatever you want is fine with me," he said. He got out of the car, came around to my side, and opened my door. "Lead the way."

I got out and led us to the front of the hotel, where the fountains were. I was thinking about Cuba, and my instincts were leading me to water. The fountains weren't dancing yet—they wouldn't until later in the afternoon—which was just as well. They would only have distracted me from what I needed to think through. Dennis followed, for a moment absurdly reminding me of a Japanese wife hanging back a few steps behind her husband. I walked until I found a place out of the sun.

"OK. We'll talk here." I turned to face Dennis and looked at him closely for the first time that day. I noticed that my heart was beating a little faster than usual when I gave him a quick once-over; I was curious to see what, exactly, about him had made me feel like an adolescent girl. I soon concluded that, whatever it was, it wasn't apparent to the naked eye.

He was wearing a black cotton suit over an ironed white shirt, the same as yesterday. I wondered who took care of his clothes, because they were very clean and crisp. He didn't wear either a tie or a belt—a surprise, given that his other clothes were so formal. I was tempted to glance down at his feet, to see what kind of shoes he was wearing, but I didn't want to make him too self-conscious. The man missed nothing, and he would be able to detect my inspection if I was too obvious.

Dennis took off his mirrored glasses; that was a bit of a surprise, because I had begun to think he'd had them surgically attached to his face at some point during the night before. He folded them and tucked them into his suit pocket. I avoided looking directly into his amazing pale eyes. If he'd smiled while I was peering into them, I would have melted into the pavement.

For a fleeting moment, I wanted to forget all about what brought me to Las Vegas, instead asking him every personal question I could formulate. I had to admit, the man intrigued the hell out of me. I knew I was paying him for his time and expertise, but that did nothing to diminish my curiosity.

This is business, I reminded myself. Don't make it personal.

"What's the Cuba angle all about?" Dennis asked, looking out at the traffic on the Strip.

I glanced up at Dennis's expectant face. I had to plunge in and hope for the best. "To begin with, my sister Diamond is different from the rest of my family in one important respect—she's never been interested much in her Cuban heritage."

The wind suddenly picked up, and I raised my hand to keep my hair from flying around. "When she was in college, at the University of Montana, she never took Cuban food back with her after trips home to Miami. And she never asked Mama to FedEx food from Versailles, or sweets from Gilbert's, like all the rest of us did."

"Your mother used to send Cuban food to you when you were in college?" Dennis asked, his tone raising in disbelief. "By FedEx?"

First it was Gabriel with his cell phone, and now Cuban food being express delivered all over the country. I felt as though I was sinking fast in Dennis's estimation.

"Only when we were feeling depressed and desperate," I quickly added, trying to salvage my dignity. I could tell from Dennis's expression that I was failing miserably. "Mostly in the wintertime. Cubans don't do very well in wintertime in the North. You know. Cold. Snow. Darkness."

"I get the point," Dennis said. "So what does all this have to do with what you found in your sister's apartment?"

"The tin of Pilon coffee I saw in her refrigerator," I said. "I've been thinking. Diamond only drinks decaf."

Dennis looked at me as though I had been smoking the weed we found in Diamond's apartment.

"And then there was that card for Mass schedules at the Guardian Angel Cathedral," I continued. "Diamond has always been an atheist. And those two credit card receipts for the Cuban Café. Diamond is a vegetarian."

"Esmeralda." Dennis took a deep breath. "I'm not sure exactly what you're trying to tell me."

I must have looked supremely dejected. Dennis gave a little I-don't-get-it shrug. I was so upset that I actually reached out and grabbed his arm, releasing it instantly when I realized what I was doing.

"Don't you understand?" I pleaded. "Can't you put it all together?"

Dennis shook his head slowly. He looked at me as though seeing me for the first time, perhaps reconsidering his opinion of me.

"I really don't get it," he said. "Connect the dots for me."

I half-turned and looked at the water shimmering in the fountain. "Put it all together," I said. "The photograph of Maria Mercedes. The Cuban coffee in the fridge. The Guardian Angel Cathedral. The receipts for the Cuban Café. Don't you see?"

"No," Dennis said flatly, and a little annoyed. "I still don't see. Explain what you're saying in more detail."

"Diamond had to have gone back to her Cuban roots for a reason," I said. "She never cared about Cubaninity until just recently—and in secret from her family. I know my sister. It's all connected to Maria Mercedes, all the Cuban stuff she's gotten into in Las Vegas. Diamond *hid* that photograph for a reason. And that's why she's missing."

"Because she suddenly got into being Cuban?" Dennis asked.

"We have to follow the Cuban trail here in Las Vegas," I told him. Once we do that, then we'll find her. I'll bet you anything on that."

We stood side by side, looking out at the fountain.

"I never thought much about the Cubans in Las Vegas," Dennis finally said, the doubt largely missing from his voice.

"My parents always used to bring me here when I was little," I said. "They kept in touch with the men who used to work in the Havana casinos before Castro took over, especially the ones employed at La Estrella, our family's casino. A lot of them came here after exile and took jobs in the gaming industry, and now many of their children are here working in the same casinos. Sometimes it seemed like my parents knew each and every exile who lived here."

Dennis listened attentively to what I was saying. "So we could ask some of the Cubans here about your sister, and they might know something about her?"

"I used to think she was permanently cut off from her Cuban past. Now I can see that wasn't true," I said. "Anyway, what else do we have to go on?"

"You said your parents knew a lot of Cubans here. Do you know them as well?" Dennis asked. In the corner of my eye I could see him looking at me, which was unsettling.

"No, I don't know them all personally," I admitted. "I mean, I was a little girl when we used to come here all the time. But I think some of the workers in the casino will remember my family name. Maybe I can get my parents to help us."

"Your parents aren't here," Dennis gently reminded me. "And wasn't it a long time ago, when your folks left Cuba? I mean, how long can we expect them to have kept in touch?"

I sighed and looked away. "Forty-three years," I said. "They left Cuba right after the revolution."

"A lot has happened since then," Dennis pointed out. "Maybe the Cubans here don't have such a long memory. Maybe they're not in as strong a position to help your sister as you think they might be."

I wasn't willing to give up. Only a member of my family could understand the importance of Diamond suddenly taking an interest in her Cuban past after decades without doing so. She hadn't become a Cubana in Las Vegas without a reason, not after her indifference to her heritage in Miami.

"There are other avenues we could explore," Dennis said.

I rummaged in my purse until I found the packet of papers I'd taken from Diamond's apartment. "Here," I said. I held up the two credit card receipts for the Cuban Café and read him the name and address where it was located. "This is a Cuban restaurant she visited. Might as well start there."

"Fine. Let's go."

Dennis took my elbow and gently guided me back to the limousine. At first his touch startled me, but then a moment later it felt perfectly natural.

24

"ESMERALDA? IS THAT YOU?"

Even though I had spoken with her on the phone only once before, I was instantly able to recognize Adrianna's voice.

I admit that I'm superstitious, and I won't deny that I took Adrianna Gomez's phoning me just as Dennis was pulling into the Cuban Café parking lot as an omen. How much of a coincidence could it be, the only Cuban I knew in Las Vegas contacting me at the very moment I began to look into Diamond's Cuban connections? Well, maybe I didn't personally know Adrianna— she was a friend of Dorcas—but my friend's friend automatically became mine as well.

"Adrianna, hi," I said. Dennis had just parked the car in one of the empty spaces across from the restaurant. I motioned for him to keep the car running until I was finished talking. He nodded and sat back in his seat.

"Esmeralda, how's it going?" Adrianna asked. "Any news about your sister?"

"No. Nothing yet." I told her a little about my meeting with Detective Morris that morning and what he had told me.

"Yes, I know Detective Morris," Adrianna said when I was done, startling me.

"You do?"

"He's very thorough," Adrianna said, without going into any explanation. "From what you're telling me, he'll do all the right things, follow all the proper procedures and all that. But you're doing some looking around on your own, aren't you?"

"Yes," I said, impressed with Adrianna's concerned manner. "It turns out that my sister has gotten back in touch with her Cuban roots recently. I'm looking into that."

I was circumspect enough not to bring up Maria Mercedes, the cash, and of course I said nothing about my parents' stash in Miami and Mama's vision. Still, I could feel Dennis tense up next to me as I spoke. I figured he thought I was being rash by telling this woman anything about my sister. I appreciated his concern, but I knew that Adrianna had already spoken with Dorcas; since she seemed to know a lot of the background, filling her in on my latest thoughts couldn't hurt. It wasn't Dennis's fault; there was no way he could comprehend the ties of friendship that bound Cubans together, nor could I expect him to. The exile experience was hard for outsiders to understand.

Adrianna was silent for a moment, thinking. "Well, how are you planning to look into your sister's sudden interest in Cuba?" she asked.

Which was a natural enough question. Unfortunately, the only honest answer was that I was making it up as I went along.

"I'm not quite sure," I said. "I'm parked in front of a restaurant she ate at a couple of times."

"If you need my help, you call me," Adrianna said insistently. "I live here. I know my way around. I might be able to help you."

"Thanks, I just have to sort this thing out," I said. I was about to hang up when something occurred to me. "By the way, how many Cubans are living here?"

Adrianna didn't let a beat go by. "If you go by the 2000 census, there are almost eleven thousand five hundred."

Although Cubans can be notorious bullshitters, I didn't doubt that Adrianna was giving me the correct number. She recited the figure with a note of pride in her voice.

"*Gracias,*" I said.

"You have my number. Call if you need anything," she said and hung up.

As I put the phone back in my purse, questions buzzed in my mind. I still didn't know who Adrianna Gomez really was. Dorcas said she was "well connected." Adrianna had heard of Detective Morris; she was up on the latest census count. The way she talked, it was almost as though she owned a hefty portion of the town.

Dennis looked over at me with a quizzical expression. "A friend?" he asked.

"Someone offering help," I said. "The same woman who called yesterday."

"Are you going to take her up on her offer?"

"As soon as a figure out how," I replied.

Dennis nodded, got out, and came around to open my door. "Have you ever been here before?" I asked him when we were walking to the front door of the Cuban Café.

"No. And in case you're wondering, I've never heard of it, either," he said, shaking his head a little. That wasn't encouraging. The man knew his way around Las Vegas, and if the place would have been worth patronizing, then he would have known of it.

Just before he opened the door, Dennis leaned close to me. "I don't mean to press you," he asked quietly. "But what exactly are you hoping to find here?"

It was the second good question I'd been asked in five minutes for which I had no answer. Then I remembered the museum curator in Cincinnati, when asked about how he planned to identify the pornography in a Mapplethorpe photo exhibit during a Supreme Court case:

"I'll know it when I see it," I told him.

The Cuban Café was carved out of an unused corner of a third-rate hotel. We were pretty much on the fringes of town, so I knew this wasn't going to be an upscale four-star dining experience. The location itself didn't put me off—the best Cuban restaurants are often hidden in the dingiest, roughest places. But from all appearances, this one was going to have to be a real diamond in the rough to be any good at all.

We had to pass through the hotel lobby on the way in. I tried to compose my face into bland neutrality when I had a look around. From the street, no one could have imagined what was inside this place. I knew all about Art Deco—I lived and worked in Miami, after all. But Ertè would have turned over in his grave if he knew of this place—right after he threw up, that is.

Whoever had designed the place was infatuated with etched glass—and purple. Not just one purple, but every variation and every shade of purple. I looked around and started cataloging: mauve, lavender, plum, and a garish shade I hadn't seen since the boys stopped watching Barney on television. For the first time in my life, I felt as though it would have been a blessing to have been born colorblind. Sheets of etched glass covered the walls and most other surfaces, including nooks, crannies, ornaments, lamps, fixtures—anything on which glass could be glued. And, for some mysterious reason, the designer—and I used the term loosely, and felt my own work somehow dirtied by the comparison—had deemed that fake white flowers in pink plastic baskets would be the perfect element to tie all the décor together. The flowers were cheap and lived their artificial lives in worn rattan baskets that looked like leftovers from a chintzy funeral.

The furniture was purple, big surprise there, mostly plastic chairs but with a few chaise longues thrown in for a Florida effect. It all looked thrift-shop, Salvation Army castoff to me, without the cache of being camp or retro.

"Nice-looking place," Dennis muttered as we walked together.

There were a dozen or so slot and vending machines along the walls; I glanced at the latter and felt positively ancient when I realized I was completely unfamiliar with the products for sale. The condoms, for instance, were sorted by size, shape, and for a particular variety of sexual outcome. I decided that I had led a sheltered life.

The most bizarre aspect of the lobby—the one that convinced me the owners, or designer, or both, had been on heavy drugs—was the wedding chapel set off to the side of the Cuban Café entrance. I looked in and was treated to the sight of what had to be the only wedding chapel in America that featured a lavender rug leading up to a mauve altar. The six rows of pews on either side of the space had been painted a shade of lilac that almost gave me vertigo when viewed in concert with the rest of the chapel.

The place was called the House of God—what god, I wasn't sure, maybe Bacchus—and on a printed card by the wall was a list of services offered by that nuptial heaven. I might have been old-fashioned, but I didn't feel a lasting marriage should be paid for by credit card, nor with the bride renting a bouquet of, what else, white plastic flowers. Out of the corner of my eye I spotted a counter that displayed the necessary accoutrements for a perfect Vegas wedding: his-and-hers rings, disposable cameras, veils and garters for the bride, cummerbunds and black ties for the groom. In my background, a wedding with five hundred guests was con- sidered intimate and nothing short of rushed if it took only a year to plan. Had it been up to me, I would have gone into the chapel and checked everything out, but I could tell that Dennis wasn't in an indulgent mood. We moved together through the double doors, decorated in etched glass, that constituted the entrance to the Cuban Café.

In comparison to the hotel lobby, the restaurant turned out to be a testament to good taste. Taken on its own, I probably wouldn't have been so kind. If I were pressed for a description of the décor, I probably would have compromised on post–Spanish Conquest, pre–Cuban Revolution; it was almost as though the owners couldn't quite come to terms with the fact that it had been more than a century since Cuba had been a Spanish colony.

It was a big, open room, featuring a very large faux stone fountain shooting jets of bluish water. The walls displayed oil paintings in heavy wooden frames of past members of the Spanish royal family, interspersed with portraits of José Martí, Carlos Manuel de Céspedes, Máximo Gómez, Francisco Vicente Aguilera, and other Cuban liberators. Dennis and I stood together inside the entrance while we waited for the hostess to come show us to our table. Only three tables were occupied—not exactly a bustling lunchtime rush. About a dozen booths covered in dark red leather lined the walls.

The hostess was a no-nonsense middle-aged woman in a plain server suit; she started to seat us at one of the tables strategically placed around the fountain, but Dennis motioned instead to one of the open booths near the back.

We slid in and started looking over the menu. Our waitress came over, a slim young girl in a too big white cotton uniform. She couldn't have been much older than fifteen. We watched her fill our water glasses, and then she asked in Spanish for our drink orders.

"What did she say?" Dennis asked.

"What do you want to drink?"

"Coffee," Dennis grumbled, staring at the Spanish menu with a helpless expression.

I ordered iced tea for myself and café con leche for Dennis. The waitress soon returned with our drinks as well as a basket filled with a small mountain of hot, delicious-smelling garlic bread. She asked, again in Spanish, if we were ready to order. Her huge brown saucer-shaped eyes dominated her pretty face.

Dennis dropped the menu. "Hey, you're the Cuban," he said. "You know what's good. Order for me."

I ordered *palomilla,* a Cuban version of skirt steak, for Dennis, and the garlic chicken for me. Both dishes came with black beans and rice, sweet plantains, and French fries. It was your basic artery-clogging meal served throughout the Caribbean. I had checked out the menu in full before ordering, and I saw that there was nothing even remotely close to a vegetarian option.

So why had Diamond been here?

I looked around the room. The hostess sat behind the cash register, going through some receipts. The waitress tended to a couple at one of the tables. At a booth, a man and a woman sat sipping coffee from tiny cups.

Nothing in the room told me why Diamond had been here twice in the past few weeks. The Spanish royalty and Cuban patriots on the walls weren't offering any answers. All I could determine for certain was that this was the kind of place that would have once sent my sister running, screaming for a plate of spinach, tofu, and bean sprouts.

Dennis hadn't said a word; instead, he watched me checking out the place. Soon our waitress returned with a heavy iron tray bearing our lunch. She carefully unloaded all the dishes, and after she had left we arranged our plates to our liking. Dennis looked skeptical at first but then pushed everything aside until he had uncovered his steak. For the first time since we entered, he began to look comfortable.

"Now what?" he asked.

I picked up my knife and fork. "At least you can learn something about Cuba," I told him. "Come on. Let's eat."

25

DENNIS AND I MANAGED one concrete achievement at the Cuban Café—we stuffed ourselves with platefuls of delicious, greasy food. I was used to such heavy Cuban meals and at an early age developed a cast-iron stomach. One look at Dennis after he returned from the men's room told me that he hadn't developed such a strong constitution. I would have thought a former homicide detective would have fortified himself for years on chili dogs and overstuffed sandwiches, but he still wasn't up to the task of facing down a Cuban meal.

After I put away a delicious flan, I was tempted to linger over a double Cuban coffee—enough to make my heart beat at twice its normal rate—but, given Dennis's state, I thought we should leave quickly instead. Instead, I asked for the check. The bill totaled twenty-seven dollars, splitting the difference between Diamond's two credit card charges. That confirmed what I suspected—that Diamond hadn't been alone at the Cuban Café. I kept staring at the bill, as though that printed piece of paper was going to yield the reason why my sister had been there twice within the span of a few days.

"Ready?" Dennis asked as soon as I replaced my credit card in my wallet.

We had barely spoken during our meal. And conversation after lunch wasn't done—Cuban custom was to order, consume, pay, and get out. By that time, we were the only patrons left in the restaurant.

"Sure," I said as Dennis started to slide out of his booth. He seemed relieved to be leaving.

"Let's go," he said.

We walked together toward the door. Dennis ushered me quickly through the hotel lobby, probably sensing how taken I was with the incredible tackiness of the décor. I made a promise to myself to return for another look once Diamond was found.

We were almost to the car when Dennis said, "Well? Did you learn anything?"

"I know for sure that my sister was here twice with someone," I told him. "And, believe me, it's totally out of character for my sister to eat in such a grease pit. Something in her life changed recently."

"OK," Dennis allowed. "Now what?"

I looked at my watch. "Now I'm going to call Oscar Maxwell." I took out my cell phone, found a slip of paper in my pocket, and punched in the number for Maxwell's direct line at the newspaper.

"Maxwell here," a man's voice answered after a couple rings.

"This is Esmeralda Montoya, Diamond Navarro's sister," I said. "I called earlier."

"Oh," Maxwell said, sounding oddly disappointed.

"I'm going to come over for our meeting. Should I come up to your office?" I asked.

"No. Don't do that." Maxwell paused. "I'll meet you in the parking lot in front of the building."

He hung up.

"Are we ready?" Dennis asked.

"I suppose," I said. "He doesn't exactly sound thrilled to hear that I'm coming."

Dennis pointed his keys at the limo and clicked twice to turn off the alarm. He ushered me into the car, then took his place and started the motor. His manner had returned to his earlier official, gruff mode.

"The *Herald*'s office is a short ride from here," he said, pulling the limo out of its parking space. "It should not take long to get there."

Less than five minutes later, after we had traveled only a couple of miles, Dennis turned on his blinker to signal our turn off Las Vegas Boulevard. We took a side street for a block until we reached a nondescript four-story building; a sign on the top read LAS VEGAS HERALD in worn-out neon hues.

The lot was only partly filled, but Dennis drove around a couple of times until he found a spot to his liking, near the entrance, but with a view of the front slightly obscured by a large concrete planter. He lowered the window, and we waited for a minute.

"Sure you don't want to listen in?" I asked him.

"No. This is your show," Dennis replied. He pointed to a wooden bench under a tree in the corner of the parking lot. "I'll be waiting over there. I don't want to scare off your contact."

I could see Dennis's logic, but I was still disappointed. I watched him get out and walk slowly across the hot asphalt, thinking how fortunate I was to have met him. It was sheer beginner's luck that I had the benefit of his advice and his steady presence, and I supposed it was a bonus that I felt so warmly toward him that I was able to overlook his prickly personality. Watching him walk to the bench, and with a slight limp that I hadn't noticed before, I was able to distance myself from the intensity of my earlier reaction to his smile. Surely, I thought, it had been a moment of weakness.

The more time I spent with Dennis, the more I was fascinated with him. I knew better than to ask him any personal questions, knowing that he would volunteer information about himself when he decided that the time was right. It was strange, how drawn I was to him. He was probably fifty years old and I was thirty, but I had probably spent more time sitting in cars with him than I had with my high school boyfriend. Of course, all Dennis and I had done was talk and wait—a marked difference to my teenage days.

It was less than a minute later that a young man opened the front door of the *Herald* building and visually scouted the parking lot. It seemed Oscar Maxwell had been waiting for me. I got out and waved.

Watching him approach the car confirmed my earlier impression that Oscar Maxwell would have preferred to face a firing squad rather than talk with me. He had already made it clear to me that he didn't know where Diamond was since he took her position at the paper, other than having heard she took a job at one of the casinos. But something led me not to believe his version of the facts, and the more I dealt with him, the more I was convinced that he was being purposefully evasive. Every instinct told me that he was hiding something, it was just a matter of figuring out what it was. The thought flashed across my mind that Diamond herself had sworn him to secrecy, but I quickly discarded it. She would never have told someone to hide her whereabouts from her closest family.

"Ms. Montoya?" he said when he was near. I heard resentment and anxiety in his voice.

Oscar was an attractive, if slightly disheveled, man in his midthirties. He was tall and rangy, reminding me of an adolescent boy whose body had shot up so quickly that he hadn't had time yet to learn to coordinate his movements. His hair was black and thick, though in need of a vigorous trim. Even though he was obviously unhappy, he had a loose, casual way about him. In different circumstances, he was probably a nice guy. I could imagine Diamond being friends with him.

Oscar shoved his hands in his pockets and looked at me with a hangdog slouch. He had warm brown eyes framed by eyelashes so long that they almost fluttered when he blinked. My eyes lingered on a flurry of light brown freckles across the bridge of his nose.

"Ms. Montoya?" he said again, deliberately accenting his use of formal address. I could tell he had decided that any intimacy between us would break his resolve.

"Thanks for getting together with me," I said.

"Sorry about meeting you out here," he said sheepishly. "I'm on a deadline for a story."

"That's fine," I said. The last thing I wanted was to alienate this man, when he might be in a position to help me. I smiled at him and stuck out my hand.

He was startled, and moved back a bit, but finally extended his own right hand. I held on a little longer than usual, feeling as though I had to grab him to keep him from running away from me.

"I know you're busy," I added. "So I really appreciate your taking a few minutes for me."

I finally released his hand, suspecting that he wouldn't extricate it on his own. He refused to look me in the eye, and his body language spoke of total discomfort. He glanced back at the newspaper building, as though anxious someone might be watching us from inside.

"No problem," he mumbled.

"You already told me you don't know about Diamond's disappearance," I said gently. "But could you please try to think back? Maybe you heard something, anything, about where Diamond might have gone after she left the paper."

I moved a little closer, blatantly infringing on his personal space. Normally I never would have been so aggressive, but I sensed I was in a moment of opportunity that would slip away if I allowed it. Finally Oscar looked up and met my eyes: in that moment, I knew I could get more out of him than he was letting on.

"Look, I don't know where your sister is," he said miserably. "I took over her job. That's it. That's all I know."

"Did you ever meet my sister?" I asked. My hands trembled with the desire to grab him and shake him. I remembered reading once that police interrogators used the names of victims during interviews, in order to personalize the situation. So I added, "Did you ever meet Diamond?"

Oscar thought for a moment. "Yes," he said. "I met her."

My heart began beating fast. "Really? When?"

I watched the wheels turning in his mind and knew that he was calculating how much to divulge. He was so miserable that I almost felt sorry for him—a reaction that I quickly shook off.

"When I took over her job." Oscar crossed his arms and stared down at his wingtips.

"That was about a year ago," I said. He nodded. "Well, did she tell you anything about what she was going to do next, where she was going to work?"

I remembered the voices on Diamond's answering machine— Angie, saying that Mickey, their boss, was furious at Diamond's absence, then the man swearing at Diamond because she had stood him up.

"No, she really didn't say anything," Oscar said. I wasn't convinced. I wished I had Dennis there to help. No wonder Oscar had been so reluctant to meet with me—he must have known he was a lousy liar and that he couldn't maintain his story during a face-to-face conversation.

Still, it was becoming painfully obvious that I wasn't going to break Oscar down by asking him questions. It was time to get rough.

"Wait here," I ordered him, and went to the car.

I reached into the open window and picked up my purse from

the passenger seat. I found the manila envelope inside, then pulled out Diamond's photograph. I went back to Oscar and shoved the picture right up to his face.

"Look," I said. "Look at Diamond!"

My hands were trembling with anger and frustration; Oscar tried to inch back, but I moved the photo even closer.

"I'm holding you personally responsible if anything has happened to her," I hissed at him, in a voice I hadn't heard from myself before. "I'll come after you, Oscar, I swear it. Because you're hiding something from me that would help me find her."

Oscar's eyes were bulging when he looked at me. He instinctively held up one hand, as though to fend me off.

"All right, that's enough!" he shouted. He pushed the picture away. "I get the point, lady!"

I carefully replaced Diamond's picture in the folder, next to the photo of Maria Mercedes. I was about to put the folder back in the car when I had an inspiration. I took out the photograph of Maria Mercedes and showed it to Oscar.

"Ever seen this before?" I asked, as I carefully studied his reaction.

Oscar blinked, looked at me, then back at the picture. I saw his resolve break in an instant. Clearly this was not the first time he had seen that photograph.

"I think we should talk more," I said. "But not here."

Oscar nodded miserably. "All right," he said. "Just tell me where you want to go."

26

myself back at our booth inside the Clipped Chip—apparently I was joining Dennis as one of the regulars inside the dimly lit bar. I had my customary rum and Coke in front of me, and one look around told me that all the other habitués were also in attendance. It was déjà vu all over again, except, this time, we were joined by Oscar Maxwell.

I watched the reporter sipping off his second Corona—he'd consumed his first one in about a minute, in a display of nervousness—I could barely believe I'd gotten him to agree to talk more about Diamond. I know I had been threatening with him, which was out of character for me, but I also remembered that it had been the picture of Maria Mercedes that had finally broken his resolve. What remained was for me to find out why that aged photograph had resonated with him so deeply.

When Oscar had agreed to speak with me, I had gone over to where Dennis was waiting. I had been so excited when I told Dennis what had happened that I surely sounded barely coherent. It was probably my enthusiasm that convinced Dennis to accompany me to talk with the reporter. When I introduced the two men, they had regarded one another with wary expressions— and, in Dennis's case, with what I took to be professional cool.

When Dennis suggested we head over to the Clipped Chip, Oscar said it was fine with him, even though he had never heard of the place. We offered Oscar a ride in the limousine, but he had preferred to ride in his own car. I was a little worried that he might try to ditch us, but every time I looked out the back window I saw the reporter's gray Toyota following us.

If Oscar wondered why I wanted my limo driver to come inside with us and listen to our conversation, he did a good job of hiding his curiosity. Oscar, for all his outward affability, was incredibly difficult to read. I suspected that, in his line of work, he had grown accustomed to behaving as though strange things were ordinary.

In that spirit, he showed absolutely no reaction to the scene inside the Clipped Chip. I was still trying to adjust to the darkness, after coming inside from the light of day. Oscar merely turned off his cell phone, put it on the table in front of us, and gave Dennis his order for a beer. He ran his hands through his unruly hair and let out a deep sigh. He looked at his beer, seemingly fascinated with the words on the bottle.

"Can we talk now?" I finally asked Oscar.

He glanced around as though looking for an escape route. He took a long drink of his beer, then dug in the pocket of his shirt for a pack of Marlboros. He shook one out, lit it with a stainless steel Zippo, then laid the pack carefully on the table. He took a long, deep drag, then emitted a series of perfect smoke rings. I was almost afraid that he was going to set off the smoke alarm, until I realized that it was very improbable that the Clipped Chip owned one.

"OK, look," Oscar said, glancing up at Dennis. Even in the darkness, Dennis's eyes were glowing. "I told you I met Diamond only once. I wasn't being completely honest with you."

Oscar tapped an inch of ash into the glass tray in front of him. I felt my heart begin to quicken as I took a sip of my drink.

"How well do you know my sister?" I asked, trying to hide the excitement in my voice.

Dennis didn't say a word, but I felt him tense up next to me.

"You know I took over Diamond's job at the *Herald*. That was about a year ago." Dennis and I both nodded. "She gave the paper two weeks' notice. She told the editors she was going back home to Miami, that she wanted to be close to her family. She said something about wanting to live close to the water again."

I took another sip from my drink. "Oscar, she never told us anything about that," I said. "We thought she was still working at the newspaper."

Oscar shrugged and blew another smoke ring. "Diamond spent the next two weeks training me," he said. "She showed me the ropes at the paper, introduced me to some of her contacts. She was a pretty good reporter."

By then Oscar had finished his cigarette. He instantly took out another one and lit it from the Zippo. The lighter's flame was so high that I winced.

"So you got to know Diamond?" I asked.

"Yeah. The paper was pretty shorthanded—still is—so they couldn't spare anyone else to train me," he explained. "She was the only environmental reporter, so we ended up spending a lot of time together."

Dennis stood up and cleared his throat. "Drinks all around?" he asked. Without waiting for an answer, he groped his way through the darkness to the bar.

Getting answers out of Oscar was like watching an iceberg melt. If I wasn't afraid of frightening him off, I would have grabbed him and made him talk. Instead, I tried to adjust to his infuriating recalcitrance.

"So you talked?" I asked. "About things not related to work?"

"Yeah. We talked," he acknowledged.

Dennis came back with fresh drinks on a tray. Happy hour must have started because there were two drinks for each of us.

"What was the real reason she quit her job?" I asked Oscar. "Did she give you any idea what she was going to do next? She didn't come home, I can tell you that."

Oscar grabbed one of his new Coronas and took a swig. He was thinking, obviously calculating how much to say.

"One time she said something strange," he mumbled.

"What was it?" I actually sat on my hands to keep them from shaking.

"She mentioned that she sort of wanted to follow an angle on a story she'd been working on," he said. "Something she'd stumbled across."

"What story?" I asked. "What angle?"

Oscar took a drink, then a drag on his cigarette.

"I don't know all the details," he said, glancing at Dennis. "I know she was working on an ongoing story about how the casinos disposed of their waste, whether they were environmentally friendly or not. She said that she had interviewed someone at a casino in charge of waste disposal, and that she'd come across something she found interesting."

Dennis sat up straighter. "What was so interesting?" he rumbled.

"I didn't know much of what she was talking about," Oscar said. "She got sort of mysterious on me, and said she didn't want to talk about it with me."

Oscar looked at Dennis, who was glowering.

"Something about Cuba," Oscar added. "Some casinos in Cuba."

I knew it.

"Tell us more," Dennis said, spreading his hands across the table.

Oscar looked even more miserable than before.

"I don't know," he said. "We talked about some weird stuff. She gave me some line about having to get in touch with her 'inner Cuban.' I don't even know what that means."

Oscar had no idea how much he was helping me. It hadn't been random, the way Diamond had gotten in touch with her long-lost Cubaninity in Las Vegas. There had been a reason for it.

"When was the last time you had contact with Diamond?" Dennis asked.

"Oh, I'm not sure." Oscar looked at his beer bottle.

"You're a reporter," Dennis said. "You're paid to remember things."

Oscar looked up. "It's been several months," he said quietly.

"What was the occasion?" Dennis asked.

Oscar suddenly ground out the cigarette he'd been smoking, picked up his pack of Marlboros and the lighter, and stuffed them back in his pocket. He slid quickly out of the booth and stood up.

"Listen, I have to get going," he said, and he began to move for the door of the Clipped Chip.

Dennis was on his feet and after Oscar before I even realized what had happened. He caught up to the reporter in two strides, grabbed his arm, and twisted it behind his back. Even in the darkness, I saw the painful grimace on Oscar's face when Dennis applied pressure. He said something in Oscar's ear; the reporter nodded, winced, and they came back to the table.

"I just explained to Oscar that the interview isn't finished," Dennis said, giving the reporter a little shove back into the booth. This time, Dennis sat next to Oscar, blocking his escape route. Then he smiled, and patted Oscar on the hand.

"Comfy now?" he asked. "Good. I'll repeat my question, just in case you forgot. For what purpose did Diamond contact you?"

Oscar hung his head and rubbed his arm where Dennis had

grabbed him. I glanced over at the bar and noted that the bartender made a show of studying his newspaper. Apparently a little arm twisting wasn't out of the ordinary at the Clipped Chip.

"She wanted me to conduct a search on one of the newspaper's databases," Oscar said quietly.

"You mean a computer search?" I asked.

"Yeah," Oscar muttered. "A computer search."

"What was the subject?" Dennis asked. I could tell by his tone of voice that he had lost his patience with the reporter. The way he had taken charge of the situation, I could tell he had fallen back into his police detective mode. I didn't know what I'd have done without him.

"About casinos in Cuba, and their Mafia ownership," Oscar replied in such a low voice that I had to strain to hear him.

"The Mafia?" I repeated.

No wonder Oscar hadn't wanted to speak with me. No one wanted to mess with the Mob.

For the first time since Diamond disappeared, I wasn't so sure that my little sister was alive. There was an awful lot of desert out there surrounding Las Vegas, and it went in every direction as far as you could see.

27

I WAS SO SHAKEN BY THE bomb Oscar had dropped that I didn't say much of anything for a few minutes. Oscar sat nervously, daring the occasional glance at Dennis to survey his prospects of getting out of the Clipped Chip. Dennis watched me calmly, as though understanding that my mind was in overdrive. Something in the back of my head kept nagging at me—considering the state of my nerves at the moment, I couldn't remember precisely what it was. I wished the light in the bar was better, so I could get a good look at Oscar's expressions. As it was, I could see the outlines of his eyes and mouth as though through a sheet of gauze. I hadn't trusted Oscar before, and I trusted him even less now.

"So, were you able to get much information for Diamond?" I asked him.

Oscar nodded. "Some."

Dennis and I waited for further clarification, but none was apparently forthcoming. That didn't concern me too much; I knew Dennis could pat Oscar on the arm to instigate a Pavlovian response of cooperation. I knew I would be lost without both Dennis's experience and his sheer physical presence.

"Would you care to elaborate on that?" Dennis asked in an

ostensibly friendly tone of voice. "I'm sure Esmeralda would like to know more."

Oscar sighed, resigned to the fact that he wasn't going anywhere soon. I noticed that all talk of his impending deadline had dropped away. He took out his pack of Marlboros again, lit one, and blew out a perfectly circular smoke ring. He took a sip of his beer and sat up straighter in the booth. I sensed a change in his attitude.

"Diamond was interested in the Mafia families that used to own the casinos in Havana," Oscar said. "You know, that whole history of the Mob in the Cuban gambling business."

Apart from one course on Native Americans at the University of Montana, Diamond had never shown the slightest interest in history. And I knew she had thought the Mafia was boring—she was never even interested in watching *The Godfather* or *Casino* on HBO, when all the rest of us were lined up with our sofa cushions and bags of popcorn. She believed in living in the moment and didn't like to sit still for movies. And I remember her sneering once that the Mafia was something Hollywood invented to sell tickets.

"What do you think she was really after?" I asked Oscar.

He shrugged and made more smoke rings. I stared at him. My every instinct screamed out that he was hiding something. Dennis must have agreed, because he patted Oscar's arm and motioned toward me, giving the reporter a silent signal to talk. The gesture had the desired effect, because Oscar winced and almost flinched.

"This is what I thought at the time," Oscar offered. "I don't know for sure, but I got the impression that Diamond found out something that had to do with the Mob guys who had casinos in Cuba. It was something about that whole angle that somehow pertained to the present."

"Like what?" I asked.

"I really don't know," Oscar said with another shrug. He

looked at Dennis as though begging my driver to accept his answer.

I almost felt sorry for the reporter, seeing how intimidated he was. But I understood something important: this was a kind of dance that Oscar Maxwell had to go through in order to assuage his conscience. He wanted to talk, or else he could have left. Dennis was intimidating, but he had no legal power over Oscar.

"Apart from asking you for help at the newspaper, how else did Diamond plan to get information?" Dennis asked, his face expressionless. Oscar didn't answer right away, so Dennis nudged himself a millimeter closer. "You said that Diamond had left the paper to work in one of the casinos, right? Was that related to her search?"

Of course! The moment the words left Dennis's mouth, I knew what he was getting at: Angie and Mickey, the voices on the answering machine. It made sense suddenly. Diamond had quit her job at the *Las Vegas Herald* because she had wanted to look into something—something big, if she was willing to quit her job over it.

"Diamond didn't go into details," Oscar said. "I would have told you if she had."

Oscar looked at me, then at Dennis. His cigarette had burned almost down to the filter, though he didn't notice.

"Really, you have to believe me. That's all I know," Oscar said. "I even asked her a lot of questions. I thought she was acting strange. She was really being evasive, so I couldn't get a straight answer out of her."

"Why would she hide her motivation from you?" I asked, knowing that I sounded as though I didn't believe him.

"I don't know," Oscar said, miserable. "I guess I didn't ask the right questions."

I took a deep breath and tried hard to keep my composure. On a normal day I would have been closing up my office and picking the kids up at school, worrying about nothing more than what my family was going to have for dinner that night.

Oscar finally put out his cigarette. I couldn't help thinking that he couldn't be much of a reporter, if he hadn't been able to get any answers out of my sister. Diamond had always been an open book, even when she thought she was successfully hiding something. If Oscar Maxwell was telling the truth, he was worthy of exile to whatever was the journalistic equivalent of Siberia.

"Look, Oscar, I appreciate how much you're helping me." I said, trying to keep the situation from becoming purely adversarial. "Maybe you could tell me what you found out for Diamond, what information you passed on to her?"

Oscar let out a surprisingly deep breath, given the amount of tar that must have been in his lungs.

"Actually, it was pretty interesting," he said with relief, glad to be able to give us something. "I didn't know anything about the Mob, or Cuba, before I looked into it. It turned out there was a lot of information available through the computer searches."

"Why did Diamond need you?" Dennis asked. "Couldn't she have just gone to the library?"

Oscar shook his head. "We have access to databases at the paper that are a lot more advanced," he explained. "They're really expensive, though, too much for individuals to afford."

I remembered what had been gnawing at the edges of my memory. A couple of days ago, when Mama and Papa had told us about the apparition and showed us the secret room, they had talked about their "friend" in the Mafia who had helped them get their cash and jewelry out of La Estrella. The same person had helped them buy their Miami Beach penthouse and assisted in the construction of their safe room. There might have been a link between the two, but I couldn't concentrate on it while Oscar was still talking.

"I didn't grow up in Vegas," Oscar said. "I'm from Philly, so

I didn't know much about the gaming business. It's all new to me. My family's owned a newspaper for four generations—the Philadelphia *Business Market*—a financial daily. You might have heard of it?"

It was my and Dennis's turn to shrug.

"Well, anyway, I'll go back and work there eventually," Oscar said. "Everyone in my family goes and works at other papers around the country before coming home and working for the business. It's kind of a family philosophy. I applied for a job here because it seemed like an interesting place to live for a while."

Oscar certainly wasn't tight-lipped about his background. I hoped he didn't digress into a story about how his family came over on the *Mayflower*. I'm sure Dennis could get into the Irish potato famine, and I could go into the history of all the Cuban refugees. Mercifully, Oscar seemed to run out of gas, and I had an opening.

"That's when you met Diamond, after you applied here and came out to take her job," I said, getting him closer to the point.

"Right. I met her when I took her job." Oscar lit yet another cigarette. I noticed that Dennis simply breathed in Oscar's smoke without showing any sign that it bothered him. Maybe all those years as a detective had inured him to second-hand smoke. Or else he was an ex-smoker who would take a nicotine fix any way he could get it.

"I didn't know much of anything about Las Vegas, or the gaming business, when I took the job," Oscar admitted. "I'd been to some of the Atlantic City casinos with my family, but I'd never been here before. When I started looking into things for Diamond, it was a real eye-opener."

I looked over at Dennis, who was staring at Oscar with a hard, stony look on his face. Even in the dim light, Dennis's eyes were focused like two searchlights.

"What do you mean?" Dennis rumbled.

Oscar smiled, showing more animation than at any time since I met him. Maybe he was a real reporter after all. As he told me, it was in his blood.

"I found out that Fidel Castro screwed things up," Oscar said eagerly. "If it hadn't been for him, Havana could have easily rivaled, if not surpassed, Las Vegas as the casino and entertainment capital of the world. When Castro came along and shut down the Havana casinos, it was the best thing in the world that could have happened to Las Vegas. It got rid of most of Vegas's competition."

I nodded. "My parents told me the same thing," I said. I pictured all those New Year's Eves, with Papa saluting the mementos of La Estrella. "Both the casinos of Havana and Las Vegas were run by the American Mafia. After Castro took power, the Mob simply concentrated their energies on Las Vegas."

Oscar leapt in, suddenly enjoying himself. "In most places, the Mafia muscled their way into the gaming business," he added. "But the situation in Cuba was different. Batista actually *invited* the American Mob into Cuba, asking them to build and run the casinos. He approached Meyer Lansky, who was in charge of the Mob's gambling concerns. Batista had a vision—he wanted a clean, crime-free operation for the customers. And, really, who better than the Mob to put that in place, if you really think about it?"

Dennis shifted in his seat, a flicker of interest playing at the corners of his eyes.

"In '55, Batista decreed that any hotel built in Havana at a cost of more than a million dollars could feature a casino," Oscar said. "As you can imagine, that was a license to steal, with the Mob and the government taking their percentages off the top—not just of the casinos, but of the construction costs as well. Pretty soon the government was completely in bed with the Mob. One of Batista's brothers-in-law, for example, owned all ten thousand slot machines in the casinos. No one complained, though. Even after paying taxes, expenses, and bribes, the Mob still made a fortune. It was a great arrangement for everyone involved—except, of course, for the Cuban people."

"Why's that?" Dennis asked.

"Those profits could have been used to build schools and roads, or to improve the health-care system," Oscar explained. "Instead they went into Batista's pockets and into the pockets of his family and his cronies. It was no wonder Castro shut down the casinos as soon as he grabbed power. To him and his followers, the gaming industry represented graft, corruption, and social inequality. Castro came into power New Year's Eve, 1958, and mobs of Cubans ran through the casinos and destroyed them."

Oscar made a world-weary gesture, as if to say that people always got screwed, that was just the way it was. I remembered my parents' story about getting out of Cuba that night, and about La Estrella's fate.

Still grinning with the memory of his discoveries, Oscar spread his hands out on the table like a born storyteller.

"See, for gamblers, going to Havana was really appealing," he continued. "There was sun, sea, and sin on the island, and gamblers knew that even though the percentages were in the house's favor, they weren't going to get ripped off playing crooked games. The Mafia loved it, they were making money hand over fist. Just imagine, in the heyday of the Cuban casinos, the Pan Am Clipper flew from Florida to Havana six times a day."

"Did you know all this?" Dennis asked me. He had seen me nodding in agreement as Oscar spoke. I had told Dennis that my family had been in the casino business in Cuba, but I don't think he had known what that meant until now.

"Yes," I said. I also knew that graft and corruption were rampant, even if the games themselves were clean. My siblings and I always figured that our parents were paying off both the Mafia and the Batista regime, but we never knew the details.

"And you knew about the Mob?" Dennis asked me.

"I heard a story," I told Dennis. "Every night, Batista's bag man would go around to the casinos to collect his thirty percent."

"Thirty percent," Oscar whistled appreciatively.

"Then, the bag man's wife would follow up for her ten percent," I added. "Things in Cuba were so corrupt that Batista's brother-in-law owned all the parking meters in Havana. He collected all the money himself."

"His personal piggy bank," Dennis commented.

"I found out that there were eleven casinos on the island," Oscar broke in, on a roll now. "Ten were either owned or controlled by the Mob. There was one independent casino that was actually owned by native Cubans. That one actually wasn't totally ransacked. It was pretty much left alone the night Castro came to power."

"I know," I said. "It was called La Estrella. My family owned it."

Oscar looked as though he had been slapped in the face. "Oh, my God," he said. "That's you? Your family? Diamond never said anything about that!"

Suddenly everything seemed to click in Oscar's mind. He was no fool. Now he could see that Diamond hadn't innocently disappeared.

"No wonder you're so worried," Oscar said. "As soon as you heard Diamond was looking into the Mob, you connected it to your family's old casino business. Damn, and I helped her get the information!"

"Calm down, Oscar," Dennis said gruffly. He glanced at me and shook his head, just a fraction. I guess nothing like this happened at the Philadelphia *Business Market*.

"It's all right, Oscar," I said, seeing the reporter suddenly near panic.

"Think, Oscar," Dennis commanded. "Where do you think Diamond went to work after she left the newspaper?"

Oscar lit up a fresh cigarette and took a series of deep puffs. I couldn't really blame him for being upset. No one wanted to know their path had touched on the Mob's, even if it was only via an Internet search engine.

"I think I'd better quit while I'm ahead," Oscar said, squirming in the booth. "Honestly. I think I'm done."

Neither Dennis nor I moved. We had come this far, and Oscar had to know we weren't going to stop now. Detective Morris seemed to be perfectly competent, but I doubted he had much experience searching for girls from Miami who disappeared looking into Cuban-Mafia ties to the Las Vegas casinos.

"You're not going anywhere," Dennis said calmly, "until you put on your thinking cap and give us a solid lead."

The way Dennis spoke sent a chill of fear down my spine. I could just imagine the effect Dennis was having on Oscar. Oscar suddenly seemed near tears, and his hand holding the cigarette began to shake.

"There's one thing. I remember now," he said. "There was an old man waiting for Diamond outside the building one day when we were going to lunch. An old guy. I think he was Cuban. Skinny, wiry. He had some kind of patch over one of his eyes."

Dennis said nothing. I could tell he wanted to comment on how odd it was that Oscar suddenly remembered such a figure, after apparently suffering amnesia until now.

"They talked for a minute," Oscar continued. "I didn't understand what they were saying, because they were speaking Spanish. I did get the impression that the guy was helping her somehow, and that it definitely wasn't the first time they had met."

My heart started beating fast. "Keep talking," I ordered him.

"The guy was really old. His skin was leathery," Oscar said. "I remember the eye patch. That was pretty hard to ignore."

"Why do you think Diamond knew him?" Dennis asked.

"I could just tell," Oscar said. "They seemed familiar with each other. At the same time, the way they were talking made me think that they had business. It was like the old man was giving Diamond an update or something."

Silence descended over the table. It seemed obvious that Oscar was tapped out, that he had nothing more to offer.

"Look, I've tried to help you people," he said quietly, putting out his cigarette. "I didn't want to get involved, and now I've given you everything I have. I just want to go back to work. I don't want anything to do with this. I'm sorry your sister is missing, and I hope she's all right, but if I knew where she was I would tell you."

Dennis looked at me. I nodded.

"All right," Dennis said. He slowly got up from the booth to let Oscar leave. The reporter looked at Dennis warily, as though unable to believe we were actually letting him go.

"Good luck," Oscar said, sliding out of the booth and reaching for his keys.

"Thanks," I said, exhausted, feeling a little defeated. After all the effort we had put into interrogating Oscar, I didn't feel as though we had all that much to act on.

Oscar disappeared, leaving me and Dennis alone. I looked around. For all the drama that had taken place at our table, none of the patrons inside the Clipped Chip seemed to have noticed.

"Ready to go?" Dennis asked, still standing.

In the car, I asked Dennis to take me back to the Bellagio. I needed some time alone to think things through.

"I hear you," Dennis said, his shades covering his eyes. I glanced over at him, surprised by the note of sympathy in his voice. I probably unfairly wished that I could hear the same tone when I talked to Tony about my search for Diamond.

We drove back to the hotel in silence, and I said good-bye to Dennis at the entrance, promising to call him later. I walked through the casino like a zombie, again not even tempted to try my luck at one of the tables. As I rode up in the elevator, I leaned against the wall and closed my eyes.

Once I was in my room, I looked at my bed. It was only about six, but I felt the pull of sleep so strongly that I couldn't fight it. I lay down on top of the blankets, telling myself that I would close my eyes for just a couple of minutes.

I fell asleep so quickly that I didn't even have time to take off my shoes.

28

THE NEXT THING I KNEW,
someone was knocking at the door. The room was pitch-black. I
sat straight up, struggling to remember where I was. Then it all
came back to me. *Las Vegas. Diamond.*

I looked over at the lighted dial on the bedside clock and saw
that it was eight o'clock. I had been asleep for about two hours.

My door opened, and I jerked, startled. "Who's there?" I
called out in a voice groggy with sleep. "Who is it?"

"Oh, sorry. I didn't know anyone was in here," a woman's
voice replied with a soft accent. "It's housekeeping. Do you need
your bed turned down?"

"No, no, thanks. I'm fine," I managed to answer as I reached
over to turn on the light.

"All right. Have a good night," the housekeeper called out to
me. I heard a rustle, then the sound of the door closing as she left
the room.

The moment she was gone, I regretted not asking her to leave
me some of the chocolates the Bellagio placed on their guests' pillows. Just the thought of food made my stomach growl. It had
been a heavy lunch at the Cuban Café earlier in the day, but it had
also been eight hours ago.

I leaned back on my pillows and considered my options for the evening. The most tempting choice was to order room service and take a bath while I waited for the food to arrive. I could watch TV, eat, and then go back to sleep. But that wouldn't help me find Diamond.

I wondered what Dennis was doing. He didn't say anything about having any other clients at the moment, so maybe he had gone home. I tried to picture the place where he lived but failed. One thing I knew for sure—his living space would be neat, ordered, tidy, like his mind.

The next thing I needed to do was to follow up on the old man Oscar had seen with Diamond, but I had no idea where to start. Something about Oscar's description of the man struck a chord in my memory, but I wasn't sure why.

My brain was muddied with sleep, I decided. I felt rumpled and dirty, and I could taste the rum and Cokes I had consumed at the Clipped Chip while Dennis and I were interrogating Oscar. I needed a scalding shower and then a little time to jot some notes and think about what I had learned. I knew there was something familiar about the leathery old man Oscar described.

Just as I was about to get out of bed, my cell phone rang. I thought guiltily about Tony and the kids, and my parents, and my brother and sisters. Everyone was probably worried about me.

But when I saw the area code on the phone's screen, I noted that it was 702: a local call. After a moment, I recognized the number. Adrianna. She had been so kind, offering me assistance in finding Diamond, and I had basically blown her off. In spite of everything I was dealing with, I had to admit that I had treated her badly. I hoped that I could make things right before she told Dorcas how I had behaved.

"Adrianna, hello," I said.

"How's it going, Esmeralda?" Adrianna asked in a warm voice, sounding concerned. "Any news?"

"Thanks so much for calling back," I said. "I really appreciate your concern, but there isn't any news. I'm still waiting."

"Sorry to hear that," Adrianna said. "It must be terrible, not knowing what happened to your sister."

Adrianna sounded so nice, I could see why Dorcas was her friend.

"I'm hoping for the best," I said.

"What about the police?" Adrianna asked. "Anything from the detective assigned to the case?"

"No. I met with him, and he took down some information, but that was about it," I replied.

Suddenly I had a thought. Something clicked into place, a thought about that little old Cuban man.

"Adrianna, this might be a strange thing to ask," I began.

"Ask me anything," Adrianna said.

"Well, since you're Cuban, and since you live here, I guess I will," I said with a nervous laugh. "It's about the Cuban men who worked in the casinos before Fidel. You know, the dealers and floor staff. I know a lot of them got jobs here. Do they hang out at any special place that you know of?"

Adrianna was quiet for a moment, thinking.

"Well, I heard that Caesar's Palace had some Cuban dealers, and the Flamingo took on some guys who got out of Cuba," she said. "But, Esmeralda, any of the guys who worked the casinos before Fidel would have to be really old now."

"That's true," I agreed.

"Yeah, Caesar's and the Flamingo," Adrianna said. "Those hotels have been here almost since Vegas began."

I jotted down the hotel names on the pad next to my bed.

"But things could change," Adrianna said, a little more slowly, backtracking a bit. "Maybe they work and hang out at different places now. If there are any of them left."

"Thanks a lot," I said. I had other questions—such as what she actually did in Las Vegas. Dorcas said Adrianna was connected, but it didn't seem like an appropriate moment to press for details. For some reason, I did not feel comfortable confiding in her just then.

"Remember. Just call me if you need help. Any time. Day or night." Adrianna made me promise I would, and then we hung up. I looked over at the clock. It was close to eight-thirty.

That meant it was getting close to eleven-thirty in Miami. It was too late to call home and check on the boys. It would have been nice to hear from Tony, but I decided I should be kind and assume that he was busy dealing with the household—even though I knew that his mother had taken charge of everything and that Tony had probably already reverted back to spoiled-son mode. I was also surprised not to have heard from Dorcas, but then I realized she was probably checking in with Adrianna and getting reports that way.

After one look at my sleepy face in the bathroom mirror, I decided that it had been a mistake to turn the light on. I had deep sleep lines, my hair was a fright, and my eyes were two little slits. I turned away from the mirror, stripped off my clothes, and left them in a heap on the floor. I made a mental note to put them in a laundry bag later to be cleaned.

Stepping into the shower, I was glad that the Bellagio didn't charge its guests on the basis of how much water they used. I stayed in the shower so long that my skin started to turn pink—no mean feat, for a Miami Cuban. Finally I dried off, put on the terrycloth robe, and wrapped my hair in a towel. I sat down at the table next to the window and took out my folder of notes and pictures.

Finally, I was waking up. I had a few ideas what to do next. I jotted down a few notes from my day, just a few observations, but by that time the growling in my stomach was drowning out my thoughts, so I broke down and ordered room service. I had planned to grab a bite at the café downstairs before going out, but my appetite wasn't cooperating. I picked up the phone, ordered dinner, then sat alone with my notes while I waited for the food to arrive.

It was while I was jotting down a few new facts that a persistent image came to my mind: the little leathery old man with the eye patch. I remembered the trips to Las Vegas with my parents, and the people they introduced me to from the time when I was a little girl. It was then that I remembered something.

I also remembered telling Dennis that I would call him later, but I decided against asking him to come pick me up. I didn't really need him for what I planned to do, and I didn't want to bother him unnecessarily. I was paying for his time, but I couldn't expect the man to follow me everyplace I went. I was capable of handling some things on my own.

Looking at Dennis's business card, which I pulled out of my folder, I picked up my cell phone and punched in his number. My heart beat a little faster as I waited for him to answer.

"Hello, Esmeralda," Dennis said after picking up on the second ring. I couldn't be sure, but it sounded as though he had been waiting for my call.

"Dennis, I'm just calling to check in."

"Need me to pick you up?" he asked.

"No, not tonight," I told him. "I had a nap, and I'm waiting for room service."

"Sounds good," Dennis replied.

"Listen, thanks for all your help," I said. "I really don't know what I would do without you."

"Don't mention it," Dennis said. "And you'd do fine. Give yourself some credit."

"Will you be available tomorrow?" I asked, hope rising in my voice.

"I don't know," Dennis said, his voice suddenly rough and businesslike. "Let me check my calendar."

"Oh," I replied. "All right. I'll hold."

There was a long moment of silence.

"Esmeralda?" Dennis finally said.

"Yes?"

"That was me being funny," he said. "Of course I'll pick you up tomorrow. Ten o'clock, in the usual place?"

I laughed, releasing more tension than I knew I'd felt.

"People don't always know when I'm joking," Dennis said in a surprisingly embarrassed tone.

"It's my fault," I said. "This thing has me wrapped pretty tight."

"So you're staying in tonight?" Dennis asked.

"Probably," I said evasively.

"Probably?" Dennis repeated. "Look, if you're going out, I can—"

"I'm fine, Dennis," I said. "I'm a grownup. Get some rest. I'll probably run you all over town tomorrow."

"OK," Dennis said. "In the morning, then."

"In the morning."

There was a knock at the door. Dennis said good-bye, and I went to sign the room-service charge. I dug into my meal, and within twenty minutes I was ready to go.

As I locked my hotel room door, I thought about what Dennis had said and decided that he was right. I needed to give myself some credit. I was going to do this. I was going to find Diamond.

29

THE STRIP IN LAS VEGAS
runs from Mandalay Bay to the Stratosphere along Las Vegas Boulevard; it's only seven miles long, and the heart of the city is only half that length. It isn't a great distance, and it's easy to imagine all the hotels and casinos as close together. In reality, appearances are deceiving, so, as a result, the walk between one hotel and the next can be quite a long hike. All along the Strip are trams, escalators, and elevated walkways that connect one site to the next—and each covered passage is all the more necessary during the unbearable summer months in the desert. Still, I knew from experience that getting around Las Vegas on foot was tricky and time consuming.

I held the piece of paper on which I'd written the two hotels Adrianna had cited as hangouts for the old Cuban dealers: the Flamingo and Caesar's Palace. The Bellagio was pretty much equidistant from each of them, so it was just a toss-up to determine which one I would visit first. I left my room at around nine and walked down the hall to the elevators. By the time I reached the ground floor, I had decided to start the evening off at Caesar's Palace. I had based the choice on a simple fact: the view outside my room at the Bellagio faced that casino.

A born gambler, I took superstition seriously. I knew that

my being assigned a room facing that casino was no accident. The more I pondered it, the more logical it became. Thinking of Caesar's Palace, I was also reminded that the hotel was architecturally similar to Mama and Papa's apartment building in Miami Beach. All roads led to Caesar's Palace.

As the power of chance took over my consciousness, I decided to try my luck for the first time since I arrived in Las Vegas. I headed straight for the Bellagio casino, feeling a familiar itch that compelled me to reach for my wallet inside my purse. I felt like a dieter who couldn't resist a salty potato chip, telling myself that I would play only one game, just for luck, in Diamond's name. I would have liked to have sat down at one of the tables where blackjack hands were being dealt, but that would have taken too long. Blackjack was always my preferred casino game and the one at which I always enjoyed the most luck. I scanned the tables and saw that they were beginning to fill up with gamblers who were settling in after dinner.

I wouldn't join them. Instead, I decided to play five dollars in a slot machine—not exactly my usual choice, which was why I opted for it. I walked up to the casino cashier station in the center of the room, slid a five-dollar bill across the counter, and asked for five one-dollar coins in return. I must have been feeling lucky, because I also picked up a plastic cup from the stacks next to the counter that were provided for holding winnings.

A slot machine in a long row next to the cage beckoned me. I sat down, taking in all the lights and noise all around me. I closed my eyes, listening to the din of machines, metal, rustling bills, clinking coins, and voices expressing excitement and disappointment. The texture of the moment felt like a microcosm of my life. Again, I felt like Marcel Proust with his Madeleines.

I opened my eyes and saw that I was the only person working a machine in my row. It must have been an omen, good or bad. I played the machine four times, and lost each time. I decided then to change my tactics, so instead of pulling the handle myself on the next play, I pushed the button on the side that told the machine to take over.

Almost instantly, the bells rang and lights on the machine flashed on and off in sharp succession. It happened so fast that I barely had time to understand that I had won. I looked up and saw bright red cherries lined up in a row like three tart soldiers. The torrent of coins pouring from the machine was so loud that people stopped to stare, a couple giving me a thumbs-up. I gathered as many coins as I could in my plastic cup and, to my amazement, had to reach for two more in order to hold them all.

I walked over to the cage to exchange the coins for cash, happy that I had won, but even more elated that I was going to have a lucky night. I watched the cashier pour all the coins from the cups into the counting machine and found that my winnings totaled a little more than five hundred dollars. As the cashier counted out the bills on the counter, I felt more than ever that I was closer to finding my sister.

Tucking the cash away, I walked through the hotel's reception area. It struck me, as I took in the busy scene, that this was the first time I was looking for Diamond without Dennis's help. The deep sense of loss I felt was surprising, given that I had only known the limousine driver for a couple of days. This was my third night in Las Vegas, although it felt as though I had been there a lot longer.

To get to Caesar's palace I had to walk past the Bellagio fountains. I stopped and watched them for a moment, feeling that I was adding to my good luck for the night. I drifted for a second on the illusion of the design, feeling transported to a village in Tuscany with a lake ringed with old-fashioned black iron lampposts. I almost expected to see villagers strolling around the water before retiring for the evening—a notion that swiftly vanished when I focused instead on the hordes of tourists dashing into the hotel in pursuit of their own slice of good luck.

There were so many people filling the sidewalk on Las Vegas Boulevard that I was jostled with every step. I kept my shoulders squared and walked quickly, and eventually was relieved when I was close to Caesar's Palace. I had been there many times before on previous visits, but I was still taken aback by the sheer spectacle of the place. My designer's eye enabled me to be fascinated, rather than simply appalled. I could just imagine how much fun it must have been to put a piece of ancient Rome in the middle of the Las Vegas Strip—and I would have loved to have gone on one of the designers' buying trips.

Walking toward the main entrance, I decided to forego the people movers that would have carried me directly inside. I stood, mesmerized by all the statues, fountains, and fake ruins. I couldn't imagine what present-day residents of Rome must have thought when they saw the Vegas forum at Caesar's Palace. Probably their first instinct was to run to one of the many bars nearby and drown their sorrows while thanking the gods that Julius Caesar wasn't around to see the enormous statue of him that graced the hotel's entrance. After seeing his likeness reproduced in front of a resort hotel, I imagined the emperor would have thanked the senators for stabbing him on the Ides of March. The same went for the life-sized statue of Michelangelo's David (renaissance, not classical, but why quibble over details), which might have inspired the artist to concentrate exclusively on the Sistene Chapel ceiling. Looking at the vast white expanse before me, all bathed in blue light, I thought it impossible that there was any marble left in any quarry in the world. I felt like a rubber-necker checking out a highway accident: I couldn't stop looking, even though I knew I should move on.

I moved toward the casino entrance, my thoughts again turning to Dennis. I had a few reasons for not asking him to come with me tonight, but the main one was that I hadn't told him everything that had happened since we talked to Oscar at the Clipped

Chip earlier in the day. I had been forthcoming with him about everything else, but I hadn't shared my memory of the skinny, one-eyed old man who matched the description Oscar had given us of the man who met Diamond one day outside the newspaper.

Oscar had painted a picture of a man who I had finally remembered while sitting in my hotel room waiting for my dinner. His name was Armando Solis, and I recalled Diamond being with me when my father introduced us to him. We were little girls at the time, and I was sure that Diamond would have recognized the patch over his eye—the kind of detail that would have stuck with a small child.

My father had told me that Armando Solis had been one of the best dealers in Havana and that he had worked for my family at La Estrella. Papa also told me that Armando had been fishing as a boy when a hook became embedded in his eyeball; Armando had waited too long to see a doctor, and an infection had set in that made it necessary to remove the eye. The story had scared me away from fishing pretty much permanently. Papa had said that Armando made up for his impaired vision with physical dexterity, for his fast hands were the stuff of legend.

He was a roulette dealer—a wheel dealer, as they were known in the business—and was a fixture at La Estrella. After Castro closed the casinos in 1959, Armando received a lot of job offers in Las Vegas—not surprising, since the same people, save for my family, ran the casinos in both cities. I had met him too long ago to remember at which casino he worked, but he was probably retired by now. Most of all, I remember Armando as one of Papa's success stories—he loved to brag about how desirable his old employees were and how any casino would be lucky to employ them.

Papa's voice had filled with pride when he told me that Cuban wheel dealers were in demand in Las Vegas casinos because of their ability to perform a specific feat: they mastered the art of pushing ten stacks of chips with a single hand. Considering the fact that there were twenty chips in a stack, it was a technique that required considerable skill and ability. When the Cuban dealers came over, their American counterparts hadn't seen the move before, and had to learn it in order not to be left behind.

I knew there were two casinos in the Caesar's complex—one at Cleopatra's Barge, the other at the Garden of the Gods. I decided to try the latter one first because it was closer.

I was about to go inside when I heard someone call out my name. I looked around at the milling crowd, squinting into the dizzying array of lights.

"Is that really you?" called out a man's raspy voice with an accent, speaking in Spanish.

I turned around and saw that I had already found Armando Solis—or, rather, that he had found me.

What is this? I asked myself, wondering for a split second if I was moving through a dream.

There was nothing to do but go to the source of the voice. He was standing by the casino entrance. Suddenly I had a strange sensation that he had been waiting for me, almost as though thinking of him had somehow summoned him in the flesh. The odds against it were astronomical. I believed in chance and coincidence, and I knew I was going to be lucky that night, but this was too much. I decided not to let my skepticism show.

Never tip your cards, Papa told me once. *And don't let them see you sweat.*

"*Hola,* Armando," I said. I kissed him quickly on the cheek and said, in Spanish. "What a nice surprise to see you here after all these years!"

It had been at least a decade since I had seen Armando, but there was no mistaking him. His appearance hadn't changed a bit. I did a quick calculation: if Armando had been about thirty when he left Cuba, then he must be at least seventy by now. He didn't show it, although as I looked closer I saw that he had dark circles under his uncovered eye, and that his café con leche skin now looked more café than leche.

Armand was about my height and, as Oscar had noted, was very skinny. He was, as always, a dapper dresser, in a white linen suit over an open-necked lavender shirt. His black leather lace-up shoes were shined to a buff sheen. He looked prosperous and healthy, which in spite of my suspicions about the timing of our meeting, pleased me.

"I know why you're here," Armando said, drawing close. "We need to talk. But not here. Come with me."

It had been a lucky evening so far and, if I was being set up, at least I had found the man I was looking for. So, without asking any questions, I followed the skinny, one-eyed old man in the white linen suit.

30

ARMANDO TOOK ME BY THE arm and ushered me away from Caesar's Palace. He was stronger than I would have thought, and he pulled me fast, almost as though he was worried that someone might be following us. In minutes we covered ground that had taken me much longer to walk through on my own. I had to rush so much to keep pace with the seventy-year-old Armando that I barely had time to wonder where we were going. I thought I was in good shape from working out at the gym, but trotting along with Armando made me feel like an old lady.

At Las Vegas Boulevard, Armando stepped out into the street and raised his arm to hail a taxi. Almost instantly, a car pulled over for us. Armando opened the door and motioned for me to get in, which I did.

"Take us to Landry's, please," Armando instructed the driver. To me, in Spanish, he said. "It's quiet there, away from the Strip. It's a place where we can talk."

I had no idea what Landry's was, but I raised no objections. Whether finding Armando was my good luck or someone else's design, at least I had found someone willing to talk to me. I figured I was safe with him—after all, he had worked at La Estrella and had been a family friend of sorts for decades. Also, I had a physical advantage over him if things got ugly—I was forty years younger and probably outweighed him by ten pounds or so. I also had the added advantage of two working eyes. I had taken a self-defense course a year ago at my gym in Coconut Grove, and I was confident that I could punch my way out of trouble. What made me feel safest was Armando's dapper white linen suit—there was no way a Cuban man would risk getting blood on such a garment.

Armando leaned back in the seat, gave me a neutral smile, and took in the sights outside the taxi's window. It was clear that he didn't plan to tell me anything until we reached our destination. I knew that nothing in Las Vegas was ever very far away, so I resigned myself to waiting. Wherever we were going, it was almost sure to be a change of pace from the Clipped Chip and the watery rum and Cokes I drank there.

I looked out at the crowds passing by, having already given up scanning faces in hopes of seeing Diamond. The people went past in a blur, but I still wondered whether any of the anonymous thousands on Las Vegas Boulevard knew my sister, had ever seen her or talked to her.

The cab turned west on Sahara Avenue; soon after that, the driver pulled into the parking lot in front of a shopping strip. He made a few turns before stopping in front of a one-story place with a bright red sign on its roof: Landry's Seafood House. Armando handed the driver a few bills that he'd earlier tucked inside his clenched hand. We got out together, and I followed Armando up the wooden ramp that led into the restaurant.

As soon as we entered the foyer, a hostess came over to greet us. We opted for the smokefree section of the large main dining room—something for which I was grateful, after spending the afternoon inhaling Oscar's Marlboros at the Clipped Chip.

As we followed the hostess, I looked over the dining room. Almost all the tables were occupied, mostly by families; even children got to stay up late when they were visiting Las Vegas, a fact that my boys always loved. The place was loud and lively. It was definitely a seafood house—which the décor made sure no one forgot. Every square inch of the restaurant was covered with a nautical theme: the carpet was dark green with undersea motifs, and there were fish traps, stuffed fish, and fishing poles all around. It was like SeaWorld on steroids. With each step, I thought of the Old Man and the Sea, Robinson Crusoe, Captain Hook, and Captain Ahab. I was just starting to think about Jaws when we finally reached our table.

"Excuse me for a moment," Armando said as I sat in the dark green leather booth. "I'll be right back."

I watched Armando heading off for the men's room, giving myself a moment to look around. I sort of liked the searchlights suspended from the ceiling—probably to invoke night fishing—but I could have done without the carriage lanterns on lighthouse poles placed all around the room. I was glad to see that the maritime motif didn't exclude a reminder that we were still in Las Vegas—the plastic card on the table advertised specials such as the "Double-Luck Thursday."

It seemed significant to me that Armando had chosen to take me to a place that so aggressively evoked the sea. The wheel dealer might have lived in Las Vegas, a city built in the middle of a desert, but he was a Cuban at heart. Thoughts of the sea would never be far from his mind.

I picked up the menu. I'd had a chicken Caesar salad in my room at the Bellagio an hour or so before, but that didn't keep me from looking over the list of fare with growing enthusiasm. The more I read, the hungrier I became. By the time Armando returned I was famished; if there had been a tablecloth in front of me, I might have been nibbling on it by then.

Armando sauntered over to the table with measured strides. He might have been old, but he knew how to wear a suit. When he settled into his seat, he gave me a sly smile.

"So, Esmeralda, first we order a little something to drink, then a bite to eat," he said. He picked up the menu and looked it over. Our waitress appeared and Armando glanced up.

"A little wine?" he asked.

"Sure," I said.

"White?" he asked.

I nodded.

"Very good. We'll have a bottle of the sauvignon blanc, please." Armando pointed to a wine on the list, to make sure he was getting what he ordered. "Would you like to order?"

I nodded again, feeling a bit like a bobblehead doll. "The salmon, please," I said. The Caesar salad was long forgotten. "Cooked rare."

"Good choice," Armando said. "I'll have the same. We'll have the fried calamari for an appetizer."

The old man brought his hand to his mouth and kissed his fingers. "The calamari are delicious here," he said in Spanish.

I smiled at him, transported back to my childhood, when my parents were always introducing me to characters such as Armando whom they had known in Cuba.

"Now we can talk," Armando said. "First, tell me about your family. Your parents, your brother, your sisters—all the children. You know, it's been a while since I talked to your father."

I gave Armando a quick sketch of how my family was doing, surprising myself midway when I realized that I had left out Tony. It was true that my marriage hadn't been going well, but I hadn't thought things were so rocky that I would fail to mention my husband. It was as though I had subconsciously eliminated him from my life, something that I chose not to ponder for the moment. I hadn't mentioned Diamond, either, but there was a reason for that.

I was almost finished when the waitress returned with our wine. Armando quickly went through the tasting ritual, gave his assent, then watched as she poured the pale liquid into our wine-glasses. As soon as she was gone, Armando raised his in a toast.

"To La Estrella," he said.

I echoed his words and took a drink, feeling my eyes watering as I tasted the white wine. It was the first time I could remember someone outside of my family drinking a toast to our old casino.

A minute later, the waitress returned with a huge platter of fried calamari. I picked up the serving implements and scooped up a healthy amount onto a smaller plate, which I handed over to Armando. Then I did the same for myself, and we munched for a while. Armando was right—the calamari was out of this world. Landry's décor might have been enough to instill aquaphobia, but the food more than made up for it.

After we'd eaten for a minute, I looked up at the old man. I expected him to take the hint, but instead he just ate his food and sipped his wine.

"You said you were expecting me back at Caesar's Palace," I finally said. "What did you mean by that?"

Armando flashed a deer-in-the-headlights look at me. He finished off his glass of wine and poured another.

"I have to tell the truth," he said, looking down at the table. "It's all my fault. You have to forgive me."

When he looked up, his good eye had filled with tears. His black eye patch began to quiver, forcing me to imagine what was going on behind it.

"What do you mean?" I said.

Armando clutched his wineglass so tightly that I feared he was going to break the stem. He took another long drink. "Your sister, Diamond. It's all my fault."

My heart began to pound. Armando let out a sob that made the people at the next table stop talking and look over at us.

"Armando, please, you have to calm down," I whispered to him. The last thing I needed was for him to have some kind of medical episode. "Please, I'm sure you're not to blame for anything. Just tell me what you have to say." I put my hand over his. My touch seemed to calm the old man down.

"Diamond came to Caesar's Palace about a year ago," Armando said. He paused and took a bite of his calamari—he was a Cuban man, after all, and meals were important. "She saw me there, hanging out with Mario."

"Mario?" I asked.

"You remember him," Armando assured me. "Mario Mendoza. He worked at La Estrella, too, at the blackjack tables."

I shook my head. My father had introduced me to a lot of people.

"Well, Mario and I were playing the slots at Cleopatra's Barge when we saw your sister come into the casino." Armando shook his head at the memory. "She remembered me, but not Mario—just like you."

Amazingly, Armando didn't seem to think there was anything particularly memorable about his appearance.

"She said she was working here as a newspaper reporter," Armando continued. "She was investigating a story that had to do with casinos and pollution. Garbage, something like that."

"Diamond was working for the *Las Vegas Herald*," I said to help the old man out. "She was the reporter assigned to cover environmental issues."

"Well, Mario and I decided to show off." Armando looked down at the table again. "We told her that we were retired but that we were still in touch with the people who run the casinos. The administrators, the managers, the floor bosses. We started telling her how important we were, just shooting off our mouths. You know, two old guys talking to a pretty young girl."

I could easily imagine it. Diamond was the kind of girl who was capable of making two old geezers fall all over each other trying to impress her.

"What happened next?" I asked. I finished off my wine and poured another glass. At the rate I was going, I would have to start attending AA sessions at the church in Coconut Grove once I returned home.

"Diamond went to a meeting at Caesar's after that," Armando said. "We waited for her for a couple of hours, but she didn't come out. You know, we wanted to say good-bye to her."

"I don't understand," I said to him. "What happened that you think is your fault?"

Armando sighed. "It was what happened two days later. Diamond called me at home—she said she had found my number in the phone book. She sounded really excited, and she said that she wanted to meet with me about La Estrella. Of course I said yes. I was very curious, asking her what she wanted, but she said we had to talk in person. So we met at a coffee shop off the Strip."

"What did she want with you?" I asked.

"Well, first she told me she was looking into how Caesar's disposed of its garbage," Armando explained. "You have to understand, Esmeralda, I don't know a lot about this environmental stuff. Your sister was talking about clean air and water, but I wasn't really following her. When I was growing up, we just threw things away. No one worried about it."

Armando gave me an apologetic smile and took a bite of his calamari. I suddenly had sympathy for police interrogators who put their subjects under harsh lights in order to get them to talk.

"Diamond said she had found out something about La Estrella," Armando said quietly. "She said it was very important, and that she needed to learn more. She said I had to help her."

"She found out something here in Las Vegas that had to do with La Estrella?" I asked.

"That's what she said," Armando replied.

"So what did she need your help with?"

The waitress returned then with an enormous tray loaded with food, which she proceeded to serve with alarming efficiency. Despite my need to hear more from Armando, I felt my mouth begin to water when I caught the smell of cooked seafood. We waited while our waitress fussily arranged our plates to her satisfaction. When she was about to leave, Armando pointed at our empty bottle of wine.

"I think we're going to need another one of these," he said. The waitress beamed at him. By her reaction, I figured that the families who ate at Landry's seldom ordered much from the wine list.

"Your sister said she remembered talking to me and Mario," Armando muttered once we were alone again. I leaned closer. "I guess all our bragging made an impression on her. Diamond said she needed my help getting a job at one of the casinos."

A casino job. That made sense, given what I knew and what I'd heard from Oscar, and assuming the Mickey calling on the answering machine in Diamond's apartment was Diamond's boss.

"What kind of job?" I asked.

"She said she wanted to look into some business that had to do with La Estrella," Armando said. "I'm not sure about the details. Sometimes I forget things."

The waitress came back with a new bottle of wine. Armando and I watched her open it, both of us showing as much rapt attention as if we were residents at a hospital watching a surgeon perform a complex operation. I waited until we were alone to speak again.

"What kind of job would tell her about La Estrella?" I asked. It was hard for me to put together the idea of Diamond leaving a journalism career for a casino. But La Estrella had a powerful hold on every member of my family—that fact alone made me think it was all true.

"She wanted access to the whales. She was very clear about

that." Armando must have seen my dumbfounded reaction, because his old face opened up in a smile. "You know what the whales are, don't you?"

We were in an aquatic-theme restaurant, but I knew what Armando was talking about—and it wasn't sea life. Las Vegas "whales" spit out money from their blowholes.

"Whales are gamblers with high credit limits," I told Armando. "Their credit can go into the hundreds of thousands of dollars. Mostly their game is Baccarat."

"That's right." Armando picked at his salmon with his fork. I suddenly had the impression that he was about to clam up on me. I could tell he was reluctant to say more, probably because he thought I was going to blame him for whatever happened. I tucked into my own salmon, which I had to admit smelled divine. We ate in silence, with low-grade tension between us, until we had cleaned both our plates. Finally I decided that Armando might be more cooperative now that he had a full stomach.

"So were you able to get her a job where she would be in contact with the whales?" I asked gently. I waited for a few seconds, then continued. "At which casino?"

"Yes. Well, it wasn't easy. Those are high-paying jobs, you know, and there's a lot of competition for them."

"Which casino was it, Armando?" I repeated.

"The Star," he told me. "She wanted a job at the Star."

I had heard of the Star, although I hadn't been there before. It was a newly renovated place occupying the shell of one of Las Vegas's first casinos. The joint was advertised on splashy billboards coming in from the airport and was obviously being aggressive in trying to attract customers.

I could see the old man was torn between pride over having gotten Diamond a coveted job and guilt over the role he might have played in her disappearance.

"I made her promise to keep in touch, to call me from time to time," he added. "I made her give me her home and cell phone numbers. You know, I felt responsible for her. I got her the job, her papa wasn't here—she begged me not to call him and tell him. She said she wanted to surprise your family."

"So, did she keep in touch like she promised?" I asked.

"Yes, in the beginning," Armando told me. "We didn't talk for a long time. She just told me she was doing fine, and that she was getting what she needed. She always told me not to worry, that I wouldn't regret getting the job for her."

"When did you know something was wrong?" I asked, apprehensive of even asking the question.

Armando frowned miserably. "When I hadn't heard from her for more than a week—about ten days. I started to call her, but I didn't reach her. She was out here on her own, with no one to help her."

"Did you leave messages?" I asked.

"I should have." Armando rubbed his cheek. "But I never liked those damned machines. Still, I was very worried about her. I would have called your papa, but Diamond made me swear on La Estrella that I wouldn't."

Armando smiled at the irony of that oath. That was a promise Diamond must have known he wouldn't break.

"I knew one of you would be coming out to find her," he said. "I looked in the papers every day, hoping maybe I would see something about her. I called the hospitals, I asked around. *Nada.* That was when I knew I would be seeing one of you. When I saw you outside Caesar's Palace, I was so relieved. Finally someone else knew what was going on."

It was a very strange coincidence that I had run into Armando that night, but the old man took it as perfectly natural. Once a gambler, always a gambler, I supposed. Armando was used to long odds.

"So you weren't surprised to see me?" I asked him.

Armando shrugged, as though things couldn't have turned out any other way. He sipped his wine and looked into the middle distance until a small smile played on his features.

"You know, Esmeralda, there are so many Cubans here now," he said slowly. "I just called in a few markers and—there it was— Diamond had her plum job with the whales."

Even though he had changed the subject, I was glad to see Armando getting chatty again. I nodded for him to go on.

"Cubans have such an impact in Las Vegas, but hardly anyone knows it," he said with a chuckle. "Someone should write a book about us. We had the best wheel dealers. We set the standard. And Baccarat, even though it's an old game that's been played for hundreds of years—the version of it they play here today originated at the Capri Casino in Havana. Now how many people know that?"

I smiled at him, thinking how much he sounded like my father. Something about what he had told me nagged at me, but I couldn't put it together in the din of the restaurant.

As soon as we had finished off the wine. Armando signaled for the check. When it arrived, I whisked it away from Armando before he had a chance to know what had happened. Without even looking at the amount, I handed the waitress my American Express card. The old man protested for a moment, but I could tell that he was secretly pleased by my gesture. I had no idea where Armando's money came from these days, but I noticed that his shirt was a bit frayed and that his suit could have used a good cleaning. From a distance he looked as dapper as ever, but up close I could see that it would be a stretch for him to pay for our meal.

"Next time I pay," he said solemnly.

When the waitress arrived, I asked her to call a taxi for us while we got ready. It was almost eleven, and the place was starting to empty out. I took one last look at the décor, thinking that I would have worn a bathing suit if I had known where I was going to end up that night.

Armando told the taxi driver to take us to the Bellagio; he said that he would walk back to his apartment from there. We traveled in silence, almost like two strangers sharing a ride from the airport. When we pulled in, I let my eyes linger on the fountains.

After Armando paid the driver and we got out, the old man took my arm as we watched the taxi pull away.

"What is it?" I asked him.

"It's about Diamond, and her job with the whales," he explained slowly, looking away from me.

"You remembered something?" I asked. I felt my heart thump in my chest.

"She said something funny." Armando looked up at me with a bittersweet smile. "She told me that if she was right about what she was doing, pretty soon I would be going back to being the head wheel dealer at La Estrella in Havana."

Hearing what Armando had said, I put my hand over my mouth in shock. What did she know? Where was my little sister?

31

I HAD BEEN SLEEPING SO deeply that I had a tough time identifying the shrill ringing in my ears as the sound of the hotel phone next to my head. I reached for it, cursing the fact that I was never to wake up naturally—it was always phones, alarms, or knocks at the door. Just once I wanted to wake up without something pressing to do.

Reaching over, I glanced at the clock and did a double take. It was ten in the morning. My grogginess instantly vanished. I sat up in bed as though I had been shot out of a cannon.

"Esmeralda?" I immediately identified Dennis's voice. "It's me. I'm downstairs, outside, waiting for you."

"Oh, God, I'm so sorry!" I cried out. "I overslept! I can't believe it's so late!"

I felt a pang of guilt, knowing I'd slept late because of last night's outing—which I hadn't yet told Dennis about. I would fill him in soon enough, but not until I'd had my morning coffee.

"No problem, take your time," Dennis said. "I was just worried because you've been so punctual before. I'll be waiting in the usual place. Just come on out when you're ready. I'll grab a quick bite to give you time to get down here."

I was about to apologize some more when I realized that he had hung up. Dennis was certainly a man of few words.

I lay back in bed and closed my eyes. I sat up so quickly that I had made myself dizzy. I stretched out, starting with my feet and working up to my head, the way I'd been taught at yoga class at the gym. Pretty soon I felt more composed, if not completely alert.

Dennis had said he would wait, so I decided to take him at his word. I felt better knowing that he was going to eat something. I picked up the phone and dialed room service for breakfast—I figured that by the time it arrived, I would be showered and dressed. I got up and walked over to the little table by the window, pausing there. I flipped open my notebook, where I'd written more than two pages before finally going to bed the night before. I had been exhausted when I got back from dinner with Armando, but my mind had been working on overdrive. I couldn't help but notice that I'd already filled up more than half the notebook—I hoped I wouldn't reach the end of it, or at least that the last sentence on the last page would be that Diamond was back with us.

I had finished writing the night before with Armando's comment outside the Bellagio—that Diamond had said that soon he would be the head wheel dealer at La Estrella again. It was strange. Mama and Papa hadn't been able to reach Diamond to tell her about Maria Mercedes's prophesy. Apparently Diamond had reached the same conclusion on her own, and it had something to do with the casino whales.

Staring at the notes, I waited for everything to make sense. My run of luck from the night before was apparently over and time was passing. I closed the notebook and put it in my purse. Just as I was about to climb into the shower, my cell phone rang. When I picked it up, I looked at the number on the ID screen. *Coño!* It was Adrianna. I should have thought to call her to thank her for her tip on where the old dealers hung out. I couldn't have found Armando without her.

As I answered the phone, I realized that, for some reason, I had been keeping Adrianna at arm's length since I arrived in Las Vegas. I told myself that I needed to change my attitude; after all, she had put herself out for me with nothing to connect us other than our shared friendship with Dorcas.

"Esmeralda?" she said, her breathy voice now familiar. "*Hola,* this is Adrianna. How are you?"

"Fine, good morning," I said.

Without waiting for me to say anything else, she went on. "I'm calling to see if you've heard anything about your sister," she said.

"No, there's no news yet," I said.

"Did you find the Cuban men you were looking for last night?" she asked. "The ones who worked in the casinos back in Cuba?"

"I found the man I was looking for at Caesar's Palace," I said. "I really want to thank you for your help. I'm so appreciative of all the concern you've shown."

"Well, I'd like to help more, or at the very least keep you company while you're looking for your sister," Adrianna said. She paused. "I know you're busy, but feel free to call me any time. Any time at all."

I felt like such an ingrate. This stranger was offering so much, and all I wanted to do was avoid her.

"I appreciate the offer, but I'll only bother you if it's an emergency." I told her. Then I went ahead and asked her what I had been wondering for a while. "I mean, you're probably busy with work? With your job?"

Dorcas had said only that Adrianna was connected, but I still didn't know what the woman did for a living.

"I do a little of this and that, and I pretty much set my own hours," Adrianna said. Clearly she didn't want to volunteer anything more, so I didn't press her. "You can call me any time you want. Don't worry about bothering me."

"I will," I said. *"Gracias."*

I thought our conversation was over when Adrianna surprised me by asking, "Any news from the police? Have you talked to Detective Morris since the last time we spoke?"

"No, I'll probably call him today," I said.

"Well, let me know," Adrianna said.

I thanked her again and, not really knowing how to take advantage of her continued offers of help, signed off. If I hadn't been so short of time that morning, I would have called Dorcas right away and asked for more information on Adrianna. As I walked to the shower, I tried to picture Dorcas's friend in my mind—her husky voice had a smoker's rasp, and she was certainly open and giving. I resolved to buy her dinner as soon as I had time.

After rushing through my shower, I dressed comfortably in khaki pants and a black cotton T-shirt. Anticipating the temperature outside—I could already see heat waves rising off the asphalt on the Strip below my window—I combed my hair into a braid. I had just finished putting on my makeup when I heard a knock at my door telling me that my breakfast had arrived. I had the waiter put the tray on the table by the window. After he had gone, I glanced through my free copy of *USA Today* while I ate everything on my plate, washing it all down with three cups of coffee. I didn't know whether it was nerves or fatigue, but I had eaten everything I could get my hands on during the brief time I had been in Las Vegas. If food was fuel, I was ready to race at Le Mans.

I thought about making a quick call to Tony before I went downstairs. It was almost eleven, which meant it was about two in Miami. Tony seldom left the office for lunch, so I knew I would be able to reach him. I also knew I would be on the run for the rest of the day, and I didn't want to talk to Tony in front of Dennis. I stood by the door of my room, not sure what I wanted to do.

The truth was, I was in a good mood, which was a rarity these days. I knew that talking to Tony would squash the good feeling with which I was starting my day. I was riddled with guilt; after all, I had been gone for four days, leaving my husband with the boys and a dog that was probably still farting. But I reminded myself that this was no pleasure trip and that I still had serious business ahead of me. Sometimes I thought that Cuban women had a lock on guilt—until I talked to some of my Jewish friends, who convinced me that it was a gender thing, and not one having to do with ethnicity. I finally decided not to call Tony. If he wanted to talk to me, he had my number. I would have called Gabriel, but he was still in school. Unless I wanted to have another conversation with him and the sound of toilets flushing in the background, I would have to wait until he was out for the day.

It was fairly amazing that my parents and siblings were leaving me alone while I looked for Diamond, aside from Sapphire's minor transgression of two days before. I was grateful for their restraint because I was feeling enough pressure as it was.

I decided that it would be a good idea to call my parents at the end of the day, although I was going to have to think long and hard about what I was going to tell them. I didn't want to lie, or withhold information, but I didn't want to worry them, either. I could easily picture Mama and Papa, and my sisters and brother, worried sick over Diamond and feeling helpless.

Once I had tucked my notebook in my purse, I realized that I wasn't going to find my sister easily, or quickly. I had little hope that the police were going to find her. Sure, they could follow all their traditional avenues of investigation, but what did Detective Morris know about Maria Mercedes and La Estrella? It wasn't his fault—it wasn't his history—but I knew that telling him about my family and their past would result in little more than a blank stare.

I considered hiring a private investigator—especially when I thought realistically about how completely overmatched I felt looking for my sister. But, the deeper I got into the search for my sister, the more I thought it would be hopeless to bring in an outsider. It was the same problem with Detective Morris: how to explain about La Estrella and Maria Mercedes? It was too chancy, and too time consuming to get into. I was Diamond's best hope, and I simply had to be up to the task. I felt that Dennis was starting to understand, but he was a special case—he had been with me since I arrived in Las Vegas, and I sensed that he was deeply smart and perceptive. Maybe it was superstition, but I felt as though he had been sent to help me.

As I closed my room door behind me, I said a little prayer that Dennis wouldn't be too annoyed when I told him about what I had done the night before. After all, I had asked for his help—which he had given reluctantly at first, then willingly. I might never have searched Diamond's apartment so thoroughly if he hadn't been there, and I almost certainly wouldn't have found the strength to grill Oscar the way we did.

But there was more to it, wasn't there, this worry about offending Dennis or making him angry with me?

I had hired Dennis as a limousine driver, I was paying him by the hour. But we both knew that, at some point, our relationship had moved beyond business. Which certainly complicated things.

We could sort that out later, I thought, after we found Diamond. After *I* found Diamond.

I didn't know him well enough to discern how he felt about my tardiness. I figured that he was used to his clients running late and, since he was on billable hours, the situation didn't present him with much hardship. Still, our relationship had begun to transcend business. He still hadn't presented me with any kind of bill, a situation I needed to deal with—the hours had to be adding up, and I needed to know where I stood, as far as his fee was concerned. I knew my family wouldn't object to paying, but I also didn't want to abuse my parents' generosity.

"Where do you want to go?" Dennis asked as he opened the door to the front passenger seat. I was pleased that he had assumed I wanted to ride up front with him.

"You're Catholic, right?" I asked. Since he was an Irishman, it was a pretty solid assumption.

Dennis nodded warily. "Sort of."

"Well, we'll start off by being holy," I said as I slid into the seat. After Dennis had come around and gotten buckled in, I added, "We'll go to the Guardian Angel Cathedral."

"Fine." Dennis started the car and put it in gear. "Still following the Cuban trail?"

Now would have been a good time to tell Dennis about Armando, but I let the moment pass. Instead, I reached into my purse and took out the Mass card I had found in Diamond's apartment. Dennis had reached the end of the Bellagio driveway, and he had to stop before merging onto Las Vegas Boulevard.

"Here," I said, handing him the card.

"I know where it is," Dennis said as he eased into traffic, heading north. "It's on Desert Inn Road, not far from here."

I didn't know what I was hoping to find at the church, but the fact that Diamond had the card in her apartment left me no choice but to go there. I hoped it wasn't a dead end—as, I had to admit, the Cuban Café seemed to have been—but I had to follow up on the few leads I had.

32

DENNIS WAS WAITING IN his usual spot, just outside the Bellagio entrance. I was starting to think of his black Lincoln Town Car as my second home in Las Vegas. He was standing by the limo, expectant, as though waiting for something to happen that would require his full attention. As I observed him, he reminded me of a soldier at ease.

That morning he was dressed in the same crisply pressed white shirt and black pants that he seemingly always wore, along with his ubiquitous mirrored shades. I couldn't help but wonder wha he looked like when he wasn't on the job. Did he wear Hawaii shirts? Did he dress like a conservative preppy, or like a Harl Davidson tough guy? I was so used to his driver's outfit th seemed like part of his personality. I wondered if he drove ferent car when he wasn't on the job—a pickup truck, or a vative sedan?

The more time I spent with Dennis, the more I want rage him with personal questions, but his manner did encourage the exchange of confidences. I simply could him off the job, living a personal life. Maybe that was

"Sorry I'm late," I greeted him.

"No problem," Dennis said, dismissing my apo it was of no consequence.

As we drove out, I kept thinking about Diamond, seeing her face so alive and vibrant. I slipped her photograph out of the manila envelope, which Dennis noticed without comment. I ran my hand over the picture's surface and tried not to give in to my frustration. I had learned more about her life in Las Vegas, but I hadn't made any sense of it. For instance, the Mass card itself—which I found in the apartment of a nonbeliever and nonobservant Catholic. Maybe my sister had gone there looking for spiritual guidance, or maybe she had gone there following up on something she learned from her job with the whales. If the latter was the case, then perhaps I would find out something she had as well. I hoped that the Guardian Angel Cathedral had been aptly named and that its namesake was looking out for Diamond.

The one thing that was clear to me was that everything I had learned so far in my search for Diamond had led back to Cuba. All the roads in my life led there, one way or the other. Even though my siblings and I had been born in America, we all considered ourselves Cuban. It was typical for our generation. Cuba was always inside us, as deep as our blood type, which could be diluted or transfused but never changed. No exile I knew had completely come to terms with his or her Cubaninity, something I fear we never would.

"We're almost there," Dennis said when we had been on the road for about ten minutes. I had been so engrossed in my thoughts that I barely noticed where we were going.

"Thanks," I said. I carefully put the photograph away and blinked back the tears that were on the verge of pouring out onto my cheeks.

A few moments later, Dennis signaled that he was making a turn. Soon we were on a small street that ended at a church. I let out a little gasp when I saw it, because it reminded me so much of the Ermita de la Caridad, the chapel in Coconut Grove in Miami that had been built by Cuban exiles in honor of the patron saint of the island, the *Virgen de la Caridad del Cobre*. Although the Ermita in Miami was on a parcel of land next to Biscayne Bay, while the Guardian Angel Cathedral was just off a busy avenue in Las Vegas, the similarities between the two were striking—from the palm trees that lined the street to the white color of the building against the brilliant blue sky.

Dennis drove slowly, and I tore my eyes away from the church to take in its surroundings. Across the street from the chapel was a shopping strip with a Chinese restaurant, a Taco Bell, and something called the Royal Hotel and Casino. It didn't exactly strike me as a spiritual setting.

Dennis pulled into a parking slot diagonal to the building, lowered the windows of the car, and turned off the motor.

"I assume you're going in," he said.

I started to open the door before he could go around and do it for me. "Are you coming with me?" I asked.

"If it's OK with you, I'll just wait outside." Seeing my disappointed look, he added, "I spent too many years on my knees. You know . . . the nuns."

"The nuns?" I repeated.

He held out his hands and showed me his marked-up knuckles. "I was intimately acquainted with the ruler," he said.

"I understand," I said with a shrug. "I'm not sure how long I'll be. I don't really know what I'm looking for."

"No problem," Dennis assured me. "Take your time."

"*Gracias.*" I got out of the car and squared my shoulders. Dennis was being so nice that I felt terrible about not revealing to him what I had done the night before. I would tell him when the time was right, I figured, although it was getting harder the more time passed.

The church wasn't very big; it was a small chapel, really, built in a stark modernistic style. I went inside and saw a triangle theme carried on from the exterior to the interior, especially in the shape of the big mural behind the altar that depicted Christ in modern, bright colors. The mural at the Ermita de la Caridad del Cobre in Miami was designed the same way, although there the mural depicted the heroes of the Cuban wars of independence against Spain. I stood back for a moment, looking the place over, then decided to say a few prayers. I certainly could use them.

The church was almost empty, but I glanced at Diamond's card and saw that a Mass was scheduled to begin within the hour. I wouldn't stay for the entire Mass, so I chose a pew close to the back, where I could sneak out without causing too much disruption.

As I had done in so many other churches, I knelt down and genuflected before I took my place in the pew. I had just begun to pray to the Virgin when two older ladies of about seventy, dressed in black from head to toe, took their places in a pew directly in front of me.

Instead of praying quietly, they began to talk. The place was so quiet that I heard them, and was surprised to realize that they were talking in Spanish—and with unmistakable Cuban accents. I looked up, immediately curious.

I couldn't see the women's faces, but I could clearly hear what they were talking about. Instead of praying, they were talking about their last trip to Miami, and the sales they'd taken advantage of at the Dadeland shopping center in the Kendall area of the city. They may have been elderly and devout, but they also seemed to be borderline shopaholics.

My attempts at prayer were finished; instead, I listened with fascination to the two women talking. I didn't really consider it eavesdropping, because their voices were so loud that I didn't even have to strain to clearly hear their words. From the gist of their conversation, I gathered that they were long-term Las Vegas residents. I wondered how they had ended up here. Papa had explained about the two distinct groups of Cuban exiles who had settled out here in the desert—the first had been in 1959, after

Fidel Castro closed the casinos in Havana. They were the dealers and casino staff who took jobs at the Las Vegas joints, like Armando. It had been a logical transition, since for the most part the gaming houses in the two cities were run by the same outfit—the American Mafia.

The next two waves of exiles who had filtered into Las Vegas had come in 1980, during the Mariel boatlift, and then in 1994, during the Guantanamo exodus. Papa had explained that those two groups of exiles were largely young men who arrived in the United States without family or sponsors. They needed employment, and the American government had asked those families who were established in the Las Vegas gaming industry to take in these new exiles and provide them with jobs. I looked at the two ladies in front of me, who were clearly in their seventies. The math was simple—they must have arrived in the first wave, in 1959, the same as Armando.

I listened to them describing the dresses they had bought on sale at Burdines—not only on sale, but with extra discounts from coupons clipped from the *Miami Herald*. I considered getting up and moving, so I could pray for Diamond without all the distraction, when one of the ladies asked her friend what time it was.

"Not quite noon," came the answer.

"Ten minutes until Mass," said the first woman in Spanish. "Just enough time for a cigarette."

I watched the two women make their way down the aisle to a side door. They were so eager for a smoke that they were already fumbling in their pockets for their packs of cigarettes. Without even thinking about it, I picked up my purse and stood up. Once I reached the aisle next to my pew, I knelt down, made the sign of the cross, and followed the two old women out of the church.

When I was outside, I hung back a little, pretending to study the dried-out garden next to the building. I waited while they lit up their cigarettes. The ladies were in all black, standing in sharp contrast to the stark white walls of the church—they made me think of pictures I'd seen of widows in Greek villages. Watching them inhale furtively, I thought they were secret smokers, the kind who hid it from their families.

After they'd inhaled a few puffs each, I decided to approach them. When I spoke, it was in Spanish.

"*Señoras*, I hope I'm not interrupting you," I said politely. They both looked up with surprise, instinctively hiding their cigarettes behind their bodies. I smiled to let them know I wasn't some kind of antismoking militant. "I was sitting behind you in the church, and I couldn't help overhearing some of your conversation."

The two ladies frowned and exchanged a look. Out in the light, I was suddenly struck by the similarities between their features. I would have bet that they were sisters.

The taller of the two took a step toward me. "I hope we weren't disturbing you," she said.

"Oh, no. Not at all," I said. "But I was wondering if I could ask you a question or two."

They looked at each other and, apparently deciding I didn't look too threatening, shrugged in unison. I took that for an affirmative reply.

"You're Cuban?" I asked. They both nodded. "I thought so. But you live here in Las Vegas?"

"For quite a long time, dear," said the taller one, wincing with slight suspicion.

I smiled. "I'm Cuban, too," I explained. "I live in Miami, in Coconut Grove."

My words had the effect of forming an instant bond between us, as I knew they would. They moved to each side of me and began asking questions—primarily how long I had been in the States, the first question that Cubans ask one another. The answer always determines who the individual had been back on the island. The first wave that came over, between 1959 and 1961, were mostly the landowning upper class—they had known right away that Fidel Castro was a Communist and that they would suffer most under his rule. During the consequent agrarian reform, Castro confiscated their land and took over their properties without compensation. The next wave of exiles left Cuba in the mid- to late sixties. After that, the primary exiles were basically anyone who was able to get out. There's an unfortunate stigma attached to the later groups who fled the island, a feeling that hopefully will eventually fall away.

"I was born in the United States," I told the ladies. I registered their disappointment, but then they politely nodded. Given my age, that fact wasn't particularly unexpected. They asked about my family and what part of Cuba they were from. I didn't want to reveal too much, so I simply told them that we were from Havana. They probably had heard of La Estrella, and I didn't want to get into my family's connection to the casino.

We ran through our history and geography—they were also from Havana, from a family of university professors and doctors—and what we thought was going to happen after Castro died, the subject near and dear to every exile's heart. Once I felt they were comfortable with me, I decided to get to the point.

"*Señoras*, I'm working on my Ph.D. at the University of Miami," I said, the lie coming out of my mouth before I could take it back. "I was wondering if you could give me some information to help with my dissertation?"

I hated to lie to them, but I also knew that they would love to think I was studying for an advanced degree. Cubans have learned the hard way that everything can be taken away—except an education. And there's nothing a Cuban wants to do more than help another Cuban.

Sure enough, they both clapped their hands together with eagerness. "Your Ph.D.!" said the shorter of the two. "How wonderful."

"Of course we'd love to help you," said the taller sister. "What can we do for you?"

I knew I had to tread carefully now, because I knew nothing about these women—other than that they were Cuban, and that they were ferocious bargain hunters.

"Well, the topic of my dissertation is the casinos in Havana around the time that Castro closed them," I said. "Specifically, what happened to the people who worked in the gaming business—the dealers, the money people. That's why I came to Las Vegas. I understand that quite a few people ended up here."

"Oh, yes, quite a few," said the taller of the two, obviously the more chatty one. "You know, some of them left that very New Year's Eve. They were so talented that a lot of them came here and got jobs right away. But, if you've done your research, then you know that already."

The shorter of the two women poked her companion in the ribs, as though telling her not to give me a hard time. They both had their cigarettes out in the open now and started puffing away.

"You know, it was the Catholic Church who brought a lot of the Cubans here to Las Vegas," continued the first sister, in the same tone of voice she'd employed to discuss the sale at Burdines.

"The church. Really?" I said. "I didn't really know that. I thought it was mostly the U.S. government."

The taller one moved closer and looked around, as though making sure no one was listening.

"The government helped some, but not all," she said. "Well, you know who owned the casinos in Havana, don't you?"

I nodded.

"Well, except for that one owned by a Cuban family," she continued. "What was their name, the Montalvos? They owned a casino called La Estrella. But the American Mafia owned the rest of them."

The shorter one tugged at her companion's dress. "That's enough, Carmen," she said. She tossed her cigarette on the ground and stamped it out. "Mass is starting soon. We'd better go inside."

"We have to help this young lady, Marisa. She's getting her doctorate," insisted Carmen. "This isn't information she's going to find in books and newspapers. You know about the money, don't you, dear? Now that's a story!"

Carmen had a wicked look in her eyes. Marisa looked as though she was about to have a stroke. Obviously this was one of Carmen's favorite topics of discussion.

"What money?" I asked. I could tell from Marisa's reaction that this was going to be interesting.

"The money in the American casinos in Havana," Carmen said. She stood so close to me that I could smell the cigarettes on her breath. "They say it's just a rumor, but I've heard it from so many people that there must be some truth to it. They say the Vatican helped the American Mafia get their money out of the casinos in Havana. They even gave them a plane to do it, so that Fidel Castro couldn't get his hands on it."

Marisa exhaled nervously. This was dangerous talk, even though Carmen seemed to be loving every minute of it. Marisa grabbed Carmen's arm and tried to pull her back toward the church.

"Carmen, stop spreading rumors," she hissed. "You don't know if that's true."

Carmen ignored her and kept talking. "They say the Church even changed the Cuban pesos into dollars for the Mafia at the Vatican bank," she added triumphantly. "Can you even imagine?"

I had no idea what to think about what I was hearing. Was it the ramblings of an elderly lady who read too many supermarket tabloids, or was there truth to what she was saying? I remembered Papa telling us about a friend of his in the Mafia helping him and Mama get the money and jewelry out of the safe at La Estrella. If the Mafia had helped my parents, had the Vatican helped the Mafia?

Carmen was watching me very carefully to see what I thought about her story. I struggled to put on a neutral face.

"*Señoras*, I've been looking into the subject for a while, but I never heard anything like that," I said. "It certainly is interesting."

Carmen took a final puff from her cigarette and looked at her watch. "Mass is starting in a minute. We have to go inside," she said, clearly thinking she had done her duty in furthering my fictional academic career.

"Yes, we should go," Marisa said with relief, obviously hoping to get away from me before Carmen could do any more damage.

I moved toward the door and started to open it for them. "Thanks for talking to me," I told them. "I really appreciate your taking the time."

Carmen and Marisa busied themselves straightening their clothes before going inside. I watched them tug at their dresses until they felt they were presentable. Just before I stepped aside, something else occurred to me.

"May I ask you one more question?" I said.

Marisa shot daggers at me, but Carmen smiled. "Yes?" she asked.

"How do you really know all that, about the Vatican and the money?" I said. I knew it was a hell of a question to ask, but I would have kicked myself later if I hadn't. It was Carmen, naturally, who answered me.

"We were nuns back in Cuba," she said. "But not any longer. The Catholic Church brought us here to Las Vegas more than forty years ago."

"You were nuns?" I asked, astonished.

"Used to be." Carmen grinned. "My dear, we know where all the bones are buried."

And with that, she and Marisa breezed past me and went inside. I was totally flabbergasted as I watched them head back to their pew, crossing themselves.

33

WHEN I GOT BACK TO THE parking lot, I found Dennis waiting in the precise spot where I'd left him. Even though I hadn't specified how long I would be gone, I felt guilty when I saw him standing next to his car, not leaning on it, as though not wanting to mar its shine.

I had ducked into the church for Mass, which had taken about an additional forty-five minutes after I was finished speaking with Marisa and Carmen. What Carmen had told me, after I mulled it over, had left me frightened and somewhat numbed. So I stayed inside for a while and prayed for my sister, all the while extremely conscious of the Mass card that I had found in her apartment and the fact that she recently might have been kneeling in the very same pew.

Dennis gave me a half-wave and walked around to the passenger side, waiting until I neared before opening the door. Even though he still wore his sunglasses, I could see the edges of his mouth wrinkle with amusement.

"So, did you have an interesting talk with those nuns?" he asked me. "Did you learn anything?"

"How did you know they were nuns?" I asked. Dennis might have been an ex-homicide detective in New York, but as far as I knew, that job description didn't entail possessing superhuman powers of perception.

Dennis laughed, a loud, barking sound. "I told you I went to Catholic school," he said. "I can spot a nun from a mile away. You don't forget what they're like."

"Well, they're *former* nuns," I said, for some reason wanting to have the last word.

Dennis shrugged. "Whatever you say. But as far as I'm concerned, there's no such thing as a *former* nun."

He waited until I was inside, with my seat belt snapped, before closing the car door. He walked around, got in, and started the motor. I held my hand up to the air conditioner vent for relief— the sun was high in the sky, and the trees were casting few shadows.

"What now?" Dennis asked.

"There's something I need to talk to you about," I said. "But not here, not in the car."

Dennis nodded. "Well—" he began.

"But not at the Clipped Chip. Please!" I interrupted. "Not that there's anything wrong with the place, but three days in a row would be too much."

"Don't worry, we don't have to go back to the Chip." Dennis looked away for a moment, suppressing a smile. "Just tell me where you want to go and that'll be fine with me."

I considered our options for a moment. "You're probably hungry," I said. I hadn't lived with Tony and our three boys without learning a very basic fact—that the male species is always ready for food. "We could go back to the Bellagio. There are lots of restaurants there where we could talk."

That decision made, Dennis put the car in gear; a few minutes later, we were motoring on Las Vegas Boulevard. As we drove back, I thought about what the ladies at the church had told me— and about how much I had been eating since I arrived in Las

Vegas. If I wasn't careful, I was going to turn into an emotional eater who drowned her worries in food. I supposed there were worse fates.

Once we were at the Bellagio, Dennis parked in his usual slot, which was miraculously open despite a commotion of cars, taxis, and airport shuttles. It was almost as though the spot was reserved for him alone, I thought, as we got out and walked to the hotel entrance. I glanced back at Dennis's car before we went inside.

"It's all right to park there?" I asked. Somehow it seemed as though the spot should have been reserved for a VIP.

Dennis waved to a fellow dressed in a suit, a rough-looking man in his fifties who was talking to one of the valets.

"No problem," Dennis said. He nodded toward the man he had waved at. "See him? He's from New York. We worked together undercover for a few years. He's retired and works security here."

"Very impressive," I said.

Dennis shot me a look, as though making sure I wasn't poking fun at him. Once we were inside the reception area, he put his hands in his pockets and looked around.

"Do you have a preference?" I asked him. "It's after one, so the lunch rush will be on. Most of the restaurants are going to be pretty crowded."

"Whatever you want is fine with me, Esmeralda," he said.

I had to admit, I could get used to being with someone who was so deferential to my desires. I mentally listed all the dining options available to us and had an inspiration.

"You know, I haven't been outdoors much since I got here," I told him. "How about the pool area? There's a café there that serves salads and snacks."

"Fine with me," Dennis said. "Lead the way."

All paths in Las Vegas led through the casinos, and the way to the Bellagio pool was no different. I led Dennis through the gaming area and the corridors past it, following the signs to the pool. After we went through a set of doors, I showed my room key to one of the attendants standing guard. Once I was cleared, we were allowed to pass.

I had been to the pool before, albeit not on this particular visit. One quick look around showed me that little had changed; the area was huge and well-kept, with rows and rows of chaise longues filled with guests relaxing, sunning themselves, reading, or taking naps. A few athletic types were swimming laps, no doubt swimming off the excesses of the night before, or preparing for the excesses of the night ahead.

The landscaping was fabulous, and totally in synch with the meticulous design of the rest of the hotel. There were burgeoning planters everywhere, and bushes and trees trimmed with such precision that they seemed interchangeable. The area was divided into several pools and lounges, and as I walked past the bodies lying in repose I wanted nothing more than to join them in blissful rest. But there was going to be no rest for me until I found Diamond.

A young, perky hostess led Dennis and me to one of the tables in the corner of the dining area. We looked over the menu, and by the time the waitress arrived I was starving. Dennis ordered a cheeseburger and a Coke, while I asked for a tuna salad and iced tea.

"There's something I have to tell you," I said to Dennis when we were alone.

"So you said." Dennis took off his sunglasses and laid them on the table, fixing me with the direct power of his opaque X-ray eyes. "Come on, talk. I won't bite you, Esmeralda."

I took a deep breath. "It's about last night," I said, trying and failing to look into his eyes. "I did something other than just stay inside and go to sleep."

Dennis nodded. "I figured that one out. I called you right after we talked because I wanted to tell you something, but you didn't answer. So I tried calling you every half hour until midnight. You didn't pick up, so I figured you'd gone out and that you'd tell me about it today. And no, I didn't try you on your cell phone. It wasn't that important, and I didn't want to interrupt whatever you were doing."

His voice was so calm, so kind, that all my dread about this conversation slipped away. Dennis wasn't nearly as scary as he looked. Our lunch arrived and, by tacit agreement, we ate before getting into the subject of my nocturnal wanderings. It took us only a few minutes to eat, during which time I decided to first tell Dennis about Armando, then to move on to the content of my conversation with Marisa and Carmen. It was all related, I knew that, but I needed more time for it all to come together in my mind.

Our waitress removed our dishes and brought us coffee—American for Dennis, a double espresso for me. Then I told Dennis about my dinner with Armando the night before. As was his custom, he listened quietly, keeping his thoughts to himself until I was finished.

"Well, that certainly sheds new light on things," Dennis said softly when I was done. "Now we should think about what to do next—without putting you in any danger."

"Diamond's boss was this Mickey, and her friend was Angie," I said. "And Diamond was working with the whales. That's something to go on."

Dennis poured another cup of coffee from the carafe on our table. He had inhaled the first, and I could tell that he was used to consuming vast quantities of caffeine.

"You were right about looking into the Cuban angle, Esmeralda," he said. "I have to give you that."

I found myself beaming and was a little surprised by how good his praise made me feel. "Nothing else made sense," I said. "But what about Maria Mercedes's picture in the apartment, hidden with the money? What do you think that means?"

"I don't know," Dennis admitted. He smiled. "I guess we'll find out as we go. But now we have a starting point. That's how it works. Now things can start falling into place."

We spent the next couple of minutes talking about what I had learned from the ladies at the church. Dennis seemed interested but reserved—he wasn't one to get excited about a rumor. I was glad to have spoken to the old women and Armando on my own, because I now knew that neither conversation would have been as candid with Dennis present. Things were happening for a reason, even if it wasn't clear at first.

It was almost four o'clock when we got up from the table. I had made some notes in my book, the first of which was to call and check in with Detective Morris. I was sure he would have called me if he learned anything important, but Dennis suggested I stay in touch to keep Diamond's disappearance on the front burner. When we reached the door leading to the pool promenade, my cell phone rang. I looked at the caller ID and saw that it was an unfamiliar local number.

"Just a second," I said, ducking into an alcove to answer it.

"Esmeralda? This is Oscar Maxwell," said the voice on the line. I paused, surprised. We hadn't exactly parted on the best of terms.

"Oscar," I said, loud enough for Dennis to hear.

"Listen, I don't have much time," Oscar said. "Yesterday, at that bar, remember how I told you about the skinny old guy with the eye patch? The one who came up to Diamond outside the newspaper building?"

"Yes, I remember," I said. I had a sinking feeling in the pit of my stomach. Oscar sounded agitated, almost panicked. "Why, Oscar? What's wrong?"

"You know I work the environmental desk, right?" Oscar

didn't wait for me to reply. "Well, the guy who works the crime desk here, Mark Reynolds, he's out sick today. He has the flu or something. Anyway, I'm covering for him."

"What are you trying to say, Oscar?" I asked, although I feared I knew the answer.

"I'm waiting for the crime scene unit to finish up," Oscar said. "But I can see enough from where I'm standing."

"What are you looking at, Oscar?" I heard Dennis behind me, hovering, his curiosity coming off him in waves.

I heard Oscar take a couple of deep breaths. "It's the same guy. Skinny, old, a black patch over his eye. I know it's him."

"Oh, no," I cried out, so upset that I almost said Armando's name. "What happened?"

"The guy got strangled," Oscar blurted out. "I'm standing by the alley where he's lying. He's in a bunch of garbage cans. There's still a cord around his neck."

"Are you sure it's the same man?" I almost shouted into the phone. "It could be someone else. You could be mistaken."

"It's the same guy. I'm not mistaken," Oscar said with a dark, hoarse laugh. "One of the techs told me that the old man was strangled so violently that his eye patch fell off. They found it next to him on the ground."

"Thank you, Oscar. Thank you for telling me." I was in shock, but I managed to keep my wits. I couldn't help the flood of images in my mind—Armando at dinner, Armando lying dead—but I knew enough not to reveal my connection to a murder victim while talking to a newspaper reporter. I needed to hang up before he thought to ask me any questions. It occurred to me that I wouldn't have received this call from Oscar if the other reporter hadn't called in sick. Chance was everywhere.

"I thought you'd want to know," Oscar said. "By the way, what do you think—"

"I'll call you later," I interrupted, and hung up.

I turned to Dennis and told him about Armando. He thought for a minute, his expression pinched and serious.

"We're going to have to change our to-do list," he said. "And we're going to have to do it fast."

We went back into the hotel, with Dennis leading and me following. I believed in luck, but I also knew when I was running out of time.

34

Bellagio casino—the point from which all roads diverged—my cell phone rang again. Again it was a local Las Vegas number, one I didn't recognize. Just before I answered it, I shrugged at Dennis to indicate that I didn't know who was calling.

"Is this Esmeralda Montoya?" a woman asked.

"Yes," I said. The reception in the hotel was never great, but at that moment it was terrible. I could barely make out what the caller was saying.

"This is Rose Martin, the manager at Mountain Peaks," she explained formally, as though I would have forgotten her.

"Oh, of course, Rose," I said. I covered the receiver with my hand and mouthed the name "Rose Martin" to Dennis.

"I hope this isn't a bad time," Rose said, considerate as always.

"Have you heard from my sister?" I asked, hope rising in my voice even though I knew it was unlikely that Diamond would have showed up at her apartment.

"No, I'm sorry," Rose said quickly. I shook my head at Dennis, letting him know that Diamond hadn't surfaced. "But there is something I think you should know."

"What is it?" I asked, knowing already that it wasn't going to be good news.

"Your sister's apartment has been broken into," Rose told me.

"Broken into? When? What did they take?" I asked. I glanced over at Dennis, who had folded his arms and was watching closely.

"I don't know much right now," Rose explained. "One of our security guards was making his rounds when he saw your sister's sliding door open. He knew your sister is missing and that you are looking for her, so he went upstairs and knocked on the door. No one answered, and that's when he came to tell me what he'd seen."

"And you went inside with your set of keys," I finished for her. "And that's when you found the place had been broken into."

"I'm sorry to have to give you the news, but I thought you should know right away." Rose explained. "If you want to come by and have a look, you can. I'm just about to notify the police."

"I'm on my way," I said, and hung up.

"We have to change that list again," I said to Dennis, who had figured out already what was going on. It all seemed surreal, with the bad news piling up so fast. I felt a flash of fear. Armando's murder and my sister's burglary had happened almost at the same time.

"Rose said she'd let me back into the apartment," I told Dennis. "And she hasn't called the police yet."

"Interesting," Dennis said. "Looks like we have more to talk about."

We almost ran through the Bellagio to get to Dennis's car which, given Dennis's relationship with the hotel's head of security, was right where we had left it hours before. A minute later we were back on Las Vegas Boulevard headed for the highway that would take us to Summerlin. I knew it was only a few miles away.

"What do you think happened to Armando?" I asked Dennis as he merged onto the midday traffic on US-95, which was heavy, forcing Dennis to concentrate on what he was doing.

"As I see it, there are two possible reasons for Armando's death," Dennis said, letting out a frustrated snort as a BMW cut us off. "Either he got killed because he talked to you last night, or it was a random mugging that just happened to take place right after your conversation. Given his distinctive appearance, we can rule out mistaken identity. And it certainly wasn't a suicide."

"Well, what do you think?" I asked.

"Look, all we have is what Oscar told you over the phone," Dennis replied. "He talked briefly to a crime scene tech, but he didn't really have too much information. It's hard to come to any conclusions based on what a spooked reporter told you from what he saw at a distance."

"But you have, I can tell," I said. "You have an opinion."

"Well, don't hold me to it, but I think the old man was killed because of you," Dennis said, staring straight ahead. "Somehow you're involved in this."

I thought the same thing, but it wasn't exactly comforting to hear Dennis say it. Up until then, the only person I considered to be in danger was Diamond. I didn't think I presented any threat to anyone because I had shown up and started asking questions about her. But now I thought there was someone who didn't want me to learn anything more.

"Do you think I'm in danger here?" I asked. He didn't reply, so I turned sideways to look at him. I could see his hands tighten on the steering wheel.

Dennis turned off the freeway onto the Summerlin Parkway. Instead of slowing down, he pressed on the accelerator; suddenly, the palm trees on the exit ramp were speeding past in a blur. The engine moaned in protest.

"Dennis, slow down," I said.

A moment later, Dennis regained control of himself. He slowed the car to a smooth stop at a red light. I realized he had lost his cool, which really made me feel frightened.

"Look, Esmeralda, we don't have any facts. All we have is speculation." Dennis said. "Let's focus on your sister's apartment and what happened there."

"I'll call Rose," I said. I pulled up the apartment manager's number on the phone's memory and called her. We were already on Town Center Drive, just seconds away.

Rose was waiting for us next to the security gate when we pulled up; she was flanked by the same two security guards we had met the first time we visited. The older one had abandoned his golf cart to stand at attention, as a sign of the gravity of the situation. Rose waved at us and pointed to the place where we'd parked before, next to the rental office. After we parked and got out, she joined us.

I couldn't help but notice that Rose looked pale and worried, although she was dressed nicely in a smart red-wine suit and black leather high-heeled shoes. I knew that one of the selling points of a place like Mountain Peaks was the tight security. Now a young woman had gone missing there and her apartment had been broken into. It wasn't a pleasant situation for Rose Martin.

We shook hands and were joined by the two guards. She introduced me and then waved vaguely at Dennis. Then she turned to the younger of the two guards.

"This is Dan Messenger," Rose said. "He's the guard who noticed the sliding door of your sister's apartment was open."

My heart sank. I remembered Dan as the dumber of the two, the one who struck me as possessing a single-digit IQ. I knew that an elephant could have been carting possessions out of Diamond's apartment and Dan would have barely noticed. Still, I had to give him credit for seeing that something was wrong.

Dan Messenger was unimposing, about fifty years old, tall, thin, with sparse wispy hair combed across his head. He wore black plastic glasses with frames so thick that it was impossible to tell what color his eyes were. He wasn't exactly a figure who would frighten off a would-be burglar. Understandably, he also seemed upset and ill at ease.

"Can you tell me what happened, Dan?" I asked.

Dan pretty much repeated what Rose had told me, adding a couple of details. The poor man was so scared that he spoke in a low voice and tripped over his words.

"Did you call the police?" Dennis asked Rose.

"I'm about to," Rose said, nodding to me. "I assume you want to go inside your sister's apartment, right?"

"Yes, please," I replied.

Rose turned to the guards. "I'm going to take Ms. Montoya and her friend to Ms. Navarro's apartment. If you need me, call me on my cell phone."

Rose led the way quickly through the grounds of the complex. I didn't see anyone around, which I thought was kind of strange. As I remembered, the grounds were meticulously kept. It was too bad Mountain Peaks didn't place as high a value on security guards as it did on landscaping.

"I have to warn you, it's a mess," Rose told me when we reached the stairwell leading up to Diamond's apartment.

"I'm ready," I told her.

We climbed the stairs and waited on the landing while Rose fiddled with her keyring. Finally she found the one she was looking for.

"Was the door unlocked when you came to check things out?" Dennis asked.

Rose thought for a moment. "Actually, both the front door locks were locked when I came. It looks like the burglar came and went through the sliding door on the porch."

"Can you wait a little while before you call the police?" Dennis asked.

Rose paused, and looked away. "That's what I'm doing," she said. "All I ask is that you don't tell anyone. I'll call them the minute you're done looking around."

"Thank you," I said, feeling my eyes water. Rose had only met me once, but she was risking her job for me.

"I feel terrible for you," Rose said quietly. "It was the least I could do to help."

Dennis reached into his suit pocket and pulled out three pairs of latex gloves. He handed a pair to me, then one to Rose.

"Let's cover ourselves," he said matter-of-factly. "We don't want to leave prints if we touch anything."

Rose, shocked, started putting on the gloves. "Dennis is a former New York homicide detective," I explained, not wanting her to think my companion was some kind of a freak who traveled around all the time with latex gloves.

"I see," Rose said, seeming reassured.

"Can we open the door now?" Dennis asked when all three of us had donned our gloves.

Rose carefully inserted the keys in the locks and turned them. The door opened easily.

"Remember what I said," she warned me. "The place is a real mess."

Dennis walked in first, with me right behind him. I cried out involuntarily when I got a look and saw how completely Diamond's home had been trashed.

Diamond didn't have much furniture, but what she owned had been destroyed. The green canvas couch had been ripped to shreds and white stuffing was scattered all around the room. The coffee table had been overturned, its legs taken apart. The plants had been pulled from their pots and the dirt was ground into the floor. The posters on the walls had been torn down, and the wooden table and chairs in the dining area had been smashed and flung against the wall. The contents of the kitchen cabinets had been spilled out onto the floor. The sliding glass door stood open.

I stood there, just taking it all in. I saw Dennis moving toward the bedroom. I followed him, while Rose remained outside.

The scene in the bedroom was even worse than the living room. The sheets and blankets had been yanked from the bed, and the mattress had been ripped to shreds. The pillows were slashed open, and a layer of feathers covered everything in the room. The chair in the corner had suffered the same fate as its counterparts in the dining area. Diamond's closet was emptied, with her clothes, bags, sweaters, and shoes scattered everywhere, many of them apparently ripped apart.

In the bathroom, the medicine cabinet had been emptied out onto the floor, and the contents of all the bottles had been emptied. The little room smelled sickly sweet, a combination of shampoo and conditioner, hand lotion, and perfume. Even the toothpaste had been squeezed out of the tube and into the sink.

I broke down and sobbed, tears pouring onto my cheeks. Whoever had done this was an animal. If they could do this to an apartment, I was terrified to think what they could do to a person.

Dennis found me in the hall and put his arm around me. I turned to him and buried my face in his chest.

"Esmeralda, it's OK," he said softly.

"What were they looking for?" I thought of the bag of marijuana hidden in my room safe at the Bellagio. I whispered, "It wasn't the weed, was it?"

"No, that wasn't what they were after," Dennis replied confidently.

He left me standing there and walked into the bedroom, where a bedside table had been turned over and its contents scattered on the floor. He knelt down next to it and, touching it very gently, moved it a couple of inches.

"Well, this might not have been all they were looking for," he said. "But they did find something."

I walked to him, moved over the chaotic landscape of my sister's things on the floor. Then I saw what Dennis was pointing at.

"My God," I said. "The tape from the answering machine. They took it."

"That's right," Dennis growled. "It's a good thing we listened to it before. Someone didn't want that tape to be heard."

"But they don't know we listened to it. Right?" I asked.

Dennis stood up and headed back to the living room. "I'm going to check out the photographs on that altar table," he said.

Like everything else, the altar table had been turned over. The framed pictures were scattered on the floor, opened up, with their backings ripped. Thinking of what I had found there, behind the picture of our family, I said, "I guess we got here just in time when we did."

"Good thing you rescued your ancestor and the cash," Dennis said. He picked up the picture of my family and stared at it.

Rose came into the apartment. "Is anything missing?" she asked. "Did whoever did this take anything?"

"No," Dennis and I answered simultaneously.

Rose looked at us with an expression that suggested she knew we were lying to her. "Are you finished looking around?" she asked in a nervous voice. "I need to call the police now."

"One last thing." Dennis walked over to the sliding door and inspected the lock. "Yeah, it looked like they came in through here. The lock's broken."

"Please call the police now," I said to Rose. "I really can't thank you enough for letting me come in here."

"You're going through a bad time. It's the least I can do," Rose said. She stepped aside for Dennis and me to leave the apartment. Once all three of us were outside, she locked the front door.

When we were walking down the stairs, I thought of something. "Has someone named Detective Morris been in touch with you about Diamond's disappearance?" I asked Rose.

"Detective Morris?" Rose repeated. "No. No one by that name has been in touch with me."

I explained who Detective Morris was and added that he would probably be calling Rose about Diamond. I was a little surprised that he hadn't been to Mountain Peaks to look inside Diamond's apartment, but I figured that he must have been pursuing other leads. It seemed more obvious than ever that I was going to have to find Diamond on my own.

Once we were on the road, I looked over at Dennis. He had both hands on the wheel, and he was staring out at the highway.

"Looks like we're going to have to tear up the to-do list," I finally said.

Dennis tightened his grip on the wheel, a grim expression on his face.

"Looks that way," was all he said.

35

"I KNOW WE HAVE TO TALK, but I can't deal with the Clipped Chip," I said to Dennis as we approached the freeway exit taking us back to the Strip. "Unless you have some other place in mind, let's just go back to the Bellagio."

"The Bellagio it is," Dennis agreed.

Before I felt it coming, I realized that I had a splitting headache—thinking about how I hadn't talked to Tony lately seemed to trigger a particularly nasty burst of pain behind my forehead. I dug into my purse for some Advil and popped three into my mouth, gulping them down without water. I slouched back against the seat and closed my eyes as soon as the pills took effect. I must have dozed off because the next thing I knew Dennis was softly saying my name. I opened my eyes and saw that we were parked in Dennis's usual spot in front of the Bellagio.

"We're here!" I exclaimed. "I fell asleep." I looked at the clock on the dashboard and saw that it was almost nine o'clock. It had been just after seven when we left Mountain Peaks.

"You seemed so exhausted," Dennis explained. "I thought it would do you some good if I let you sleep for a while."

I was embarrassed that Dennis had seen me slip into such a deep sleep and imagined him looking at me slumped in my seat. The only good news was that my headache was gone.

Everything suddenly weighed on me—my lack of success finding Diamond, my deteriorating home situation, the threat represented by Armando's murder and the break-in. Whose idea was it for me to deal with all this, I asked myself. I should have been back in Miami picking colors for an office building's lobby.

Then I reminded myself: I was the one doing this. If it wasn't for me, then it wasn't going to get done. And I had Dennis to help me.

"Are you ready?" I asked him.

Dennis nodded and we headed for the hotel entrance. I was so preoccupied this time that I barely glanced at the fountains.

"Where to now?" Dennis asked, waving to a valet who was busily helping hotel guests into and out of their cars. The flow of humanity around the hotel was unceasing.

"My room," I said. To hell with propriety. My life was on the line. And no one had to know.

"OK." If Dennis was surprised by my suggestion, he didn't show it. "Lead the way, Esmeralda."

We walked through the casino toward the elevators. I showed my key to the security guard, and Dennis and I joined a Japanese couple in the nearest elevator. I punched in the floor and we rode up together in silence.

We got out on my floor and mumbled good-bye to the Japanese couple, who smiled and looked away uncomfortably. I led Dennis through the interminable hallways, searching in my pocket for the room key. After about half a dozen turns, we reached my room. As I put the key in the slot, I hoped that I hadn't left the place in a mess.

Once the door was open, I stepped aside. "Please," I said, motioning Dennis inside.

"Thanks." Dennis walked into the room and looked around. "Very nice," he said.

In his black pants and white shirt, Dennis contrasted starkly with the cream colors in the room. The room was distinctly feminine, which in contrast made Dennis looked extremely tall and masculine, almost tough and dangerous. For a second I saw him as someone I had picked up in a bar somewhere, someone capable of anything. After all the time I had spent with him the past few days, it was almost surreal to see him in this new light.

"It's pretty comfortable," I said. I saw that the night maid had been in to turn the bed. Unfortunately, she had also spread out my nightgown on the bed, arranging it artistically so that it covered a large portion of the comforter. Dennis stood in the middle of the room, seeming not to know what to do with his hands. He was as uneasy as I'd ever seen him.

"Do you want something to drink?" I motioned to the minibar. "There's food in there, too."

"No, thanks, I'm fine for now." Dennis glanced around, obviously trying not to look at the bed.

It struck me that I didn't even know if this man was married. And, if he was, I didn't know what his wife would think about his being in this circumstance. The situation between Tony and me was strained, but I certainly wouldn't have wanted him to know that I had invited my limousine driver up to my room. Diamond might have been missing, and my life might have been in danger, but I was still a Cuban woman married to a Cuban man. That meant some lines couldn't be crossed—especially when I had left my husband at home to deal with three boys and a flatulent dog.

I took a deep breath, then walked to the table by the window. "Might as well start figuring out this whole mess," I said.

"Fine." Dennis took the chair closest to the window.

I sat in the other and took my notebook out of my purse. For the next couple of hours we talked through the situation. Dennis wanted to go all the way back to the beginning, asking for details about Maria Mercedes's appearance and subsequent prophesy. We talked through the break-in, and I went through the facts of what the two nuns had told me outside the church that afternoon. Dennis listened carefully while I recounted everything Armando had told me before he got killed. At one point I put my head in my hands and tried to remember what my life had been like before Mama and Papa called us all together in their apartment just days before.

I had taken the nap in the car, but pretty soon I started yawning.

"I think the next step is getting into the casino, where the whales play," I said to Dennis. "That way I can see what Diamond saw and maybe find someone who knew her."

Dennis had been quiet and supportive until then, but now his face dropped and he forcefully slapped the edge of the table with his open hand.

"You want to get involved at the casino, after the old man was killed for talking to you?" Dennis barked. He started to stand. "No, Esmeralda. Absolutely not."

"It's the best way, and you know it," I said. "I'll just go in and look around, that's all. No one has to know who I am."

"Look, this situation is getting dangerous. Whoever is behind this has something to hide." Dennis started pacing. My room, which had seemed so large before, suddenly seemed claustrophobic. Dennis folded his arms, trying to contain his temper as he moved back and forth. "We have to think of something else."

"It's my sister who's missing," I said, my voice breaking. "I have to find her. I'll do anything to find her."

Dennis's eyes widened and he looked at me. "I know that," he said, sounding stunned.

I got up, and he came to me. He pulled me close to him, so tight that I could feel his ribs. I began to cry, giving in to the despair that tugged at me, trying to bring me down.

"I have to do something, Dennis," I said as I tried to regain my breath. "You have to understand that. If I'm in danger as a result, then so be it. That's the way it is."

I pulled back a little and looked into his eyes. A flash went through me, a strange feeling that I couldn't quite recognize.

"I can't live with myself otherwise," I said.

"I knew you would say that," Dennis said, his arms still around me. "Otherwise you wouldn't be you."

I put my head against his chest, happy just to be comforted. I was glad Dennis couldn't see my face, because I must have been a mess. My nose was running and my eyes burned. I was never able to pull off ladylike crying. When the tears came, they took over.

"Help me figure out what to do," I said to Dennis. "One way or the other, I'm going to find my sister."

Dennis pulled out my chair for me to sit down. "All right," he said. "Let's talk it through."

"One thing," I said. I went to the closet, knelt down, and opened up the safe inside. I took out the bag of marijuana and the cash, then the pictures of Diamond and Maria Mercedes. I arranged everything in the center of the table, then motioned for Dennis to join me.

"What's this?" Dennis asked.

"I told you I work as a designer, right?" I asked.

"Of course you did," Dennis said.

"Well, one thing I've learned—it never hurts to have props in place when I'm trying to close a deal."

Despite himself, Dennis smiled.

36

WE SAT ON EACH SIDE OF the table, the photos, cash, and grass between us. Dennis and I were jotting notes—it turned out we shared the trait of thinking clearer when we were able to write things down. Dennis's page contained diagrams, boxes connected by lines, as though he were tracing family trees.

"What if Diamond was kidnapped?" I asked.

"Kidnapped?" A look of caution flashed across Dennis's face, so briefly that I thought I might have imagined it. "Why? Your family hasn't received a ransom demand, have they?"

"No, but isn't it a possibility?" I asked. "People don't just vanish into thin air. As far as we know, she hasn't turned up at a hospital, or in jail, or at the morgue. And her car hasn't turned up, either."

Dennis laid down his pen. "When people are kidnapped, it's because whoever has kidnapped them wants to get something," he said. "That means a ransom. I don't get the feeling that's what's going on here. Kidnappers wouldn't have waited so long to make a move. The longer they hold someone, the greater the risk they take."

"You're right," I said quietly.

Dennis looked down at his page of diagrams, going back to

studying them. I suddenly felt a swell of acute frustration that surprised me with its intensity.

"Well, where is she, Dennis?" I said, my voice louder than I'd intended it to be. "What's happened to my sister?"

Dennis fixed those crystalline eyes on me. "I think right now would be an excellent time to raid the minibar," he said.

Without waiting for my consent, he jogged over to the small refrigerator, picked up the key resting on top of it, and opened it up. "What do you want?" he asked. "It looks like they have just about everything in here."

"White wine," I said. I had looked through the minibar, and I remembered that there was a decent bottle of chablis inside. Dennis brought it to the table, along with a wineglass and a bottle of beer for himself. He poured me some wine and cracked open his beer.

"Cheers," he said.

A few minutes later, the tension in the room had begun to lessen. Dennis sat back in his chair and allowed himself a heavy sigh.

"I have to gain access to the whales at the Star Casino," I said. "Obviously Armando can't help me, but maybe his friend can—Mario Mendoza, the old man who also worked at La Estrella."

Dennis sipped his beer. "This Mario Mendoza—do you know him?"

I shook my head. "Maybe I would if I saw him. Right now I don't remember him. My father introduced me to a lot of people."

"Why do you think he'll help you?" Dennis asked. "He's going to know the situation is dangerous."

"Maybe he'll want to find out who killed his friend," I said. "Armando said that they were close. And Mario is probably still loyal to my family—most of the old La Estrella employees feel that way."

I put as much conviction as I could manage into my voice, hoping that Dennis would buy into my optimism. I was happy that he was no longer totally opposed to my idea of getting close to the whales at the casino where my sister once worked.

We talked on, and it was about three in the morning when the grumbling in my stomach grew so loud that I felt embarrassed by it. Dennis and I had grown close enough to share drinks in my room, but somehow ordering food and eating there together seemed too intimate. Tony might not have been treating me well lately, but I was still married to him. Finally, though, I couldn't take it any more. I looked at my watch and calculated that it had been almost twelve hours since I'd had a proper meal.

"Are you hungry?" I asked Dennis. "Would you like to go downstairs and get something to eat?"

Dennis stood up right away. "Sure, yeah." he said. He folded his paper and put it in his pocket. "We're about done here, anyway, don't you think?"

I started to collect the money and the marijuana. "I'm going to put these back in the safe," I said.

"Good idea," Dennis agreed. "You don't want the housekeeper walking in and seeing those lying around."

I put the contraband back in the safe and locked it. I would have liked to go to the bathroom to freshen up, but I felt awkward about doing so with Dennis around.

"Ready?" I asked. Maybe it was the late hour, but I was suddenly as uncomfortable as a teenager on her first date.

We walked through the long hallways to the elevator, then went downstairs to the Café Bellagio. It might have been three in the morning, but the place was packed—there was even a line of customers waiting to be seated. When our turn came, we followed our hostess to an open table. I looked around and saw that people were eating all different kinds of food—some had ordered breakfast, some sandwiches, while others were eating full-scale dinners. There was no such thing as time in Las Vegas, not if someone decided to ignore it.

Dennis ordered a rare steak, I asked for pasta, and we both ordered salads. I asked for the wine list and ordered a bottle of cabernet sauvignon. We ate quickly, without saying much. When we were done, we walked outside to where the car was parked.

"See you later today," Dennis said, reaching for his keys. He was right. It was today.

"Today," I repeated, my mind feeling numbed with sleeplessness. I looked around at the bright lights, thinking that somewhere in this city was a person who had killed Armando. And perhaps someone who was responsible for Diamond's disappearance.

Dennis paused before getting into his car and was watching me.

"Don't worry," he said. "You'll find her."

Dennis drove away as the first faint light of morning started to tint the sky. I went back to my room and had a steaming hot bath. It would be time to get up soon, but my mind was still racing with everything that had happened.

Just as I was about to get in bed, I realized that my cell phone hadn't rung during the long evening. The last time I had used it was to call Rose at the apartment complex to tell her we were about to arrive. I turned on the lamp next to my bed, wincing at the bright light, and took my phone out of my purse.

I was about to plug in the cell phone to charge it when I realized that it wasn't turned on. That meant that if anyone had called, they would have been delivered directly to my voice mail. I looked closely at the screen and saw that I had seven messages.

"*Ay,*" I whispered to myself. I scanned down the list of numbers. Two were from Gabriel, one from Sapphire, one each from my mother and my father, one from Dorcas, and one from Adrianna.

I quickly listened to Gabriel's messages, and laughed out loud when I discovered that they largely dealt with Buster and his digestive problems. Because of the dog's constant farting, Tony had gone out and bought a low-fat special-diet dog food.

"Mom, Buster's so miserable," my son said on the recording. "I hope you don't mind, but I dipped into the money you gave me. I've been buying Buster Whoppers from the Burger King down the street and giving them to him when Dad's not looking. I didn't know what else to do. Buster's really happy now, though. So everything's fine."

I knew Gabriel wanted to talk about more than Buster, but this was his way of letting me know that he was handling my absence.

Sapphire had called just to check in with me. Mama and Papa had done the same, though I sighed to myself when I heard the borderline desperation in their voices. Dorcas had called to tell me to contact her if I needed anything. Adrianna had done the same. It was still night, so there was no point contemplating calling anyone back.

I noticed that Tony still hadn't called.

I turned off the light and lay back in bed. I should have gone to sleep right away, but my mind was too active. I thought about Dennis and how I still knew nothing about his personal life. I also thought about how he carried a cell phone but that it never rang. I assumed that, at some point, he would receive calls about other limousine-driver jobs, but that hadn't happened. Maybe he retrieved his calls when I wasn't around. Maybe what really troubled me was that we had spent an evening together in my room, but that he hadn't made any kind of romantic advance toward me at all.

We had hugged when I was in the depths of despair about Diamond but that had been it. I didn't have an ego that required every man I came into contact with to make a play for me, but I also knew that Dennis and I had established a bond that went beyond looking for my sister. Maybe he was so aloof because I was married, or because he was technically my employee, or because of the difference in our ages. Or maybe it was the simplest reason of all—that he wasn't attracted to me. *Dios mio.*

The sky was lightening outside my window. I had to get some rest or else I was going to be useless the rest of the day. The last time I remembered staying up all night was when the twins were both teething, seven years ago. It had been so dreadful that I had basically tried to erase it from my memory as quickly as possible. It hadn't been one of my shining moments as a mother, with two babies up all night screaming in pain over their inflamed gums. None of the remedies my American pediatrician had prescribed had been effective, so I decided to take matters into my own hands.

It had been at four in the morning on my third consecutive sleepless night that I truly became desperate. Tony was blissfully asleep in the guest room, as he had been during the entire episode, so he knew nothing about what was going on. I took the boys out of their cribs, strapped them into their car seats, and drove straight to Little Havana. In my hand was the address of a Santería priestess whom Dorcas had told me about. It was close to dawn when I banged on her door, but she was awake, as though she knew I was coming.

I tried to ignore the goat tethered in the yard as I went inside. Three scary spells later, the priestess gave me some herbs with instructions for what to do with them. The boys were still awake, still crying, while I boiled the herbs in the kitchen and poured the resultant green liquid into their bottles. I was so desperate that I made a pledge to myself: If the herbs didn't work, then I was going to hand the boys over to a responsible adult—not Tony— and walk away. By "responsible adult," I meant anyone who had slept at least two consecutive nights in the last month.

After they drank their bottles, the twins slept through the next day, and most of the following night as well. I threw the rest of the herbs away, knowing that I might be eventually tempted to use them again. I had no idea what was in the solution the priestess gave me. Apart from Dorcas, I never told anyone what I had done.

Why was I thinking about this now, I asked myself as light filtered through the window. Because I felt guilty, probably. The boys had gone days without me, and I was barely closer to finding their aunt than when I first arrived in Las Vegas.

And I was lying in bed thinking about a man other than their father.

Contemplating my life back home, I wondered how I ever was going to step back into the role of Tony's wife. It had only been a few days, but those tense mornings and silent dinners felt like features of a past life I didn't like remembering.

As I drifted off to sleep, I wondered who I was becoming.

37

at least four hours. That was shot when my cell phone started to ring. It felt as though I had just closed my eyes when I picked it up and saw that it was Ruby on the line.

"Esmeralda, I'm so glad I reached you," she said, her voice a hoarse whisper. "Were you asleep?"

"Sort of," I mumbled. "Why are you being so quiet?"

"I'm in the courthouse waiting for my case to be called—you know, the big one I've been working on," Ruby replied. "I just had to call to see how you're doing."

At least that's what I thought she had said—between her whisper, the bad reception, and the background noise, it was hard to be certain.

"I'm fine, but it's been really hard out here," I said. "I think I'll know more in a day or so. How's everyone at home holding up?"

Even with the bad connection, I could hear my sister sigh. "Not well, I have to say."

Her words sank into my fuzzy brain, and I sat bolt upright in bed. Ruby was the mistress of understatement, and for her to say such a thing, conditions must have been really bad back home.

"Ruby, I'm doing everything I can," I told her.

"I didn't mean to imply you aren't," Ruby said quickly. "Please don't think that's what I meant. It's just that . . ."

Her voice trailed away. "I know," I told her. Ruby was typically so composed that I shivered at the sound of her struggling to express herself.

"Listen, they're calling my case, so I have to go," Ruby said. "Contact Mama and Papa when you can. They're really worried."

She hung up. I looked over at the clock on the night stand and saw that it was seven—ten in the morning in Miami. I thought about calling my parents—they usually slept until noon, but I knew they would welcome my call. The problem was what to say to them. I didn't want to make them more worried than they already were. I held the phone for a long time, almost calling them but not. The news about Armando alone would have sent them into a panic.

I had turned off the light at around six, which meant that I had gotten almost exactly one hour of sleep. It was too early to call anyone in Las Vegas, so I lay back in bed and closed my eyes. After half an hour, though, I gave up and went to the table to look at my notebook. I read through my notes in bed, thinking, hoping, that I would remember something I missed. I knew what was in the notebook by heart and barely had to read to conceive of every line I'd written.

I had to believe that I would somehow know if Diamond were dead. Some inner voice would tell me that. Instead, the voice was telling me that I was the only one who could find her. I stared at the notebook, almost feeling Diamond's presence out there somewhere in the city. I finally noticed that it was almost eight. I ordered another continental breakfast and took a shower while I waited for it to arrive. By nine I had showered, dressed, and eaten. I took out the Las Vegas phone book and found Mario Mendoza's number—thanking God that he was listed. I jotted the number down in my notebook and picked up the phone.

Mario, I figured, was bound to be awake—no one who knew Armando was going to be sleeping well anytime soon. I made the sign of the cross as I dialed the number. Mario picked up on the first ring. It was almost as though he had been expecting my call.

"This is Esmeralda Navarro," I said, using my maiden name. "Is this Mario?"

"Esmeralda, *niña!*" Mario exclaimed. "Armando told me that you were here. Did you hear what happened to him?"

The line went silent, and I heard Mario attempting to stifle a sob. "Yes, Mario, it's awful," I said. "I'm so sorry."

"You know, we were like brothers," Mario said in a broken voice. "We lived next to each other for thirty years. I saw him lying out there in the alley. Like garbage. That's how they left him—out there with the garbage."

Mario exhaled so loudly that I heard him quiver with grief. I tightened my hold on the phone, almost overcome by his emotion.

"Mario, I would like to come and visit you," I said gently. "Would that be possible?"

"*Ay,* Esmeralda, I'm not fit for company," Mario replied.

"Mario, please. You're part of the Estrella family," I said. "Nothing can change that."

"All right. If you really want to." As soon as he said that, I knew that Mario had been hoping I would insist. He gave me his address and directions for getting there.

"I'll be there soon, Mario," I told him.

After we hung up, I replayed the conversation in my mind. Armando had told Mario that I was in Las Vegas. I wondered what other information Armando had confided to his old friend. I could picture the two old men, retired, with so much in common and so much time on their hands. I imagined them after Armando and I talked, in the hours before Armando died, the two old men exchanging memories of the Navarro family and La Estrella.

I looked over at the clock. I had an hour still before I was due to meet Dennis downstairs. I knew Gabriel was in class, but I called his cell phone, anyway; I left a long message on his voice mail, reassuring him that it was all right that he had fed Buster Whoppers. I added that it wasn't a great idea to be sneaking around behind his father's back, but I knew it was a special situation, and that we would talk about it as soon as I was home.

After punching in another familiar number, I immediately realized that I might have made a mistake—Sapphire's unmedicated voice was so loud that I had to pull the phone a full two inches away from my ear.

"Tell me you've found her," she said.

"I haven't," I said quietly. "I'm still trying."

Sapphire was silent for a moment, and I swore I could feel her vibrating in her chair.

"I have an idea for another show," she said, changing gears instantly. "It's going to be about a woman's rebirth—but instead of being born from a woman, or from the sea, she's going to come from a giant vat of *arroz con pollo*. It came to me last night, when I was thinking about Diamond, and about my own life. This is the only direction my work can go in right now. It's so obvious, I have to laugh."

She proceeded to do just that, a nervous cackle that had me wincing. Only Sapphire would seriously consider the idea of a performance-art piece based on the artist emerging from a platter of chicken and yellow rice—one of the unofficial national dishes of Cuba. Listening to Sapphire talk more about her show, I wondered how she was going to incorporate her trademark blue color into it. I didn't ask her, though, because I was afraid she might disclose it. I listened to her for another five minutes before I cut her off, telling her I would call her back later. She was still talking when I hung up. I wondered how long it would take before she realized I wasn't any longer on the line.

I debated whom to call next—Dorcas or Adrianna—and decided that my Miami friend had priority. When I called her, though, I was put straight through to her voice mail. I left a message and hung up, then decided to skip calling Adrianna. I didn't really feel like dealing with her.

Soon it was almost time to meet Dennis. I checked my makeup in the bathroom mirror—avoiding for the moment asking myself why I was so concerned about my appearance. When I went down, I found him waiting by his car in the same spot, wearing the same outfit. I think I would have fainted from shock if I ever saw him wearing anything else.

"Good morning," I said. "Did you get some sleep?"

"Some," he answered. "You?"

"Some." I walked around to the passenger side. "I talked to Mario, and he's expecting me."

"Let's go," Dennis said. He walked around and opened the door for me. I should have opened it for myself, I realized, that was our protocol now. But I was so exhausted, and burnt-out from fear, that I felt as though I was about a half-second behind the rest of the world. I wondered how Dennis was really holding up—probably fine, after the horrors he'd surely witnessed in New York.

I handed Dennis the slip of paper containing Mario's address. "He lives in the same building that Armando did," I said. "They had apartments next to each other for thirty years."

Dennis nodded. "Tough business," he muttered, starting the car.

Mario's apartment was in a modest three-story building on Stardust Road, off the older part of the Strip. Its stucco was cracking, but it looked as though the residents were making an effort to keep the place up. As we turned into the parking lot in front of the building, I saw a flash of a back alley that apparently ran parallel to Stardust Road.

"I think that's where they found Armando," I said, pointing it out.

"Do you want to go have a look?" Dennis asked, expertly maneuvering the limousine into a space marked for compact cars. "I'll go with you, if you want."

We got out of the car and stood there for a while, looking in the direction of the alley. I finally shook my head and replied, "No." It somehow seemed disrespectful and ghoulish to go to the place where Armando had died.

"I'm just going to go inside to talk to Mario," I said.

"OK," Dennis replied. "I'll be waiting."

I went up a rickety, shaky elevator to the second floor. When the door opened with a lurch, I made a mental note to take the fire escape on the way down. I slowly walked along an open corridor until I found Number 202, at the very end, with Mario's name on a plastic card next to the doorbell. Mario must have seen me coming: he opened up the door before I had a chance to knock.

Mario hugged and kissed me as I stepped into the apartment. I took a whiff, making me almost wish I'd arranged to meet him someplace else. It was a little apartment, a studio, and it smelled of unwashed clothes and stale cigars. Mario's open, welcoming expression made me feel a pang of guilt for minding the odor of the place. Still, he had obviously been alone in there for far too long. He needed to open the doors and windows and let in some light and air. I realized that this was probably true of his life as well.

"Can I get you anything?" Mario asked, heading toward the kitchenette. "Coffee? Orange juice?"

"No, thanks," I said. I wasn't going to dwell on the smell of Mario's apartment, but I also wasn't going to feign an appetite or thirst.

Mario Mendoza could have been Armando's brother. They were both small, leathery-skinned, and bald. They even moved in the same spry way and shared a self-deprecating manner. Mario wore a tan suit, a pink shirt underneath, and two-toned lace-up shoes. I suspected that he had dressed for my benefit, and I was touched by the gesture.

I didn't remember ever meeting Mario specifically. Armando I remembered because of the eye patch, but Mario could have been one of many older former workers at La Estrella. I decided that it would make him happy if I behaved as though I did remember him.

We sat on the ratty old couch and made small talk—mostly about Havana and about La Estrella. He had talked to Armando, and, as a result, was also convinced that one day soon he would return to take his old job as a wheel dealer at the casino.

Finally I decided to try to focus his thoughts. "Mario, I know you and Armando were very close," I said.

Mario shook his head slowly from side to side. "*Ay*," he whispered. "I loved him like my own brother."

"Do you know about my sister Diamond?" I asked.

"Yes, I know how Armando got her a job at that new casino, the Star." Mario shook his head and sighed. "Armando felt very guilty about that. He thought she had gotten into some trouble, and that it was his fault. He wanted to call your family, but I told him to wait. I told him someone from the Navarro family would come out here to look for the girl. And I was right, wasn't I? Here you are."

"You *were* right, Mario," I said, trying to smile.

Mario's smile dissolved. "And look what happened, Esmeralda," he sobbed. "It got him killed."

This turn made me shift forward on the sofa cushion. "What got him killed?"

"Meeting with you. Talking with you. Telling you about Diamond." Mario talked flatly, without rancor or accusation. "I told him to stay away from you, to let the Navarro family handle their own business. But he wanted to do the right thing. He was loyal. Armando was always that way."

Mario got up from the sofa with a heavy sigh and trudged off to the kitchen. He took out a glass and poured himself some water from the tap. He downed half the glass, refilled it, then came back into the living room. He stopped in front of the window and held the glass up to the light.

"See?" he said proudly. It was a glass from La Estrella, with the image of the casino etched onto the crystal. "I took it with me when I left Havana. I hope your father wouldn't mind."

"Of course not. He'll be very happy to know that you have it," I reassured the old man. Somehow I suspected that the glass wasn't the only thing he had taken from La Estrella, but that was his business.

"Maybe Armando was mugged," I said, my voice falling flat in the stale, stagnant air. "Maybe it was a random robbery."

Mario gave me a sad look, as though I shouldn't allow myself the luxury of entertaining such foolish thoughts.

"Be careful," he said, his voice grave. "Armando came straight here after he had dinner with you at Landry's. We talked until very late. When he left, I thought he was going back to his apartment. I went to bed."

"You never saw him again?" I asked.

Mario's nose twitched. "I woke up when I heard the police cars in the alley," he said. "My neighbor, the widow two doors down, she was out in the hall. She said there was a body found in the alley. I knew right away that it was Armando."

"You must have some idea who killed him," I said.

Mario shook his head slowly. "I know one thing," he said, his voice raspy and quiet. "Whoever did it will come after me next. After all, here I am talking to you. They have no way of knowing what I said."

"You can't think that!" I said with alarm. "The police will investigate and find out who killed Armando."

Mario waved that idea away, as though it was an annoying fly buzzing around. "Think about it, Esmeralda," the old man said, perfectly composed. "Someone is watching you."

"Then you have to go," I told him. "Go away for a little while, until this thing is settled."

"I don't think I will do that," he said slowly. "I have no place to go."

I followed his gaze to the wall, where there were two framed photographs: one of Armando and Mario smiling on a Havana street, another of the two men decades older on the Las Vegas Strip.

"I have nothing left," Mario said.

"Don't say that," I insisted. "What about La Estrella? What about what Diamond told Armando?"

I had no idea why Diamond had led the two men to believe they would resume their old jobs, but I was willing to try anything to make Mario protect himself.

Mario looked up at me and smiled.

"Your family was very good to me," he said. He stood up straight and buttoned his jacket. "You gave me work, you helped me find a job here when I needed it. Now I am an old man. Maybe I should not cling to ridiculous stories."

"Mario, there's always hope," I said.

"Yes, there is," he agreed, leading me gently to the door. "And it belongs to the young. Look out for yourself, Esmeralda, and do me one favor."

"Anything," I said as he opened the door.

"Find your sister," Mario said, taking my hand. "She is a beautiful young woman. A true jewel. I don't believe she did anything to deserve this kind of trouble. If there's one thing we don't need, you and me, it's any more trouble."

Despite the morning heat, I felt a chill. Mario kissed me twice, then closed the door before I could say anything else to him. I heard the sound of three locks being thrown, then I walked down the fire escape to the parking lot below.

Dennis checked me out carefully as I approached.

"How did it go?" he asked. "Is this guy going to help you?"

"I didn't really ask for his help." I said as Dennis opened the door for me. "This turned into a condolence call."

Dennis looked at me with disbelief, then slipped his glasses down his nose to fire those laser beam eyes at me.

"I see," he said dryly, then came around to his side of the car.

"Now what?" he asked.

"Now we go to Plan B," I told him.

"There's a Plan B?" he asked as he steered the car onto Stardust Drive.

I started thinking fast and furiously. For a Cuban, for a Navarro, there was always a Plan B.

"*Sí,*" I said.

Never let them see you sweat.

38

WE WERE STOPPED AT A red light on Las Vegas Boulevard when Dennis turned to me. "So what about this Plan B of yours?" he asked. "Are you going to tell me about it, or is it some kind of a secret?"

I pulled myself out of my swirling thoughts. Dennis had been so opposed to my trying to get at the casino whales that I figured he would hit the roof if I told him what I was considering.

"I'll tell you about it," I said slowly. "But I have to think everything through first."

Dennis sighed. He had seemed almost relieved that I had come away from Mario with no new information or ideas, but I knew that was because he thought I was in danger and he was trying to protect me. I surely wasn't going to tell Dennis about Mario's sense of fatalism about his own immediate future.

But the fact was, seeing Mario had only cemented my resolve to gain access to the world of the casino whales. That was the realm in which Diamond was last known to be working, before her disappearance. My next plan of action, though, was going to be my own—it wasn't going to rely on the help of others.

The light turned green, and Dennis went back to concentrating on his driving. We hadn't talked about where we were going next, so Dennis was automatically taking us back to the Bellagio.

We never spent a lot of time making small talk, but during this drive the silence was uncomfortably thick between us.

Once we had arrived at our customary parking space—miraculously open, as always—I turned to Dennis. He slipped his glasses off, and I found myself assuming an awkward expression.

"What's on your mind?" Dennis asked.

"It's a delicate subject," I began.

"Go ahead," he replied, looking distinctly nervous. He lowered the car windows and turned off the motor. "Look, Esmeralda, I've been chased down and shot. I'm reasonably certain I can deal with whatever you're about to tell me."

"It's about your bill," I said.

Dennis looked at me in disbelief. "I thought it was going to be about this great Plan B."

"No, I want to talk about your bill," I said. "It's been four days, and I haven't paid you a dime. I'd like you to submit to me a bill for your services."

Dennis considered this for a moment, seeming both relieved and disappointed. "I usually bill my clients when they no longer need my services." His eyes narrowed. "That's my policy. What, are you telling me you don't need me anymore?"

"That's not what I'm saying at all," I hurried to reply. I could have kicked myself; Dennis might have been a semiretired ex-cop, but I had forgotten that he was a man with feelings.

If only I could get a better idea of what those feelings really were.

Dennis shrugged. "Well, that's what I thought you were saying," he explained. "Especially since you're shutting me out of your thoughts on what to do next."

"Look, I have a lot of thinking to do," I said. "That's all."

"Sometimes it's better to talk things over. After all, I pretty much know everything that's gone on since your sister went missing." Dennis looked away and seemed to be searching for words.

I could tell he wasn't used to asking for much of anything. "I could help if I knew everything you're thinking, but right now I'm not feeling particularly useful. Do I have to remind you that someone got killed right after talking with you?"

I could see where Dennis was going—and the fact that I'd met with Armando without Dennis's knowledge was certainly part of what he was implying. Up to now, Dennis had been very considerate in not pointing out that I was out of my league, that I was a working mother from Miami. The truth was, I had pulled him into this situation. Now I was cutting him out when things got hot.

What Dennis said made sense. But the fact was, I was thinking about taking a major risk, and I didn't want Dennis standing in my way. I knew he cared about me, one way or the other, and that he would try to stop me.

"I'm sure you're right," I said, trying to smile. "Don't worry, I'm not going to go off the deep end and do something stupid."

Just then, with exquisite timing, my cell phone rang. I was so grateful for the distraction that I answered it without even checking the screen to see who was calling.

"Esmeralda?" said Adrianna. "I left a message for you earlier. Is everything all right?"

"Yes, I'm fine, Adrianna," I replied, saying her name out loud so that Dennis would know who was on the line. "I'm sorry I haven't had a chance to call you back."

"Do you have any news?" asked Adrianna.

"No, nothing," I said, a bit shortly.

My clash with Dennis must have left me feeling a bit touchy, because I found myself resenting Adrianna's inquisitiveness. I told myself not to be defensive and mean-spirited, that the woman was simply trying to help me.

"I'm sorry to hear that," Adrianna said. "What about Detective Morris? Has he found out anything?"

"If he had, he hasn't shared it with me," I said. "Listen, Adrianna, I'll be sure to call you when I know anything for certain. All right? Thanks again. We'll talk soon."

I didn't want to go over the details of the situation, even to my friend's friend. As I hung up, I hoped I wasn't being rude. But I was almost past caring.

I looked back over at Dennis. "Sorry about that," I said.

"You don't know that woman, do you?" Dennis asked.

"She knows my closest friend from Miami," I said. "She just wants to make sure I don't feel alone here."

"Well, she seems pretty interested in what you're doing," Dennis said, casually. "I mean, for someone you don't know, she sure seems to be calling all the time."

"It's a Cuban thing," I told him. "Because of my friendship with Dorcas, she has to offer her help. That's just the way it works. I'd be expected to do the same thing if she was in trouble in Miami."

"If you say so." It was getting warm in the car, so Dennis started the motor and sent the windows up again. A welcome blast of cold air came out through the vents. "What now?"

"I think I'm going to go upstairs for a while," I said, as delicately as I could. "Just for a couple of hours at the most."

"Should I wait for you here?" Dennis asked, his tone rising on the final word. "Whatever you want is fine with me."

I smiled.

"What?" Dennis asked.

"Nothing," I said, thinking how great it would be if Tony ever said my wishes were the most important factor to consider. "I won't be long, really. I can call you before I come back down."

"Don't worry about it," Dennis said. "I've been on a lot of

long stakeouts. A couple hours of car time isn't going to kill me. Anyway, it's on the clock."

I could tell his pride was wounded, therefore I gathered my things and got out quickly.

"I'll be here," Dennis said after he'd gotten out. He patted the top of the car with his open palm.

Once I was in my room, after having brought inside the copy of *USA Today* from the little table in the entryway, I hung the Do Not Disturb sign on my door. I sat down by the window and opened up the newspaper to the business section. I got out my tiny Hewlett Packard calculator from my purse and opened up my notebook to a clean page. I looked up some figures from the newspaper, then punched some figures into the calculator. I checked and rechecked the numbers to ensure that I hadn't made any mistakes.

After about a half hour, I was ready to call my parents. This time, I had something definite to talk about.

Mama answered on the first ring and shouted my name with happiness. It was wonderful to hear her voice, but also worrying—I could hear her fatigue and weariness through the phone line.

"Listen, Mama, I have to talk to the whole family about what's been going on here," I explained. "I have something to propose, but, before I do that, I think we should all talk about it at the same time."

I spoke in a businesslike tone that I knew Mama would recognize; she immediately understood that we had no time to waste.

"Whatever you want, I will do it," she said solemnly. "Just tell me what to do."

I sighed with relief. I hadn't expected my mother to be difficult, or to give me a hard time, but it certainly made things easier that she was resisting the temptation to make me jump through hoops and tell her everything first.

"I need you to get yourself and Papa, Sapphire, Ruby, and Quartz together in front of a speaker phone so we can all talk together," I said.

"Give me a few minutes," she said. "I'll call you back to let you know when I can do this."

"I'll be waiting," I said. *"Gracias,* Mama."

It was almost an hour before I heard back from my mother. Instead of calling to tell me a time to talk, she had a surprise for me that made things much easier.

"We're all here," Mama announced, her voice slightly distant on the speaker phone. "We're all in Ruby's office."

"Hello," I said. I grew so emotional at the thought of all of them being together that I felt a lump in my throat.

"We miss you! We love you!" said all the voices I knew so well, my crazy family that I loved so much.

"Everyone get comfortable, because I need to talk to you for a while," I said. "There's so much to tell you."

I talked for about an hour, using my notes as a guide, so as to make sense for them of everything that had happened since I arrived in Las Vegas. They listened without interrupting once. Their only reaction was a collective gasp when I told them how Diamond's apartment had been trashed, then expressions of sadness from Papa and Mama when I told them about Armando's murder. It was an immeasurable relief to finally be able to share with them about what had been going on.

I left out the part about the cash and the weed. I hoped there would be no need to tell Mama and Papa about that.

When I was done, and they started asking questions, I could tell right away how much faith they had in me. They accepted what I had told them then listened carefully when I explained what I thought we should do next. As always, they were behind me.

Dennis ended up waiting a lot longer than two hours. It was almost six when I called him on his cell phone and told him that

I was coming downstairs. I was happy not to hear annoyance in his voice.

Finally I had a plan. I had to go to Diamond's world, the last place she was seen. My family knew about it, and they were prepared to let me take the risk. Because they understood that any of us would do absolutely anything for the other.

39

"SO THIS MUST MEAN YOU'RE ready to fill me in on Plan B," Dennis said. We were looking over the menu at Circo, an Italian restaurant inside the Bellagio. He was trying to sound casual but was failing miserably.

I had already apologized about keeping Dennis waiting so long after my extensive conversation with my family. The next thing I had done was suggest that we share an early dinner—six in the evening qualifying almost as a late lunch by Las Vegas standards.

"Not yet," I sighed, suggesting that the issue was beyond my control.

"Esmeralda, look, I don't know why you're being so close-mouthed about this," Dennis said. "You keep telling me how much of a help I've been. I don't understand this change that's come over you. I really don't."

Mercifully, the waiter came to take our order. I perused the wine list and picked out a good Barolo. I nodded to Dennis to see if he wanted to order anything else, but he simply gave a gruff nod to indicate that he would be content to stick to wine.

"A good choice," the waiter said, then left Dennis and me sitting uneasily across from each other. The place was full of people talking and laughing, but the silence that had settled on our table provided nothing less than an excruciating counter-point.

"So you're from New York originally?" I asked brightly, at the same moment feeling silly, as though I was making small talk on a first date. Dennis looked up glumly. "What part?"

Dennis stared at me as though I had gone bonkers. "Esmer-alda, just because you don't want to share your plans with me doesn't mean that you have to fake an interest in my past."

The waiter returned with the wine and two glasses. I was so re-lieved, I promised myself to add to his tip. If he kept showing such great timing, he was going to make a fortune that night.

"Shall I pour?" he asked while showing me the label.

"Yes. Now," Dennis and I said simultaneously.

The waiter was a clean-cut, wholesome-looking guy of about thirty; without showing any sign of noticing our mutual outburst, he calmly poured some wine in my glass. He waited for my ap-proval, which was of course pointless. At that moment, I would have given the nod to Ripple.

"Ready to order?" the waiter asked after he had poured two full glasses. I thought he sensed there was trouble at his table and that he wanted to be done with us as quickly as possible.

Circo specialized in Tuscan cuisine—I love all Italian food, and Tuscan in particular, so it wasn't easy to make a selection. I would have liked to have taken my time ordering, but given the atmosphere at the table, I quickly opted for the Steak Floren-tine. Dennis ordered the same, asking for his cooked medium while I ordered mine rare. We both passed on a first course. The waiter topped off our glasses—Dennis and I had both managed to start on the wine in the minutes it took us to order—then left us alone.

Dennis and I looked everywhere but at each other. It made me miserable to have him angry with me. I had no good excuse to give him for my reluctance to share my plan with him. The fact was, I didn't want to deal with his disapproval. I had my family on board for my latest idea, and perhaps part of me simply didn't want to bring Dennis into that inner circle of my life, no matter how much help he had been so far.

There might have been another reason: I was attracted to Dennis as a person. No, even that was edging away from the truth. I was attracted to Dennis as a *man,* and part of me was very cautious about getting any more involved with him. The more time passed, the more comfortable I became with him—and the more appealing he became. Dennis hadn't made any advances toward me, but I knew that he cared. I hadn't been close to a man other than Tony in more than a decade, and Dennis was a limousine driver from Las Vegas who was about twenty years older than I. On the surface, it was nothing short of crazy. I was married, with three children. I was an interior designer from Miami who had been thrown into a potentially dangerous situation. I hadn't come to Las Vegas looking for someone to rescue me from my stagnating marriage.

The longer I sat there, saying nothing, sipping wine, the worse I felt. I was jerking Dennis around. It was almost as though I was penalizing him for his honesty and goodwill.

I was just about to start talking to Dennis—without any real idea what I would say—when the waiter came to our table.

"Everything all right?" he asked.

Dennis and I each mumbled that it was.

"Very good," he said with a tense smile. "Your entrées will be out shortly."

Less than a minute later, he returned with two oversized plates bearing the most delicious beef I'd ever smelled or looked at. The steaks looked so succulent that they would have transformed the staunchest vegetarian into a carnivore within seconds.

The waiter fussed with our plates and table settings. I saw Dennis eyeing his plate with a food lust that matched my own.

"*Buen provecho,*" I said when the waiter had gone.

"Same to you," Dennis said with the smallest hint of a smile.

Pretty soon, we had both cleaned our plates. As my mother would have said, we left nothing for the *cucarachas*. The wine was long since gone, but I resisted ordering another bottle as I wanted to be clear-headed the rest of the night and the following morning.

"Look, Esmeralda, I don't want there to be a problem between us," Dennis finally said, pushing his plate away. "I know this is an extremely difficult situation for you. The last thing you need is a load of pressure from your limousine driver."

I was so relieved that I broke out in a grin. "Thank you for saying that," I told him. "And you know by now that you're more to me than just a driver."

Dennis showed no reaction to my statement. "You're trying to find your sister in a strange city, and now you're dealing with a dead body and a violent break in. I know you're doing the best you can under the circumstances."

"Thanks," I said, grateful for his apparent compassion.

Dennis looked around for something to drink, settled for a sip of water. "You have to make your own decisions," he said. "I'm glad I've been able to help you. And I'd like to continue providing that help however possible. And that's it."

For Dennis, this was the equivalent of a tearful confession. I actually felt slightly uncomfortable, but I was happy to accept the olive branch that he was proffering.

"I appreciate it," I replied. "And I'm glad you still want to help. I don't know what I would have done without you so far."

We smiled at each other, but we both knew that I still hadn't told him what I was planning to do next. For some reason, the details of Plan B were of inordinate importance to him—in my opinion, his interest was beginning to border on obsession. He was prideful, I could tell, and protective. But was there more?

It was barely eight o'clock, but suddenly a great weariness came over me. I suppressed a yawn.

Dennis must have noticed. "Sleepy?" he said.

"I don't know what's come over me," I answered. My mother had taught me it was rude to yawn in someone's presence, but I couldn't control myself. "I think I'm just going to ask for the check and go upstairs."

"You need a good night's sleep," Dennis agreed.

I signaled for the check, and the waiter brought it within seconds. I think he had taken a look at Dennis and me and feared that we were a couple on the verge of having an all-out fight. I gave the waiter my American Express card and, when the slip came back, added on a generous tip before signing my name.

"Ready?" I asked Dennis.

"Thanks for the meal," he said, gruff again, uncomfortably looking around the upscale restaurant. "It was damned delicious."

Dennis walked me to the hotel's reception area, where we paused.

"I'd like to get a later start tomorrow, if that's all right with you," I told him.

Dennis folded his arms. He was too smart not to know that I planned to do something without telling him.

"You're the boss," he said tightly. "I'll be waiting for your call whenever you're ready."

"Thanks," I said, striking a wrong note and showing how happy I was to be let off the hook so easily. "I'll call you."

I turned to walk away. Before I turned the corner, though, I looked back. Dennis was still standing there, his arms still folded, those eyes still shining in the artificial light.

"Go on," he said, reaching out his hand to shoo me across the lobby. Somehow it was the warmest gesture he'd given me so far.

"See you tomorrow, Dennis," I said softly, although he was too far across the noisy lobby to really hear me.

40

I WAS AWAKENED BY A KNOCK
on the door of my room. That was strange, because I knew I'd put out the Do Not Disturb sign before I collapsed into bed the night before. I opened one eye and focused with difficulty on the bedside clock. It was eight in the morning.

I closed my eyes. Whoever was out there had made some kind of mistake. Surely they would figure that out and leave me alone.

I moaned into my pillow. The knocking came again, louder this time. I resolved to count to thirty—slowly. If the knocking was still going on, then I would get up and see who the hell it was.

I reached thirty. *Knock knock.*

"Come back later!" I called out. Whoever was out there was persistent. And annoying.

It was hard to believe that one of the hotel's housekeepers wanted to come in and make up the room so early. Maybe I had received a fax, or maybe the card had fallen off the door. Maybe, I realized, I had put it on backward and instead asked for immediate room-cleaning service. I wouldn't have put it past me—after dinner with Dennis last night, I had barely been able to take a bath and watch a TV show before I basically passed out. One thing was certain—whoever was out there wasn't going to go away.

I cursed as I put on the hotel's terrycloth bathrobe over my nightgown and made for the door.

"Who's there?" I called out. No answer. "Who is it?" I said, my voice louder. Still no reply.

Had it not been so early in the morning, I might not have opened the door. I figured that the security at the hotel was tight and that I was in no immediate danger.

Although, as I unlatched the lock and turned the knob, I remembered Diamond's apartment. And Armando, lying dead in the alley behind his home.

I was about to pull the door shut again and call hotel security when it was pulled out of my hands and thrown open. I gasped, thinking that I had just made a very serious mistake.

Then my eyes cleared, and I blinked, then blinked again.

"Mama, Papa," I said. Tears fell from my eyes, and I felt my hands trembling. "Sapphire, Ruby. Quartz!"

We all started hugging. I put my nose into one of my sister's hair, breathing the smell of her to convince myself that this wasn't some kind of dream brought on by exhaustion.

"My God, I can't believe you're really here," I blubbered. It was hopeless trying to control my emotions; they all came out in a torrent, all the repressed fear and frustration of the past few days coming out of my heart like a fountain.

I stepped aside to let them into my room, babbling about how happy I was to see them. Mama came in first, followed by Papa and my siblings. I hadn't thought of the room as small previously, but when it was filled with our six outsized personalities it seemed as though there was little space to move.

There were so many questions to ask them, I just picked one out of thin air. "When did you get here?" I asked, breaking into happy laughter.

"After we talked yesterday, we thought it wasn't fair to leave you here alone in Las Vegas," Mama said, settling into the chair by the window, speaking as though they had taken the only logical course of action. "But don't worry, we still agree with your plan. We just want to be here in case you need us."

I couldn't stop looking from one to the next. Mama and Papa were dressed up as usual, looking as though they were escapees from a fifties TV sitcom. Mama was done up as Donna Reed, and Papa was the spitting image of Ricky Ricardo. Sapphire was dressed like a genie in light blue gauze, while Ruby wore a severe Armani-type suit. Quartz was in black from head to toe, your basic Goth lounge lizard.

I realized that, to other eyes, they may have looked as though they were out on work release for a program for the mentally disturbed, but they were my family. And, I realized, other than my sons, they were everything to me.

"I don't know how to thank you," I said through a fresh round of tears. We weren't usually a family that touched much, but still I went around and kissed and hugged them one by one.

"We got here late last night, to answer your question," Papa said. "It was lucky that Ruby's case settled, so she was able to come with us."

"My show isn't scheduled yet, so I was able to get away," Sapphire added, as though being born from a plate of chicken and yellow rice in front of a deranged audience was as high-pressure as Ruby's litigation. Well, maybe for her it was.

"I got a friend to cover my deejay commitments," Quartz said gravely.

"I'm sure that took some doing," Papa said. As usual, none of us could tell whether or not he was being sarcastic. "Anyway, it wasn't a problem for your mama and me to get away. We wanted to be with you, after all the things you told us."

It was obvious Papa was proud of himself, and considered himself the ringleader of this impromptu Navarro exodus.

"There were so many of us that I didn't feel like dealing with an airline," Papa added. "So I made a few calls and chartered a plane. And now here we are!"

"There's a little more to the charter plane than that," Ruby said, frowning a little, always a stickler for detail. "Día and Noche had to come along with us. No airline would let them both into the cabin, so they would have had to go into the baggage hold."

"And that would not do," Mama said adamantly.

"The dogs are here?" I said, amazed. "Where are they?"

"We checked in late last night, so they're in our room." Mama said. "We took four rooms on this floor. You sounded so tired on the phone that we wanted to let you sleep."

"It was hard to wait until now to come see you," Sapphire added.

I might have been a thirty-year-old mother myself, but Mama gave me one of those looks that told me I would always be her baby. "Thanks so much," I said, trying not to start crying again.

"Can we have breakfast now?" Quartz asked.

For someone who barely weighed more than a hundred pounds, Quartz was always ravenous. He ate like a horse and never gained a pound. It was his only trait that I disliked intensely.

"Yes, I'm hungry, too," I added. What could I say? It was a family trait, if not a national one—save for the part about never gaining a pound.

We decided to meet downstairs at the Café Bellagio in thirty minutes, giving me time to get ready. I was so happy to see my family, I probably would have otherwise assented to going in my nightgown.

As soon as they were out the door I dashed into the bathroom to shower and get dressed. As I soaped up under hot water, I thought about what their presence might mean for my plan. I soon realized that there would be few modifications and—to my relief—they hadn't come to try to stop me from putting myself in danger. Any of them would have done the same for Diamond.

There was a long line of customers waiting at the Café Bellagio, which was fairly astonishing to me. It's always been a source of amazement when I saw people who got up, showered, and dressed to go out to breakfast—when they could have had a late meal in their own place instead. I looked around and saw my family seated at a round table in the back, far away from the crowded middle of the restaurant, affording us some privacy. I took the empty seat that had been saved for me between Mama and Papa.

"We went ahead and ordered," Mama explained apologetically.

"No problem," I said. I had been a guest of the Bellagio long enough, and enough times in the past, to be able to order without looking at the menu. I asked the waitress for my usual: the Continental breakfast with a double café latte, heavy on the espresso. All our food came at the same time, and we ate quickly, knowing there was important business to discuss.

After the waitress cleared our plates, Papa said, "Esmeralda, we had a long talk after our phone conversation yesterday," he said in his deep voice. "Mostly we talked about how we could help you."

Mama and my siblings nodded somberly. "We all agree you've done a wonderful job of looking for your sister," he said. "And we owe you very much for what you've done."

"But I haven't found her," I replied. "I've tried. I've tried very hard, but I still don't know where she is."

Mama reached over and patted my hand. "You've done your very best. And I'm sure Diamond will thank you for that once she's back with her family."

I hoped that was true. "What about my plan?" I asked.

"We talked in my office yesterday about the best way to finance your idea," Ruby said. She gave a familiar throaty laugh. "You should have heard some of our proposals."

"Well, I was just glad that the banks were still open," Mama commented. "We had the option of using their services if we needed to."

Quartz had a helpless expression on his face as he sipped his espresso. "Nowadays, you don't have to actually physically *enter* a bank to make a transaction," he said, long-suffering. "It can all be done electronically, although just try convincing Mama and Papa."

"But this isn't a normal kind of transaction," Sapphire pointed out.

"That's right," Ruby said. "We couldn't do this one electronically. It would have been impractical."

"I'm just saying," Quartz said, looking into his coffee cup.

"I'm not sure I follow," I said. "I thought you were simply going to transfer the funds into my account. That shouldn't have presented too many problems."

Ruby took a deep breath. "I could probably be disbarred for being part of this scheme," she said. "But it's my sister who's missing, and I'm up to my neck in it already. So that's why I agreed to come along and do this in person."

I was completely lost. "Tell me what you all decided."

"Noche and Día weren't the only reasons we decided not to fly commercial," Papa said. "There was another, more important reason."

I looked from one to the next, my stomach turning. I knew that they were capable of anything.

"And what was that?" I asked warily.

Quartz got up and came around to where I was sitting. He was holding a black leather satchel, one that I had never seen before.

He looked around to make sure no one was watching us before he put it in my lap.

"We'd never have gotten through security with this," he said, settling into the booth next to me. "They're really strict at the airport these days."

My brother unzipped the bag and moved aside a thick black cloth inside. I gasped when I looked in and saw two gold bars, comfortably resting against each other. I reached in to touch them, to make sure they were real. I was surprised how cold they felt. Mindful suddenly that we were in a public place, I zipped up the bag again.

"I can see how you might have had some explaining to do to airport security," I said.

"That's only two of the bars—they're ten pounds each," Ruby explained. "There are a few more upstairs, in the safes in our rooms. We split them up between us."

"How many more?" I asked. I pictured the secret room in my parents' apartment filled with valuables.

"Ten more," Papa replied. "All together we brought twelve gold bars."

"*Dios mio,*" I whispered.

"You suggested we finance your plan from the gold in the safe," Papa said with pride. "Why deal with middlemen? We just decided to bring the stuff in person."

In spite of my shock, my mind started to calculate. "Well yesterday the newspaper quoted a troy ounce of gold at $319. There are sixteen ounces to the pound."

I got my calculator out of my purse and started punching in numbers. "That makes each pound currently worth $5,104. Since each bar weighs ten pounds," I punched in a calculation. "Then each bar is worth $51,040."

Quartz sipped his coffee, his free hand on the bag.

"That's right," Mama said. "So we brought twelve in all, just to make sure we'd have enough."

I punched in some more numbers. "So you carried $612,480 in gold bars on a charter plane."

Even for my family, this was extreme.

"Yes, but remember that the exchange rate is fluid," Ruby told me. "That's why we covered our bases by bringing more than the half-million you asked for."

I stared at my family. "So this was your little change in the plan."

They all nodded at the same time, as pleased as they could be. They were crazy, every one of them, but I loved them for it.

41

with breakfast, we went back to Mama and Papa's suite. Their bedroom and lounge were furnished in the same creme motif as my single room, which somehow comforted me as we pulled all our chairs around the table to form a circle. Papa and Mama sat next to each other on the two-seater couch, with Día and Noche passed out on their laps.

Part of me kept looking for my boys, as though they would naturally appear at such a family gathering. I had been away from them for almost a week—the longest time I had ever gone without holding them, talking to them, hearing about how their days had gone. I knew they were in good hands with Tony and Magdalena, but I also knew that no one could take my place.

"All right, I told you yesterday that Diamond disappeared after she got involved with the high-roller casino whales," I said. It seemed logical that I should chair this impromptu meeting.

"We understand," Papa replied.

"I estimated that it would take me about half a million dollars to gain access to that world," I added.

"It seems the only way," Papa said. "Especially with Armando gone. I've always said the best way to get inside is to go through the front door."

I took a deep breath. "Well, as you all know, the whales get special treatment at the casinos. They stay in the best suites, and they get to gamble in private rooms. And sometimes, from what I've heard, they even get rebates for their losses."

Papa shook his head and let out a snort of derision. "Rebates," he muttered. "We never would have done that at La Estrella. You win, we pay. We win, you pay."

"There are some good reasons for the way the casinos do business these days," I said. "A lot of today's whales lost a lot of money in the stock market over the past few years. And the Asian high-rollers have been hurting as their economies have suffered."

"Not to mention the loss of tourism after 9/11," Ruby added.

"So the casinos are competing for a smaller pool of big-time gamblers," Quartz said. "And that's why they offer these new incentives?"

"Right," I said. "That's why the whales are courted with all these perks. I stopped off at the casino yesterday here at the Bellagio and asked a few questions. I assume the Star casino is operating under the same conditions—if anything, they'd offer more incentives, since they're not as established as the Bellagio."

"What kind of money are these whales playing?" asked Sapphire.

"From what I understand, winnings and losses from the whales can actually impact a casino's bottom line," I explained. "On a good night, a single whale might drop several million dollars at a Baccarat table."

"But what about these private rooms you mentioned?" asked Ruby, ever the attorney. "I didn't think that was legal."

"They're new," I said. "I managed to get one of the dealers downstairs talking about them before I called yesterday. The state legislature voted a couple of years ago to permit gambling in private salons—the claim was that closed-door gambling was permitted in some other places internationally, and that the high-roller income was being diverted as a result."

"What was Diamond doing, working around these people?" Quartz asked. "I mean, all this sounds pretty exclusive. I never even knew about it."

"I don't know," I replied. "All I think is that she worked with a woman named Angie at the Star, and that her boss was named Mickey. I assumed that from the calls left on the answering machine."

"Where is this limousine driver you told us about, the one you said has helped you so much?" Mama asked.

I looked over at her. Her expression was hard to read, but I could see that she was curious about Dennis, who I had probably built up in their minds into a semilegendary figure.

"He's not involved in this," I said.

"That's good," Papa nodded. "No one on the outside should know what we're doing."

"What kinds of games do they play in these rooms?" asked Sapphire.

I was glad to get the subject off Dennis. "Baccarat and blackjack are the most popular games," I said. "The minimum bets are in the hundreds of dollars. That's why I wanted half a million—that way, even if I was losing, I would be able to hang around the private room at the Star for quite a while."

"That makes sense," Papa said. "But, Esmeralda, you're a hell of a blackjack player. Who says you would lose."

"I like to cover my bets," I said, smiling at the gleam in Papa's eye. "I don't like to bet against the house until I've had a look at my cards."

Everyone in the room nodded. That was the philosophy of gaming that we had been taught.

Ruby got up. "Water, anyone?" she asked. Without waiting for an answer, she started slinging ice into tall glasses and filling them with bottled water from the bar. I helped, then took the glasses to Mama and Papa.

"I was intending to go over to the Star and show them a cashier's check for half a mil to gain admission," I said. "Now I'll take the gold bars."

"You don't have to show them all at the same time," Sapphire said. "Just take two or three—whatever you can carry—and tell them you have more. That'll buy you plenty of time."

I paused, noting the fact that Sapphire was exhibiting common sense for the first time in recent memory.

"Does everyone agree, then," I finally asked. "Is this our best shot at finding Diamond?"

I looked over at Mama, whose eyes were full of tears. Quartz looked miserably at his water glass and nodded. Papa got up and put his arm around me.

"We have faith in you," he said.

"One thing I have to ask," Mama said, both dogs in her lap now. "Is Esmeralda going to be in danger?"

Of course all of us were wondering the same thing, although no one had brought it up until now. I shook my head, trying not to think of Armando, Mario's prediction, and Dennis's apprehension.

"Of course not, Mama," I said. My hands moved behind my back, as they did when I was a child and I wanted to hide the fact that I was crossing my fingers.

"All right, then," she said. "But you must be careful."

"I will, Mama," I promised.

Silence descended on the Navarro clan. All of a sudden, I realized that I was terrified. For me, and for Diamond. If I was wrong about her disappearance being linked to the whales at the Star, then this was a dead end. And if she was already dead, then all roads led nowhere.

"We're behind you," Papa said. "And don't worry about losing the money. I know you're a little rusty, and you're going to be nervous—not a good combination at the tables. It can't be helped. Remember, there are more gold bars where those came from."

"Thank you, Papa."

"And we will spend them all if we have to," he added.

I kissed my father, then everyone else stood up. I motioned for Quartz to bring me the black bag.

"Are they really heavy to carry?" I asked him.

"Not really," Quartz said. "Here, let me show you how to do it."

Quartz pulled the bag's straps together and pulled them over my shoulder, fussing with the balance of the gold bars' weight.

Finally, I said. "That's enough, Q."

My brother smiled, a little embarrassed. We both knew he had been delaying the inevitable. After I said my good-byes and made for the door, though, I realized that I was carrying a hundred thousand dollars in gold as though it was light as a feather.

From over my shoulder came my father's voice, saying my name. When I looked back at him, I tried to freeze him, then all of them, in my memory. It was like a snapshot that I would keep looking at to get through the next several hours.

"It isn't lost on me that this new casino is called the Star," Papa said seriously. "It seems very auspicious."

I thought so, too.

42

WHEN I WAS IN THE HALL-
way, I looked back and forth, painfully conscious of the value of
the bars I was carrying in the black satchel. I forgot about the les-
son Quartz had given me on carrying it, and clutched it to my
chest as I moved quickly down the corridor and opened the door
to my room. Once inside, I double locked the door behind me. I
sat on my bed, the bag in my lap. Even though my family was just
down the hall, I felt exposed and alone.

I realized how I was behaving and that I was going to have to
teach myself to seem at ease, even nonchalant about the fact that I
was carrying more than a hundred thousand dollars on my shoulder. I had to act like a true whale, someone who had millions to
burn. Finding Diamond depended on it.

I looked at my watch and saw that it was almost noon. *Dennis!*
I gasped, realizing I had completely forgotten to call him. I didn't
know what to say to him. I had to think things through—and decide whether or not I was really ready to go forward without
Dennis's help and knowledge.

Outside the window were the mountains in the far distance. I
searched in my purse for the photos of Diamond and Maria Mercedes, then went to the minibar and poured myself a glass of
wine. I toasted my sister, then my ancestor. I was almost waiting

LUCK OF THE DRAW

for those pictures to talk, to tell me that I was doing the right thing.

Time was passing. I coached myself, thought about what I was going to say when I got to the Star. I was a recent divorcee, I told myself, just separated from a cheating husband. I had received a massive settlement and was going to gamble away some of my ex's hard-earned money just to spite him. My ex-husband was a well-known man, though, and I wanted to have some fun without being seen in public. I didn't want to use a credit card, because that would leave a trail. I had plenty of cash for tips—the loot I'd won from the slot machine downstairs—and, now that I thought of it, I also had the money I'd found in Diamond's apartment.

First of all, I had to look the part. I went through the clothes hanging in my closet and realized that I had nothing that was remotely suitable. There were stores at the Via Bellagio, so that wasn't going to be a problem. It would take a little time to shop, but that couldn't be helped. Anyway, I figured the action in the private gaming rooms didn't really heat up until evening.

I decided against calling Dennis, because I didn't want to lie to him. If he asked me where I had been, I would tell him the truth— I had gone shopping. If I knew Dennis, that would be as effective a deterrent against further questioning as it had been telling my high school gym teacher that I was having my period.

An hour later, I came back to my room with several shopping bags. My first stop had been at Armani, where I bought two suits, three silk blouses, and a blazer. I had spent the equivalent of the GNP of a small nation. I had been tempted by a silk dress in the window at Chanel, but that seemed too much, and, instead, settled for some accessories—a couple of pins and some tasteful pearl earrings. Last, I had stopped off at a shoe boutique and splurged on a pair of black leather Manolo Blahniks. I had always wanted a pair of Manolos, but I had never been able to justify the expense.

Even though I was spending a shitload of money, I made sure to pick out things that I could wear to client meetings once I was home again.

Client meetings. Miami. Home. I fought off the urge to give up, racing across the room to clutch tight again the picture of Diamond.

"I'm coming, baby sister," I said to her.

I changed into one of the Armani suits, put my hair up into a French chignon, and put on makeup. I slipped on the shoes and walked over to the mirror on the back of the closet door. As I wobbled around in those pointy high heels, I understood why they were called "limousine shoes"—they certainly weren't meant for walking.

My reflection in the mirror shocked me. The person peering back at me in no way resembled the woman who had arrived in Las Vegas the week before: the good girl from the crazy family, the Cuban Catholic, the married mother of three.

But I had to admit, I looked really good. It was hard to tear my eyes away from the mirror. It was amazing, the effect of five thousand dollars worth of designer clothes.

I double-checked the gold bars in the satchel, then added two thousand dollars in cash from Diamond's stash before I zipped it up. I had just started to pick up the bag when my cell phone rang. It was only when I sighed with relief over seeing Gabriel's number on the caller ID that I realized I was avoiding Dennis altogether.

"Honey!" I said when I picked up. "How are you? Is everything OK?"

From the noises in the background I could tell my son was calling from the boys' bathroom at school. His day would be almost over.

"Mom, I can't talk too long," Gabriel whispered.

"Is everything all right?" Even through the annoying sounds

of flushing toilets and running water, I could detect a note of anxiety in my son's voice.

"I have to tell you something, Mom," Gabriel said, talking faster than usual. "You know how I told you I was feeding Buster Whoppers from the Burger King?"

"Is Buster sick?" I could have kicked myself for condoning feeding the dog fast food. And I wasn't even there to shove Kaopectate down Buster's throat. Tony was probably going to end up making good on his threat to take Buster to the pound.

"No, no, Buster is fine," Gabriel said. "It's something else. It's just that Abuela Magdalena keeps cooking us Cuban food every day. Me and Carlos and Alex can't stand it anymore."

"She means well, Gabe. Your abuela wants you to eat well and be healthy." More than ever I hated not being home. My poor boys weren't used to a daily diet of home-cooked food—they thrived on anything that came wrapped in plastic. They were probably going to come down with some kind of a stomach flu as a result.

"Mom, I just want you to know that I've been spending some of the money you gave me to buy food for us. For Buster, Alex, Carlos, and me. We've been eating at the BK. Is that OK?"

Gabriel sounded so concerned that I wanted to laugh. Compared to what was happening in Las Vegas, the fact that my boys were secretly overloading at BK was somehow comforting.

"That's fine, honey, just as long as your father and abuela don't find out." Still, I wondered what kind of mother I really was—first I told them it was all right to subsist on fast food, then I instructed them to hide it from their father and grandmother. My parenting techniques were going to land me in hell one of these days. I knew from previous experience that Magdalena hated when I telephoned while I was away, so I did not feel guilty for not speaking to her. I suspected she thought that I was checking up on her if I did so. She once told me that if anything went wrong, she would call. That was fine with me, as I did not need to hear her first-hand account of the goings-on at home.

"Gotta go, Mom," Gabriel said. "The bell rang."

I heard a cacophony of toilets flushing in the background, indicating that the boys' bathroom time was indeed finished.

"I love you," I blurted out. "I love you a lot."

"When are you coming home, Mom?" Gabriel asked, suddenly not in so much of a rush.

"I don't know for sure," I told him. "As soon as I can. I promise."

"We miss you. Come home, Mom," Gabriel said. "Now I really gotta go."

After I hung up, I just stared at the telephone. I wanted to speak to the twins, but I knew that would upset them, as they did better when they did not hear my voice. I should have been at home with my family and poor Buster. Instead I was in Las Vegas, hatching crazy plans. I was out of my league, and it suddenly seemed absurd that I could even imagine I was capable of finding my sister. I had another life, and three boys for whom I was responsible. My children and my dog shouldn't have been secretly nourishing themselves at the local Burger King while I was living at the Bellagio in Las Vegas—and planning to gamble half a million dollars.

I took a deep breath to remain calm as I told myself that one way or the other, it was going to be over soon. I would play with the whales, and then I would think about getting out of this mess. Maybe if nothing happened at the Star, it really was time to bring in a professional. Even if that person would be an outsider to the Navarro clan.

I still hadn't contacted Dennis. I remembered that Dennis had known I was up to something when I sneaked out to meet Armando—and I could tell that fact bothered him. I decided it wasn't fair to keep Dennis on standby.

Dennis picked up on the first ring. "What's up, Esmeralda?"

"I'm sorry I didn't call earlier," I said.

Dennis let that one pass without comment. "What time do you want me to pick you up? Are you ready now?" he asked, all business.

"Actually, I'm exhausted from shopping. I just hit all the stores at the Bellagio," I said in what I hoped passed for a lighthearted manner.

"You went shopping?" A pause. "You mean, like, at a store?"

"I've been here longer than I planned, so I needed a few things," I said even as I knew how lame that sounded. "Anyway, I'm beat. I don't think I'm going to need you to drive me anyplace today."

Dennis said nothing.

"Go ahead and charge me for a full day, though," I said. "I asked you to be on standby, so it's only fair."

"Listen, Esmeralda, it's your right if you're doing something you don't want me to know about. But don't treat me like a fool." His voice was cold and emotionless. "I was drawn into this situation, and I've been helping you—at least that's what I've been led to believe."

I felt like shit. "You *have* helped me. So much."

"Then treat me with some respect," Dennis said. "Look, you don't owe me anything at all. You hired me to be your driver, and I helped you when I could. Maybe that's all there is to it. You have no need to lie to me. I won't stand for it."

"Dennis—"

"I'll submit my bill to you tomorrow. I'll leave it at the front desk."

I remembered that Dennis only billed out when the job was completed. I couldn't believe my relationship with him was going to end this way—bitterly, and over a cell phone.

"Please, hold off on sending me your bill," I said. I wasn't going to beg, but I might come close. "Please, Dennis."

I knew what was going on here. I wanted Dennis, but only on my terms. Dennis wasn't the kind of man to accept those conditions.

What, I asked myself, exactly was I talking about?

"Look, maybe we're both getting a little worked up here," Dennis finally said. He sounded a bit more conciliatory. "Why don't we talk later."

"OK," I said. "But Dennis, please, no bill. Come on."

Dennis laughed. "All right. No bill. Yet."

We hung up after saying good-bye. I felt as though I had dodged a bullet. Not only did I need his continued help finding my sister, but I was surprised how panicked I had been at the prospect of never seeing him again.

I hoped that when Dennis and I talked next, we would have something good to discuss. With that in mind, I took one last look around my room and picked up the satchel. I was as ready as I was ever going to be.

43

THE STAR MIGHT HAVE BEEN a startup only in business for less than a year, but it didn't show on the surface. The remodeled hotel was all Vegas glitz, with big chandeliers in the lobby and a plush carpet that sighed under my feet as I made my way to the concierge's desk. A placard next to where I stood announced a variety of shows and tours, attempts to draw in the dwindling tourist dollar.

I checked out the three men stationed at the desk and chose the one who I thought would be the most sympathetic to me—a slim, slightly built man in his early thirties who gave me a big smile when I approached. I clutched tight to the satchel slung over my shoulder.

"I wonder if you can help me," I said.

"Yes, Ma'am," he replied with a smile, taking in my expensive outfit. "What can I do for you?"

"I heard there was good high-stakes action here at the Star," I said with a nervous laugh. "You see, I've never been here alone, so I'm not sure how to go about gaming at the high-stakes tables."

The concierge looked me over. "Well, ma'am, we certainly do have games for casino patrons who wish to play for significant amounts. In fact, I think the Star has the best high-stakes tables in Las Vegas."

He spoke as though conferring an insider's secret. The guy was good.

"Well, I'm here to play," I added, in a whisper. "But I'm not going to be comfortable playing for large sums in public. You know, out in the general part of the casino."

The concierge nodded, as though he understood my distaste for mingling with the riffraff and shared it himself.

"I'm going to take care of this lady," he announced to his colleagues. "I'll be back as soon as I have her comfortably settled in."

They both looked up from what they were doing and nodded. Apparently it wasn't entirely unusual for someone to make such a request. My new ally came around the desk and joined me on the plush carpet. I looked at his nametag, which read "Cedric."

"Thank you so much for understanding, Cedric," I said.

He led me through the casino—as expansive and bustling as any in town, successfully creating that Las Vegas Twilight Zone feel—then through a door in the back. I imagined Diamond taking the same walk, when she had been prying into someone's secrets.

Cedric stopped in front of a door marked "Private" and knocked on it. There was no answer.

"This'll take just a moment," he told me. "I'm going to get Mickey, the host, for you. I'll have him paged and he'll be with you right away."

Mickey. My heart almost stopped. I almost repeated the name out loud. *Diamond's boss.* My knees started shaking.

"Thank you," I mumbled. "Of course."

Cedric, seeming not to notice my shock, left me alone for a minute. When he returned, he was accompanied by a big, dark, beefy guy in a black suit. Mickey looked tough and more than a little scary. I tried not to react to the sight of him.

"My name is Mickey Paladino." He stuck his big hand out to

me, and I had no choice but to shake it. His hand was as cold as a steak from the meat counter at Publix.

"I'm Emmy Saunders," I replied, taking the last name of my roommate from college.

"Please. Come into my office." Mickey swiped a plastic card across the slot on the door. I looked around for Cedric, but he had already vanished.

Mickey's office was small but surprisingly tasteful, with a glass table that apparently served as his desk. There were three black leather chairs—one behind the desk and two across from it. On his desk and an adjoining table were vases filled with white lilies. I couldn't help but remember how lilies were associated with death.

"This is a lovely office," I said, just to say something. There was nothing on Mickey's desk other than a sleek high-tech telephone and a Star Casino cup holder full of pens. Clearly, Mickey wasn't bogged down with paperwork in his capacity as a casino host.

"Please, Ms. Saunders." Mickey indicated one of the chairs and took a few steps toward a credenza behind his desk that served as a bar. "Make yourself comfortable. Would you like a drink?"

I noticed there were bottles of champagne cooling in buckets. *No, thanks, I don't need a drink. What I need is for you to tell me what happened to my sister, you thug.*

"No, thank you. I'm fine," I said. Mickey was nothing but cordial. I burned with desire to say my sister's name, if only to see how he reacted.

"Cedric told me you'd like to play in a high-stakes setting," Mickey said, settling into his seat. His mouth was locked into a smile, but his eyes were cold and appraising.

"That's right, but I don't want to play in public," I said, smiling back. "I've heard you offer private gaming rooms—for guests playing for high enough stakes, I assume."

"That's right." Mickey's smile dropped a fraction. "You look sort of familiar. Have you been to the Star before?"

I almost panicked. There was a family resemblance between Diamond and me, but I never thought a stranger would pick up on it—especially if we weren't standing next to each other. Besides, Diamond would never have worn an outfit like mine that day. I decided Mickey was on a fishing expedition.

"I've always come here with my husband," I said. "Oops, I mean ex-husband. He liked high-end gaming. You know, you have a terrific memory."

"It's part of the job," Mickey replied. "I thought I had seen you before. Well, what games do you like to play?"

I put my hands on the leather armrests to keep them from shaking. "Mostly blackjack, maybe a little Baccarat," I said.

Mickey nodded. "And how would you like to arrange the financial end of things?" In spite of his cool, intimidating appearance, I could see that Mickey could handle the discreet side of his job. "At the Star, we aim to provide you with the utmost comfort and service."

"Well, I hope the casino can help me with that." I picked up the satchel from the floor and put it in my lap. "I have a form of payment that might be out of the ordinary."

Mickey stood up and put his hands on his desk. "We can handle just about anything, Ms. Saunders, I can assure you of that."

"Good." I unzipped the bag and opened its sides as far as they would go. "This is how I want to finance my gaming here."

Mickey peered down at the bars of gold. His expression remained unchanged. "May I?" he asked, motioning toward the satchel.

I nodded and watched as he took the bag and placed it on the credenza. He opened a drawer and pulled out the kind of scale I'd seen at jewelry stores, along with a small leather case. He took one of the bars from the bag and laid it on its side on the scale.

"Exactly ten pounds," he said, his voice a little hoarse.

He opened up the case and took out a test tube from a neat row and half-filled it with a clear liquid. He scraped a bit of gold from the bar with a little metal pick, then put the shaving in the test tube and waited for it to change color.

"Eighteen carats," he said. "Very nice."

I watched Mickey take the other gold bar from the bag, weigh it, and test its purity.

"You have twenty pounds of eighteen-carat gold here," Mickey said. He gave me a piranha's smile.

"I know," I told him.

"I have to look up today's exchange rate," he said. "But off the top of my head, I'd estimate that you have more than a hundred thousand dollars here."

I was tempted to give him the exact figure, but I didn't want him thinking I was too sharp. This man wasn't my friend, I reminded myself.

"I have others," I said.

Mickey almost had to bite his tongue to keep from asking me how many more I had in my possession—and where they were.

"Ms. Saunders, where are you staying in Las Vegas?" he asked instead. Before I could answer, he moved toward me with that toothy smile on his face. "Let me answer for you. You're staying at the Star. As our very special guest, and for as long as you would like."

"That sounds lovely," I said.

I was in.

44

IT WAS CLEAR THAT MICKEY saw me as an opportunity to make a lot of easy money for the Star Casino. I was an apparently ditsy woman, recently divorced, who was eager to blow a lot of her ex-husband's money in as discreet a fashion as possible. The scenario I outlined for Mickey worked as well as I had hoped it would.

I left his office as soon as I agreed to be a guest of the Star.

"I can send someone with you to get your things," Mickey said. "Where did you say you were staying until now?"

"I didn't say," I told him sweetly. "I think I mentioned my need for discretion?"

"Of course, Ms. Saunders," Mickey said, still smiling but slightly rebuffed. He handed me a business card. "This is my cell phone number. Please call me as soon as you get back to the Star. It would be my honor to personally show you up to your room and our private gaming facilities."

"That would be splendid," I said.

I left the Star thinking that the whales must have indeed become scarcer in Las Vegas, if I was receiving such a royal treatment with only about a hundred thousand dollars to spend. I had told Mickey there were other gold bars, of course, but he hadn't seen them. I knew one of the primary rules of running a casino—

don't take the gambler's word for his or her assets until you've seen them with your own eyes. Casinos saw all kinds of cheats and swindlers, and they were always on their guard against getting ripped off.

On that level, at least, I was legitimate. As soon as I got back to the Bellagio I returned to Mama and Papa's suite to tell them what had happened. Sapphire, Ruby, and Quartz were all there, and they were all feeling apprehensive now that our plan had reached a critical point. It took a lot of reassurance, along with hugs and kisses, to get away from them again. I understood why they were worried about me but, if they thought about it, they had to understand why it was impossible for me to stop now.

"Well, we're going downstairs to the tables," Sapphire said, herding Ruby and Quartz into the corridor.

"Good idea," I told them, opening the door to my room. Our family was always soothed in times of crisis by some high-quality gambling.

I packed a bag with enough things for a brief stay at the Star— a nightgown and an outfit for tomorrow. I packed my toiletries and took one last long look around at the room that had been my home for the past week. The woman who had first entered these four walls had changed, I knew that for certain. The question was who was going to walk out of the Star, and if she was someone that I would recognize.

Mickey had offered to store the gold bars in the hotel safe, but I was still carrying them. Mickey hadn't been too thrilled with that arrangement, but I wanted to hold as much power for as long as I could. I was carrying two bags when I returned to the Star at a few minutes past seven. I asked the concierge to call Mickey and let him know that I'd returned. It wasn't Cedric this time, but he seemed to recognize the made-up name I supplied him with.

"Right away, Ms. Saunders," he said. "We've been expecting you."

Mickey showed up almost right away. It was amazing how quickly I was allowed into the Star's inner circle, with just a hundred thousand dollars and the promise of more. It was lucky, I thought, that Diamond had last worked at a casino trying to make its name in Las Vegas—the Star was hungry for money and high players, and obviously wasn't asking too many questions about where they came from.

I followed Mickey through the main casino floor, past the jangling slots and the lip-chewing tension of the card tables. He led me past his office to a narrow hallway where we came to a locked set of thick glass doors. Mickey put a little key into a lock next to the doors, and I heard a soft click. He stepped aside for me to enter, and we reached a foyer and an elevator. Mickey swiped a card through a slot, and the door opened immediately.

"A private elevator," he explained. "Only for our most special guests."

I simply nodded and followed him inside. Mickey seemed not to notice how nervous I was. There was only one stop: the penthouse floor. The elevator ride was so quiet and smooth. I could barely tell that we were moving at all.

When the elevator door opened, I moved forward and let out an involuntary gasp. I had never seen anything like this: a glass-topped garden with an all-around unobstructed view of Las Vegas. I saw the lights of the strip stretching out like multicolored fireflies. It was as though I was standing on the peak of a high mountain right in the middle of the city.

"Something, isn't it?" Mickey said, pleased by my reaction. "I never get used to it myself. Not really."

I glanced over at him, and he gave me a warm smile. For a moment I was able to see him as a real person, not as a minor character on *The Sopranos*. Then I snapped back to the moment and what I was there to accomplish.

"Here, let me show you to your room," Mickey said softly.

I followed him down a corridor so deeply carpeted that my Manolos sank into the plush beneath my feet. I had to concentrate hard not to twist my ankles and, I feared, blow my cover: after all, I was supposed to be used to wearing these kinds of clothes. Finally Mickey stopped in front of one of the twenty or so doors that lined the silent corridor.

"Here's the room I reserved for you," he said. He swiped a card in the lock and again stepped aside for me to enter first.

If I had wished for some color in my room at the Bellagio, someone must have been listening. My room was enormous and, I suspected, reserved for female whales: the walls were a splash of color, decorated in a floor-to-ceiling floral motif. There were large English bouquets arranged throughout the room in feminine vases. The curtains were printed with big, splashy roses in every conceivable shade of pink and lavender. There was a king-sized bed, two very big armchairs, and two sofas all decorated in splashes of colored flowers. For the first time in a while, I found myself completely speechless.

"This is unbelievable," I finally said to Mickey.

"I think you'll be very comfortable here." Mickey showed me the bathroom, the closet, and how to work the plasma TV hanging on the wall. He handed me a little plastic box with a pearl button in the middle. "If you need anything—room service, maid service, anything at all—just press this button."

"Thank you," I said.

Mickey stood there for a while, and I wanted to shoo him away so I could collect my thoughts. Finally I saw his eyes stray to the leather satchel over my shoulder, and I realized that he was waiting for me to give him the gold bars.

"Of course," I said with an uneasy laugh.

I took out the two bars and handed them to Mickey. He seemed to have expected me to give him the entire satchel, but he recovered well. He went into the bathroom and returned with two small pink towels; carefully, he wrapped up the bars. I saw him glance at my overnight bag, probably wondering where were the rest of the bars I had promised existed.

"You have credit for one-hundred thousand dollars," Mickey said. "Give or take a few thousand. I did the calculations based on up-to-the-minute gold prices."

He handed me an envelope from the pocket of his jacket, his mouth twisted into a smile.

"This is your receipt," he said. "If you need additional credit, please don't hesitate to have me paged. I'll take care of everything for you."

"Thanks for your generous help," I said.

Mickey was satisfied, for now. "I'll leave you, Ms. Saunders," he said. He gave me a little plastic card. "This will give you access to just about anywhere on the property. Don't be shy about using it. You're part of the Star family now."

When he was gone, I decided that it was probably still a bit too early to start gambling. I looked around for a room service menu but couldn't find one, so I pushed my pearl button. A moment later there was a quiet knock at the door.

"Madam?" A tiny young girl with raven hair waited outside the door. "May I help you?"

"I was looking for the room service menu," I explained.

"There is no menu, ma'am," she said. "Please tell me what you'd like to order, and I'll have the chef prepare it for you. Or, if you'd prefer, you can call him yourself and discuss your dinner choice."

"I'll just tell you," I said, breaking into a smile. The girl blinked politely, too reserved to share in the ridiculousness of the moment. "All right. I'll have whatever fresh fish you have in stock, a big salad, and some fresh vegetables. Something choco-late for dessert. And some red wine—a cabernet sauvignon."

"Right away, ma'am." She memorized my order, doing every-thing but curtsying. "It won't be long."

When the meal arrived, a young man in an immaculate white uniform arranged it on my table, along with an ornate cream-colored tablecloth, real silver, and a fresh arrangement of mixed flowers. Each course came in a different serving platter. The waiter pulled the table in front of the television, then pulled up a hardbacked chair so I could watch the television while I dined. I had been in some pretty fancy places in my life, but this was in an-other league. I suspected I could have asked the waiter to cut my food for me, if I wanted it—and maybe chew it, too.

The meal was the best I'd had in years. Normally such food would have relaxed me and made me ready for sleep, but as I fin-ished I felt a hot flood of nervousness go through me. I paced and wished I had brought my notebook with me.

At about ten o'clock I went downstairs, figuring that by then the other high-rollers would have finished their meals and would be ready to play. The gentleman guarding the door let me in right away, as though he knew me by sight. I hoped he couldn't hear how loud my heart was beating.

The private rooms were sparsely occupied, with about a dozen whales spread out amid the Baccarat and blackjack tables. I caught a glimpse of roulette tables in the next room.

I stopped and looked around. No one approached me. This was a reserve of quiet, calm, and luxury.

The other whales were almost all white males, ranging from thirty to about seventy years old. They all seemed to be alone. The room was so quiet, it was as though gambling on this level was a job rather than a fun diversion. Cocktail waitresses—all young and beautiful—moved from table to table with drinks and snacks.

Diamond had once been one of those working there in some capacity.

I smiled at the dealer at the nearest blackjack table, joining one other player. The first hand I played a twenty-one. The dealer deftly moved a pile of chips toward me.

I had my ears open, my eyes peeled, taking in the chandeliers and the plush wallpaper. Although I was tempted to order a drink, I decided against it and had a ginger ale served in cut crystal.

Something strange started to happen. I stayed at the table for a while and started on a lucky streak. I was up and down, but making steady gains. A few men came to play at the table, but none of them said a word to me. One by one, they left when my winning streak deepened.

While the dealer cut new cards I looked around, wondering what had attracted Diamond to the place. The air was rarified, the mood grim. There was a sense of a lot of money changing hands. But no clue about what happened to my little sister.

I took in the décor—a sort of Las Vegas baroque, with gilt, gold, and cherubs all over the place. Other than being decorated in very bad taste, there was nothing out of the ordinary in the private gaming rooms.

At midnight, I decided that I had seen enough. By the time I tipped the dealer and headed upstairs to my room, I was ahead by fifteen thousand dollars. Papa was right, after all. I was a good blackjack player. I hoped I would get a chance to tell Diamond soon about my run of luck in the domain of the whales.

That last thought depressed me as I settled back in my bed, still fully clothed. I would have to come back tomorrow and play again, maybe using my access card in the meantime to snoop around a little. I hung up my suit in the closet and ran hot water in the bath. The bathroom filled with thick steam.

I put on a pink bathrobe with the Star Casino insignia stitched over one lapel and went to the sink to wash my face.

I still hadn't found Diamond. I couldn't give up. My sister was near, I could almost sense it.

Bending over the sink to wash my face, I had the strange sensation that I was not alone in the bathroom. However, I was not sure, so instead of turning, I reached up with my bathrobe sleeve to wipe the steam off the mirror so I could see who it was.

There was someone there, a woman holding a rag up in the air. It was so absurd that I barely resisted when she pressed it to my face.

As I started to fall, I got a good look at her.

"Maria Mercedes!" I cried out.

And then everything went black.

45

I WAS AMAZED TO DISCOVER that, all my expectations to the contrary, I had made it to Heaven, as when I opened my eyes, my sister Diamond was bending over me and wiping my forehead with a cool cloth. My head and heart were pounding, and I had an awful taste in my mouth. Knowing that Diamond was finally with me again made it all bearable.

"Esmeralda," Diamond whispered my name in my ear. "You're safe," she said.

"I found you," I mumbled. My tongue was thick in my mouth, and my words came out garbled. I tried to open my eyes to get a better look at my sister, but it was too difficult. "I found you. I think I hit my head on something, baby sister. It hurts so much."

"It's all right. Just sleep," Diamond told me. "I'm here."

"I don't want to sleep," I said. "I want to see Heaven."

The last thing I heard before I passed out was a man laughing in the background. Was it God? If it was, why was he laughing at me? It didn't seem very funny, not with my head pounding the way it was.

I FELT BETTER THE NEXT TIME I awoke. My headache had subsided, and so had the metallic taste in my mouth. I slowly opened my eyes and blinked to bring everything into focus. Diamond was sitting, fast asleep, in a chair next to my bed. She looked beautiful, radiant in a white diaphanous dress, her hair framing her angel's face.

"Diamond?" I said. "Where are we?"

I managed to turn my head. If this was Heaven, then it was decorated in the same style as the Bellagio. I looked over at the familiar clock on my bedside table and saw that it was eleven. Whether it was day or night, I had no idea. I looked down at myself and saw that I was still wearing the pink terrycloth bathrobe I'd put on before . . . before . . .

"Esmeralda, are you OK?" Diamond had moved to my side and was stroking my face.

"What's happening?" I said. I knew I was back in my room and had just started to register the fact that my sister was safe and alive.

"There's so much to tell you." Diamond put her arms around me. She smelled like incense. "I'm so grateful for all you did trying to find me. I love you so much, big sister."

Suddenly a memory came to me. I sat up abruptly, which proved to be a big mistake—my head exploded with fireworks of pain and light. I gasped in shock and lay back again. It was a little while before I dared open my eyes again.

"Diamond, you're not going to believe this," I said. "I saw Maria Mercedes, our ancestor. She was in my bathroom at the Star Casino."

Diamond slowly stroked my arm. "I know," she said.

"You do?" I sat up just a fraction. "Where were you, Diamond? I almost went crazy looking for you. Have you talked to Mama and Papa? And why does my head hurt so much?"

The questions came tumbling out in a rush, and my hands shook before me. None of this made any sense. I suddenly jerked on the bed, thinking that we might still be in trouble.

"Maybe I can help," said a familiar male voice.

Dennis walked over to my bedside and sat down in the chair that Diamond had just vacated. "What are you doing here?" I asked him. I tried to remember the last time we talked and whether he knew anything about my going to the Star.

I noticed suddenly that Dennis wasn't wearing his usual uniform black pants and white shirt. Instead he was wearing a really attractive khaki poplin suit, a light blue shirt, and matching striped tie. He looked really good. Except for his piercing light gray eyes, nothing about him looked the same.

"I know you're going to hate me for what I'm about to tell you, but you have to believe I had no choice," he said slowly. His brow creased with worry. "Diamond, I'm going to need you to back me up on this one."

What could make me hate Dennis? He had obviously found Diamond for me—why wouldn't I be eternally grateful?

"Esmeralda, Dennis has been protecting us," Diamond explained. "First me, then you. Please hear him out before you get angry. Promise me, please?"

"I promise," I reluctantly agreed. "Just tell me."

Dennis took a deep breath and looked down at his hands. "Diamond was never really missing," he said flatly. "I knew where she was all the time."

"What!" I tried to yell, and my head exploded with pain. "You lied to me?"

"Esmeralda, you promised." Diamond put both her hands on my shoulders to keep me from getting up. "Listen to him. Please."

"I promised, but that was before I knew he was lying to me!" I had my hands out, reaching for Dennis, but Diamond kept me back. My only plan at the moment was to wrap my hands around his throat and squeeze, but I was far too weak.

Dennis waited a moment until I was totally subdued by my sister. He looked as though he was about to endure a particularly painful dental procedure.

"I'm not a limousine driver," he said examining his fingernails. "I'm an FBI agent. I'm investigating Mob activities."

Dennis dug in his pocket and produced a wallet; he flashed his shield and ID card at me.

"No wonder you didn't care about your bill," I blurted out. "You're a phony—my taxes were already paying your salary."

Dennis glanced at me; he could tell that my initial rage was subsiding. Diamond clapped her hand on his shoulder and motioned to me. Dennis shrugged.

"All right," he said. "You can tell her."

"You know I was working as an environmental reporter at the *Las Vegas Herald*," she said. "Well, one of my assignments was looking into how the casinos disposed of their waste—you know, whether or not they were being environmentally friendly."

"I know that," I said. I propped myself up on my pillow, resisting the urge simply to pull my sister close.

"Well, I wanted to focus on the Star—since they're starting up, I figured they'd be the most likely to cut corners to save money," Diamond said. "I had an appointment there with their press relations person, but when I arrived, he wasn't there. I was told to hang around the office and wait until he showed up."

I thought for a moment. "So you started snooping around," I said.

Dennis allowed himself a chuckle. "It seems to be a family trait," he said.

"Well, I followed a porter through a security area—you'd be amazed where you can go, if you act like you belong there," Diamond said. "I ended up in the high-roller private gaming area. There weren't any gamblers around—it was too early."

"You were trespassing," Dennis pointed out.

"I was being a reporter," Diamond corrected him. "Anyway, I found a conference room down the hall, with the door open. There was a meeting going on inside, so I decided to eavesdrop."

"What were they talking about?" I asked. I managed to sit all the way up, my back against the headboard.

"They were talking about casino finances, how they were in the red," Diamond said. "Typical stuff. But then, just as I was about to leave, things got interesting."

Dennis glanced over at me, checking to make sure I was no longer feeling homicidal toward him. I looked back at my sister, unwilling to let him off the hook just yet.

"They started talking about the casinos in Havana," Diamond said. "There were some older guys there, and they started talking about how well the Mob did under Batista, and how Castro had made it hard on everyone. I knew all this, of course, but it was funny to hear anyone other than Papa still talking about it."

"They were talking about Cuba?" I said, unable to believe it. Proof that, yet again, Cuba is never very far away from anyone who has ever had contact with the island.

"It was like being home for New Year's," Diamond said. She smoothed her long hair distractedly. "Then one of the old guys started talking to the younger men about how it was a shame how much money they had lost from the Havana casinos, and how great it would be if they could get their hands on it now. Because they could use it to offset the money they were losing during the start-up phase of the Star."

"What about the money the Vatican helped them get out of Cuba?" I asked, remembering what the two old nuns had told me at the Guardian Angel.

"They said something about that," Diamond said. She looked a little perplexed. "That was news to me, actually. But it isn't important. What really got me interested was when they mentioned La Estrella."

"La Estrella?" I repeated. "How did that come up?"

"Remember Mama and Papa telling you about how their

'friend' helped them get their money out of the casino safe the night of the revolution?" she asked.

I thought for a moment. "You weren't there when they showed us the safe."

Diamond looked over at Dennis. "He told me," she said. "He put together what you told him and connected the dots."

"You knew everything but still let me babble on?" I asked him, almost ready to work myself up to being disgusted with him again.

"We've been after these guys' asses for years," Dennis said calmly. "We knew they were backing the Star and trying to wedge themselves back into the gaming business, but we never had anything solid on them—until your family came along."

"Just keep going," I said to Diamond. None of this really mattered to me. Diamond was safe. I could go home.

"Well, guess who was at the meeting?" Diamond asked.

"The 'friend' who helped Mama and Papa?" I said. As someone who had gambled all my life, I believed in luck, but this situation seemed especially fortuitous. Someone up there was looking out for La Estella.

"The same friend who helped them design their penthouse apartment and the secret room," Diamond said. She gave me a smug smile. "But I learned something that day that Mama and Papa might not even know. Their 'friend' had a daughter."

"A daughter?" I thought for almost a full minute, with Diamond watching me. Then I looked at Dennis. "Adrianna?" I asked. It was the only thing that could make sense.

"That's right," he said. "Adrianna. I thought you had the makings of an investigator. The fact that you didn't trust her told me a lot."

"Wait, wait, let me think," I pleaded. I had to absorb what had just been said. "Dorcas said Adrianna was connected, but that she came from Cuba on a raft. I don't get it."

"Adrianna's mother was Cuban," Diamond explained. "In fact, she worked at La Estrella as a cigarette girl. Her father was Mama and Papa's Mafia friend. Adrianna stayed in Cuba until her mother died. When that happened, her father sent her money to buy a place on a raft and then to come to Las Vegas."

"You knew all about Adrianna?" I asked Dennis. He shrugged.

"The old guys in the conference room started bitching about La Estrella," Diamond said. "They had named their new casino the Star as a kind of inside reference that only the old guys would understand. Now, after all these years, they were starting to feel greedy about the money they helped La Estrella's 'management' take from Cuba."

"In other words, Mama and Papa," I said.

"Then things started to get weird, and I started to get frightened standing out there in that hall," Diamond said. "Because the old guy in the room said he had an idea about how to get his hands on that money. He said he'd get back to them about it at the next meeting—seven P.M. Friday, he said."

Diamond went to the ice bucket on the table and wrapped some more cubes inside the washcloth. It was surreal, having Dennis sitting quietly about three feet away from me. I was about to ask what had happened to me, how I had gotten from the floor of the bathroom at the Star to my bed at the Bellagio—a topic I kept forgetting to bring up—when Diamond started talking again.

"This was when these guys must have realized they'd left the door open," Diamond said. "The door slammed all at once, and I just stood there and shook—all I could think about was what they would do if they found out what I'd heard and who I was. So I got out of there as quick as I could."

"And that's when you decided you had to be there for the next meeting," I told her. "*Ay,* Diamond. Why didn't you call us in Miami?"

"I needed to find out more," Diamond said.

"This is my sister," sighing, I said to Dennis. "She has to do things on her own."

"I figured that out," Dennis said.

"Then I asked Armando to get me a job at the Star," Diamond said. "He got me in there fast, and a couple of days later I was serving drinks to the whales."

"What did you tell Armando about getting his job back as a wheel dealer?" I asked her. "You know, the old man was clinging to that."

Diamond looked abashed. "I bullshitted him," she said. "I don't know. I half-believed it myself. I keep thinking how we're all going back home as soon as Castro dies."

"Do you know what happened to Armando?" I asked her angrily.

"I know," Diamond said, lowering her eyes. "I feel terrible about it. He was a sweet old man. I never thought I was getting him involved in all this."

"Tell me about Adrianna," I said. "What did she want? I can't see where she came into the picture."

Dennis smiled. "Funny you should say the word *picture.*"

"Adrianna passed herself off as Maria Mercedes," Diamond said.

I thought of the woman who came at me in the bathroom, with the visage of Maria Mercedes. The memory flooded back.

"I managed to listen in on the second meeting," Diamond said. "It wasn't easy, and I had to keep coming in and out. But I heard the old guy talking about Mama and Papa's secret room— this was the first time I heard about it. He said he knew where there was a fortune in gold and jewels, and how they had to get to it."

"They were going to rob Mama and Papa?" I asked.

"They started talking everyday," Diamond said. "And I

started asking for extra shifts, so I could be around when they met. That's when I guess I got careless."

"We've been tapping a lot of these guys' phones," Dennis said. "We picked up some chatter about a cocktail waitress who was always hanging around, and we got worried."

"So that's when you stepped in," I told him.

"I approached her at the natural foods store in Summerlin," he said. "I had to be careful, because it was possible that she was already being watched."

"I was relieved, to tell you the truth," Diamond laughed. "I mean, I heard all this stuff, but I didn't know what I was going to do about it. I started to call Papa about fifty times, but I didn't want to get him worried until I knew what they were thinking about doing. And, you know, I had never actually seen the hidden room. It could have been all talk, as far as I knew."

"So you took Diamond into protective custody?" I asked Dennis.

"That's right. Right then and there. That's how serious and dangerous the situation was," he said. He smoothed his tie. "Then we listened in on the Mob guys' conversations. The fact that Diamond stopped showing up for work got them really upset. They started checking into her background, and then they found out who she really was. They canvassed her apartment about the same time as we did, but not as thoroughly as we did—as they apparently did not want to risk getting caught—then came back and ransacked the place when she had not returned after a few days. You should have heard how pissed off they were when they found the picture in the entryway missing. They were so desperate they took the tape from the answering machine to follow up on any information they might glean from it. The old Mob guy knew about your ancestor, Maria Mercedes, from your parents—they always idolized her, after all—and he really ripped his guys for not checking out the picture. He had good instincts: thank God we found the money Diamond had stashed there before they did."

My headache was almost gone. "What then?" I asked Dennis.

"Well, they had to come up with their own Plan B." Dennis said.

"Plan B?" Diamond asked.

"I'll tell you later," I said.

"They knew Maria Mercedes was important to your parents," Dennis explained, "especially after the picture disappeared. That was when they decided to use Maria Mercedes to find Diamond."

I thought back to the woman who had attacked me. "So they turned Adrianna into Maria Mercedes?"

"It wasn't all that hard," Diamond said. "Think about that old picture—her features aren't really all that clear. And she would have to appear at night, with Mama and Papa sleepy. Adrianna has the same dark complexion. Dress her in the same clothes, same hairdo, hazy lighting. It wasn't difficult," she added.

"We knew their first priority was to find Diamond and shut her up," Dennis said. "So they cooked up this plan to have Adrianna impersonate your ancestor and visit your parents and demand the family be reunited. She fooled you, right, in the bathroom? Adrianna was good, very very good." They knew how to get her in there, since your family's so-called friend helped draw up the floor plan. After that little visitation in the middle of the night, they figured your parents would either hire an investigator or send one of your family out to Las Vegas—since they couldn't find Diamond, they hoped someone from your family could."

"We fell right into it," I said. "We wanted La Estrella so badly, we bought the whole story."

"We had a wiretap on Adrianna's phone by then," Dennis continued. "So we heard her talk to your friend Dorcas about how you were coming out, and how you could use help."

I had a terrible feeling in my chest. "You mean Dorcas was involved in this?"

"No, no," Diamond hurried to assure me. "She didn't know. Dorcas really thought she was helping you by hooking you up with Adrianna."

"Your friend Dorcas, without realizing it, tipped off the Mob to what you were doing," Dennis explained. "There wasn't much we could do about it, although in the end it helped us. We found out when you were coming, and where you were staying."

"How did you get to be my driver?" I asked him.

"The Bellagio helped us out," Dennis said. "As soon as we found out where you were staying, we contacted them. They let me pose as one of their regular drivers. They made sure I was in place to take the job."

"But you saw what I was going through," I said. Suddenly it seemed as though I had never known him. He looked so different, and all the trust I placed in him seemed sorrowfully misplaced. "You saw me suffering, worried sick over Diamond."

"We couldn't risk telling anyone," Dennis said. "I'm sorry. There was a lot riding on it. And Adrianna was keeping pretty close tabs on you."

"That's why you were so pissed off when I was keeping things from you," I said. I paused. "Damn it, Dennis. You used me as bait to get to these people."

"Trust me, Esmeralda," Dennis said, almost sadly. "There was no other way. And I tried to always be there to protect you."

"What about Armando?" I asked, remembering the old man.

"They got suspicious about him when you asked Adrianna where the old dealers hung out," Dennis said. "Don't feel too guilty. They were trying to figure out who had placed Diamond at the Star. It was probably just a matter of time until they found him. And then, when they located him they asked him questions

"I'll call you," I said.

I didn't know what was going to happen when I went back to the house I shared with Tony and our sons. I had no idea how my husband would react, or if he would even notice that the old Esmeralda had been replaced by a woman who had risked her life and lived through it.

I would only know when I stepped through the door. After that, I supposed I would just play the cards as they were dealt to me.

47

I LOOKED OVER AT THE
clock on my bedside table and saw that I had just thirty minutes
before the first of the three alarms would start ringing. There was
still time for me to think back about the events of the past week.
Although I was physically back in my home in Coconut Grove,
my mind was still in Las Vegas. I knew that soon enough I would
go back to my role as wife and mother, but the truth was, in outward appearance I may have looked the same, but inside, I was a
changed person.

I had been home for just over two hours, after having returned to Miami in the same private airplane my family had
chartered for their trip out to Las Vegas. I had not informed
Tony that I would be coming back that night, partly because I
was not sure of the time, but also because I did not feel up to
going into details about what had happened in Las Vegas. I
had, however, telephoned him and told him that Diamond was
safe and sound, and that I was coming home as soon as possible,
but apart from that, I had not volunteered much more information. Tony was incapable of keeping a secret, so I knew the
minute I told him I was coming home, he would not be able to
resist sharing that with the boys, who would then want to stay
up to welcome me back. I missed them desperately, but, for their

own good, I would have to wait to see them when they awoke to go to school.

Even though I had not told anyone when I would be arriving, somehow Buster knew that I would be coming home. Even though the taxi was still a block away from the house, I spotted him waiting by the front gate, his tail wagging madly from side to side in the frenetic arc that was so familiar to me. As I saw Buster there, so happy to have me back, my eyes watered slightly, and I actually got a lump in my throat. As soon as the taxi stopped, I quickly paid the driver, picked up my suitcase, and sprinted toward him. I must have stood there for a good five minutes, letting Buster slobber all over me as I hugged him, trying not to inhale the gas he was freely and continuously passing as he jumped around.

Using my key, I let myself into the house, hurrying to turn off the alarm in the thirty-second window allowed before it would go off. Although it was pitch dark, I was so familiar with its contents that I did not need to turn on any of the lights to find my way around. I took off my shoes at the foot of the stairs and crept upstairs. On my way to the master bedroom, I opened the door to each of the boys' rooms and looked inside, watching them as they slept, breathing in their particular scents. I had missed them so much that being apart from them the past week had been at times physically painful. I resisted the temptation to wake them up by telling myself I would be seeing them in a few hours, and continued on to our bedroom.

Tony had always been a sound sleeper, so I had to shake him gently a few times before I was able to awaken him. "I'm home." I kissed him on the cheek, as I lay next to him. I had been apprehensive about how I would feel upon first seeing Tony, but I was relieved that I reacted to him in a perfectly normal way. Actually, I felt a rush of affection for him as I watched him slowly wake up.

"Oh! Emmy! You're really back. Good." Tony turned to me

and hugged me. "I missed you so much!" And, with that, he turned back around and promptly went back to sleep. I was familiar with his sleeping patterns, so I was not necessarily offended that my husband's greeting had not been more effusive. It was enough that he had expressed pleasure that I was back. I had not been sure how he would receive me.

It had been a very long day and night, and I was not exactly feeling fresh, so I headed to the bathroom to take a shower. Suddenly, I had a need to wash Las Vegas from my body before getting into bed next to my husband.

Once in the bathroom, I closed the door behind me and turned on all the lights. I quickly took off my clothes and threw them into the hamper. Then, naked, I stood in front of the full mirror and critically inspected every inch of my body, as if looking for telltale signs of what it had gone through while I had been away. To my unsparing eye, I seemed the same, but I knew I was not.

For the past ten years, I had been a wife and a mother in Miami, working part-time as an interior designer, leading a comfortable but basically uneventful life. My marriage had been going through a rocky period, but I was confident if I devoted time and energy to it, I could make it work. I recognized the fact that I was truly blessed. Tony was a good man, a family man, who was faithful and hardworking. He had his weak points, but so did we all. I loved my children and had a great relationship with them. As time passed and the boys became more independent, I would have more free time to devote to my interior design business, something I looked forward to doing. Prior to my trip to Las Vegas, I could see the future clearly. However, now my instinct told me that the events of the past week would change all that.

The truth was, in Las Vegas, for the first time in my life, I had had to rely on myself to act in a way that would determine the fate of another person. My family had trusted me enough to place the very existence of one of our members in my hands. I had gone out there, alone, with no road map, no guidance as to how to go about finding Diamond. I had had to rely solely on my instincts. Nothing in my life had prepared me for that.

Eight days ago, my life could have been described as: wife, mother, daughter, interior designer. Suddenly, without warning or preparation, I was tested, thrust into the mysterious underbelly of Las Vegas, looking for my sister. I found that I could draw on reserves of my personality that I did not know were there. I had been in physical danger, yet that did not deter me from finding Diamond. Not even Armando's murder had stopped me— actually that very sad event had only strengthened my resolve to find Diamond. I was confronting situations as they occurred, with only my instincts to guide me as to how to proceed. Nothing in my life in Miami had prepared me for what I had to do in Las Vegas.

I had met a man, Dennis O'Shea, who was as different as possible from anyone I had ever known and who had awakened in me a desire for a different situation than the one in which I was. True, Dennis and I had not met under what was, in any account, a "normal" situation, but it was one which tested one's true character. What had happened between us could not be dismissed as simply having happened due to time and place. The feeling between us was too real for that. I was only thirty years old, too young for a traditional midlife crisis in which individuals jettison their current life in search of another, a more fun and exciting one.

I had changed profoundly during those past seven days. The question became just how that change would manifest itself.

I stepped closer to the mirror, standing so close to it that my breath began fogging up the surface, and looked into my eyes, as if to read the answer in them. Except for the exhaustion showing in them, my eyes did not disclose the answer I was seeking. However, the time I spent there, examining myself, was not wasted, as now I was confident that somehow, the right answer would present itself to me.

I stepped inside the shower stall and stood there, feeling the steaming hot water soak every centimeter of my body. I then shampooed my hair and soaped myself several times. As I did so, I was conscious of the fact that I could clean my body on the outside, and wash Las Vegas off, but, inside, it was still there. When I finished, I quickly dried myself off and put on my terrycloth bathrobe, which was still hanging on a hook on the back of the door. As I did so, I thought back with a measure of nostalgia to the thick one in my bathroom at the Bellagio.

I opened the door, walked across the room, and slipped into bed, careful not to disturb Tony. I closed my eyes, hoping to take a short nap before starting the day, but that proved to be impossible. There was just too much to think about, to straighten out in my mind. There was no use in trying to force myself to sleep, so I gave into the inevitable, and turned my thoughts back to Las Vegas.

48

blocked out the background sounds of Tony snoring softly next to me, then began reconstructing what had happened the last day that I had been in Las Vegas. Everything had happened so fast that I had not really been able to do so. I carefully touched the bump on my head, a very realistic reminder of my encounter with Adrianna while in the bathroom of my suite at the Star casino. As the bruise was located toward the back of my head, I thanked God the swelling did not show, as that would have been difficult to explain.

Still touching the bump on my head, I thought back to the scene in my room at the Bellagio, when Diamond and Dennis stood by my bed and filled me in not just on the details of what had happened to me but also how the events had developed around me. I could not help but smile as I thought about my last conversation with Dennis and the invitation he had issued. That, I would save until later, when I had more time, as that needed to be savored.

After Diamond had left, and we had had our private conversation, Dennis, discreet as ever, had left me alone in the room to finish packing. I knew that his reason for doing so was not because he was a true gentleman and wanted to give me privacy while I got dressed. As a law-enforcement officer, I suspected he did not want to know what, exactly, I was going to do with the bag of marijuana that belonged to Diamond, which I had stashed in the safe in my room. I had seen enough crime shows on television to be able to figure out that while the investigation was going on, there was not much he could or would do about the weed, as it would compromise it. However, now that the active part of the investigation seemed to be over, he might have to act on the fact that he knew there was a plastic bag full of weed in my safe. He certainly did not want to be a party to how that was disposed of.

I had planned to give the weed to Diamond prior to boarding the airplane for the flight back to Miami, figuring she would know how to put it to good use. As I gave her the bag, I could not help but think that it was a good thing we were flying back on a private plane to Miami and not flying commercial, where we would have to go through security searches.

After spending a few hours in the casino, the family came back upstairs to their rooms prior to checking out of the Bellagio. I then told them the sad news about Armando's murder, and how Dennis had reported that he had died protecting Diamond and me. I assured them that those responsible for Armando's murder would pay for it. I knew Dennis would follow up on that, especially since he had said that Adrianna was behind it. For Dennis, it was personal, and not just another case.

I also described how Mario had warned me of the danger I was in, and how he had placed himself in harm's way because of his loyalty to the family. Mama and Papa heard all this, and were so touched by their former employee's actions that they decided to stop by Mario's apartment on the way to the airport and visit with the old man. While there at Mario's, although I did not see it happen, I had a strong suspicion that my parents gave enough money to the old man to make his life considerably more comfortable.

I had sat next to Diamond during the flight back to Miami, so I was able to speak with her at length about her disappearance in Las Vegas. Back in my room at the Bellagio, she and Dennis had filled me in on what had happened to her, but I felt it had only been an overview, and I still had quite a few questions to ask.

Before beginning the discussion, however, I wanted to be sure that Diamond and I were speaking in private, as I did not want to upset anyone by asking what were difficult questions. The airplane that Mama and Papa had chartered for the trip to Las Vegas was a sixteen seater, certainly large enough to accommodate the seven members of our family, plus, of course, Día and Noche, so there was plenty of room to spread out. Still, I would rather that our conversation not be overheard. I looked around at the different members of the family and saw that most of them were napping, except for Q, who was listening to music on his MP3.

First, I was interested in asking Diamond where the cash she had stashed in back of Maria Mercedes's photograph had come from. As soon as I had finished asking the question, Diamond looked at me in surprise as if I should have been able to figure out the answer to that on my own.

"They were my winnings, of course, Esmeralda!" Diamond laughed. "You know how our family is with gambling—we can't stay away from the tables for long." She took a deep breath. "Every day, on my way to work, I would stop at the blackjack tables at different casinos and play—but I had to hide my winnings, because as their employee, the Star did not allow us to gamble in any casino. They were very strict about that." She suddenly turned serious. "At first, I was going to donate my winnings to environmental causes, but, as I got deeper and deeper into finding out what those guys were planning to do to our family, I figured I might need to use the cash for a quick getaway."

I thought about what my sister said. Her answer made sense in a Diamond-like way. Then I asked another question. "OK, fine. Now who is Angie?" I could never quite figure out who was the caller who had left the message on Diamond's answering machine.

"Angie?" Diamond asked, perplexed. "Oh, that's right, you listened to the messages on the answering machine. Dennis told me that. Angie's a cocktail waitress at the Star. My 'friend' there. I used to take some of her shifts with the whales, for a price, of course, so I was able to eavesdrop on the mob guys' conversations. She's a single mom, so she was perfectly happy to let me work the whales' area, so long as I paid her." Diamond now shook her head slowly. "Angie's going to miss the extra income, now that I'm no longer there. She was probably worried Mickey would find out what the deal was between us when I didn't go to work anymore. I hope she doesn't get fired, but I think she probably will."

"Yes, I suppose she will lose her job." I agreed. I sat back in my seat and began to look out the window. As I did so, I could not help comparing the differences between my trip out to Las Vegas a week before, frantic with worry over my sister, and the flight now, sitting next to Diamond, with our family all around us. "Hey, Diamond." I turned to face her. "If I ask you something, promise not to think I'm a *loca,* okay?"

"Sure, I promise." Diamond looked amused. "What's up?"

I took a deep breath. "I've been thinking about how you found out that those guys were going to steal the money from La Estrella. You know, how you happened to overhear them talking when you went in to interview the press relations person at the Star."

"Yes, that did seem to be a huge coincidence, didn't it?" Diamond agreed. "Lucky I was there, just then, right?"

"That's what I was going to ask you about," I spoke slowly. "I mean, I believe in luck, in chance—hell, we all do in our family—but, even for us that seems kind of pushing it, don't you think?"

Now Diamond had my full attention. "Esmeralda, what are you getting at?"

"Do you think our ancestor, Maria Mercedes, was looking out for us? For La Estrella? Do you think she was the one who subconsciously suggested to you that you go to the Star at exactly that time, and stand in that corridor where you would overhear that conversation about La Estrella?" I blurted out. Even to Diamond, my sister, it was difficult to broach such a tricky subject. "I mean if those guys had gone ahead with their plan and had stolen the money, then Mama and Papa would not have been able to set up La Estrella again back in Havana, ever!"

Diamond took my hand and squeezed it. Even in the dim light of the interior of the airplane I could see that her eyes were filling up with tears. "Oh, Esmeralda, I'm so happy you brought that up!" One large tear began rolling down her cheek. "I've thought that all along. That's the one thing that kept me going back to the Star to try to find out more about their plan. I felt that Maria Mercedes was looking out for me, I felt that, I promise!"

We both began crying simultaneously, mostly from relief that we were not crazy to think such thoughts. After all, Maria Mercedes had been such an integral part of our lives that it was not illogical to think that she would always be there for our family and look out for us in her own way. Even if Adrianna had partially succeeded in exploiting the importance of Maria Mercedes by impersonating her to Mama, coming at her at night, our ancestor had ultimately prevailed, and had protected La Estrella.

Just then, as far as I was concerned, listening to Diamond express her feelings, it was comforting to know that I was not the only one who thought that Maria Mercedes's spirit was protecting us. We discussed the events of the past few days a bit more, and then, drained, decided that the rest of the conversation could wait. Soon, physical and mental exhaustion took over, and we both slept the rest of the way back to Miami.

Now, lying on my bed at home, the light of dawn beginning to creep into the room, I knew that it would take me a while to sort out what had happened and to fully understand how the pieces of the puzzle connected with Diamond's disappearance fell into place. I would be asking more questions about that in the future, but for now I had to get on with my everyday life in Miami. To go back to being a wife, a mother, and an interior designer.

I looked over at Tony sleeping next to me. During the past half hour, little by little, he had been creeping toward me in bed, until we were almost touching. I wondered how long it would take him to realize that I was not the same Esmeralda who had left to go looking for her sister in Las Vegas. And, once he realized that, how he would react to the different person I had become. I still did not know how that change would manifest itself, but I was positive it would. For, I now knew that in looking for my sister, I had found myself.

The first of the alarms began ringing, catching me by surprise. As I reached over to turn it off, I could not help but calculate what time it was in Las Vegas, and what Dennis would be doing. Soon enough, I would telephone him to tell him that I had arrived back in Miami. The rest of the conversation, I would play by ear.

The one thing I was certain of, whatever I decided to do, was that Maria Mercedes would be with me in spirit, looking out for me.

It was written in the cards.